THAT TIME I TOOK DOWN A CULT

REBEL CARTER

DEDICATION

Let this book serve as a reminder to never ever join a cult, not even when the demon god is smokin' hot.

AUTHOR'S NOTE AND TW LIST

Hi Bestie!

Thank you so much for picking up *That Time I Took Down A Cult*. This book is a Cozy Dark Romance full of camp, tender moments and plenty dark humor that I hope will have you smiling the entire way through. There are few books that I've written in my life that have given me such joy and happiness, and this book is one of them.

While this is a bonafide book of my heart please know there are trigger warnings to be aware of, bestie.

That Time I Took Down A Cult contains sexually explicit scenes, to include public masturbation. There are references to emotional abuse, sexual abuse and coercion(not shown or on page), as well as on page violence, gore, misogyny, murder and mutilation, parental murder, throwing of severed heads, brainwashing, and human sacrifice.

I hope you love this book but read with caution because there's nothing more important than you!

Love y'all <3

THAT TIME I TOOK DOWN A CULT PLAYLIST

Hi bestie! I wanted to do something a little special and give you a listening treat to go along with cozy lil' vengeance book. You can listen to the playlist on Spotify here or use the handy dandy QR code as well.

Love y'all and happy listening!

Which Witch-Florence + The Machine
Undo Me- Jennifer Knapp
Bitch-Meredith Brooks
Untouched-The Veronicas
Just A Girl- No Doubt
Survivor-Destiny's Child
Bidi Bidi Bom Bom- Selena
Silver Springs- Fleetwood Mac
Virgin State of Mind-K's Choice
Lilith- Halsey, SUGA
Just Like Heaven- The Cure

Mama's Broken Heart- Miranda Lambert
Insane- Black GryphOn, Baasik
Closer-Tegan and Sara
Blackbird- Sarah McLachlan
Since U Been Gone-Kelly Clarkson
Buffy Theme-Vampire Slayers

WRAITH'S EMBRACE

THE FOUNDERS' CIRLE

THE HOT SPRINGS

THE HALL OF WORSHIP

THE GREEN HOUSES

THE GRAVE

THE ROSSI'S

THE OUTSIDE

THE
AUTUMN HARVEST
FESTIVAL

WELCOME TO SWEET TOOTH

CHAPTER
ONE

I LAY ME DOWN TO SLEEP AND IF MY SMILE SHOULD BREAK, I PRAY MY SOUL WRATH TO TAKE.

"Are you shitting my dick?"

"Those better not be your wedding vows, Buffy."

"I mean..."

"Buffy!"

I grin at Meadow and wave her off while I go back to applying my lipstick. It's a rosy pink that goes perfectly with my tawny skin, a lucky thing seeing as there are only six approved colors sold in town. It's not my favorite color, but it is the one I use the most. The red would have been a better choice, but that would have been...*too bold* for a Blossom on her wedding day.

Blossoms are perfect and I will be perfect, even if the Witch of the Woods says otherwise.

"You think you're a perfect, pretty, pretty Blossom, but you'll be nothing but dust under their heels. Crushed in the flower of your bloom. Such a waste."

I wasn't supposed to see the witch today, but magic is funny that way. The Witch of the Woods comes and goes as she pleases.

1

We all know that, it's why we stay out of the woods. But *I wasn't even in the woods when she spoke to me, which seems like a major cheat on her part.*

If she can teleport anywhere she wants then what's to stop her from catching you in the bathroom or when you're struggling to parallel park? Nothing, that's what.

Totally not fair.

When the Witch of the Wood caught me, I was walking down Main Street with a basket of fresh laundry my mother had just washed, meant for the school. I was almost there, too. I wouldn't have even been caught by the Witch in the first place if I knew how to drive, but I'd never learned. Not completely, at least. Not without hitting the curbs in town. Why were there so many curbs here, though?

We are one small town, with one cult to its name. The amount of curbs there are to hit the side of in my father's car is excessive. I'm not even saying that because I can't drive. Luckily, my wedding day is meant to be perfect, which means today was the perfect day for a walk and that's why I'd volunteered for it when all the other Blossoms were resting.

The sun shone bright and the birds were singing while children played in sight—a true treat of a day. I stopped and turned my face up, soaking up the sun with my eyes closed until I felt the cold wind of the witch blow over me as she spoke.

When I opened my eyes and looked, she was there, just a blink really, with a gnarled finger and a sneer in my direction.

"What do you mean? Under whose heel?" I asked, like an idiot. *You never speak to witches, everyone knew that. Dumb Buffy.*

"Pretty, foolish, Blossom. You'll see when they pluck your petals off tonight, you smiling fool."

Then she was gone.

Having magic doesn't mean she's right. Besides, Wrath has far more magic than she does.

Everyone knows that.

"I'd never do that, Meadow," I say, my eyes on the tube of red lipstick sitting so close, yet so far away. My fingers itch to touch it, but I won't. Nothing will ruin tonight, not even the Witch of the Woods and her cryptic popping in whenever she pleases. I don't care how Arcane and Ominous she is, she doesn't know what she's talking about.

Meadow tips her head to the side and looks me over like she doesn't believe me, which is fair. She knows me too well. Meadow Atlier is my best friend and a Blossom, like me. Which makes this her wedding night, too. I'm so happy I get to share my night with her. She raises an eyebrow at me and her lips almost turn down into a frown when I lift my eyes from the lipstick to look at her and her wobbling smile.

"Wouldn't you?"

"Don't ask questions you don't want to know the answer to," I tell her, dropping the pink tube of lipstick onto the dressing table with a flick of my wrist. The tube bounces and spins on the smooth wooden surface of the table and I let my lips curve into my long practiced smile. Now is not the time to let my smile break over something as silly as lipstick.

I'm about to marry the most handsome man in town. The smartest man in town. The man every girl wished would get down on one knee for her. Yet the Founders made me a Blossom and made the match.

They chose me.

Me. I'm the chosen one.

I'm the one marrying Callum O'Hare. Having my wedding night with him is a dream come true. I'm a virgin like every Blossom and Callum is my Prince Charming. He's tall and strong with blond hair that shines like gold in the sun and green eyes that make me think of springtime. I've never seen a more beautiful man than Callum, which might not sound like much when you're a member of a cult, but it counts for a lot to me. The other Blossoms have gushed about how lucky I am to have Callum as *my first*. We've always been chaperoned when we were together, but there have been a handful of almost kisses and handholding.

"I think I love you, Buffy." He'd said after the Autumn Harvest Festival last year. I can't wait to visit this year's festival with him next week as his wife. Callum means what he says to me too, I can tell. I know Callum will make tonight perfect.

I know it.

Callum is the first son of the O'Hare's, the most powerful family in town. They were the ones to first set down their claims in Sweet Tooth. We wouldn't have our town, cult, or community without them.

I wouldn't have tonight.

The O'Hare's are so powerful there isn't a thing denied to them. Not a council seat or board they don't have the final say in. After tonight, my family will join them. The Martinez's won't be the laughing stocks of Sweet Tooth for a day longer after tonight. Even though I know that, there's a feeling I can't shake.

It's the Witch of the Woods.

Damn her.

Her words feel sinister now that night has fallen. It was easy to ignore her when the birds sang and the sun still shone, but now her words are all I can hear. The harder I try to forget, the

4

more they loom over me and give today's joy a bitter taste in my mouth.

"You smiling fool."

"Buffy, your smile, be careful," Meadow warns and shakes a finger at me. I fight not to jump, but do it anyway, smashing my elbow into the dressing table. Her finger looks so like the Witch's that it's impossible not to flinch, but she doesn't notice and goes back to straightening her plain white wedding dress. It's floor length with a modest scooped neck and capped sleeves. I have the same dress on. There wasn't anything to decide on when it came to our wedding dresses. The Founders chose the dresses. While it left a lot to be desired, there was no way around it. Blossoms didn't get to choose their dress—no one in Sweet Tooth did.

"You didn't tell me what you thought about my new saying," I remind Meadow when she looks like she's going to lay into me. I want to think about my stolen words from the Outsiders, not worry about the witch's bullshit warning.

It means nothing.

Nothing.

Blossoms usually ready themselves alone, but it's an obvious choice to do it with Meadow, so I snuck in from my dressing room. She's the closest thing I have to a sister. I'm an only child and so is Meadow, so it works out perfect that we're best friends. Even though we're both Blossoms, her family is different. Her dad didn't fall in love with an Outsider and marry her. Meadow's dad married the second daughter of the Smith founding family, which is a pretty big deal. She's worried about me tonight because, even if we're both chosen, I'm different.

The Martinez's haven't mattered since my father took his vows with an Outsider.

The only time my mother is valuable to the Founders is when they can trot her out as a cautionary tale to anyone that tries to step out of line. She's the woman that begged to join Sweet Tooth because of how cruel the Outside is. She's proof that life out there just doesn't work. Why we need the Founders to keep us safe.

I still want to see the world, though. There's so much beyond Sweet Tooth, I know it. The Outsiders remind me every work assignment I have in the flower shop or the hot springs. We're known for both, with exclusive deals with every tourist company in the area.

Why anyone would want to come see Sweet Tooth, I don't know. I've dreamed of leaving it and the Cult of Wrath for as long as I've known the Outside exists. I've tried to ask my mother about it, but she gets tight-lipped and changes the subject. Just like when I ask her about where my name came from.

She named me, just like every mother in Sweet Tooth does, but there's no one else in town named Buffy and I can't find a record of it in any of the Sweet Tooth lineage ledgers. Wherever Buffy came from, I know it was from the Outside. Sometimes mother slips up when she thinks she's alone at home and I hear the ghost of who she was before she came to Sweet Tooth. She's really into *Christ on a Cracker* and missing something called White Claws, which I think are the pastries Ms. Donna and Ms. Fisher are in charge of making Sunday mornings when we know the biggest groups of sightseers are scheduled to visit town.

"Buffy, I swear to Wrath," Meadow huffs.

"It's a winner. You know it is," I insist.

Shitting my dick is solid gold, I know it. Even if Meadow isn't saying it, she does too. It's a saying I heard from the Outsiders when I was helping in the flower shop two days ago. It was my last assignment before my wedding. I've committed all their sayings to memory. Some I know better than others or get wrong, but I won't be forgetting *shitting my dick,* just like I won't forget to find out what a Waffle House is when I leave Sweet Tooth.

Whatever it is, *it has to be psychotic*...but with waffles. What else would they serve with a name like that?

That basically makes it the Promised Land.

I won't work when I'm married. The O'Hares will send me to the city with Callum. We'll have such a perfect life in the city. Every Blossom that's been sent to the city loves it and will be there to show Meadow and me how everything works. I think that's my favorite part. That I'll get to share it with Meadow and that Sweet Tooth won't be too far away. I'll learn how to drive and never hit a curb again, not even when I have to parallel park.

My life will be good and perfect.

My parents will visit and maybe my mother will finally tell me what a White Claw is. It's going to be amazing. It'll be nothing but red lipstick and waffles as far as the eye can see. No Witches popping up with warnings ever again.

I can't wait.

"Fine. I like it," Meadow mutters and pats her hair. "It's got a certain charm. I'll admit it."

"So much charm. Oodles of it," I say and wiggle my fingers at her as I come to stand beside her. She rolls her eyes at me when she hears *'oodles'.* It's another stolen word from Outsiders, but even so she smiles at me and this time it's real.

"Tons of charm." She takes my hand and gives it a squeeze. "Everything is going to change tonight, Buffy." She's marrying Roy Aguirre. He doesn't compare to Callum, but he's nice enough. A little boring, but maybe Meadow will liven him up with time.

I squeeze her hand. "I know."

The mirror in front of us shines bright with our reflection. Meadow's auburn hair and my jet black hair stand out against the stark whiteness of our dresses. Dressed identically, we could pass for sisters and the thought warms me through. The glow of it and Meadow's hand in mine pushes back at the heavy feeling the Witch's words gifted me.

Her warning is nonsense. *I am no fool.*

Tonight I meet my destiny and become a Blossom Bride. It's what I was meant for all of my life. It's a dream come true to finally fulfill my rite as a Blossom with Meadow at my side. There's a knock at the door and I give a little excited shimmy while Meadow joins me with a giggle. We answer the door together, not even bothering to hide that I snuck in from next door.

The usher—Mister Carmichael—scowls at seeing me. Next to him is Miss Fisher, who's banging on my door and calling my name with a strained smile in place.

"Buffy, please answer the door. Now is not the time for cold feet, my dear. Callum is waiting for you," her voice is pleasant, more of a song than anything else and she jumps when Mister Carmichael snaps his fingers at her.

"She's here," he mutters. The men don't have to smile in Sweet Tooth. It's just the women and girls that have to pay our tithes in smiles.

Relief floods Miss Fisher's face and she comes forward with a bright smile in place. "Ladies, ladies, ladies, you know the rules. You were meant to stay apart tonight."

"We're sorry," Meadow and I apologize in unison, but Mister Carmichael waves us off.

"Not much time left anyhow. Let them play," he grumps and gestures for us to head down the hallway where the other Blossoms are falling in line. I wave at another girl, Lylah, who beams at me as she hurries to take her place in front of me. The hall is full of familiar faces, all women that I've known my whole life. Each one a Blossom chosen for The Reaping.

It's with smiles and giggles that we head down the hallway to meet our husbands and begin the most valuable service a Sweet Tooth woman can do for the cult. Every year Blossoms are Reaped, to marry in Wrath's name.

There is no greater honor than to be chosen.

I'm so lucky I was chosen. Thankful for the chance to bring honor to my family and to be able to become a wife. It's the only thing I've ever truly dreamed of for myself.

"All right my beautiful Blossoms. Follow me, it's time to meet your husband," Miss Fisher's voice trills through the hall and we all fall silent. This is the moment we've dreamed of since we were chosen as children. When we start down the hall, it's with our heads held high and our hearts full. Even when Mister Carmichael glares my way, I smile like I always do. This time it's even easy.

Nothing will stop me from being the best wife ever dedicated to Wrath.

CHAPTER TWO

T he walk through the Hall of Worship and into the night is quiet. It's also faster than I would have thought it would be. For the past five hundred years, the Founders' Circle is where all Blossoms become true brides and it's where Meadow and I will join them. She's just behind me and even though Mister Carmichael glares at us and Ms. Fisher smiles nervously as she walks up and down the line ushering us towards the forest that holds the Founders' Circle, I still reach back for her hand.

There's nothing but the full moon shining to light our way. The moonlight makes the stones we walk on light up like gemstones. All around our path is darkness, but each stone shines bright. It's just like Meadow and I imagined it would be. My heart feels like it's going to leap out of my chest until Meadow squeezes my hand.

I hold it tight as we step into the trees single file and walk the white stone path that leads us to our grooms. Beyond these trees are the hot springs we're famous for. Outsiders from all over come to enjoy the healing waters of Sweet Tooth. We're blessed by Wrath for our obedience. For our smiles that never falter and serve as currency to our god.

The god that I'll meet tonight when I become a bride. Only a precious few are allowed to look upon Wrath and *only ever* the Blossoms.

I take another steadying breath when I catch sight of light up ahead. Flames. Light to see my god by. My hands tremble and I forget all about the fact that Callum will be waiting for me at the Founders' Circle. He may be as perfect of a man as Sweet Tooth has ever created, but he is still just a man.

Humans are imperfect and the god I serve *is perfection.*

He is who I will truly wed tonight. Not Callum.

I wonder what he will look like, what his voice will sound like when he speaks to me. Will he come close enough for me to touch him? Will I be allowed?

"Pretty, foolish, Blossom. You'll see when they pluck your petals off tonight, you smiling fool."

I stumble, the weight of the Witch's words alive and bright in my mind.

Just like the fires I see lit up around the circle. Torches set in the stone pillars that create the circle crackle happily and form the outer ring. White smooth stone serves as the floor and into the stone's surface, sigils are carved in twelve spots where twelve intended grooms stand waiting for their brides. At the center of it all is the obsidian altar that gleams in the moonlight. It rises up, a dark slash against the white stone. The top of it sits empty and waiting.

My eyes go to the altar, not Callum, as I approach the circle.

The dark altar is where Wrath will appear once we've taken our vows to take him as our eternal husband, with our chosen grooms serving in his place for the rest of our lives. I'll only see Wrath for a moment, but that's all that I need when it comes to gazing upon perfection. A single moment is enough to sustain me for a lifetime.

The smile on my face as I approach the altar and my spot is bright and sharp. I only want to give my god the very best of me. Even though I've smiled for lesser males, Wrath will get what he's owed from me.

"Blossoms, you've been gathered here in payment," Callum's father, Mister Draven O'Hare says. His voice booms, but it always does that, so I don't pay much mind as he begins to circle the dark altar. There are others in the shadows moving in tandem with him, I see them from the corner of my eye. The torches only reveal so much, but the moon does the work of showing me their silhouettes. There's the Aguirre's and the Smiths, the Rossi's and the Marsh's.

All of the five Founding Families are here, with the O'Hare's represented by Callum's father. He looks so much like his son that it feels like I'm looking at what my future holds. How exciting. Mister O'Hare's eyes move from Blossom to Blossom as he speaks. Meadow is on my right, Lylah on my left. I know they're smiling just as much as I am.

This is our time and we are ready to take the next step.

"You have been chosen, as Wrath decided the moment each of you were born. Celestial brides to our god." Mister O'Hare raises a hand to point at the empty altar. "Your god has chosen each of you for himself and now you will give unto him that which he has claimed. What do you say to this?"

I know my part perfectly. I've always known it.

"To Wrath we are bound as a wife to keep."

"Who gives this wife?" Mister O'Hare calls out.

Our intended grooms speak from behind us. "We do, in the name of Wrath. She is his offering to keep." Callum's voice is clear and strong and pride wells up in me at hearing it. He's going to be such a good husband.

Mister O'Hare stops circling the altar. He's in front of me now and he smiles. He has such a kind face. "When Wrath seeks, what will you give freely?"

I raise my hand and press it to my heart. "I give my mind, heart and soul as a wife bound to Wrath," I say as Mister O'Hare's eyes meet mine. His gaze hardens. I watch the easy springtime fade to winter in his eyes and when he smiles, it's not kind or soft. It's mean.

"And so shall he claim you," he says and points a finger at me. When he speaks again, I realize it's not me he's pointing at, but Callum.

"Do it. Do it now, boy," he growls.

Nothing happens for a moment. I don't understand what Mister O'Hare wants his son to do, but then a bell chimes out, the sweet sound of it mingling with a scream that pierces the night air. I look away from Mister O'Hare and see the Blossom across from me fall to the ground in a heap and mayhem falls upon us. Another Blossom cries out and I hear the men that have been in the shadows of the circle shout.

"Get her back here!"

"Bring that Blossom to me!"

I know I should be running too, but I can't look away from the girl on the ground. There's blood on her dress, so much it soaks the fabric until it looks black under the moonlight. Daniel Marsh stands over her body with a knife and raises it above his head with a whoop.

"Her soul has been reaped in Wrath's name!" My blood runs cold at the sight of his knife in the moonlight. Even from here, I can see the blood dripping off of it. I scream and so does Meadow. In the distance, I hear the men's excited shouts.

"I've got the runaway!"

Run. I need to run, but I don't know where to go. My feet feel frozen in place but then Lylah is yelling.

"Get off of me!" Lylah yells. When I whip my head in her direction she's swinging wildly at her intended groom. She falls back and lands on the ground when he swings his knife at her.

"Help us!" I scream, but the second I do, I know there's no one to help. I recognize the voices I hear shouting in the darkness.

Our grooms are *killing* us. Their families are helping drag us back. What the Wrath is going on?

My feet come unglued. I'm freed by Lylah's scream and my feet know exactly where to go. I run towards her.

"Get away from her!" I raise my foot and kick as hard as I can. I've never fought anyone, but it doesn't matter. I catch John Remus unaware and the knife wielding would-be murdering groom catches my foot up his backside.

It sends him sprawling towards Lylah. She manages to roll to the side and John's face breaks his fall. I hear his knife bounce away and skitter across the smooth stone of the circle.

"Buffy, run!" Lylah orders before she swings on John. "You jerk! You tried to kill me! I knew you were a loser, *but really,* John?"

Right. Running. I have to run. I turn to look for Meadow, but the sight that greets me makes me sick.

"Callum! Callum, what are you doing?" I hold out a hand to him and fall back a step, but he doesn't come closer. That's probably because my next step sends me smack dab into Mister O'Hare, who grabs my arms and holds me in place for his son. "Oh Wrath, help me!"

"You stupid, worthless boy. Finish her!"

Callum's hand shakes and he swallows hard. I hear Meadow shout again, but when I look her way Mister O'Hare shakes me so hard my head snaps back and I can't see Meadow anymore.

I try to fight myself loose, but he's too strong. "Meadow!"

"Buffy! Help me!"

"I'm coming, Meadow!" I promise, even though Mister O'Hare's grip on me is like iron. I'm going to have to get creative if I want to get away from him. Why the fuck did my parents join this cult? Why would they choose a murdering cult?

Oh my Wrath, did they know it was a murdering cult?

"Kill her or I'll do it myself." Callum's father drags me forward as he speaks. There's another shriek, but it's farther away. I don't know if it's Meadow or Lylah. I dig my feet in and throw myself back. I try to bring my heel down on Mister O'Hare's foot, but it's no use. I'm wearing silly soft slippers that made sense when I thought I was going to spend the night being adored by my new husband before I left for the city in the morning.

There's no city. Only death. And I'm stuck in a pair of house shoes for it all.

"Let me go! Help me!" I scream and call out to the only soul I know that can save me, *"Wrath! Help me!"*

"The only thing Wrath is interested in is your soul. The only way for you to give that is to die, you little idiot!"

"Pretty, foolish, Blossom. You'll see when they pluck your petals off tonight, you smiling fool."

Bullshit teleporting or not, the Witch of the Woods was right. I just never thought it would be my intended groom plucking my petals.

CHAPTER
THREE

Everything slows down and speeds up at the same time. I can feel my heart pounding and I hear the soft hoot of an owl in the distance. There's another scream and I wince while Mister O'Hare drags me towards Callum, who still looks unsure. Hope blooms in my chest. He said he loved me at least twice. How can he kill me?

"Callum, help me! Please!" I try, but his father is quicker and throws me at Callum's feet.

"You either kill her or I'll cast you both out. You'll be an Outsider with her. You want to be together? The both of you can roam the world lost."

"Dad..." Callum's voice breaks.

"We keep our life by giving him souls. The Blossoms are the way we keep our end of the bargain. Now, slit her throat."

I scramble to get away from Callum. I search for anything to use against him, but there's only dirt and rocks beneath my hands. "You don't have to do this," I whisper. But when Callum looks at me, it's not my Prince Charming that looks back.

It's a killer.

"I have to."

"No, no you don't."

"I'm sorry, Buffy."

That's all I get before Callum lunges for me while his father cheers him on. "That's it! You're doing the right thing, son. I'm proud of you."

Proud of him for trying to kill me? *Are you shitting my dick?!*

I grab a handful of the rocks and dirt under me and fling it at Callum. He cries out and stumbles when I land a direct hit to his stupid springtime eyes. *I hate green.* If I could, I'd burn the world to never see another green thing ever again.

The whole world could plunge into eternal winter with every green thing dying and I'd be ecstatic.

"Fuck you!" I scream and the intake of breath I hear from Mister O'Hare is almost comical. He's shocked I cussed. Good. I intend to do far more than cuss to get out of this.

Callum wipes at his eyes and I spring to my feet. He's hunched over, which makes him the perfect target for the shoulder slam I lay him out with. He hits the ground with a satisfying thump and his knife bounces away from me. I don't even think twice. I go straight for the knife, with Mister O'Hare screaming at me to *'get my ass back here'* while Callum is ass up on the ground. I take off running into the night.

I make it a few steps before I run straight into one of the men guarding the circle. They shove me back into the circle and they're strong, whoever they are. I can't see their face with the moon high above them, so I do the only reasonable thing anyone, but especially someone in a cult that almost got sacrificed and doesn't know how to fight can do and I stab him.

I stab him so damn good and twist the knife for extra measure when he hollers in pain. He falls to his knees and I bring the knife down again.

"How do you like it?" I scream in his face. The moon shines bright and when he turns his face up, I know who it is. Victor Marsh. He's my next door neighbor. I sat beside him in school all my life. His mother visits mine on Tuesday and Friday for cards. When we were twelve, his dog Lady had a litter of puppies so they gave them out to some of the families and mine was one of them.

I named her Blossom because I was so proud to be one. I had her until she was three and was bit by a snake one summer afternoon. I cried for days while my mother begged me not to. She was so scared I'd lose my place as a Blossom, because with my constant crying there wasn't a smile to be found.

Nothing happened to me. Not really. I used to think it was because Victor was there to sit beside me in our front lawn to keep me company and let me pet Lady. The Marsh's were influential. *A Founding Family.* Nothing could really happen unless they okayed it and Victor and I were friends. He did that until I stopped crying. Even then, he still offered to let Lady come over and sit with me.

And he just tried to kill me.

"Buffy, I swear I didn't-" Victor starts, but I don't bother to let him finish. I bring the knife down as hard as I can and slam the butt of it into the top of Victor's head. He drops like a stone and I have to bite my tongue from the pain that shoots up my arm. No fighting my whole life has made me soft and turns out fighting *hurts*. Doesn't help that Victor has a hard head either. I shake my arm out and wince at the dull ache, but all it takes is one shouted *"Get her"* for me to leap over Victor's body and run unto the trees.

It's not safe to be in the forest at night, not when this is the Witch of the Woods' domain, but I'm beyond worrying about the cryptic crone right now. My grip on the knife turns sweaty and I squeeze it tighter. I'm not losing it, not when I'm going into the forest.

There's no telling what I'm about to find in the trees. Whatever it is, I know it's safer than the men behind me. I prefer the witch's riddles and bullshit of her possibly popping in on me in the middle of the forest, because I just executed a twenty point turn to being murdered by my next door neighbor and the jackass that said he loved me twice.

Twice.

Why are men?

I heard an Outsider say that to her friend once at the hot springs. She'd been on her phone and rolling her eyes while a group of older men whispered and stared at her and her friend until one ventured over to them to ask for their number.

She was my age and he looked like he could have been her father.

Blech.

When she told him no, he got upset. I don't know what he said because I was closer to the girls than him, but I saw his face. *Anger*. The same look Callum's father gave me. The same look I'd seen on so many men in my life but pretended not to. The girls had passed me, pressed close together with annoyed looks, their question ringing in my ears when I had to take towels to the same group of men a minute later.

They'd asked for my number, too. I'd just smiled like I'd been trained to do by my backstabbing murderous cult.

Why are men? That's the only thing that burns through my mind. I trusted them. I trusted every single one of them. Every man that came to me as a leader and swore Wrath had given them authority over me and the other Blossoms, over every woman in town and the cult.

I believed them and it was all lies. The leaders they pretended to be weren't murderers. We were peaceful, a safe slice of life in the wasteland of the world. A place where you didn't have to lock your doors and a smile was always directed your way.

At least, it was when it was on a woman's face. Men could frown and glare, they could be angry and sad without their mothers worrying if someone would take their title from them. And now, they could lie and kill. I run faster, my dress catching on branches. I stub my toe on a rock so hard that I nearly fall, but I keep moving. A limb slaps me across the face but I don't slow down, because I think I know where I am.

Up ahead I can see a break in the trees. The moon is still high in the sky and it looks like the light at the end of the tunnel from where I am in the dark forest. I pump my arms faster when I hear someone behind me.

"Buffy!"

Oh Wrath. It's Callum.

Shit. Shit. Shit.

I look around me. The hot springs are up ahead and there's outcroppings of rock along the way and around the springs. To the left of me is the concessions stand where the towels, snacks and souvenirs we sell to tourists are kept. To the right there's nothing but an open space that usually has tables and chairs set up, but we brought those all in just last week for maintenance. I feel sick remembering how I helped carry those tables and chairs with a smile on my face, because I was so excited for my wedding night.

"I'll be Mrs. O'Hare this time next week. I can't wait," I'd told some of the other girls that weren't chosen to be Blossoms. By the time The Reaping happens again, they'll be older than I am now.

"Don't forget us when you move to the big city," they'd told me, because we all believed the lie. A life in the city, the perfect husband, permanent status in the cult.

All you had to do was follow the rules.

My stomach clenches painfully. Just because they'll be too old to be picked as Blossoms next year doesn't mean their daughters won't be one day.

"No," I whisper. "I have to stop it."

"Buffy! Where are you?" Callum's voice floats to me and anger builds in my belly. It's unfamiliar and feels too big for my body, but it settles when I press my hands to my chest. I know what I have to do.

I have to stop the cult.

And I'm going to start with my ex-fiancé.

CHAPTER
FOUR

nger is great for clarity, but it does little for strategy. I have my knife, which is helpful, but I won't be able to take Callum in a fair fight.

Good thing I have no intention of fighting fairly.

If he can lie, I can cheat. Fairs fair.

Hiding is the first order of business and I take a deep breath as I scan the area. The concessions are too easy of a target. Callum will go there immediately and there's nothing inside to use on him other than towels and snack size bags of cheddar cheese chips. My stomach growls at the thought of chips and I wish I'd been smarter and eaten dinner when I'd had the chance.

I'd been too excited for tonight, like an idiot. Now my stomach is going to give me away while I try to get the drop on my ex-fiancé. I rub my stomach and run past the concessions and straight for the hot springs. Steam rises up from the pools and mists into the night. The Witch's woods surround the hot springs, there is nothing out here but her territory for days. You'd never know it with the hot spring's steam blanketing the area.

The Witch of the Woods could be staring me down right now and I'd never know, but it's good. If I can't see, then Callum can't possibly see me.

"Hide now, chips later," I promise myself, dropping behind an outcropping of rocks large enough to hide me.

"I just want to talk, Buffy! I swear. You know I would never hurt you. Come out and talk to me, please." Callum sounds sincere and as honest as he did when he told me he thought he loved me. My anger flares when I realize he'd been lying then, too. I can't believe I counted that as one of the times he said he loved me.

"Wrath, help me," the plea slips from my lips easily. My god is the only thing I have known to pray to, to ask for help and it's only when I stop, drop, and roll behind the rocks on my hands and knees that a thought occurs to me.

What if Wrath isn't real?

The perfect life in the city isn't real, so why would Wrath be any different?

What if the cult is just a bunch of lies the Founding Families use to control us? I feel sick, then dizzy, and then sick again before I take a deep breath and focus.

It doesn't matter if he's real or not. I'm going to get out of this alive, but I'm not going to get anywhere freaking out if Wrath is a lie or not. I raise my hand and my knife shines bright in the moonlight.

My lips curve up in a smile. "This is the only god you have now."

"Come out, come out, wherever you are..." Callum's voice

floats to me and I almost frown. Even with all of the revelations of tonight, my mouth just doesn't know how to do it. I peek around the rocks and see Callum by the concessions stand. He's looking around the corner for me and I don't miss that his hand behind his back has a knife in it. The knife glints under the moonlight and somehow I'm disappointed in him, even though I know he is trying to kill me.

Despite it all, I wanted Callum to be different.

How did I fall for his lies? How? Sure, he just wants to talk with a knife hidden behind his back, but who am I to criticize? I have a knife, too. I watch as Callum circles the concessions stand and kicks the side door with a frustrated swipe of his blade.

He's ticked.

Oh yeah, he's definitely going to try and kill me this time, even without his Daddy watching.

"All of this is just a misunderstanding, Buffy. You'll see that soon." He turns my way and I jerk back behind the rocks. Oh no. What if he saw me? I swallow hard and listen for Callum, but there's nothing but the wind in the trees and the soft bubbling and swirling water of the springs.

"I wasn't lying about loving you. *I do,* you know that," Callum lies. His voice is closer, he's walking towards me. I slide around the rocks and get my knife ready. *Wrath, help me,* I pray silently. The second I see his back I'm going to stab him. If I'm lucky, I'll be able to surprise him like I did Victor.

"And then what?" A voice whispers to me and I jump at the sound. That was totally an outside voice, not an inside one.

Who else is here?

What if it's another one of the men from the circle? I turn and look over my shoulder, but there's nothing behind me except a steaming hot spring. There's no one here. Even so, fear twists in my belly. *Oh Wrath save me.* Foolish as it may be, I can't stop myself from praying to the only god I know.

Someone said something, I know they did.

"What will you do, Buffy?"

There it is again. *Oh shiiiiit.*

"Buffy!" Callum yells and I gasp loudly at the sound of his voice before I clap a hand over my mouth to muffle the sound. "I heard you, I know you're here."

I press closer to the rock and try not to think about the fact that Callum's voice doesn't sound as close as the one that just whispered to me. One crisis at a time. First I handle Callum, then I get cheesy cheddar chips and maybe somewhere in there I investigate the ghost man whispering in my ear.

"It doesn't have to go like this, you know," Callum says and I know he's on the other side of the rocks. He's so close. I move as carefully as I can, which is tough considering I'm wearing a wedding dress and in a crouch. I manage to shuffle silently around the rocks just as Callum clears them. He's quiet and I wince when I hear the scuff of his boot through the dirt.

He's found my tracks.

"We could leave together, Buffy."

"He's lying, don't listen to him."

The voice is there again, but it doesn't make me jump this time. I know it's telling the truth. Callum wouldn't leave with me. He tried to slit my throat when his father told him he'd be thrown out with me. When I thought I was marrying Callum, I thought he was a lot of things: brave, honest, gorgeous and generous. Even though it turned out he's none of those, there is one thing Callum O'Hare will always be.

A cult member.

"You know I would never hurt you. Come out and we'll leave, I promise you. We'll get married, have kids, move to the city," Callum lies. I hear his steps, he's closer by the second but I'm faster. "I'll even teach you to drive."

I raise my eyebrows, impressed at that little lie. Wow, Callum is really pulling out all the stops to make me come out. I'm surprised he hasn't tried to tempt me with Waffle House.

"Buffy, I know you're there..." Callum's voice trails off and I make it around the rocks just as he moves to the spot I was in and swings his knife down with a grunt. Callum stumbles when his knife catches nothing but air.

Sucks for him.

When I swing mine, it's right into his back.

"*Aghh!*" I've never heard anything as sweet as Callum's pained yell when I rip my knife out of his back and slash at him as he turns to face me. My knife catches his forearm and the tuxedo jacket he's wearing shreds as I bring my knife down again.

He falls sideways, landing funny on the rocks at his side and his knife goes flying. "You fucking bitch!" Callum explodes, clutching his arm to his chest. "You stabbed me three times, Buffy. *What the fuck?*"

"You tried to kill me," I shoot back. "And it wasn't three times, it was just the one time in the back. The other two were more of a slice." I bring my knife through the air as an example and Callum shakes his head.

"You're insane."

I shake my knife at him. "You chase me out here after fake marrying me just so you could slit my throat and *I'm* the insane one? No way, buddy. You're not reverse Uno-ing me. I'm trying to survive."

Callum winces and shoves himself away from the rocks. There's blood on them from his back. It shines in the moonlight and I feel conflicted at seeing it. I've never done a violent thing in my life until tonight, but there's delight in my heart at seeing Callum's blood.

I'm glad he's bleeding. I want him dead, but killing Callum really doesn't play into me getting out of this night alive.

"You're going to drive me into the city. You're getting me out of here."

Callum shakes his head. "No."

"Wrong answer. The one you want to say to me starts with a Y, rhymes with mess. Try again."

"I'm not doing it, Buffy. I take you into the city and we're both dead."

I shrug. "I can deal with that. From where I'm standing, nothing really changes, but at least I take you with me."

Callum glares at me. His handsome face twists in fury. How did I ever think he was attractive? I feel nauseous thinking about the hours I lost daydreaming about what marrying Callum would be like. I could have taught myself how to parallel park. I lost more hours than I want to admit, just to end up here in a show-down with him.

"You're so fucking selfish, Buffy! Do you understand what you're asking me to do? I don't know why you can't just do this *one thing* for me. It's not even that big of a deal."

The screams of the other Blossoms come to me. I can still hear them. The sight of the girl across the circle that crumpled with all that blood on her dress. Meadow's back there. I left her. I remember Lylah screaming at me to run.

"*Not that big of a deal?*" I ask Callum, taking a step towards him with a smile on my face. The habit is too deep for me to break, even when all I want to do is claw Callum's eyes out. All around us, the hot springs bubble and steam rises. It swirls and blows in the wind between us. Not the best for visibility, but looking at Callum makes me sick.

Still, I smile.

"You think me and the other Blossoms dying is *not that big of a deal?* You selfish ass! I can't believe I thought I was in love with you."

"Your family sold you from the second you were born. Every day of your life has been borrowed time, Buffy. So no, it's not that big of a deal. Not when I have my entire life ahead of me," Callum surprises me when he interrupts his villainous speech to lunge at me. The steam billows and for a wild second I can't see before he slams right into me and we both go flying.

Callum swings his fist down and I catch him with my knife. It's enough to stop the punch coming my way, but Callum rips my knife away from me with a roar. I hear it hit a rock nearby.

Uh oh, my knife fight just got turned into a fistfight.

Shit.

CHAPTER
FIVE

Callum swings on me again, but I roll away just in time. As angry as I am, I know I can't take Callum in a fist-fight. I've never even *been* in a fight until tonight. I don't think the stabbing people and running I've been doing counts as one.

Even if it did, my best bet at staying alive is to stay out of Callum's reach.

I manage to get to my feet but Callum is right there, grabbing my ankle and yanking my leg out from under me.

"*Umph.*" I hit the ground with a thud and the air gets knocked out of me.

"All you had to do was *stand* there. You didn't have to look at me. Why did you fucking look at me, Buffy?"

I tire of him. End this.

My ears ring with thoughts that are not my own but I can't think straight. I gasp and roll onto my side, trying to take in a breath, but it's no use. I can't get my lungs to work right. All I manage is a garbled wheeze. I hear the scrape of a knife against stone before Callum comes close. His shadow falls over me. A second later, he rolls me over onto my back with his foot. My vision blurs as the rising steam hides Callum from view, but I know he's there from the shadow making me shiver.

"You were supposed to die in the circle, but I'm not dragging you back there. It's not worth it." There's the bright shine of metal in the light, a bright spot in Callum's shadow.

"*You're* not worth it."

Callum crouches over me. I'm reaching up, ready to block the knife I know he's about to use on me, when I hear the voice again. This time it's not just in my head.

"*Who touched my wife?*"

Someone else is here.

Callum freezes. "Who's there?"

"You tried to kill my wife."

Callum rises from his crouch and slashes at the air in front of him. "I said, *who's there?*"

I cough and sit up to watch Callum edge into the steam. It takes just a few steps before he's gone from sight.

"I'm going to gift your worthless head to my bride, mortal."

I don't know who it is that's speaking, but I like them. They've got the right energy for dealing with Callum the almost-killer.

"You don't know who you're messing with! I'm important. My father will have you gutted for this."

I roll my eyes and get to my knees. Of course, Callum would pull the Daddy card. Pathetic. I'm struggling to my feet when I hear something that makes my blood run cold.

"No-no, Wrath! Please no! Wrath, I beg you! *We did it for you!*"

31

It's Callum. He's screaming and it sounds like he's begging someone. Begging *Wrath*. But that's not possible.

The Founders lied about the weddings. I thought that meant they lied about Wrath, too. They are liars, so they had to have lied about him, right?

Violence is new to me but I hear the unmistakable sound of bone crunching and the smack of a fist to flesh. A second later, Callum screams. It's only for a second before the sound is cut off. I stand shakily and wobble as I head into the steam after Callum. I shouldn't follow him, but I can't help myself. I've always been too curious for my own good.

I have to see what happened to Callum.

I take a shaky step forward but stop when I feel something funny. It's like a warm, gentle pressure on my chest, almost like a *tap tap tap* that confuses me. I've never felt anything like it before. I freeze when I hear someone walking. Pull or no pull, I should probably let them come to me. Steam hides the person, but I hear a body drop to the ground. I squint into the steam and a gust of wind comes, blowing things clear. That's when I see the figure walking towards me.

It's big.

He's big.

It's a man. A man with a horned hat? I freeze. My feet won't go another step and my legs stop working. He's carrying something in one hand and it looks like a bag from the way he swings it at his side.

"There you are, dear wife. I've brought you a gift."

His voice is like silk, buttery smooth and luxurious. If I could, I'd clothe myself in this voice for the rest of my days.

"W-who are you?" I stammer as the figure emerges from the clouds of steam.

My heart leaps into my throat when I realize it's not a man wearing a hat at all.

It's Wrath.

It's the god that I've dreamed of. The one my family devoted their lives to and offered me up on a silver, murderous platter to and he's absolutely beautiful.

My lips pull up into a smile as I drink up the sight of the god. Wrath is every fantasy I've ever had about the opposite sex come to life. He is easily a full head taller than me and it's no hat that he wears. It's his horns. They're beautiful, twin spears of onyx that pierce the sky and add to his stunningly imposing figure. He's broad-shoul-dered and muscled, so big that even from where I'm standing I can tell how well he fills out his clothing. He wears a matte black suit that reminds me of shadows from how beautifully it clings to him. Snowy white hair blows in the gust of wind that clears away the rest of the steam and gives me a clear view of the god walking towards me.

He raises his arm and I see it's not a bag at all that he carries.

It's Callum's head.

"A gift for my darling wife."

"*Me?*" I croak. Even though fear washes over me, my lips pull up in a smile.

He tilts his head to the side, his hair sliding over one shoulder. I would give my right arm to touch it.

"I see no other brides that took their vows here tonight, do you?" he asks. I blush hot because, duh, there's no one else here but me.

But still. He means me?

"No, it's j-just me," I tell him and my legs magically start working again. It's like I'm on autopilot, my legs carrying me right to Wrath. As heartfelt a gesture as bringing me Callum's head is, it's not one that I can accept.

I push past his arm and throw myself at his feet. "At least right now, my Lord," I tell him from my position face down in the dirt, my hands outstretched in supplication to Wrath. "There are more brides o-or, there were."

There's a thud in front of me and when I lift my eyes I almost scream at seeing Callum's shitty green eyes staring back at me. Wrath just dropped Callum's head in front of me and a war begins inside of me.

Do I scream and try to put space between me and the severed head of my enemy, or do I stay exactly where I am, because it's my god's feet I'm face down and ass up in front of?

I swallow hard when Callum's head rolls an inch closer to me. Before I have to choose fight or flight, Wrath takes the decision out of my hands, reaching down and cupping my chin. He tips my head back to look up at him and I forget how to breathe.

"There are other brides?" he asks, voice low and rumbling in a way that makes my toes curl.

I smile up at my god. "There are. I mean-there were. Before t-they, before they-" My voice breaks off and I'm not sure if I can say the words out loud. Especially not to my god. Wasn't it in his name the other Blossoms were sacrificed? Why Callum was after me in the first place?

His fingers flex on my chin when I stop speaking. "When they *what*, wife?" Wrath asks.

Wife.

The title that I coveted most in my life. The goal I worked

towards with utter obedience in each and every facet of my life. There has never been anything else in my world but Wrath. Even so, I never thought he would touch me. I keep still while he strokes my chin, his thumb sliding along my bottom lip.

"You have a beautiful smile. Never have I had such beauty offered to me."

"What?" I whisper in surprise. "But the Founders—is that why they raised us the way they did?" My question makes me wonder how many of the Blossoms are left and my stomach cramps painfully at the thought.

"Raised you how?"

"To smile for you," I say. I don't know what else to say while I'm on my knees in front of Wrath with a decapitated head on the ground a foot away from us.

"Humans are deceitful, dirty creatures, but for you I could be persuaded to change my opinion on the species."

"Me?" I shake my head and move to pull away from Wrath. "I'm no one."

"You are everything." Wrath moves faster than I ever imagined possible. The hand on my chin leaves, but it's only to catch me around my waist and lift me to set me on my feet.

My knees buckle and I try to lower myself once more with a shake of my head. "I'm not worthy," I start, but Wrath's eyes darken.

"You bow to no one, wife." His words steal my breath. It feels like my heart might burst from my chest when Wrath drops to his knees in front of me. There's nothing in my life that's prepared me to see my god on his knees. All my life I've been prepared to submit, but here he is, so freely lowering himself to me.

He gestures down at Callum's sightless head. "Is this not gift enough? Who among the living do you seek vengeance on? Tell me and I will tear their limbs from their bodies. I will offer their hearts to you on a silver platter for your enjoyment. Their screams will be your wedding song. Who will it be that I claim in your name?"

Everyone. I want them dead. All of them.

The thought is so quick that I almost mistake it for the voice I heard earlier, but I know this time it's me. Wrath was the voice in my head earlier, I'm positive. Even so, I still ask him.

"You spoke to me earlier. In my head," I say.

He smiles up at me. "I did."

"How?"

"Am I not a demon? And even if I was not, I am your husband."

"A demon?" I whisper-scream, because it was not on my bingo card for my god to tell me he's not a god, but a demon. Just like it wasn't for him to offer to be my own personal hitman. "How are you a demon?"

"What else would I be?" Wrath asks with a raised eyebrow.

"A god?" I answer truthfully and he laughs.

"A god? I am anything but, wife. Gods have concerns and duties far greater than anything I care to deal with. I have but one I give a damn about," Wrath holds up a finger.Though he's on his knees in front of me, his head is easily at my chest. I lick my lips and force myself not to notice how beautiful Wrath's hands are. How perfectly lickable they are. That is *not* what I should think of. Especially when he's just told me he's a demon and not a god. Even so, Wrath's hands are like every part of him. Perfect. Big and strong with well formed fingers. Ones that I remember were the only things Wrath needed to take Callum's head clean off.

I flush and force my eyes away from his hands and to his perfect eyes. They're a shade of silver that I've only ever seen in moonlight. He's so achingly beautiful.

"What is it? What's the one thing you care for?"

"You," Wrath replies, "you are the only thing I care for, darling wife. The rest of the world can burn," he declares. I nearly lose my battle not to lick his fingers.

CHAPTER
SIX

"Me?" My voice comes out in a squeak. I'm nervous, so damn nervous that my smile feels strained. I nearly lose it but manage to keep it in place when Wrath smiles back at me.

"Yes, you. In five hundred years, I've not met another human like you. You are stunning."

The warmth I felt early in my chest blooms until it's impossible to ignore. It feels like a summer morning shining down at me with clear blue skies. Like every good thing I've ever known. The feeling grows and stretches, snaps right into place and connects me to Wrath. The pull of it makes me take a step closer to him. I reach a hand up to brush my fingers along the golden thread linking us together that pulls me closer to Wrath, despite how little room there is between us.

Even without the bond, I'd want to close the space between us, because the fact is...even when I was chosen to be a Blossom, I was not special. Not truly. My entire worth came from the cult and their decision to give me standing.

If I fell from grace, there would be no way to earn redemption with the Founders or the followers I've known since birth. Would I even want such a thing? They raised me to want nothing but marriage, the role of a dutiful wife was the only thing I ever worked towards. How little such a thing to want is when you consider the grand scheme of things.

When you think of life, death, even in a cult, the idea of marriage shouldn't be far less realistic than the possibility of human sacrifice. But not in the town of Sweet Tooth. Not in the cult that raised me.

They sent me to die.

My blood burns with rage but I swallow it down and smile up at Wrath. Those silver eyes are trained on me. He's looking at me so softly. Such a tender way to look at someone and this feels like the first time I've ever seen it.

No one has ever looked at me like this.

"What do you mean?"

"Do you know that in all the time your people have sacrificed brides to me, you are the only one to follow the rules, dear one." He strokes his thumb down the side of my neck as he speaks and I shiver. It's impossible not to be affected by Wrath's touch. I've never been touched this way by anyone before, not when I was supposed to be saving myself for my groom. But his head is on the ground at our feet now.

"My ruthless little bride." Wrath comes forward another half step more and I don't move. I stay where I am and let the demon crowd into my space. "You brought me forth by blood and by

vow, no others have managed to do so. You are special. You are meant to be mine."

I feel dizzy from where his body is against mine. The warm feel of it, the hard muscle against my softer curves, the crisp fabric of his suit under my fingertips. It's intoxicating being touched, being this close to a man—no, not a man. A demon.

He's a demon.

"Only you, dear one," he says, his voice a mix of comforting rumble and seductive rasp. I feel it shoot through my body and down to my toes. "You are my wife and I find that *most* interesting."

"I-is it because I'm human?"

He shakes his head. "Human or not is of little consequence to me. I have no use for humanity. In all the time I've walked the worlds, I've never had a wife before. How fortunate for me you are clever. Time would pass far slower if you were not."

"I'm not clever. I can't even drive," I tell him. The words come out by default. I've been trained to downplay my worth–it was only ever safe for me to receive praise from others and even then the words were never mine to keep.

"I have no use for a driver. I want a wife. That is what I shall enjoy with you." Wrath is still holding me close and every place he touches feels like it's on fire. It's so damn hard to think that when I speak, it comes out in a stammer.

"I-I, I don't know how to be a wife. Not to you."

I couldn't even get married without my groom trying to murder me, so what am I supposed to offer a demon? Not just a demon, but a demon that the cult thinks is a god. One they worshiped and tried to sacrifice me to. How am I supposed to function in this role?

How?

"Do I not please you?" Wrath asks and his brow furrows. He looks down at himself with a frown, his horns flashing in the moonlight. I ball my hands into fists to stop myself from touching them. First I wanted to lick his fingers and now I want to stroke his horns...what is wrong with me?

"Would you care for another form? I can assume a more pleasing figure, if you wish."

"You're perfect," I blurt out, losing the battle with myself. I do the unthinkable. I reach up and touch his horns. The polished onyx is warm beneath my hands and far smoother than I thought it might be.

Wrath moans at the brush of my fingers and I freeze when I realize what I've done. I stare in horror at my fingers still pressed to his horn.

I have lost my mind.

Why do I feel this way? Like all common sense, all the careful discipline and restraint beaten into me, is melting away by the second.

Why am I still touching him?

I internally scream at myself and hastily pull my hand away. Before I can bring my hand back to my side, Wrath's fingers are around mine.

My hand shakes under his as I start to apologize. "I'm sorry. I shouldn't have touched you. I don't know what-"

He holds my hand tightly and brings it back to his horn. "I'd rather you keep your hand right where it was," he says, tilting his head down to give me better access. "I quite like your hands on me."

"You do?"

"There is nothing more that pleases me than my wife's touch."

I feel my soul practically vibrating as it leaves my body quick, fast and in a hurry.

"Oh, okay."

I swallow hard and barely breathe while Wrath moves my hand to firmly curl around the base of his horn. I flex my fingers and slowly slide my hand up the length, cupping my palm to its surface. I lift my hand higher and when Wrath rumbles in approval my heart starts to pound. I raise myself up on my tiptoes when there's more horn for me to touch than I can reach and we both moan when my breasts brush against his chest.

One of Wrath's big perfect hands comes to rest against the small of my back. "Is there anywhere else you would like to touch me?" he asks and I freeze. The bond I felt earlier flares to life. I let go of his horns and grab onto it with both hands. I want to keep touching him, but I'm too nervous. He is everything I have ever been raised to want. While his form was unknown—the Founders swore it would be far too much for any of us to look upon—I knew he would be perfect.

Wrath raises an eyebrow and looks down at where I'm gripping the shining bond. I don't understand what it is, but I like that it's there—that it connects us to one another. I can feel what he thinks of me through it. His pleasure hums brightly down the bond and through my fingertips to warm me through and through.

Wrath wants me. Adores me.

To know that I want to touch such a being makes my legs feel like jelly, but to know that he wants me to touch him is quite another thing entirely.

My hands shake but I don't dare raise them from where they're clutching our bond.

"Yes," I confess.

Wrath lifts his head then and looks down at me. The demon is so tall that the movement forces me closer to him. He wraps an arm around me, lifting me up when I wobble on my tiptoes.

"I was hoping that would be your answer, but I can tell you've never touched any but your own flesh. Isn't that right, wife?" He raises a hand to the bond and gives it a gentle strum of his fingers.

I nod because my tongue is incapable of helping me make intelligible words right now. I'm lucky that I don't drool on him with how hot my blood has turned. I'm on fire for this demon.

"Then I shall teach you. There are a great many places I would have you begin your exploration."

"What is this?" I ask, looking down at the bond. "I don't understand what this is."

"Blood for blood," he murmurs, a smile curving his lips. Silver eyes meet mine. The light of our bond makes his eyes glow as he speaks to me, "You paid the blood price and I returned it tenfold when I claimed you as my wife. This is our bond eternal, dear one."

The moon slants across his face. Shadows and light play across the bridge of his nose and over his high cheekbones and full lips. Those beautiful silver eyes glow in pleasure and reflect the bond's soft light back to me.

My heart flips in my chest. "Callum," I whisper and look to where his head lies near us, "when you took Callum's head you sealed our bond? W-we really are married?"

"I would prefer you not say his name. It fills me with jealousy and I wish to take his head again. Yes, we are married in truth. Your soul to mine, your heart to mine, your body to mine."

Wrath is jealous. Jealous over me and I love it. That's not even counting the fact that our souls, hearts, and bodies are magically tethered to one another.

Our freaking bodies.

I shouldn't love it, but I do. Confusion over what's happening doesn't stop me from loving it. I blush hot and squeeze the bond in my hand when I feel it pulse beneath my fingers. I give the bond an experimental tug and Wrath moans, his eyes drifting closed. I smile.

"This is interesting," I pause and then test out the word that's been sitting on my tongue, *"husband."*

I hear the sharp intake of Wrath's breath. His eyes open immediately, but they're dark now. "Give your hand here, wife" Wrath tells me, holding his palm up to me. It is then that I truly understand the meaning of being *'chosen.' Of* what it is to be blessed and favored among others.

I thought I had achieved that as a Blossom of the Cult of Wrath, but I didn't know better. I didn't know there *was* better out there.

Men will sacrifice you for their own selfish gain, *but a demon?*

A demon will make an honest woman out of you, claim you as their wife and destroy your enemies while an eternal magical mystery bond binds you to one another.

I blink, looking down at the golden tether between us and swallow hard. How was I chosen by this demon to be his wife? Favored and exalted. It has my brain short circuiting and I don't think, *I act.* I put my hand right where he tells me and I know without a shadow of a doubt that I'll continue to do so tonight.

Where Wrath wants me is exactly where I'll go. *No questions asked.*

Wrath hums in approval and rubs his thumb across my knuckles. "There is a charm to you following directions so prettily for me, wife. Is that what they raised you to do?"

I nod. "A wife is to obey her husband," I tell him. The words are not my own, but they come easily all the same. The words are the Founders'. They belong to the cult, the people who tried to kill me. My belly turns and my hand trembles in Wrath's grip.

I think I'd like to answer to Wrath.

He raises an eyebrow at the tremor and his thumb stops moving over my knuckles. "You do not obey me, wife."

I'm confused. All my life men demanded submission. It was currency to keep my place as a Blossom, but Wrath doesn't want it?

"I-I don't?"

"No," he purrs and resumes stroking my knuckles. "Now, tell me your name, dear one."

"Buffy," I tell him, once more giving into what he asks of me with little thought, "My name is Buffy Martinez."

He raises his free hand and strokes our bond. I barely stifle the moan that almost slips out of me at the gesture. It's possessive, but in a gentle sort of way that makes me want to curl close to the demon.

"A beautiful name for a flower such as you."

Flower. He means Blossom. Oh, Wrath, what happened to all the other girls?

I jerk my hand away from him at his words. "I'm not a flower."

"The other girls are safe. Mostly," he says and I freeze.

"What? How did you know what I was thinking?" I ask, looking down at our bond with wide eyes. "Is it this? I-I, oh no, is this letting you hear my thoughts?"

"It's not our bond that gives me your thoughts." Wrath taps a finger against his temple. "I'm a demon, dear one. Invoking my name gives me access to your delicious mind."

Calling out to Wrath when I was in distress was as natural as breathing for me. Of course, I had called on him when I was running from Callum and the others. I'd given him a direct link to my thoughts without even knowing.

"Is that the only way you can read my thoughts?" I'm curious to know just when my demon husband will be able to help himself to my inside voice—there isn't anything quite like being paranoid your new demonic husband will know when you think his ass looks great.

A smile plays over his lips before Wrath answers me. "It's not, but it's the easiest for now." He moves quickly, dropping down into my space just a little more so that our mouths are only an inch or two away from one another.

Oh Wrath. My first kiss.

I hear the undeniable intake of Wrath's breath before he hums for me. "Such a prize for me to claim. I'm going to enjoy defiling you, Buffy."

Oh no. He heard me. He heard me because I keep calling on him. I'm going to have to think of something else to say, but there's no time for that. Not now. Wrath has me right where he wants me.

"Your mouth, sweet Buffy. Offer it to me. Give me your first, dear one."

And just like I knew I would, I obey my demon husband.

CHAPTER
SEVEN

I've never been kissed. I might not know much about it, but I know kissing a demon is a better experience than any human man could give me. Wrath is patient with me, slowly kissing me, letting me learn his mouth and figure how I might like to be kissed.

He's paying attention to what I like. I know from the whimper he pulls from me when he nibbles on my bottom lip. He's done it twice now and each time is better than the last. I press my mouth harder against his and try to do it to him. He lets me, even hums encouragingly when I do it right.

Learning to kiss via a demon teacher on my wedding night is not how I imagined my first kiss. Why he asked, I don't know. Not when we both know he's capable of taking what he wants from me. I don't think taking is Wrath's game, though. Not when it comes to me. It can't be from the way the demon holds me close and kisses me.

He kisses me like I'm a princess.

Like this is our happily-ever-after and he's my prince charming come to rescue me.

Well, he did rip Callum's head off, so I guess that much is true. If I was going to get the best happily-ever-after, I suppose it would be with the god-turned-demon the cult who tried to kill me worships. Even still, this kiss is brain-altering.

It's everything.

Wrath cradles me close. The arm around my waist is strong and firm, holding me right up against him while his other hand is tangled in my hair. He strokes his fingers through it, combing out the tangles I got in my run for freedom, before cradling my head in his large palm.

I feel safe.

Cherished.

Both are new feelings and I drink them hungrily. I part my lips when Wrath licks at the seam, eagerly opening my mouth to him. When his tongue moves against mine, the kiss transforms from tender adoration to frenzied hunger. I wrap my arms around his neck and arch my back to press closer while Wrath moans into my mouth. Steam rises from the hot springs and coils around us. It wraps itself so firmly around us that the outside world ceases to exist.

For a moment there is no cult out to murder me. Or the dead body of my almost husband a few feet away. There is only us and that's the way I like it. So does Wrath, if the way he takes control of our kiss is anything to go by.

He devours me through our kiss and I enjoy it all. When he lifts me higher and drops the hand in my hair to my thigh it only takes a moment to register the cool night air on my hip. Wrath's warm palm teases my skin a second later.

Wrath. Yes.

I've waited for this for so long. I raise my leg when he cups a large hand under my thigh and lifts it. I wrap my leg around his waist and it only takes the slightest nudge to my hip for me to raise my other leg and hook my ankles together. Wrath practically purrs in satisfaction.

"Ruthless little bride," he rumbles against my lips and I smile.

"I didn't think I would ever want to be called ruthless by anyone, but from you? I could get used to it."

He chuckles and kisses me hungrily again. Heat travels down my spine and I feel it between my thighs—my clit throbs and it makes my breath catch. I've never been kissed until tonight, but that doesn't mean I've kept my hands to myself when it all became *too much.*

Wrath inhales deeply. "You smell divine."

"Y-you can smell me?" I freeze. That isn't what I thought he would say. To be fair, I haven't been able to predict much about what Wrath will say, but even so. Oh Wrath, bury me now.

"I'd rather not. I like you right where you are," he says and I wince.

"I have to find another word to use," I groan and duck my head, but Wrath's hand at my chin forces my head back to look up at him.

He scowls. "I like knowing I am your god. Using my name is just fine or do you want to make me jealous?"

"Jealous? Who would you have to be jealous of? You're perfect."

"Now that is the right thing to say, wife. Flattery will get you everywhere. Though there already isn't a thing I would not give you."

49

"Tell me, demon. Is giving your little virgin sacrifice your dick on that list of things she can ask for tonight?" A voice drawls and I scream.

"Who's there?" I try to twist to look around, but I can't manage it in Wrath's embrace. "Someone's here. We have to go."

Wrath snorts. "Like hell we do. It's only the witch," he says dismissively, leaning in to kiss me again, but I'm not about to let the witch get the drop on me twice in one day.

"The witch as in The Witch of the Woods?" I shake my head and try to get free from Wrath, but all I manage to do is kick out, my feet paddling nothing but the evening air while he looks on unbothered.

"We have to go. She's dangerous," I tell him. "We shouldn't be here if she's creeping in the woods."

Wrath scoffs and keeps his eye on me while I try to shimmy out of his arms. "Dangerous? She's more annoying than anything, really."

"I heard that, demon," the Witch calls out to us. Her voice echoes and bounces back to us from the hot spring pools. I hear the crunch of her foot on the ground but still can't see her. It's impossible to see anything with the steam swirling around us. "And I'll have you know, dear Blossom, I do not creep. It's called *reconnaissance*, look it up."

Wrath sighs. "You know my name, Sunday. Quite rude of you to pretend you don't after all this time."

"Well, I'm quite rude, if you don't remember."

"Don't remind me."

I tap his arm. "Can you put me down, please?"

Wrath makes a face at my request. "I'd rather not, but since you wish for it I'll make an allowance," he grumbles, setting me on my feet.

The second my foot touches the ground, I spin around to try and catch sight of the witch, but there's nothing. "Where is she?"

"I'm here, you silly goose," Sunday says, suddenly appearing at my arm. She looks different than I remember. This afternoon when she appeared, she had on a tattered gray robe and her hair was long, almost to the ground, shining a silvery gray. I'd thought she was old then, her hood hiding her face from me. The only thing I'd seen was her gnarled hand.

She's not old, not at all. The Witch of the Woods is young and beautiful, wearing a white pantsuit with midnight black hair cut in a sleek bob. She looks more like someone suited to sit on the Founders Council than an teleporting witch.

It's a good look on her.

Still doesn't mean I'm okay with seeing her again.

I shriek, throw a wild punch and hide behind Wrath. I shake a finger at her from behind the comforting bulk of my demon husband. "Will you stop doing that? That's twice today!"

"Stop doing what? This?" she asks and in the blink of an eye, she's gone. Just to tap me on the back a second later. "You surely mean this, I think?"

"Oh my Wrath!" I take another swing at the witch and hit nothing but air. "I mean it! I didn't think it was funny this afternoon and I don't think it's funny now. How would you like it if someone did that to you? What was with that cryptic warning?" I forget my fear for a beat and step out from behind Wrath.

"You had me *right there*. At no point did you think it would be helpful to tell me *I was going to be murdered tonight*?"

"But I did clearly tell you," Sunday says and makes a show of looking at her nails in the moonlight. "Quite benevolent of me to warn you at all."

"You said they were going to pluck my petals off, does that sound clear?" I ask and throw my hands out in a *'what the hell'* gesture, "You said I was going to be ash under their foot. You called me a fool! How is that helpful when I didn't know about my entire life being a lie or the knife waiting to cut my throat?"

She hums and takes a step closer. The move has Wrath growling a warning. I feel him take a step closer to me, his chest to my back. As angry as I am, I have to force myself to focus on Sunday and not the places Wrath's body touches mine. It's hard to think of her as anything but The Witch of the Woods, but I manage it.

"Stay there, witch," he orders and *Wrath,* I nearly moan from the rumbling growl his voice sends through me. Of all the times to get ambushed by her, it had to be now?

"Touchy, touchy, Wrath, but..." Sunday's voice trails off and she stops with a smile, "I think I see why you like this one. Little human has fire to her, doesn't she? Seems I judged your fair wife prematurely." Sunday makes a show of bowing in apology to Wrath and I think about what might happen if I close the space and kick her before she zips away again. I can go back to exploring Wrath then. He squeezes my shoulder and pulls me back against him.

"I know your thoughts, dear one. No hitting the witch," he whispers in my ear. I wince. Old habits die hard, it seems. What else do people not raised in a cult say when they're in a panic over how close their demon husband is?

"The way you say *witch*, like I'm not *The Witch.* It's The Witch of the Woods. *Not a witch* of the woods," Sunday *tsks* and crosses her arms. "And this is the thanks I get for warning her about what was going to happen? It's because of me that she's alive at all, you know."

If I hadn't been conditioned by a murdering cult to smile when I was angry, I would scowl. Seeing as I wasn't, the best I can manage is not a smile. I think I heard one of the Outsiders call it Bitch Face. Whatever it is, I give it to Sunday in spades.

"That's not true. All you did was confuse me and scare me this morning."

"Ah, ah, ah, but you were on your guard, were you not? That has to count for something."

I ignore her. "And you didn't save me. *I saved me*," I pause and think of Lylah screaming at me to run while she fought her groom. "The other girls are the reason why I'm alive. *Not you*."

"Tomato, Potato."

Wrath sighs. "That's not how the saying goes."

Sunday flicks her hand at us. "One little human wife and you think you're the human expert now, eh? Well, you know what? I think I've had enough pleasantries. Before your little hellcat tries to sucker punch me again, you're going to want to listen very carefully. Especially if you want to rescue the rest of your pretty little Blossoms."

I freeze. The Blossoms. She means my friends. Even the Blossoms I don't know as well as Meadow or Lylah deserve saving. I have to help them.

"They're alive? Really?"

She inclines her head. "They all are, at least for now. I don't expect they have long, though."

"But how are they alive? I saw that girl, the one they-the one they killed." I don't know who it was, not in the chaos that went down. It could have been any of the girls I knew with how panicked I was trying to get away.

The only thing I can hold on to is that Meadow is still alive.

For now.

"Oh, my sweet hellcat, do you mean *that girl?*" Sunday asks and nods to the left. I follow her movement and feel my stomach drop to my feet, but in the best of ways. It feels like one of the almost moments I had with Callum when I thought he might try and sneak a kiss.

He never did though and this moment is so much better, because the girl I thought was dead is alive and well.

CHAPTER
EIGHT

"Nina?" I whisper and the girl I thought was gone is standing in front of me. We went to school together and she was always sweet. The kind of shy and quiet person that mostly goes unnoticed, at least she was when we were kids.

She was picked later than the rest of us. She was twelve when the Founders named her a Blossom. I thought it was wonderful when she was announced as a Blossom—it brought her out of her shell. She became chatty and outgoing, a completely different girl. We had fun at the Autumn Harvest Festival together when we were in charge of the hayrides.

"*They killed me!*" She screams and starts to stomp towards us. "*He* killed me!"

"Almost killed. I explained this to you," Sunday sighs and crosses her arms. "You think she'd get over being dead for a minute or two. Some of us have been dead for a lot longer, you know?"

I blink at Sunday's words. "You're dead?" I ask. She could be, I don't know. She looks different now than she did before, with her power pantsuit and hair. Maybe she's dead?

"Who hasn't been these days?" Sunday asks.

I point to myself. "Me?"

Wrath says nothing, but chuckles. The sound is...nice. It's almost as good as when he growled, but a different kind of good. This makes me think of fresh baked cookies and sunshine. The kind of lazy morning when I could sit with Meadow and gossip. I lean back against him and the arm around my waist gives me a squeeze. He's perfectly content to hold me in silence while I have it out with Sunday, only stepping in when he thinks she's stepping out of line. I even tried to punch her and I know it's only the threat of Wrath that kept her from doing something magical and terrifying to me. I don't know what I was thinking when I tried to swing on her, but I did it and Wrath supported it.

Support.

I don't think I've ever had that from a man, but then again, Wrath is no man.

"Just barely, but fair point," Sunday mutters as we watch Nina storm through the steam like an avenging goddess. The sweet and nice girl I remember is gone. This Nina looks like she wants blood.

I completely understand. I'm bloodthirsty now, too.

"*He cut my throat!*" Nina points at her throat which looks as perfect as I remember, but her dress is still stained red from her blood. "That little shit! Do you know how terrible he was? The only thing he ever talked about was himself and how great everything in the city was going to be. He made me look at apartment floor plans and interior design magazines for *hours*! And for what, when he was just going to kill me? Do I look like I know the difference between Tuscan Sun and Yellow Mirage, Buffy, because let me tell you, *I. Do. Not. Know.*"

I wince. She's right. Her intended, Daniel Marsh had made a show of getting ready to leave for the city. I remember the stacks of magazines he had Nina carrying. Considering Callum is now dead, I got off easy on this one.

I clear my throat. "Nina, I'm sorry, I-"

"Is that...oh my Wrath, is that him?" Nina freezes a few steps away from us. Her eyes aren't on me anymore, they're over my shoulder on Wrath. Then, just like I did, she throws herself down on the ground with her palms facing the sky.

"My Lord, I didn't know it was you. I will gladly die again in sacrifice if you order it!"

"What the hell is this?" Wrath mutters while Nina starts to pray.

"I pray my soul Wrath to take," she chants.

"I never wanted a single one of you dead. I hope you know that," he assures me. "Waste of a perfectly good virgin, if you ask me," Wrath says while my thoughts wander to what exactly he would do with a virgin.

"To Wrath we are bound as a wife to keep," Nina rattles on and jealousy spikes hot and fresh in my blood when she looks up at him with adoration in her eyes. "I am ready to be your bride, my Lord."

"Sorry, the position is filled at the moment, dearie. On the bright side, you have your life," Sunday chimes in before I can say anything. It's irrational to feel jealousy. We were all raised to be wives. We were all raised to think of Wrath as the one we would marry.

It's not her fault. It's not. *Wrath, it's not her fault.*

"I'm ready to offer you my body. No man has touched me, my Lord. I saved myself for you. Take me as you please!" Nina starts to pull at the top of her dress as she stands.

She's totally getting naked.

"I should have known this was going to happen," Sunday mutters while Wrath coughs. When I look up at him, I see him making a show of looking away.

"Now, I know you're feeling a bit hot, dear one," he says, eyes on the moon and I realize that I've once again let him into my mind by invoking his name. "My eyes are only for you," he says quickly while I rush forward to stop Nina from ripping her dress off.

"What? No! Please keep your clothes on, Nina. Stop!" I have to fight with the woman for a full five minutes before she finally stops fighting me and gives up.

"Wow." She pants and hunches over, hands on her knees and groans with a smile. "You've been totally working out. I saw you at the gym, Buffy."

She's right. I was working out a lot more to be ready for tonight. Thank god the weights did something for keeping Nina's dress on. She can get naked all she likes, just not in front of Wrath. Just thinking about it makes me angry.

I smile at her. "Thanks."

"You're welcome. You're so strong. I like it."

I smile at her words and I mean this one. "Are you going to stop trying to get naked?" I ask when she stands up with a deep breath.

"I thought I was supposed to get naked for him, though," she says and points at Wrath, who holds up his hands.

"That was never *my* decree."

Nina looks as confused as I feel. Even so, she smiles as she speaks. "But the Founders said-"

"Your Founders are nothing but heartless, greedy men with no souls. The deal they struck was with my former master. I've entertained it out of curiosity. Nothing more."

"Your master?" I ask.

Wrath's silver eyes meet mine and he nods. "Yes. My master. I served him for five hundred years. It was he who made the deal with your Founders."

I don't know what to make of his words. We worshiped Wrath as a god, but he had a master. The most powerful being I thought existed was bound to serve another.

"Why do you think he's so keen to help you take revenge?" Sunday asks and comes to stand with Nina and I. "He knows exactly what it's like to have to do things you don't like for a master you despise, don't you Wrath?"

"Quiet, witch or I'll cut out your tongue," Wrath snaps. When he steps forward, his eyes are brilliant and bright, his teeth as sharp as knives.

"Ugh, back to that I see," Sunday mutters while Nina gives a yelp and hides behind me.

"I'm scared, Buffy. I didn't know he was going to be so scary."

"It's okay, he won't hurt us," I whisper to her. The second I speak, the light goes out of Wrath's eyes.

He smiles but Nina doesn't stop shaking behind me. "You're right, I won't hurt you. I will hurt *them*. I intend to bring you your revenge, wife."

CHAPTER
NINE

"If you want to save the other Blossoms, you'll have to go back."

She means back to town. I'll have to go back to Sweet Tooth.

"Not happening, witch." Wrath sweeps me behind him. "She isn't going near those beasts. I'm going to kill every last one of them and gift her their heads."

I never thought my heart would warm at the mention of maiming and murder, but Wrath has changed my outlook on the whole murder, crimes of passion thing.

"As romantic as that is, if you want to save the brides, you're going to have to give her to them," Sunday flicks a finger at me. We're at the concessions stand. I remembered where the spare key was hidden and opened it up. There were a few plastic chairs inside to use, but mostly the cheesy cheddar chips I promised myself are here. Seeing as I'm real big on keeping my promises to myself after the night I've had, I'm eating chips by the handful on a rickety plastic chair while Wrath stands behind me, a few bags of chips in his hands. He grabbed them when he saw just how much I liked them. Nina rummages in the concession stand out of sight.

Wrath glares. "I'll see that town burn before she sets foot there."

Sunday sits across from me with her own packet of chips. She went with salt and vinegar.

"The only thing keeping those girls alive is that they think they need your wife to complete their ritual."

"If that's true, then exactly how is serving my wife up on a silver platter keeping the brides alive?" Wrath grumbles. When my current bag of cheesy chips runs out, he's right there handing me a replacement.

"Thank you," I tell him. I'm not used to being served–not even in the capacity of a bag of cheesy chips. In the cult, I was the one expected to keep a careful eye on the others. At least the male Founders and the grooms.

There wasn't anyone that cared about what I wanted. But here I am now with my once god and now husband worried I'll run out of chips.

"Anything for you, dear one."

I smile and Sunday sticks her finger down her throat and mock gags. "Honeymoon periods, I swear."

I pop open my bag of chips and ignore her. "He has a point. How is going back helping the Blossoms stay alive, if me escaping is keeping them safe?"

"Because they'll kill them whether you come back or not. They just haven't given up yet. You have three nights," she says, pointing to the moon overhead, "before the full moon is gone.

They'll kill them before that happens. The Blossoms will die no matter what, but you going back means you can control when and where, because they'll come for you, hellcat."

"She's not doing it. It will be me that darkens Sweet Tooth's doorways. It will be me they see before I gouge their eyes from their skulls and rip their still beating hearts out for my wife's pleasure."

Sunday leans back in her chair. "Oh shit, you're into that, hellcat?"

"I'm not-I mean," I stop speaking. Before tonight I would have said no, but listening to Wrath say it is definitely giving me butterflies. Knowing that he's committed to not only acting as my hands in a revenge scheme, but committed *to me*. Well, that does a lot for me.

"I don't know," I finally settle on and Sunday grins. "Maybe."

"You almost frowned there, Blossom. Good to see the brain-washing is wearing thin."

"We weren't brainwashed!" Nina shouts from inside the concessions stand. There's a clatter and something big falls with a thud, but she doesn't appear.

"Yes, we were, Nina. We were getting married to a demon in the middle of the night. Yet we didn't think anything bad was going to happen to us," I call out to her.

Nina pops up holding a fire extinguisher and a pool noodle. She sighs. "Okay, you got me there, Buffy," she says, pointing the pool noodle at me before she drops out of sight again.

I don't know what she's planning on doing with the pool noodle, or what she's doing in the concession stand, but I don't ask. It's probably better for me not to know.

Wrath kneels at my side and takes my hand. "I will gladly

bring their bodies to you in pieces. Name your revenge and it will be done, wife. I am yours to command."

Wife.

When Wrath calls me that, I'm done for. I give right in to my hot demon husband and I'm shameless enough not to feel bad about it.

I probably should, but once again, I was brainwashed. So it all adds to his sex appeal when Wrath threatens the cult.

Sunday snaps her fingers at us and I jump. "Focus. Stop mooning over your demon."

She's right, I was mooning. I'd forgotten all about her.

Wrath sighs heavily and gives her a glare. "I'm growing tired of you, witch. I'm taking Buffy and leaving you. She needs her rest."

"You can whisk her away to your little honeymoon demon suite *after* I finish explaining our genius plan, lover boy."

Wrath scowls, but when I put a hand on his arm, he relaxes. "She has a point about the Blossoms," I tell him. The weddings always take place on the first night of the full moon. We don't have much time left to save the rest. "Please, I need to save Meadow and the others."

Wrath settles beside me, still on his knees. "As you wish, Buffy," he says and jerks his chin at Sunday. "Make it quick, witch."

"Rude ass demon," she mutters before looking at me. "As I was explaining, we have two more nights to free the other Blossoms. That means you take your cute little newlywed butt back to town and take the Founders out. Once they're dead, there won't be anyone to run the cult and you'll get the girls back. Easy peasy."

I cross my arms and consider her words. "If it's so easy peasy, how am I supposed to take out the Founders?"

"The old-fashioned way. *Murder.*"

"I can't kill anyone," I whisper. It's true, I can't. I might have wanted to kill Callum and the rage that poured out of me at Victor's betrayal blinded me, but I don't think I could have done it if I wasn't forced. Not if it hadn't been about survival. "There's no way I can walk back into town and just kill them."

Sunday points at where Wrath continues to glower beside me. "That's what your surly demon husband is for. He's happy to maim and kill that entire town to please you. Let him get his hands dirty. I happen to think it will be wonderfully ironic for him to destroy the cult that worships him, don't you think?"

Murder. Sunday is insane with how casually she's talking about all of this. I shake my head, my smile wobbling.

"I can't ask him to do that. Not for me."

Wrath isn't having it. "It is my duty and my honor. Show me who, Buffy. I will handle the rest. There is no greater honor than bringing you your revenge."

Wrath's eagerness to help makes sense, but what doesn't is Sunday. Even if she looks like she belongs on the Founders Council and has an actual name, that doesn't change the fact that she's still The Witch of the Woods.

"And what does The Witch of the Woods gain from helping us? Why do you care if the Blossoms are dead or not? You could have stopped this or warned me before tonight and you never did."

She leans forward and smiles at me. "Oh, now that, my pretty Blossom, is easy. I hate greedy men and their willingness to break others for their own gain. As for the timing of everything, well...it was never quite right. Not until now, not until you."

"Is that the only reason, Sunday?" Wrath rumbles and her eyes flick to his for a second before they come back to me.

"Why are you bringing up old shit, demon?"

"Tell her the truth, witch," he growls and this sounds different than before. It's dark and deadly. Sunday is treading on thin ice.

Sunday's eyes narrow into a glare before she sits up straight. "You show me yours, I'll show you mine. You first, demon."

Wrath falls silent and I look his way. "What does she mean?" I ask.

"Nothing, she's meddling."

"I've not yet begun to meddle, but I'll tell you what. You agree to trot back in there to wipe out the Founding Families and I'll step in to buy you more time, should you need it."

"More time? How?"

Sunday throws her arm up at the full moon. "The moon, ninny. How else? I'll add more time to the clock if you need it, but you have to go back now. The wards I created won't hold for much longer."

Wrath sniffs and looks around with a nod. "She's right. Her magic grows weak, and the mortals are close. They know we're here."

My stomach twists. "They're out there looking for us? Like, right now?" I scan the area but there's nothing but us. The hot springs bubble away in the clearing. The dark lump I know is Callum's decapitated body and head wink in and out of sight with each cloud of steam that billows up from the springs. The trees I feared before, when I thought Sunday was the scariest thing in the world, don't seem so bad anymore. Yet I don't see or hear anyone else but us.

"Hunting more like it," Wrath says as he rises and holds a hand out to me. "I promise you've nothing to worry over, Buffy. You're safe with me. I won't let a single one of them touch you."

I take his hand and nod. "I know. I wouldn't do this if I didn't have you."

Sunday chuckles. "Don't lie to him. He's got a few tricks to read your mind. You would do it, even without him. We all know it. You're braver than the brains you have, Buffy. The only difference is now you won't get yourself killed. Now, listen closely to me. I want you to go back to town and pretend nothing is wrong."

"How am I supposed to do that? Callum is dead and he's the-"

"First Founding family's eldest, yes, I know," Sunday interrupts with a wink. "Good start on the murdering with that one. There's no reason to worry, because you're coming back to them with a husband."

"Do you really think they'll just accept me back if I come walking into town with him," I ask her.

"The entire point of the sacrifice is to wed you to Wrath. You're already married, so you're kind of off the table for immediate death. Yet, you *have* been marked for death since birth, Buffy. They won't give you up just because you have a husband. The cult elders will look for a way to finish what they started with you. Should buy the time we need to get your friends out of there before they complete the ritual to Wrath."

I jerk a thumb at Wrath. "Yeah and Wrath is their god. Husband or not, once they see Wrath with me there's no way they'll let me near the other Blossoms. They'll kill them on sight as offering to Wrath."

"As much as I hate to admit to any shortcomings in Sunday's presence," The witch kicks her feet and shakes her bag of salt and vinegar chips at Wrath in acknowledgement, "my magic is strong, but not strong enough to stop our dear cultists from killing all the Blossoms. This Meadow you speak of would be at risk if it were to come down to it."

"I have a plan for that," Sunday says and smiles encouragingly at me. "But you'll have to trust the process. Can you do that, Buffy?"

I feel sick thinking of Meadow in danger, but it's my reality. She's in danger and so are the other Blossoms. I've known them all my life and I'm not going to abandon them now.

"Yes, I have no other choice. I have to go back." Wrath lets out a disgruntled rumble beside me, but I don't back down. It only takes a second before he sighs and nods.

"Where you go, wife, I will follow."

CHAPTER
TEN

"You're sure this will work?" I ask nervously and Sunday hums with a nod.

"It will. You're married, that means they can't touch you. At least, for now."

"She's right, dear one. I've been bothered by this cult for five hundred years. They won't touch you while you have a husband. But they will look for a way to claim you. A lot of preparation goes into Blossoms. This particular ritual *is* rather outdated."

I tilt my head and consider Wrath's words. "Rituals can become outdated?"

"Verily. There's little need for virgin sacrifices, but for some reason humans still insist upon it."

A shout goes up from the woods and I freeze. "They're close."

"My wards are about to fall," Sunday says, walking ahead of me. She holds out her hand and *tsks*. "Yeah, about to bite the big one here. I'm guessing your acolytes are right on the other side."

"They are not mine," Wrath mutters and comes to my side.

"They were a job assignment that hasn't been passed on to the next yet."

"What the heck does that mean?" Nina asks. She's with us, still toting her pool noodle and fire extinguisher. She's got a bag full of pilfered items to add to her stolen loot.

"Timing, like I said," Sunday answers, motioning for Wrath and me to join her at her ward's edge. "Lucky for us, really. Here we go, my newlyweds. Are you ready to meet the cult?"

I look down at my wedding dress. It's stained with dirt and grime, with a smattering of blood on it. I have zero idea who it belongs to. I haven't seen myself, but I'm sure I'm just as rough looking as my dress.

In contrast to my level of wrecked, Wrath looks utterly perfect. He's hornless now but perfect all the same.

Even in his human form.

Wind ruffles his wintry glossy hair. Wrath's face is beautiful and still achingly perfect. He has full lips, lush and inviting. His mouth is made all the more perfect by his high cheekbones and aquiline nose. Wrath's eyes are no longer silver, but they're stunning all the same. So brown I almost think they're black.

Sunday purses her lips and looks Wrath over. "You're basically the same as a human. Just, you know, smaller."

Smaller or not, my demon husband is still big, not demon mistaken for a god big, but he's big.

A head taller than me, with muscled broad shoulders and a trim waist. He looks like a tree I'd like to climb, which is good considering we're married now. I don't think there's any real way to get out of a demon marriage. Maybe under normal circumstances, but seeing as there's a cult involved, my guess is no dice.

I wouldn't want to either. Something has settled into my

chest when I look at Wrath and think about being his wife. That could be the effects of a lifetime of brainwashing, but I don't care enough to question it right now.

Everything I've ever believed was a lie, so what's the harm in keeping just this one thing for myself? I'm owed something, aren't I, for everything I've been through? Why not let it be Wrath?

"I give you my vow that I will keep you safe, Buffy." Wrath comes close and takes my hand. "I am ready to meet the soulless beasts."

Out of all the things I could possibly call my own, the demon I worshiped is easily the best.

"I know you will," I smile up at him and let him draw me close to his side.

"Such a beautiful couple," Nina sighs and hugs her pool noodle close. "I can't even be mad that you got to be his wife and not me. You look perfect together. Really, the other Blossoms are going to lose their shit. When Callum sees you with your new husband *he's going to die.*"

"He won't," Wrath says while he rolls his shoulders and stares straight ahead at the boundary between us and Sunday's ward. The air shimmers the way it does on a hot day when you think there's water on the road but it's nothing other than a mirage. "Die, that is. I've already killed him and I am *not* using the resources necessary to resurrect him."

I open my mouth and then close it again, because what do you say to that?

"Do you think I should have a human name for this little excursion?" Wrath asks me and I shake my head. He *would* call this a little excursion, rather than us returning to the cult that raised me to revenge kill a lot of people.

"A human name?"

"Yes." He nods and reaches over to tuck my hair behind my ear. "I don't much think my being called *Wrath* will allow us to go unnoticed, dear one."

"Oh yeah, that's true..." I bite my lip and think hard for a name worthy of Wrath.

"He looks like a Reginald," Sunday offers.

Wrath rolls his eyes. "Shut it, witch."

"Well, you do. But pick quickly, because Nina and I are done here. It's all on the two of you from here on out. Remember, the cult will not kill you until they find a loophole. You have until the full moon's end to rescue the Blossoms or it's all going to be wrapped up in one giant sacrifice. If you need me, call me!"

"Call you? But how am I supposed to call you when I-" My words are cut off by a flash of light. I have to shield my eyes from the burn of it. I rub my eyes with my free hand and blink. "They're gone, aren't they?"

Wrath squeezes my hand. "They are. Good riddance."

"You really don't like her."

"I know better than to trust that witch. You'll learn in time, Buffy."

I crane my neck to look around the clearing. Everything looks the same, even with the ward failing. There's no sign that Nina and Sunday were ever here.

"How am I supposed to call her? Does she even have a phone, because I don't."

Wrath chuckles. "Sunday always has a way of turning up when you need her. You won't need a phone to call her."

"I see the springs!"

We both turn towards the shout. It's to our left and through the trees. "They're close."

"They are, but you are safe with me. Have you decided what to name me?"

I can hear the shouts of horror as the band of men searching for me find Callum's body and head.

"*Wrath*, how could you allow this!? There's his head!"

"We will have our revenge in Wrath's name!"

"*In Wrath's name!*"

The shouts bouncing and echoing through the trees remind me that we don't have much time. It's easy to forget when I'm with Wrath.

"Oh right, your name." I rack my brain while I hear the voices getting closer. They'll be on us any minute now.

"*When you lie, it's best to keep it simple. That way you don't get confused.*"

Meadow told me that. Of course, she'd meant it in the context of us playing hooky from our duties cleaning up the Hall of Worship, but like Sunday said—*tomato, potato.*

"How would you like Damon? I mean, we wouldn't exactly be lying, since it does mean Demon. It seems easy enough to remember because, no matter what Sunday says, you do *not* look like a Reginald at all. Not that I would know because I've never met one." I'm rambling, I know that. I can't seem to stop myself with the smile Wrath has fixed on me. "If I'd known I was going to go on this long I would have brought a glass of water."

"Would you like me to conjure you a glass of water, dear one?" His smile is like every beautiful thing I was raised to believe in, but this time it's all true.

I smile back at him and shake my head. "No water needed. What do you think of the name?"

Wrath nods at me. "Damon it is. Truth be told, you could call me Reginald and I would answer to it."

"You would?" I ask in surprise and Wrath shrugs. We hear a crash in the woods. There's no way they aren't on the path with us now.

"My name is not my own. It's yours to command. Any name you see fit to call me by is worthy of answering, wife."

I've heard of flutters in your stomach, but that's not what Wrath's words do to me. No, a whole army of butterflies floods my entire system and I feel my heart start to race.

"You really do say the most romantic things."

"I know no other way to be when it comes to you."

"There she is!"

Wrath lifts his head and looks away from me. His eyes are on the men charging towards us and a growl rumbles in his throat. The men are carrying torches and I spot the telltale gleam of steel in their hands. They've brought knives with them to finish the deed.

"We will try this Sunday's way, but if it fails, I'm killing them all."

I follow Wrath's gaze and fear courses through me, but a smile pulls at my lips. "Only if you promise to make it hurt."

Wrath inclines his head to me. "You have my word, dear one."

"You killed my boy!" Mr. O'Hare snarls. He's at the front of the mob with a torch in one hand and a knife in the other. He fumbles the knife when he swings it in my direction and it lands on the ground with a thud. "Grab her now and take her to the circle. I want her dead within the hour!"

Oh, goodie. Yet again, another threat to my life tonight. I eye the knife and consider making a dive for it when the men I've grown up with start forward, their knives raised high. They stop dead in their tracks when Wrath crosses his arms and stands in front of me.

Even in his human form, he's formidable. Easily taller and bigger than the rest of the men by far. "Who put this mortal in charge? He wouldn't last a day in hell." He looks back at me with a frown and wags his finger. "It was a vote, wasn't it? This is the trouble with you mortals and democracy. You never learn."

"Whatever do you mean, husband?" I grit out between clenched teeth as I smile broadly at the men who want to kill me. How are we going to pull this off with Wrath already talking like this? There's no way they won't know he's totally not human.

Wrath *tsks* at Nina's intended, Daniel Marsh, when he steps forward. My eyes land on his knife and I swallow hard. Is that the same knife he used on Nina?

Oh Wrath, I bet it is.

Wrath narrows his eyes at Daniel and immediately the other man stops approaching. "He can't even handle his weapon properly and you expect me to hand my wife over to him?" He points at Mr. O'Hare with another tut. "You're sorely mistaken."

"Damon," I warn. My smile is strained but it holds. "This is not the way we should meet the, ah," I stammer and my mind goes blank, because what do I even call my almost murderers? I clear my throat and step in front of Wrath. "My uh, we need to be more friendly to *the others*," I finally settle on and put my hand on his chest.

Wrath rumbles low in his chest but stands down the second I touch him. "As you wish, wife."

"This is none of your concern," Mr. O'Hare demands. The man is bent low, grabbing at his knife in the dirt and it strikes me as odd that I feared him for so long. Even before I knew he wanted to kill me, I worried about stepping out of line, or disobeying any order that came from the Founders' Council—every order was from Mr. O'Hare, when it really came down to it.

He looks so small now.

So insignificant. I'm not scared anymore.

"I'm not going with you. I'm married now," I tell him and look at the other men's angry faces, "You can't sacrifice me anymore."

"Don't listen to her," Daniel snaps and clears his throat as he stands taller. Wrath hasn't moved an inch and neither has Daniel, but he's trying to be brave. "Step aside, this has nothing to do with you. You're an Outsider."

"Outsider or not, I married her." Wrath sniffs and adjusts his cuff with a cold smile. "Allow me to introduce myself to you. I am Damon, so named by the god I serve. I've been appointed to clear up a few things here by right of jurisdiction. Your little full moon ritual can't have a married woman in the mix. I'd think you would know that in a cult devoted to Wrath, would you not?"

Daniel falls silent and looks at Mr. O'Hare, who's managed to get his knife up and in hand by this point. "Is that true? You promised we'd kill them all when you paired us with the Blossoms. You swore I'd get to rip her throat out. That we all would!"

Daniel's angry. He's angry that he can't touch me. He killed Nina, even if Sunday resurrected her. I saw him. My stomach sours and I have to grab onto Wrath's arm to steady myself. How can anyone be so eager to hurt someone else? I never thought Daniel had it in him, but now that I look at the faces, I realize I never thought any of them wanted to hurt me.

Sunday was right. I was a fool.

"There are certain aspects of the agreement that do state only unmarried virgins are allowed," Mr. O'Hare grumbles and glares at me. "Though none but the Founders are allowed to read the texts, so how is it that you know that?" He levels his knife at Wrath in what I think is meant to be threatening, but only earns a disdainful look from Wrath.

"I'm a mage, you idiot," Wrath returns with a sigh. My smile wobbles and nearly falls off my face. I have to hide my face behind Wrath's shoulder.

Mr. O'Hare's mouth drops open. "A mage? Y-you truly are a mage? But they all died out a hundred years ago."

"Not all, just the ones here with your little enterprise. Most likely the result of you botching the agreement made some five hundred years back. If you studied the text more thoroughly you would know that, but then again, I wouldn't be here if you had."

I have zero clue where Wrath is going with this, but I trust him so I stay silent while he leads the cultists further into his plan.

"What does he mean?" Someone calls out and Mr. O'Hare looks like he wants to rip his hair out.

He glares at us before he turns a placating smile to the men. I recognize this look. It's the one he gave us before each sermon he delivered. "He means the curse we thought was a result of the Blossom's lack of smiles is not-is not on the women, but-"

"*You*. All of you have displeased your master Wrath. I was sent to take a wife from among you in order to correct your failings. By my estimation, you have until the full moon's fall. As I've chosen Buffy for my wife, she's off the table for your offering. You'll have to find another to take her place."

Mr. O'Hare snarls. "Jurisdiction or not, how am I to know what you say is true? You could be lying, someone sent to sow dissent in our community. Why, you could even be from the cult two towns over for all we know."

Wrath snorts. "Trust me, the cultists there have little interest in you. Their interests are far more benign than killing women."

Mr. O'Hare snaps his fingers and ignores Wrath. "Grab him, bring her to me. I'm going to crack him open and see just what this mage is made out of."

The men are too gleeful to commit violence. Daniel's not the only one that wants to hurt me, hurt the other Blossoms they pledged to marry. Violence is heavy in the air and I grab Wrath's shoulder.

We'll find another way, we have to. I look up at the moon and try to think what a call to Sunday might look like. She'll know what to do.

"We have to run, this isn't going to work, please," I beg and grab Wrath's arm. He pulls his arm out of my grasp and ushers me behind him.

"Dear heart, stay there. These naughty mortals need to be taught a lesson."

"Someone dedicate her death to Callum," Mr. O'Hare says and I fall back a step when the men advance, but Wrath smiles at me.

"Don't look at them. I don't want you to see this."

I nod. "Okay." I fix my eyes on my husband and not the angry mob. The view is certainly better than the raggedy men who lied to me.

Wrath rolls his shoulders and takes a deep breath. "I tried to be merciful, but if that's how you want to play it. By all means, be my guests." There's a burst of blue light from his hands that makes me jump. When he raises his hands, the flames leap from his fingertips and shoot out to the men. There's screams and a whoosh as the forest floor catches fire.

"How is he doing this?"

"Should we revisit the faces of Blossoms sacrificed? I think they might like to have a word with all of you." The wind kicks up and my hair flies into my face, which makes it easier not to look at what Wrath is about to do. I don't need to look to hear the voices that are starting to moan and scream all around us.

I hear women, so many women. And they're angry. Shrieks of frustration rise up out of the wind and wrap themselves around us as they get louder.

"You stole my life!"

"You promised you loved me!"

"Liars! Liars, all of you!"

"I hope he rips you apart and eats your heart!"

"I'm waiting for youuuuu!"

Men's screams join the anguished cries of Blossoms. I clap my hands over my ears and drop down to hide my face. I'm smiling because my body can't help it. I bite my lip so hard blood floods my mouth and it's only then that the winds die and the screams stop.

Wrath crouches in front of me and pushes my hair back from my face. "You're hurt."

"I'm fine," I lie. I'm shaking under his hands, but it helps having Wrath touch me. I lean into his touch and drink up his strength. I feel safer with him this close to me.

"He really is a mage," someone says. I look past Wrath to where Mr. O'Hare is on the ground, clutching his knife like it will protect him from the Blossoms he sacrificed.

"We can work out a deal, I'm sure!" He calls out to us. "Name your price, mage."

"Damon," Wrath replies without looking away from my face. "My name is Damon. You will not address me as anything else." He pulls me up to my feet and holds me close. "Now, my wife is tired and needs her rest. Take me to your town and give me your best house or I'm going to gut the lot of you and feed you to your hungry Blossoms just for fun."

CHAPTER
ELEVEN

"I've never been in here," I whisper, staring at the closed door. We're in the house at the top of the great hill. It's one nobody has ever stayed in because it's meant for Wrath. It's a three story Victorian house that's as old as the town.

Every person in Sweet Tooth knows about The House on the Hill—-*Wrath's Embrace.* Over the centuries, it's been maintained by each and every Sweet Tooth Cultist. From the grounds to the furnishings. Blossoms weren't allowed to see inside. The most I was allowed to do was maintain the flowers outside on account of my green thumb.

I was always too nervous to do what the other Blossoms did and peek inside the windows. I never thought I'd set foot inside but here I am, on my wedding night with Wrath, while he wears his human form. I can't see our bond when he's in his human form but I can still feel it. I rub my hand across my chest. The comfort that floods my fingertips lets me breathe easier.

This might be Wrath's home, but we're still in Sweet Tooth.

The cult that raised me has my friends hostage while they figure out how to kill me now that I've got a husband. I still can't believe we were able to get away from Mr. O'Hare and the mob of men after they found Callum's head and most of his body.

Of course, men like them only respect another man's claim. Or, in this case, a demon masquerading as a man.

"In a town as small as Sweet Tooth, you've never been here? Why is that?" Wrath walks the length of the living room.

Despite the Victorian architecture, it's decorated with modern furnishings. Plush couches with sleek lines and thick rugs over the hardwood. There's even a glass coffee table stacked with photography books beneath the green glass chandelier above it. I can see the kitchen through an archway with quartz countertops and stainless steel appliances that gleam under the lights. The entire house is lit up like the Fourth of July for us. Someone came ahead to make the home ready for us. Outside, it's freezing, the cold wind rattles the trees around the house and I hear the *tap tap tap* of branches against windows. A roll of thunder echoed just a few seconds ago.

No doubt a storm is on the way. Despite that, it's warm and bright in the house. There's even fresh cut flowers sitting on the tables in the living room and hallway.

"Because it's your house," I tell him, walking to the stairs in front of me. A bookcase on the landing leading to the second floor catches my eye and curiosity gets the better of me. I can't wait to explore the house now that I'm finally inside. I wonder what's on the next two floors.

He stops pacing and looks at me over his shoulder. I don't see him so much as feel him look and I meet his curious gaze.

"What? My house? Why would I need a house here? That's

the silliest thing I've ever heard." He glances around the space with disdain. "I don't like modern contemporary furnishings. This looks like an ad for one of those godforsaken design shows."

Nina would agree, but I like it well enough. It's nicer than the house I grew up in. I shrug and clasp my hands behind my back. "The Founders swore you ordered it. It's not like any of us thought to question it."

Wrath hums and resumes walking the length of the room. He pauses in the archway and looks into the kitchen. "At least the kitchen is updated. I'd be offended if I saw a white fridge in here." We have a white fridge in my home. My mother was beside herself that she would finally get all the latest upgrades.

"It's going to be wonderful my Buffy Blossom. You'll see just how perfect everything will be once you marry Callum, you're so very lucky!"

I want to believe that my mother didn't know what was going to happen to me, but Callum told me differently when he spilled the beans before Wrath took his head off.

"Your family sold you from the second you were born. Every day of your life has been borrowed time, Buffy..."

She knew. My father knew. Every last one of the Founders knew. How else would they convince us to be happy about our fate as Blossoms? With a secret that big, there's only one answer that works.

They all knew.

I want to cry, but I refuse. They've taken enough from me. *So much from me.* They took my entire life and twisted it, formed it to their own liking with lies. They made me scared to be myself, to question things. Even now when I want to cry, I can't. My lips won't even turn down in a frown—the only thing I can do is smile.

The only thing that comes out of my mouth when I want to scream is a laugh, because it's what I've been built to do.

I laugh and I hate the sound of it, but something beautiful happens. Wrath looks my way when I laugh. I nearly melt.

Of course I melt under his attention. He's the only beautiful thing in the world to me.

He takes a step towards me and a smile pulls at his lips. His human form falls away immediately when his eyes meet mine. Silver eyes flash as his true form appears in front of me. I gasp and fall back a step but his arm is there, steadying me and drawing me closer to him.

Our bond is back. The gold shine of it flares once before it falls away. I follow the tug of it to my demon husband.

"You have a beautiful laugh, dear one," he murmurs, brushing my hair away from my face.

"It wasn't real," I confess and tears well up in my eyes unexpectedly. "Neither are my smiles, not really. It wasn't real when I laughed.

Wrath is quiet for a second before he speaks, "I will not rest until it is. I will not stop until your laughter, your smiles, your joy, all of it will be your own."

His words hit me with a force that nearly has me rocking back a step but I stay where I am while he holds me upright. His words lodge close to my heart. They tuck themselves into our bond as he continues to speak to me.

"I think I would like to hear you laugh a good deal more."

His words warm my heart. True laughter in Sweet Tooth is rare. Yes, there are plenty of fake smiles, simpering and giggles that are hollow. Done because it is what is expected of us, especially Blossoms, but true laughter? Joy truly my own?

It feels like a dream come true.

"You make me feel like I'm in a fairytale. I don't understand how I'm here with you."

"And you give me the same, Buffy. A demon such as me is not meant to have a wife, but you called to me, even before you blooded that fool in the circle. My soul recognized you as my match. After all my years of service, your laughter is the sweetest sound I've ever heard, dear one. I would gladly endure it all over to hear you do it again." Wrath slides his thumb across my cheek and cups my face. The warmth and weight of his palm against my skin makes me lightheaded.

I think I've only laughed truly with Meadow and a few of the other Blossoms. With Wrath, laughter comes easily and freely. The demon sets me at ease. The careful walls I've built around myself without even realizing crumble into nothing in his presence.

I lean my forehead against his shoulder. "I'd like that...maybe once the Blossoms are rescued, I'll-"

"No, not after, *during*," he says and kisses me before I can say another word. His kiss sets my heart racing and I lean into him eagerly. Wrath breaks our kiss and his lips brush against mine when he whispers to me. "I would have your laugh ringing in my ears as I rain your retribution down on every last one of them. Your laughter will be the finest music to my ears while I rip this town apart, dear one."

Wrath wants to hear me laugh while he rains my revenge down on the cult, on the entire town of Sweet Tooth. I should tell him no, but the woman worried about what is right according to the teachings of Sweet Tooth is gone.

I'm not her anymore. When he talks about revenge it makes my blood sing. I want him to do it, because he would be doing it for me.

I nod and lean up on my tiptoes to return his kiss. The move surprises me. I've never been kissed before tonight and yet here I am, kissing Wrath all on my own. Nearly being sacrificed does a thing to a woman, I suppose.

"During, then," I agree, dropping back down. "I think seeing you take them apart will put a real smile on my face."

Wrath hums in approval. "Bloodthirsty little thing, aren't you?"

I grin and nod. "What can I say? You bring it out in me. Why don't we take this to the bedroom? There's something I need and I think you need it, too," I say and hold out my hand to Wrath. When he takes my hand, our bond hums happily.

CHAPTER

TWELVE

S *leep.*

Sleep is the thing I need and thought Wrath would welcome too, but apparently demons don't need sleep.

"Demons do not need sleep. I'll keep watch while you rest."

I stop making the bed and glance up at him. He's standing guard beside the bedroom door, peering down the hallway like he expects the enemy to come charging at him.

"We set the security alarm," I tell him, pulling back the quilts. "I'm sure it's fine."

"A security alarm won't keep out the cultists, Buffy. Lazy humans that they are, there's hardly a ward around this home. For something they claim to be mine they are quite remiss in the protection of it. I'll set the wards in the morning with the sunrise."

I smile as I watch Wrath pace in front of the door. "We might not have wards, but the alarm will give us a heads up. Can't you throw magic at them if they decide to pay us a visit?" Wrath stops his pacing and turns to give me a *'What The Fuck?'* look and I laugh. "I'm kidding about the alarm, okay? I know it won't keep them out. I just wanted to see what you would do at this point. I blame the sleep deprivation."

Last night I was so excited about my wedding that I didn't sleep a wink, which seems naive and foolish in hindsight now that I've been awake for over twenty hours. I'm running on fumes.

"Ah, my little wife likes to tease, I see?" Wrath practically purrs in pleasure and some of the fatigue seeps out of my bones. Adrenaline floods my system and I know I'm blushing when he winks at me.

I nod shyly and drop my eyes to the bed I've just turned down. "I used to. With my friends, I mean. I *do*," I correct myself quickly.

My friends are hostage somewhere in town. They aren't dead.

I have two more nights to save them. I look out the window at the big moon that hangs low in the sky. It'll vanish soon and the sun will light everything back up again. I wonder what the other cultists will do.

Everyone in Sweet Tooth is in the cult, even those that are only on the fringes. Because it's better and easier to be a part of the cult than to be shut out. Life in Sweet Tooth would be lonely if it weren't for the cult we all serve. Or in my case, served.

I wonder how many of them knew I was supposed to die tonight. Too many to count more than likely. I don't let myself think about it and look back to Wrath.

"They won't come for us if you're here. They've accepted you're a mage of Wrath. Which, by the way, I had no idea mages were real. I'd heard stories, but there haven't been any living mages in so long."

There was a rumor that my great-great-grandmother was a mage, but it's too far back for anyone to really know. Even if the rumor gave my family a higher standing in the cult. At least, until my dad married my mom.

An Outsider trumps any mage related lineage easily around here.

"They are, but not in cults so out of compliance as this one. There's hardly anything up to code around here," Wrath mutters and comes forward when I hold my hand out to him.

"What do you mean?"

"I mean there's a lot more that goes into keeping up with the occult and arcane than taking the lives of twelve virgins at the full moon. It used to be that would work, but we've had a lot of progress in the last few centuries. Sweet Tooth's unwillingness to come along for it means no more mages."

I blink in surprise at him. Nothing he's saying makes sense, not when it sounds like there's an entire bureaucratic system and not one god like we all thought responsible for things. "What?"

"No compliance, no mages," Wrath says simply. "No exceptions."

"But who decides on the compliance?"

"The board does. I'd rather not talk about them right now. I've little patience after the past five hundred years of servitude and speaking of them, especially tonight most of all."

He mentioned serving after Callum, in the clearing with Sunday and downstairs.

"Who did you serve for all that time?" I ask Wrath and then shake my head and stop myself immediately. Just because Wrath has declared I'm free to ask him anything in the world, doesn't mean that I'll start now when he's asked me not to.

"No, don't answer that, please," I tell him and hold up my hands in apology. "I shouldn't have asked that. I'm sorry. You just said you didn't want to talk about it. That wasn't respectful of me. It's difficult for me not to ask questions. I'm curious about your world when I've known so little."

Wrath snaps his fingers and the door locks and the lights turn off. I jump with a gasp but he's immediately there beside me. "It is your world now too, dear one. I'll explain things to you in the morning after you've rested. Which, after the gift you've just given me, would not be for an entire week if I had the time to lay you down and take you apart the way I hunger."

I stop breathing. My heart pounds so loud it's the only thing I can hear. The tether that binds us threads itself through my ribs until it squeezes the breath out of me. Even if I wanted to breathe I wouldn't be able to.

"W-what?" I stammer and my breath floods my lungs in a whoosh as Wrath's hand lands on my hip. It's a gentle pressure, the warm weight of his palm against the curve of my hip makes me weak in the best way.

"I didn't give you a gift," I manage to squeak out. Not at all the seductive tone I wish I could summon, but the demon makes me lose myself. Even if I hadn't been raised to worship him, there's no way his perfection wouldn't affect me the way it does.

I'm only human after all.

Wrath's chuckle answers me from the dark. I shiver under his hand while he brushes my hair off my neck and drops a kiss to my skin. "You did, Buffy," Wrath says. He lowers his head further and

I feel his horns brush my cheek when he kisses the space where my neck and shoulder meet.

"For five hundred years I have been in service of a master that forced my hand and bent my will to fit their desires. I was nothing but a tool to them in whatever scheme they dreamed up. Tonight was my first night of freedom, my ruthless little wife."

My eyes go wide and I stare ahead into the darkness while Wrath goes on speaking. He moves his hands to the front of my hips and leans me back against him. The warmth of him at my back makes me remember the clearing when I first saw him.

He was so achingly beautiful and perfect in the moonlight. Breathtaking.

"No one has done me such a kindness as you."

I shake my head and swallow hard. "I didn't–I mean, you said no and th-that's enough. I wouldn't ever want you to do anything you didn't want to do."

"For some 'No' has no meaning. You know this."

He's right, I do know how little 'No' means to so many. 'No' meant nothing in the Founders' world. 'No' was meaningless in the Cult of Wrath. But here I am, with the being we were raised to worship and to him it means *everything*.

"You could have asked me to explain, even though I said I didn't want to, but you didn't." He speaks the words into the space between my body and his lips. I shiver while the vibration of his words sinks into my bones and when he lifts his head to capture my mouth, I'm already turning towards him.

"You are perfect for me," he whispers before he kisses me. I turn towards him and wrap my arms around the big demon's body. I hug him tight. I hug him so close and desperately try to find all the places we were both made to bend. I want to fill those spaces and cracks with the gentleness he's shown me, the mercy and care. I want him to know that he'll never have to worry over 'No' again.

Neither of us will from the way he holds me back. Wrath lifts me in his arms and walks us towards the bed while he kisses me. It's different than earlier, when I felt like my body was on fire as he kissed me.

It's slower, softer. It's the kind of kiss that makes me think we have forever.

Wrath curls an arm around my waist and holds me up while he lays us down on the bed, moving to lay beside me. I roll with him and press myself close. I've never shared a bed with anyone other than Meadow and those were only a handful of times when I could sneak out of my room to stay with her.

"Buffy..." Wrath starts and I know he's going to tell me to get my rest, but there's only one way I'll be able to sleep with Wrath in my bed.

"Hold me?"

His answer comes immediately, just like I knew it would.

"Always."

CHAPTER
THIRTEEN

When I wake up the alarm is going off. Wrath is gone. I sit up in bed with a groan and my pillow sticks to my face. Definitely going to have pillow creases when I see Wrath. But there's the little matter of where *is* he?

"Wrath?" I call out and then freeze. If the alarm is going off then there will definitely be someone other than us in the house. Leave it to me to be the one to out him as Wrath passing as a human mage.

"*Damon?*" I correct and roll out of bed. My limbs are stiff and my body screams at me when I hit the floor but I keep going, even if it is with a limp. The curtains in the bedroom are pulled and the room is dark, but I can see light shining underneath the door and I stumble towards it. I open the door and creep down the hallway slowly, each step reminding me that I ran for my life last night. That I got into not one, *but two fights*. Maybe I should grab something just in case my third is waiting for me.

I turn and grab the first thing I see, a yellow porcelain vase off a hall table and lift it over my head. If someone is here, I'm going to throw this right at the back of their head.

I try to listen for whoever might have set the alarm off, but it's hard with the constant blaring. I make it to the top of the stairs when I hear Wrath.

"I'll turn the alarm off if you leave."

I raise an eyebrow. Who the mulberry is he talking to? I poke my head around the stairs and see him standing in the living room with a cup of coffee in one hand while his other is resting on his hip. He scowls around the room with an annoyed look on his handsome face. He's in his human form, which is good considering there's an entire army of cultists running around the living room carrying boxes while they try to shield their ears from the screaming security alarm.

"Considering this town is as crooked as the rest of you, I'm guessing no one's going to come investigate why the alarm went off?" he asks and gestures towards the ceiling with the coffee mug.

"If you could just give us a few minutes," one of the cultists tries. I recognize them as a Marsh. I've worked with them in the dining hall a few times and they're pleasant enough, but what are they doing here? I run my eyes around the room and take another step forward.

What time is it?

Oh no. How long have I slept? Fear shoots through me at the thought of losing precious time when I only have two days left to save my friends. I look towards the windows and it looks dark still, the sun hasn't even risen.

"I'll set the wards in the morning with the sunrise."

93

Well, the Founders always did say the 'Early Bird Gets The Worm', but I always thought it meant we should work harder. No wonder Wrath looks annoyed. They showed up before he had time to set the wards.

I move to take a step down the stairs and the top step creaks. No one else notices but Wrath. Immediately, his eyes come to me and he smiles as he snaps his fingers. The alarm shuts off instantly. There's a collective sigh from the cultists crowding our living room and I sigh in relief along with them.

"As much as I appreciate your bloodthirsty ways, my love, what exactly do you plan to do with that?" Wrath asks.

"What?" I accidentally shout in the now silent house in confusion. When Wrath gestures with his coffee cup towards the space above my head I realize that I'm still holding the yellow vase.

"Sorry!" I lower the case quickly, "Sorry, I um, I was thinking of redecorating?" I try, hugging the vase to my chest as nonchalantly as I can. My answer comes out as a question when I see the cultists staring up at me and whispering. All my life people have watched me wherever I've gone, but that was on account of me being a Blossom. When they looked at me then, it was with admiration. Envy. Sometimes, even longing with how much they wanted to be a wife selected for Wrath. Now they're watching me with something different.

Shock. Fear.

Anger.

"Her smile," someone whispers louder than the rest and I realize that I'm not smiling. I'm not frowning, but I'm *not smiling,* either. Of all the things they *could* have noticed—I'm still in my wedding dress from last night, they all caught me about to chuck a yellow vase at them, the fact that I've married an Outsider to the cult.

But it's none of those that has them looking at me the way they are. It's the fact that my smile isn't present.

"Get out, all of you," Wrath orders and all eyes leave me to go to him. He stretches and I feel my mouth go dry when I finally realize he's shirtless.

"We were told to bring offerings to you and your bride," the Marsh speaks up and Wrath glares at them. The expression turns his face cold and haughty. He looks every bit what I imagined a king to look like—he would easily give the Founders a run for their money in the *I'm absolutely in charge so everyone zip it like good little cultists* category.

"And now I'm ordering you to *get out*." Wrath sips his coffee and levels a sharp look at the room. "Or shall I show you what an angry mage is capable of up before the sun has even risen on this miserable day?"

A whisper of fear ripples through the crowd and one by one they shuffle towards the door. Interesting. As obedient as they are to the Founders, they're doubly terrified of Wrath. There's nothing else but fear that would motivate them to leave after an order from the Founders. I make my way down the stairs. I'm halfway down when one of the girls looks back at me with wide eyes. I freeze when I recognize her.

Molly Simmons.

She's a Blossom and five years younger than me.

She smiles at me when she sees me watching her and I know it isn't real from the look in her eyes. She's scared. As much as I don't want to, my lips curve up in an answering smile.

I know my eyes don't look anything like she thought they

would when she stops moving and grabs the girl next to her, but then Wrath is there snapping his fingers so hard blue sparks fly from his fingertips and the cultists sprint out of the house.

"Good riddance!" He shouts after them and slams the door with a kick of his barefoot. The second the door closes he looks up to me and smiles.

"Good morning, dear one. I'm sorry for the rude awakening. They arrived before the wards were set properly."

"It's okay," I say and join him at the base of the stairs. "What were they doing here? I mean, what *is* all of this?" I peer around the living room and foyer and there's nothing but trunks and boxes as far as the eye can see.

"Clothing and other frippery," Wrath mutters. "As if I could not summon everything my wife might need."

"So they brought clothing?" I walk towards a trunk and pause when I see the markings of the O'Hare Clothing Shop. "This is the nicest store in town."

Wrath comes to look at the trunk and sniffs. "I'll make you nicer things. Prettier things. Anything you want to wear."

"I don't really need much. My things are..." my voice trails off when I see a familiar baby blue trunk. It's the one I packed up with my mother the night before. It's sitting dead center in the living room. "My things are there," I tell him and go to point at the trunk, before remembering I'm hugging the vase. I set it down awkwardly on top of the O'Hare trunk.

"I packed that with my mother when I thought I was going to the city. It should have all my things. There's no reason for you to go through the trouble of getting me anything."

What I'm saying is logical. It makes all the sense in the world, except that the more time goes by the more I want to drag my trunk out of the room and never see it again.

"It is no trouble at all to dress my wife in finery. It would be my honor," Wrath replies and looks at my trunk when he sees that I'm still staring at it. "Unless, of course, you want your things."

My things.

My things that my mother helped me pack before she sent me to my death. All the Blossoms had trunks like mine that they packed in giddy hope for the future. Do they have them now? Are they still wearing their wedding dresses while the cult plots how to use them as sacrifices? I swallow hard at the thought. I don't think I want to open the trunk or wear anything inside.

"I don't think I-well, I mean, I can probably just use some of these things." I point around the room. "There's enough here to choose from."

"So there is. You smell like fear," Wrath rumbles.

He smelled my fear?

"Mulberries," I mutter and he raises an eyebrow at me. "Just something I'm trying out instead of your name on account of how it puts you in my head," I say and tap my temple. "Not that it really matters, not if you can smell what I'm feeling. Is that a demon thing, a you thing or is it because we're married?"

"A little bit from column A and C. Why did you choose mulberries out of all the things you could have picked to replace my name?"

"You don't like it?"

"I just feel it lacks a certain something."

"What about *yummy sushi?*"

"Maybe mulberries is fine."

"Fried calamari bites?"

"I sense a theme developing here."

I nod. "Fair enough, mulberries stays for now. I'll keep testing things out until something feels right."

"I think using my name is just fine. What could be better than me?"

I laugh and I'm rewarded when I watch Wrath's face light up. He's so handsome when he smiles. "Nothing is better than you," I answer earnestly. "You're a wonderful husband."

"And I'm rather superb at baking. That doesn't get enough mention, if you ask me."

"You can bake?"

"You name it or dream it and I can bake it, wife."

Images of Wrath baking come to me and I let myself daydream what it would be like to wake up to the smell of his baking instead of a security alarm screaming. It's nice and sweet. What I think is supposed to be perfectly normal—*demon husband aside.*

Normal is something I haven't enjoyed much with the way I was raised. I also recognize this is how it could be with Wrath. My heart aches for what life after all of this is over might look like.

"Can you make a White Claw?" I ask, after a minute of thinking hard on what I could request Wrath to make. Sweet Tooth has the bake shop in town and we do get in some special things for the Outsiders that stop for the day in town, but I think the first thing I want to do is finally solve the mystery of what a White Claw is.

Wrath makes a face at my question. "I mean, I can, but why?"

"My mom talks about them when she thinks no one is

around, but I haven't seen them in any of the baking books in town, no matter how hard I look. She won't tell me what they are either."

Wrath laughs and takes my hand. "I'm going to assume you don't actually know what a White Claw is, dear one. Come with me, we'll get you a coffee. I'll explain it to you. If you still want one, I'll make you one in any flavor that you like."

CHAPTER
FOURTEEN

Wrath makes me cinnamon rolls and two White Claws–a lime and a black cherry–that morning. I get cut off when I ask for a third when he comes back from setting the wards around the house. It's barely sunrise and he doesn't accept my very reasonable explanation that it's *'five o'clock somewhere.'* It's totally fine.

I don't press the issue about any more drinks though, because I get a headache pretty fast. Wrath has to make me chug a cup of coffee and work on cramming another cinnamon roll in me while he fusses over how "frail humans are," that he's going to have to "toughen me up."

I get why my mom didn't want to talk about White Claws. They're addicting, like spicy happy water. A lot sneakier than the mead or wine that's served in town.

"You never answered my question about what you wanted to wear. You cannot show up in your wedding dress everywhere you go," Wrath says and I look down at my dress. It's looking a little worse for wear. I run my hand over the skirt with a thoughtful hum.

"But what if I did?" I ask. Maybe it's the White Claws that have muddled my brain, but I kind of want to. "To get my revenge of course," I say, taking another bite of my still warm cinnamon roll. It's huge, almost the size of my head.

"Revenge on the brain and the sun is barely up. Good to see what a couple of drinks does to your beautiful brain."

I smile and toy with my cup. "My goal is my friends. I will save Meadow and the rest, but...I want them to remember what they did. I want them to know I'm coming."

A purr rumbles low in Wrath's chest and when I look at him, I see his eyes are glowing. He's in his human form, like he's been all morning on account of our early visitors. But his eyes aren't dark now. They're the silver that I know and they glitter in the morning light that slants through the kitchen windows.

"When I mentioned you would be able to change my mind about your species, I meant that, Buffy. You are the most interesting human I have ever met in all my time."

My mind goes to the night before and the questions I didn't ask.

"How long have you..." my voice trails off as I search for the words but Wrath supplies them for me.

"Been in service to mortals?"

I nod. "You mentioned a master. but they couldn't have been human, right?"

"They weren't, but they were fond of making deals with humans. It's amazing what someone will do to bend time and lengthen their lifespan."

"That's possible?"

"It is. Sunday does it now in a way, even if she is more creative in her flitting about the area."

"I didn't know Sunday was human, she was...well, we've been taught she's dangerous. A witch. Though, I don't think there's anything to be worried about with her, with the cult trying to murder me."

"Sunday is a very dangerous witch, do not let her interest in Sweet Tooth or this cult fool you. Once her business here is done, no doubt she'll be back to her old tricks. That means you do not put yourself at risk for her, do you understand, Buffy?"

I hesitate. Sunday is the reason Nina is alive, but I'm only here because of Wrath. Those two feel like they balance the other out. I do trust Wrath a whole hell of a lot more than her, so I nod and do the smart thing.

"I understand. I'll be careful when it comes to Sunday," I tell him around a mouthful of cinnamon roll.

"Good, thank you. That does bring up the matter of your safety. There's something we have to discuss. There will be a target on your back now that you're my wife and I won't always be there with you to keep you safe, Buffy. We are going to have to make some changes."

I swallow my cinnamon roll with a gulp and set it down on the plate in front of me. "Why do I feel like I'm going to need another White Claw for this talk?" I ask. Wrath sighs as he reaches over to run his fingers through my dark hair.

"You're cut off for the morning."

I pout but nod and pick up my coffee cup. "Fair, fair. What changes are you talking about?"

"The changes are nothing to be concerned over," Wrath

assures me, "it's just the simple acceptance of your destiny now as my chosen one."

I think of the bond that I can feel but not see right now and rub a hand to my chest. "Is that what our bond is?"

"Our bond is the first step, but I've never taken a wife before, let alone a human. I did some research on the matter while you slept and I think I've found a solution we will both find agreeable, considering our current predicament."

"You mean the rescue mission with the murdering cult."

"Precisely. Which is why you having powers of your own will put my mind at ease. It won't make you invulnerable to mortal weapons and the like as I am, but it will be more than enough to deal with these bumpkins."

He has my attention. I'm not even thinking about White Claws or cinnamon rolls. Or the fact that my entire life is sitting in the next room packed away in a trunk. "What is it?"

"You are my chosen one, Buffy. That means you will share in my power. The bond between us is an exchange of that power, but there's a ritual to complete. After which, you will be a terror to anyone that lays a hand on you. You will be made stronger, you will heal faster. You will be a warrior."

My mouth falls open in surprise. "B-but I don't know how to fight. I can't even kill bugs regularly or with any consistency on account of how bad it makes me feel."

He snorts and does the last thing I think he will. He boops me on my nose. I jump in surprise and grab my nose while he picks up my cinnamon roll and takes a big bite.

"You held your own well enough last night," he says around a mouthful of what I know is yummy goodness. When I open my mouth to tell him that my lashing out at the cult was really an angry fluke, he waves me off, "and that was without my power or your new powers."

"Listen, Wrath, powers sound like a dream, really. But until last night I'd never-I mean, I don't think you understand what I mean when I say *I don't know how to fight*. I reacted last night. I was just trying to survive. I can't do that again."

"You will, dear one. You will do more than survive. You will thrive. You've taken me for a husband, haven't you? This is your due."

Fear spikes sharp in my belly and I feel the old urge to shrink and hide wake up in me. Fear is how I was controlled, why I didn't dare step a toe out of line as a Blossom. And it's alive and well here in the kitchen with Wrath and I.

I don't know why I almost give in to it, either. I always wanted to be special, different. I knew I was and I was so desperate for it I let other people control me. Wrath isn't doing that now, with this offer.

He wants me safe. He holds me when I'm scared and tired. He's bound his life to mine and now he's offering me some of his power for myself. Why is my first instinct not to accept?

Why is that what I want to do? Why does saying yes to him scare me so much?

Saying no feels so much safer when all my life 'No' was the meal others forced me to eat.

It's not the right thing to do. I know that, I really do. So I force myself to do the right thing for myself when Wrath holds his hand out to me.

"Will you say yes, Buffy?"

My throat goes tight and my voice shakes but still, I say the one word that I desperately deserve and need to say.

"*Yes.*"

FIFTEEN

T he ritual was just that single answer from me to Wrath. As anticlimactic as it might seem, with my half eaten cinnamon roll and empty White Claw cans sitting beside us on the counter, it was perfect.

I don't really think I have it in me to do another ceremony right now.

I kept my wedding dress, but I did change into something else that I pulled from one of the O'Hare trunks. Although I only managed to wear it for a few minutes before Wrath snapped his fingers and I was in an entirely new outfit of his creation.

"What the mulberry was that?"

"I'm finding that I'm jealous when it comes to you." Wrath *shrugged and held the door open for me. "If you're going to wear clothes, I'll be the one making them from now on."*

He got rid of every last trunk in the house. Which is a good idea, considering where it all came from. Where he sent it, I don't know but it was all gone in the blink of an eye. It felt oddly satisfying and put a smile on my face. I shouldn't have smiled, but I did. The curve of my lips made all the more special because my reason for smiling was entirely my own. I glance over at Wrath beside me and see him surveying the street like he's waiting for another group of cultists to descend on us, but there's no one in sight. Wrath's Embrace sits at the very top of the highest hill in Sweet Tooth, which gives us an advantage to spotting anyone on our way into town.

So far I've only seen the mailman Mr. Lennox. He turned white as a sheet and nearly dropped his satchel full of letters when he caught sight of me, and sprinted in the opposite direction. I'm choosing not to read too much into that reaction, but it's already setting the tone for a hard truth.

No one thought they would see me again after last night.

Yes, there was the lie about the city that I bought into just like everyone else but there's another layer to it. There are people who *did* know the truth of what was going to happen and I think Mr. Lennox was one of them. Otherwise there would be no reason for him to run like the dead are after him—though, maybe to him, that is kind of what is happening.

"You can relax. I'm super Buffy now, remember?" I remind him and Wrath grunts a reply but doesn't stop looking for attackers.

"Super or not, I don't want them to get any closer to us than necessary. This morning was more than enough for me."

"Then you won't like what tonight is," I tell him, turning my face up to the sun. I don't think I feel any different than I did before I said yes, but there is the fact that I'm not sore anymore. I shake out my limbs and inhale deeply. Everything smells new, like it's turned up to ten. My next breath brings me a lungful of crisp autumn air and the scent of someone baking floats to me in the wind. I take another breath and realize we have to be getting closer to town. It smells like Ms. Donna has apple fritters going at the bakery.

Maybe there *is* something different about me.

"What dreadful event do they have tonight?"

"The Annual Autumn Harvest Festival," I answer and open my eyes. We've reached the bottom of the hill. The houses that I grew up visiting are all around us. Up ahead there's Main Street and downtown. A bus of tourists has just pulled up and they flood out of it and into the cheery streets of Sweet Tooth. Maroon, yellow and orange banners float on the wind. Chalkboard signs, autumn wreaths, pumpkins of all shapes and sizes and bales of hay help set the scene for the Autumn Festival tonight.

It looks like a picture perfect scene. You wouldn't know the town is the homebase for the Cult of Wrath. Or that a dozen brides should have died last night.

"The what?"

"The Annual Autumn Harvest Festival," I repeat and then go on to explain because Wrath is giving me an *'and?'* look, that is entirely fair, "it's held after the weddings as a sort of celebration for them achieving the status of wife and leaving for the city."

All my memories of the festival were fun and cheery moments. I looked forward to the festival every single year and loved volunteering with my friends at the booths and stands, but I never knew the truth.

"There's going to be a carnival and fair tonight, with games, food and music. I never knew it was to celebrate a bunch of murders. I feel like an idiot now when I look back on it."

Wrath slips his hand into mine immediately and rubs his thumb along my knuckles. "You had no way of knowing, Buffy."

"I would have if I just stopped and looked around. There's no way that someone didn't know, that I wouldn't have known if I'd tried to see."

Wrath slows his steps and clears his throat. "You asked about my former master, but we did not discuss the particulars of my employment."

I look at him in surprise. I didn't want to press the issue but I never expected him to bring it up so suddenly. "That's right," I say softly. We're still a few blocks away from downtown, but there are people here. I see them looking our way with curious glances. It won't be long before they try to hear what we're talking about.

"Wrath, ah, I mean, Damon, perhaps we could continue this conversation at dinner, " I say, clearing my throat when a couple ahead of us slows their steps so they're closer to us. I know exactly who they are. Annie and Ron Bustos. The married couple is as nosey as anyone in this town. Annie Bustos is older and was in the choir with us. She saw Meadow holding hands with Eric, who was not at all her intended and everyone knew about it before dinner.

Meadow was put on extra laundry duty for that one while Eric was taken off the choir permanently and given extra shifts in the mess hall. It's a terrible sin to tempt a Blossom. Before, we thought it was to preserve the purity of her union with Wrath, but now...now none of it makes sense. Even if it did, would something as simple as holding hands or kissing warrant such harsh punishment?

Anger burns through me when Annie looks back at me. Her

face is calm but I see her eyes. There's shock and curiosity there. She didn't know I wouldn't come back, even if no Blossom ever returned from the city. She didn't know that I was going to be murdered but that doesn't mean she's innocent. She's curious about why I'm here and I bet she'll run her traitorous tongue the second she can and tell everyone exactly what she hears Wrath or I say.

She's just as bad as the rest of them for willingly playing her part in this evil little machine designed to keep us all bound to the Founders' will.

I will not let a woman like that hear the tender places Wrath would hide from even me. She's not worthy of him. I'll rip her hair out strand by strand before I let her know a single thing about him that he's not willing to share freely.

"I think now is the perfect time, dear one," Wrath says with an easy smile. Annie's gossipy gaze slides over to him the second he speaks.

She lasts all of half a heartbeat before her mouth drops open and I see something other than a hunger over gossip take over the other woman's face.

Lust.

A bird chirps loudly as it flies overhead and Wrath tilts his head back to look at it. The move sends his glossy hair sliding over his shoulders before it catches in the morning breeze. The sun plays over the planes of cheekbones and his lush lips curve into a broad smile. I watch him take a deep breath and close his eyes. His thick lashes flutter and almost touch his damn cheeks. Annie keeps right on staring at Wrath's beauty.

She's smitten with my husband.

I really want to pick a fight with her now and not just for being a filthy little snitch.

"Hey!" I snap and start forward with a finger pointed in Annie's direction. She gives a little jump and grabs on to Ron's arm but all she does is send a smile in my direction.

"What do you think you're-" I start, but Wrath steps in front of me and whisks me away in a half step move that would make any ballroom dancer proud.

"Lovely morning, isn't it?" he calls out to Annie who, despite me about to murder her, just giggles in response, which makes me even angrier. Wrath doesn't seem to notice. He just keeps moving and I realize he's spun us right into an alleyway. We're just a street away from downtown. Too close for comfort and too close for me to lose my shit on Annie Bustos.

I cross my arms over my chest and shake my head. "I don't want her looking at you. She's nosey and terrible. She got Meadow in trouble once."

"I'm sure she's positively vile, Buffy. But now is not the time."

"You were about to share very personal things with me and she was going to listen."

Wrath shakes his head. "She couldn't hear a thing. Or rather, she couldn't until you shouted at her, dear one."

"Wait, what?"

"I'm a demon and that means I have magic. Do you really think I wouldn't use it to give us a bit of privacy?" Wrath asks. I feel foolish when I see a shimmer in the air similar to what I saw when I looked closely at Sunday's ward. He's using magic now too.

I take a step towards the shimmering air and consider it. "You mean they can't hear us right now?"

Annie and Ron have doubled back to look at the alleyway. They're just a few steps away from me at the mouth of the alley, but they don't come any closer. Annie cranes her head and takes a hesitant step but Ron grabs her and stops her.

"They can't even see us, my love," Wrath tells me.

"Then what are they looking at?" I ask him quietly and he chuckles.

"Right now, nothing. Just an empty alleyway. But that one," he flicks a finger at Annie, "is persistent." He narrows his eyes and stares at her until Annie backs off and follows Ron into the street.

"She needed more encouragement to leave but she won't say anything about seeing us together. Neither of them will," Wrath tells me with a confidence that tells me he really doesn't understand the term hot goss. Then again, I barely do. I learned it from eavesdropping on the Outsiders.

"What do you mean? She's probably on her way to tell all of Main Street," I say and think about going after her.

Wrath tuts and wags a finger at me. "One day you will trust in me and my magic, wife. I've wiped us from both of their memories. The little chit will be lucky if she remembers her own name by noon."

I freeze and look at Wrath with wide eyes. "What? Wait, I just wanted to stop her from telling but you wiped her memory?"

Wrath shrugs. "You seemed to really dislike her. So I thought, why not go the extra mile for my Buffy?"

"Really? That's so sweet. You didn't have to."

"No, but I wanted to please you."

I laugh and cross the space between us and throw my arms around him. "You're the best husband I could have ever hoped for."

Wrath hugs me and drops a kiss against my temple. "And you are by far the most treasured being I could have hoped to take as a wife."

I close my eyes and smile. "You really are very romantic."

Wrath rubs my back and rocks us back and forth. "What can I say? It's all the sunshine I've missed. I haven't spent this much time on the surface while it was out in centuries."

I pull back to look up at him. "Why not? You can do anything, go anywhere, *be* anything," I say, gesturing at his human form. "Why wouldn't you spend all the time you want in the sun?"

It can't be that Wrath was concerned over attention. He can blend in with humans if he wants. So why would he not come and go as he pleased?

The breeze ruffles his hair and throws it into his eyes. When he gives me a wry smile he looks so much younger and carefree than normal. My heart squeezes when he clears his throat and speaks. "Ah, that brings us back to our earlier topic of conversation, dear one. My service to my master."

I grab his hand in both of mine and shake my head. "You don't have to tell me. Not now, not if it...I mean, only if you want to."

Wrath squeezes my hand back, the warmth and weight of his grip on mine is steady and grounding. He doesn't look young anymore. Or carefree. He looks like my jaded demon husband who has a sharp tongue for anyone but me.

"I do. It is something I have to share with you before we gallivant into the heat of battle to save your friends with you as my harbinger."

"Battle? We're going into a battle?" I whisper and then hold up a finger. "What do you mean, your harbinger? I thought I was your *wife*. What's this biz about a harbinger?" I whisper-scream.

"Yes, but only a very little battle," Wrath holds up his hand, his thumb and pointer finger pinched together so close they nearly touch. He gives me an encouraging smile, "and what is a spouse if not a harbinger? Besides, it's nothing you can't handle with your new powers. Anyone that raises a hand to you is as good as done for, Buffy."

"We're going to have to circle back to what a harbinger means to you and what it means to me, because my version has a lot of blood and violence in it. So far the only thing I can do is smell what they're baking in town." I jerk a thumb over my shoulder. "I'll trust you on the "good as done for" stuff, *for now,* but what do I have to know before we head into our very little battle?"

"My master is the one who struck a deal with Sweet Tooth's Founder, Ichabod O'Hare. He was a human who had managed to figure out how to trap demons to do his bidding."

Ichabod O'Hare is infamous in Sweet Tooth. We all know the tales about the man responsible for our home. The man that created the Cult of Wrath with all its teachings and traditions. They said the teachings were from Wrath but now I know better.

"Ichabod made a deal to trap demons?"

Wrath nods. "He was a mage, which made it easier. But it's still a feat for a human. Ichabod though, was only just barely human." A dark look passes over Wrath's handsome face and I watch it go hard. "I'd be surprised if he has any humanity living in him now. Not with what he's done."

"Are you telling me he's still alive?" I whisper, because speaking at a normal volume isn't possible for me right now.

Sweet Tooth was founded five hundred years ago. "How is he still alive?"

"That little deal he made with my master–Lethos. The pair are as thick as thieves. All the offerings Ichabod's devotees made in his name only provided extra power for them both over the centuries, to ensnare more demons."

"Ensnare them to do what? Fame? World domination?" I ask, because why else would anyone trap a freaking demon? I might be married to one but I can't imagine anyone trapping a demon without a grand scheme in place. "I mean, wouldn't it be the standard villain stuff? That's how he's still alive, isn't it?"

"'Villain stuff' isn't nearly big enough to encompass what Ichabod and Lethos are after. You were close with world domination, but they aren't just after your world. They want them all under their heels. They've been using demons to do it."

My mouth drops open. "There's other worlds?"

"Dimensions on dimensions. Your world is just one little speck in the grand plan of it all, Buffy. As a harbinger, you're going to need to know these sorts of things, beloved. Take notes."

I want to ask just how many dimensions on dimensions there are, or what exactly he expects me to take notes *with* when we're standing in an alley in a magic bubble but Wrath's use of *'beloved'* stops me cold.

I smile at him and that has his attention.

His eyes go soft and he sighs. "I love your real smiles, Buffy. I take it you loved what I just called you, if you're favoring me with one now."

I nod and my cheeks heat up with the blood that's rushing to my face at having Wrath's full attention. I know that I always have Wrath's attention, but there are times like now that it's more intense. Where it feels like my demon is taking me apart and committing each little bit of me to memory for his own perusal at a later time.

"I did. It's not something I've ever been called," I tell him and drop my eyes. Terms of endearment were few and far between in the cult. My parents were a love match, but it practically ruined the Martinez family beyond repair in Sweet Tooth—only me being selected as a Blossom redeemed us. Even still, it was precious little redemption.

"Your family sold you from the second you were born. Every day of your life has been borrowed time, Buffy..."

Callum's ugly words ring in my ears and I make sure to turn away from Wrath so that he doesn't see my face. I know my smile doesn't look real anymore.

"Beloved..." Wrath murmurs and a second later I feel his hand on my shoulder.

"Tell me about Ichabod," I whisper, preferring to think of a man that wants to rule dimensions and worlds, when I can barely exist in this one world where my parents sold me to gain status in the cult. "If he's still alive, I don't think he's going to like me harbinging all over his cult to get my friends back."

Tears blur my vision and I blink rapidly, holding them back. I haven't cried in so long. Not when everyone was watching. Not when tears would be the thing they ruined me over.

I take in a shaky breath and smile, even though Wrath can't see me. He feels me, though. I know that from the gentle tug on the bond from him. If he were in his demon form, I'd be able to see it connecting us, see where he's touching it now. It feels like he's got it wrapped around one of his fingers.

"What's Ichabod's deal?" I ask weakly.

Wrath is quiet for a long time. I hear the birds chirping as they fly overhead mingling with the idle chatter from tourists and the cultists I've known all my life. It all bounces and echoes down the street and into our alley but it's all white noise.

The only thing I want to hear is Wrath speak. He sighs then finally breaks the silence.

"Ichabod is, like all humans, a dick. That's his deal."

I grin and it helps the tears not fall. I feel steadier when I look over my shoulder to Wrath. "I'm a human and I'm not a dick," I remind him.

"No, you're not. But you're also the only one smart enough to summon me in this dreadful little town."

"It was an accident," I confess. He raises an eyebrow at me so I continue, "I didn't mean to pay the blood price when I stabbed Victor."

"You didn't mean to stab him?"

"No, I meant that. I really, *really* wanted to do more than stab him but I didn't know that it would summon you. I only did it in the circle because he tackled me. We fell into the circle and one thing led to another."

Wrath strokes his chin and nods thoughtfully. "As is often the case in such situations."

"Situations...you mean, like sacrificing type of situations? Wait, did this Lethos guy make you his project manager for sacrifices or something? Made you work with Ichabod?"

"In a way." Wrath steps up beside me and his arm brushes mine. When I lean into him he wraps his arm around my shoulder and pulls me tight. "Lethos used the demons he trapped to keep tabs on the humans he made deals with. Their rituals gave him power that he leveraged to capture more demons, you see. Ichabod understands humans better and has remained in this world as an anchor for Lethos."

"Why did he want demons? He wasn't just trying to set up a cult monopoly with y'all, was he?"

"No, he wanted demons because our blood is useful. Our souls even more so when it comes to world-walking."

"That's not like moonwalking, is it?"

"No, not nearly as enjoyable. But twice as lucrative."

"You have my interest. Tell me more."

"A demon soul can give anyone the power to move between worlds. World-walking, as we call it. Demons are able to do this on their own, but humans, mages, witches, vampires and the rest of those ghouls cannot unless they have a soulstone in their care. Ichabod and Lethos not only used the soulstones to move as they pleased, but Lethos sold them to others to gain power and standing across the worlds. Ichabod supplied the bulk of the stones and that is one of the reasons he has not died yet. The same for Lethos, but he's—well, I'm not sure he was ever human. What I wouldn't give to have ripped Ichabod limb from limb when he was human."

"How old is Lethos?"

"Over five thousand years. He is one of the old ones. That's all I or anyone knows about him."

"Five thousand years?" I gasp and I'm glad Wrath is holding me up with his arm. "How is that possible? How is *anything* alive after five thousand years?"

"He won't ever die with the souls he's consumed. It's not possible anymore. At least not naturally. It would take very powerful magic to bring him down."

I hold up a hand to stop Wrath. "Wait just a minute. *He eats them?*"

I don't know what a soulstone is or if it's an animal, vegetable or mineral, but I know eating one isn't something that's normal.

"He does," Wrath says.

"And you served him? I mean, he could have just eaten your soul for a midnight snack and you had to serve him?" I ask. I feel bitterness come to me through our bond before Wrath gives a dip of his chin.

"He could have, yes. I served him," he pauses and the bitterness takes on a darker flavor, something that reminds me of smoke, acrid and harsh, "The things I did under his thrall. There were times I wished he would have just eaten it."

"Wrath," I start, but he keeps talking so I shut my mouth and let him speak.

"Lethos knew which demons were valuable. He used their talents and ability to manage and coerce humans to make foolish promises and pledges. But he also understood that some had their own appeal that called to those he wanted to curry favor with among the realms. I was one of those demons."

"What did he make you do?" I ask. It's a loaded question, I know that. But Wrath said this was important to our little war, so I'm going to ask it. If he's willing to share his burden, I will carry it with him.

It's the least I can do for him when he's brought me this far.

He rolls his shoulders and stares straight ahead as he speaks. "The usual world destroying, as one does. But there was more. I kept the company of beings that found my form desirable. I am an Arthas demon. We are known for our ability to provide pleasure."

I swallow hard. "When you say pleasure, you don't mean from telling jokes and baking, do you?"

I don't give two mulberries about the world destroying Wrath mentioned. I care more about what he's saying now. I care about someone making him do things he didn't want to do.

The harshness humming through our bond softens when Wrath looks down at me. "No, beloved, I do not. I am skilled at pleasures of the flesh. Carnal delights, as it were. That is what Lethos chose to employ me in."

My gut tightens and I take in a shaky breath. I know two things for certain will happen in my life. One: I'm going to save the other Blossoms and Two: I'm going to fucking rip Lethos' spine out and feed it to him.

"Mulberries," I curse and turn to face Wrath. I wrap my arms around him and hold him tight. "I'm sorry. That shouldn't have happened to you. Now I've dragged you into this mess with my life and my friends and my stupid fucking cult that tried to kill me. I-I don't know what a harbinger does, but I know it's violent. I'm going to make Lethos pay."

Wrath cups my face and frowns. "None of that," he says with a tut and leans down to kiss me. "You are the first choice I have made for myself in quite some time and I won't have you fretting over it. Accident or not, you're mine and I am yours. This is a merry war we are about to wage on your deceitful cultists and there is nothing else I would rather do. I understand the rage you feel, my ruthless little wife. I know how your blood hungers for retribution and how your heart screams for vengeance. I know what it is to have your life not be your own," he lifts his hand and touches my cheek, "how not even the smiles you give are freely given, but forced. I know what it is to have weaker men rule you through no fault of your own but circumstances of birth. I will be there to watch you unleash your fury on each and every one of the souls that crossed you. As for Lethos? He is none of your concern. I will not have him even breathe your air. He is unworthy of you."

"I know I said I couldn't kill any of them earlier but when I hear you talk about it like that, it sounds like something I could get into. At least for a little while."

"Very good. There will be more than enough blood to spill. Now, by my last count there are five families responsible for the sacrifices and Sweet Tooth, is that still true?"

I nod. "Yes, there are. There's the Aguirre's, Smiths, Rossi's, Marsh's and of course, the O'Hare's," I say and then add, "Callum, you know the guy you, sorta," I grab my neck and stick my tongue out, to which Wrath indicates that yes, he does remember ripping Callum's head off, "he's an-I mean, he *was* an O'Hare. But there's still his father."

"Why stop at his father? There's far more of them than just him, beloved."

"I don't think I need to kill them all to save my friends, Wrath."

"Any job you do is worth doing thoroughly," he replies. I can't exactly tell him he's wrong, because he does have me there. I want to ask why I can't go after Lethos but I know it's delicate, so I steer away from that iceberg.

"We'll see how many get in the way. We said this was a "little war," remember?" I pinch my fingers together like he did, "We can't just change the rules to a normal sized or even a big war on a whim. It's little and it's staying little. The only heads I want are the heads of those families." I'm fine killing the father's, they knew. They're on the Founder's Council and it's them that benefit the most from the sacrificing of the Blossoms.

"Which, you know what? What are they even getting for killing the Blossoms? You said that it didn't do anything other than give more power to Ichabod and Lethos' little power time-share. But they must have gotten something out of the deal way back in the day, so what is it?"

"Prosperity," Wrath says without pause. "That's why you have the hot springs and the flowers. And I believe the candy? What is it again?"

"Taffy. Salt water taffy," I reply and have to put a hand out against the building I'm standing beside. *They did it for candy and flowers?*"

"No, prosperity. They did it for a rich township. For a place where people would kill to live. Kill to stay in. Lethos granted it in an interesting way. Ichabod's tie to the town and the cult sustains his power as well but it's not necessary as far as Lethos is concerned. The deal was struck and fulfilled by the first sacrifice."

"But what deal? The flowers and the springs, the taffy. It's all things that we can do on our own."

"That is correct. You can and have been profiting off a deal long done and settled."

"So the cult, the sacrifices, all of it was for nothing?"

"Not for nothing. Ichabod O'Hare is a cruel and greedy man. Heartless, like those that lied to you and your friends. He ensured his memory, his teaching," Wrath taps his chest, "the heart that no longer beats in his chest, lives on here with lesser men honoring his way. There is no true death for those whose memories live, Buffy."

I shut my eyes and take a deep breath. "All the brainwashing and emotional damage was because of a shitty man who wanted to live forever."

"Yes."

I open my eyes and smile at my demon husband. "Teach me how to be a harbinger. I don't care what I have to do, I'm going to wipe Ichabod's memory from this place."

CHAPTER
SIXTEEN

There's one hard and fast rule to being Wrath's Harbinger:

I'm pretty much invincible, unless someone takes off my head, sets me on fire, or drives an iron spike through my heart.

Those are the easy to remember basics Wrath gave me before we decided to head into downtown for a little recon. Plus there was the matter of me wanting to confirm it really was apple fritters Ms. Donna had just pulled out of the oven as the first test of my new senses, which is where we were now.

The yellow painted sign proclaiming Sweet Tooth Bakery in cherry red swayed in the morning breeze as we came to a stop in front of the big glass windows of the bakery.

"Are you sure this is the place you want to start?" Wrath asks while he looks over the street again. It's busy here now that we're in downtown proper and I can feel his worry.

He's nervous he won't be able to keep me safe, not when we're out in the open like this.

"Absolutely. If we're going to get people to talk to us and figure out where the Founders are, this is the place to start," I tell him and grab his hand. "Besides, I'm the harbinger around here. So don't worry, I'll keep you plenty safe, husband."

Wrath chuckles and the worry I feel pressing down on me lessens. "So you're sassy when you have a little power behind you?"

"Absolutely. Who wouldn't be?"

After what I've been through in Sweet Tooth, a little power feels...good. I'm careful not to get cocky. You know what they say about pride and all that.

Wrath holds open the door for me. "Well deserved, I'd say. Now, after you, beloved."He gives me a little bow as I pass him. I almost trip as Wrath winks at me. "Do watch your step," he purrs with a smirk while I barely manage to catch myself before I land right on the pie table.

I straighten up and clear my throat while trying to look nonchalant and not like my demon husband just made my blood pressure spike with a wink. I rub the back of my neck and my skin is hotter than normal. It's like there's an electric current humming below my flesh, like I'm a live wire and just realized it.

Is this harbinger biz? It has to be.

"Don't give a wink like that and think I won't be affected."

Wrath shuts the door behind him and walks forward with a thoughtful hum. "Ah, so a wink does it for you, eh? Well, just wait until you see what I can do with my-"

"Buffy? Buffy, is that you?" Ms. Donna's voice rings out. I'm grateful, because mulberry if I know what Wrath was about to say.

I turn to look over my shoulder at Ms. Donna. She's behind

the counter with a tray full of apple fritters and I feel a wave of satisfaction hit me. I was right. I knew it.

I raise a hand in greeting. "Good morning, Ms. Donna!"

"What on earth are you doing here, girl? And where's Callum? Is that boy around here? I've got fresh fritters and those are his favorite. Come over here and I'll pack you a few!"

Shit. She's right. Callum did love Ms. Donna's fritters.

"I, uh, that's very kind," I say and glance around at every set of eyes on me. I clear my throat and take a step towards the counter. But before I can take the next, there's a yank on the bond between Wrath and I. The sudden tug makes me fall back a half step and I whirl around to look at him.

"What are you doing?" I ask Wrath and everyone gasps the second I speak.

"Do you see that?!"

"Where did the fritters all go?"

"They just vanished!"

I look around the bakery and see every person staring with open mouths and wide eyes at the now empty display cases. The tray Ms. Donna holds doesn't even have a crumb left on it. The older woman gapes at it while she turns it this way and that, like if she hits the right angle the fritters will all come tumbling out. But I know that won't happen.

The fritters didn't just disappear.

Wrath made them disappear.

I let the tug of the bond take me back to his side. "Why did you do that?" I ask while Wrath gives a sniff and makes a show of looking at a pie display.

"I don't know what you're talking about." He holds up an

apple pie to me. "What do you think? We could split this for lunch."

I bat aside the pie and jerk my thumb at the bakery. "The fritters! You presto magicked them right into nothing. Don't think I don't know."

"That's a wild claim. Why would I do something so silly?"

I raise an eyebrow at him and tap my chest. "I felt you do it. Don't lie to me. Humans lie, demons don't."

"Oh all right," Wrath mutters and puts the pie down with a thunk. "I got rid of them because she mentioned *him*. I won't have my wife toting around a dead man's dessert. Not on my watch."

I'm so shocked that I don't know what to say first. "Wait, what?"

"If you aim to carry around baked goods, they'll be made by my hand and my hand alone. They certainly won't be for a mortal man." I don't miss the tone of his voice and I can't help the smile that pulls at my lips.

"You're jealous."

Wrath goes still and frowns down at me. "Yes. I find it disagreeable."

I shrug and take a step away from him to Ms. Donna who is still shaking her baking tray with all of her might. "I dunno, I like it," I tell him over my shoulder before I reach out and stop Ms. Donna's flailing.

"I think the fritters are gone, Ms. Donna. Like, for good."

Probably in another dimension for all we know. Too bad. I really wanted one of those fritters, too.

"But why would all the fritters be gone, Buffy? I just baked those this morning. Just look at all the customers, they're so upset." Ms. Donna drops the pan with a groan and shakes her head while calamity and mourning continue to roll through the bakery at the fritter's disappearance.

I should make Wrath return them, but I won't. Not when I know why he did it.

"Maybe they were taken in offering," I try, leaning against the counter and looking heavenward. "I mean, what if Wrath desired those fritters? I bet, well—I bet he's taken them for his enjoyment. I'm sure of it."

Wrath makes a choking sound behind me while Ms. Donna looks like she's seen the light. I get it. I would have done the same thing before the cult tried to gut me.

"Oh, Buffy! You're right, I know it. Bless you for always knowing just the thing to say. Now, where is Callum?" She cranes her neck to look for my dead-intended, but the only thing she sees is my demon husband looming a foot behind me with a glare on his face.

"Well, there's something I have to tell you about Callum... he's, well," I pause, because how do I tell her that he's dead? I don't know who knows. Judging by how she's greeted me, Ms. Donna isn't in the inner circle that knows what really happens to Blossoms.

"What is it, dear?"

I take in a deep breath and decide to rip the Band-Aid off in one fell swoop.

"Ms. Donna, Callum's dead and I have a husband now." I reach a hand back for Wrath and a second later he slips his hand into mine. "His name is Damon and he's a mage."

"I-well," Ms. Donna swallows hard, but at least she's not worried about the fritters anymore. "Callum is dead?"

"Lost his head," Wrath answers and then inclines his head to her. "A pleasure to meet you, Ms. Donna. I've heard nothing but delicious news about your ability to bake. A shame about your fritters this morning."

I squeeze his hand in warning while Ms. Donna looks at Wrath and when I say look, I mean *look*. The woman downright stares at him so hard that I think she's forgotten how to blink.

She smooths a hand over her hair and presses a hand to her throat. "Oh my, well. Look at you," she says with a blush before she catches herself and clears her throat. "I mean, well look at you two. A lovely couple indeed. You're a mage?"

"I am."

"But the mages are all dead and gone," Ms. Donna explains while Wrath simply clucks his tongue at her and peruses the baked goods on the counter in front of us. I see a display of cinnamon rolls has caught his eye and he drums a finger on the lid.

"Oh, they've only died out here, Ms. Donna...it was Ms. Donna, wasn't it?" he asks and the older woman nods and rushes to pull the display lid off for him.

"Please, just Donna. Only the children call me Miss. Would you like a taste of one of these? I can send one along with you if you'd like."

I smile, because smiling is what I've been taught to do when situations spiral out of control. I don't think we're there yet. But we're close. Ms. Donna is totally hitting on Wrath.

"I would, please. I'm something of a baker myself," he tells her while Ms. Donna fusses over choosing the biggest cinnamon roll and packages it up for Wrath.

"Really? I'm sure we'll see you all the time, then. We could use another hand around the bakery, especially now that you're... married to Buffy?"

Ms. Donna is grasping at straws now but I understand her fixation with Wrath. The demon makes a gorgeous human. No one ever sees the Blossoms that are married. Their grooms often return to Sweet Tooth but always alone and even those visits are infrequent.

"I felt it fair on account of the harm her intended suffered," Wrath explains and takes the box she holds out to him.

"Harm?" Ms. Donna blinks, confused. Wrath nods as he lifts the box to look inside.

"His death. I could not simply leave her without a groom."

"Ah, yes, that." Ms. Donna's face falls and she sneaks a quick look my way before she looks back to Wrath. "How long will you both be in Sweet Tooth?" Her question isn't to me. It's to Wrath so I turn away and look at the people in the bakery.

It's a cheery and cozy scene. The scent of fresh baked bread and sweets hangs in the air. There's even the smooth hint of coffee from the freshly brewed pot someone just put out for everyone to help themselves to.

I snag a cup of coffee and take a careful sip while Wrath continues to talk to Ms. Donna. I know all their faces. There's an Outsider in the mix looking over the tarts but other than that every face here I know well. Fritters aside, they've recovered enough to glance my way, but not for too long.

Who knew what was going to happen to me? Do any of them know where the Blossoms are?

I search their faces for clues, any trace that they were in on what the Founders planned for the Blossoms, but there's nothing

I can pick up on. It's just Maurice grabbing every cherry pie he can get his hands on and Lola giving the sourdough loaves a careful once over before she selects her bread for her evening offering.

None of them know anything.

There's a sharp tug on the bond and I almost drop my coffee. When I look up, I don't see Wrath looking my way. He's only got eyes for Ms. Donna while she loads him up with bakery boxes. *Mulberries.* Did he just con her into giving him her entire inventory? If anyone could do it, he could. Especially with the way Ms. Donna is mooning over him.

I ditch my coffee and hurry towards them before the woman starts swiping pies and pastries from customer's baskets to please Wrath.

"We would be delighted. Absolutely delighted to help," Wrath assures Ms. Donna while she piles another yellow box on top of the stack he's already carrying. There's no way he's carrying it on his own. Demon magic is definitely afoot. I squint and see the telltale shimmer that says I was right. I wonder if anyone else knows but then again, they all think Wrath is a mage and not a demon.

"Are you sure? I don't want to trouble newlyweds and all. I remember what it was like back in my day."

I don't miss the little eyebrow wiggle Ms. Donna sends Wrath's way. She can't even see him, not with the stack of boxes he's got in his arms but the woman is putting her best effort into it. I respect that.

"You called?" I ask and slide up beside Wrath.

"Oh, Buffy!" Ms. Donna gives a little start and blinks at me in surprise. "I didn't hear him say anything, dear."

Right. The almost telepathic bond with Wrath is a perk of having a demon for a husband. Oops.

I clear my throat. "Ah, well, I knew," I cover quickly and smile brightly. "Newlyweds and all."

Ms. Donna nods and sticks a box into the hand Wrath has managed to get free of the bakery boxes he's balancing on one arm. "Oh, too true, my dear. Now your delightful husband has just offered to do an old woman a favor and take these boxes to the Rossi's place for me."

"The Rossi's?" I can't hide the surprise in my voice. The Rossi's are part of the Founders. I've only ever been in their home on special occasions, even though Ethan Rossi was one of the intended grooms and one of Callum's best friends. There wasn't much time for Blossoms to mix with the opposite sex, especially not their intended. Which makes sense, because what's a virgin sacrifice without the virgin?

"Yes, dear. They have an event and will be needing enough to feed an army from the looks of it. I wish I could go to a fancy party like that, don't you? Well, wouldn't you know it with the Autumn Festival making it the busiest day of the year, I've turned up short-handed and running late today! Besides the Festival, there's the fact that I've twisted my silly ankle climbing ladders just this morning. I wouldn't be able to take such a load as this to the Rossi's on my own. And I can't leave Velma in charge of the shop, now can I?"

Velma is Ms. Donna's one-eyed cat. Why she chose her and not one of the bakers huffing and toting cakes and pies around the bakery by the ton, I have no idea, but right on cue Velma mewls pitifully from where she's sunning herself by a window a few feet away.

Wrath pokes his head around the boxes at Velma's cry and nods solemnly. "I hear you, friend. Worry not, we are here to help."

Velma swishes her tail and gives Wrath a chirp before she hops up and comes to inspect him.

"I said we would help with this. Not that we would help you," he tells the cat with an apologetic shrug that nearly sends a cake to the ground.

I catch the cake and raise an eyeball at him and Velma. "Wait, do you actually understand the cat?"

Velma swishes her tail at me while Wrath chuckles as he lifts the boxes high above his head. "Yes, I do. She's annoyed at you."

"What? What did *I* do?" I hold a hand out to Velma and try to pet her but she prances away with her head held high.

"She has a name, you know. She much prefers you use it than cat," Wrath explains.

"Sorry, Velma!" I call out, but it's no use. Velma vanishes into the bakery. From the sounds of the curse and crashing trays she's underfoot somewhere she ought not to be.

"Oh Wrath! Would you look at that?" Ms. Donna tuts and looks over her shoulder at the calamity in her kitchens. "I have to be off now, my dears. You are a true blessing from him above and I will repay the kindness you've done me today. I swear it."

I hold up my hands, ready to tell Ms. Donna that she doesn't owe us anything but Wrath beats me to it.

"It's a deal," Wrath says and cuts me off with an extended hand. Ms. Donna takes it and shakes it immediately before she's off with a little wave and a shouted *'Velma, NO! Leave Timothy be!'*

Wrath jerks his chin to the door. "Let's be off then before Velma comes back for second blood, beloved."

I fall into step behind him, which in the crowded bakery is made a lot easier because of the small mountain of baked goods Wrath is carrying. Someone rushes forward to open the door for us and it's with a cheerful 'Why thank you!' that Wrath steps out onto the sidewalk and starts to head towards the Rossi's. My demon husband is in good spirits all right, far better than I've seen him have around other humans. Something is up and I think I know what it is.

"What was that?" I ask when I've caught up to him.

"What was what, beloved?"

"With Ms. Donna? The deal? You did something, didn't you?"

"I merely took the deal she offered of her own free will. No harm in that."

"What do you mean *you took the deal*? What does that mean?" Instantly I start to think of Ms. Donna losing her soul or being dragged into the underworld. All because we helped her carry pies to the Rossi's.

"Nothing to fear, Buffy. I don't think I like that coming from you," he says and I nearly crash into him when he stops walking. I look up at him and see his dark eyes are on my chest, on the place where we know the bond lives. I press my palm to the tender place without thinking.

"First the smelling and now the bond. This is a lot to take in. Just like the fact that you're making deals an-and if I'm going to be your harbinger, that's fine. Because you know what? There's a lot of people that owe me. But Ms. Donna isn't one of them. She didn't know what was going to happen."

"Ah, so you're worried, not scared." He tilts his head to the side and nods. "I'll have to make a note of the difference. Very well then." Wrath takes off again. That's when I notice his boxes are floating in front of him while he ambles along, attracting stares from townsfolk and Outsiders alike.

"What happened to keeping a low profile?" I ask.

"I'm supposed to be a mage, aren't I? I'm merely doing as mages do."

"Are you going to take Ms. Donna's soul?"

Wrath laughs. Well and truly laughs. He throws his head back and I have to slow down to marvel at the way the morning sun washes over his handsome features. The way it makes his pale hair glow like midnight fire. He's too damn pretty, it's distracting.

Wrath reaches back, grabs my wrist and draws me close. "I am not going to steal that little cheeky tart's soul. She will merely owe me a favor that will be redeemed at my choosing. That's all."

I don't fully believe Wrath but when he's touching me and smiling at me, I'm willing to pretend. "Just a favor?"

"A small one. You'll see, Buffy. Nothing to worry over."

"I dunno..." I hedge, but Wrath rubs his thumb over my knuckles and I feel the common sense drain right out of my brain.

"Let's focus, shall we? The Rossi's are on your list, are they not?" Wrath asks. He's right, they are on my list.

"How do you know where they live?"

"This cult was part of my job. Even if I was only to stand idly by, I was meant to know the comings and goings of those in charge. I know precisely where the Rossi's live."

"You watched us?"

"I had a file on the Founders, that's all. But," he pauses and looks at me with a rueful smile, "I didn't watch the sacrifices, for the most part. But I did pay attention. "

"Why?"

"I waited," Wrath tells me quietly before he leads me across the street. The bakery boxes in front of us bounce along in the sunlight and someone points with a *'do you see that?!'*. It's a nice morning, crisp and fresh. I suddenly wish that I'd been able to visit Ms. Donna and the bakery with Wrath under different circumstances. Better ones that didn't have me ready to commit murder.

"For what?" I ask.

"For an explanation. For a reason why so many beauties were cut down in the flower of their bloom. I wanted to know what a wife was. How precious one must be to be so coveted by a cult. There was nothing more that I wanted to learn than the value of a wife. So I watched, I waited, I listened. But none of them ever summoned me."

"So what did you do?"

Wrath slips his hand into mine and laces our fingers together. "I asked around in the underworld. Went to this dimension and that. I traded for information on the merits and values of a wife until I was finally able to understand."

"And what did you learn?"

"That a wife is not something you control but cherish. That a wife is a part of their chosen partner. A wife is neither meant to be below or above, but beside their partner. There is little else in all the universes and dimensions, no greater honor or thing more lovely and precious than a wife to have and to hold," he says and my heart feels close to bursting. Warmth and tenderness flow along our bond. It hums and vibrates into my bones and threads itself into my muscle and blood until it becomes the thing that holds me together when Wrath looks my way.

"Till death do us part," I say softly, because I know it will please Wrath. He smiles at me.

"Death is such an early event for humans. I prefer an eternity, don't you?"

"Maybe. Let's see if I make it past the full moon and then we can talk."

"It's a deal, beloved."

CHAPTER
SEVENTEEN

"This place is hoppin'," I whisper, leaning forward to get a better look. We're crouched in the decorative shrubs off to the side of the Rossi house and it looks like every founding family and their entourage is here today. Our hiding spot is made of a whole animal menagerie made out of shrubs lining the Rossi's property. I always thought they were weird. My parents swore it was just eccentric, but I don't really think they know what that word is, seeing as we're hanging out in a topiary swan with a backwards hat on. There's a koala on a train, a pig in a bed and a bear on a ball to round out the scene.

"It'll make taking a look around easier after we've delivered these for Ms. Donna." The floating yellow boxes are probably giving our position away by how they're suspended just above the shrubs, but as it is no one even thinks to look our way. Everyone is too busy to wonder why there's a tower of bakery boxes poking out from the topiary swan.

"Can't we just dump them?" I ask, squinting to try and get a closer look at the caterers rushing in through the side entrance when I freeze.

"As much as I love mischief, no beloved. The deal was struck on the contingency that I would fulfill my end of the bargain and that entails delivering."

"It's them," I whisper. I have to lean forward to brace my hands on the ground so that I don't vomit. I might still, but it'll be easier to keep it together if I'm not looking at them.

"Who?" Wrath sweeps an arm in front of me and I sag against the swan's tail feathers. "Who is it? Remember, whoever it is, they cannot touch you with my power in your veins. You are fearsome. You are my harbinger and woe to any who would harm you, Buffy."

Wrath's words are nice, but they won't protect me against them. Even so, I nod weakly and smile when I feel his eyes on me. "Thank you for trying to make me feel better."

"Who is it, Buffy?"

"My parents," I rasp. I hate how weak I sound, but I can't help it. They sold me. Callum told me the truth about them. I know they did it.

Wrath swears and looks back through the leaves of our hideout. "The vermin that sold their own blood."

I nod weakly. "Yeah, one and the same. I just call them mom and dad, mostly," I joke, because if I think about it too much I might cry.

Wrath turns to me and cups my face in his hands. "I'm going to flay the skin from their bodies and make you a crown from their bleached and broken bones, beloved," he promises.

I know he means it. I know he'll do it, too.

I pat Wrath's hand. "As much as I appreciate gifts, I don't think I want to wear my parents as a crown."

"Are you sure? You would look splendid with a crown."

"Could we try something made of silver, maybe some diamonds, before we move to the medium of my parent's fingers?"

He sighs and looks disappointed but nods all the same. "As you wish, my treasure."

It's easy to look at Wrath instead of my parents deceitful forms entering the Rossi's when he says things like that. "Do you really think that?" I ask him. My parents sold me as a Blossom to die. I don't think anyone other than my friends have ever talked to me like I was worth anything. But then Victor *did* try to kill me and I thought he was my friend.

"Think what?"

"That I'm a treasure," my voice breaks but I force myself to keep speaking. We're about to go into the lion's den. I have zero understanding of what I'll actually be able to do against the Rossi's. I want revenge, but what if I can't do it? "I-I, I mean that," my voice cracks and shakes but I still have to ask him, "that I'm valuable?"

"Oh, Buffy..." Wrath sighs and brushes my hair away from my face. "You are and always have been valuable. Even if you were with vicious little beasts that could not see your worth. You are precious."

"My parents didn't think so," I tell him and Wrath gives a little shrug like it's no big deal. "They sold me."

"Happens to more people than you think. Look at your friends," he says and then rises from his crouch and holds a hand out to me. "We aren't here for them, not yet. We're here for the Rossi patriarch's head. What was his name again?"

"Old Man Rossi."

Wrath makes a face. "What a weird little town this is," he says and then sighs when I shrug. "Right then, that old man is who we are here to kill and if you do change your mind on your parents, we can take theirs too."

"As much as I like a BOGO sale, let's stick with just the one."

"Fair enough."

We move together, staying low and skirting the edge of the topiary menagerie until we're near the side entrance we've watched the staff enter and exit from. If all goes according to plan, we should be able to slip in without anyone looking at us twice.

"Are you ready?" Wrath asks me. We're on the steps to the servant's door and I nod.

"As ready as I'll ever be. Let's do it."

"You'll need this," Wrath tells me and pulls me close.

"Need what?" I ask, but he doesn't answer me. He kisses me instead. It's slow and tender and the bond between us wakes up. Warmth washes over me. I feel...good. Better than good, really. I feel invincible. Like nothing can touch me. When we part, I'm smiling up at Wrath.

"What was that for?"

"Your blessing," he tells me and brushes a thumb over my bottom lip with a smile. "There are other ways to anoint you, but they're so mundane in comparison."

I grin and follow our mountain of floating bakery boxes into the Rossi's. There's a clatter and the smell of spices in the air so I know we're in the kitchen. I remember where we are more or less now. The kitchen is sprawling, big enough to feed the entire town, even if it is just Ethan and his parents that live here. Through the kitchen, there's a long hallway that takes you to the massive dining room, the den and the library they have. I know there's other rooms on the bottom floor, but I didn't explore those when I was here previously. At the front of the hallway is the foyer and the front door I watched my parents enter. There's a spiral staircase to the second floor where all of their bedrooms are, but I'm not interested in those rooms or any of the others. The room that I want to look at is the basement. It's just down the hallway before you get to the dining room, which means we're going to have to go near the front door. It's risky, but it's not terrible.

If there's anything of worth the Rossi's are going to hide, it's going to be down there. My gut is telling me that's where I'm going to find Dylan Rossi aka Old Man Rossi.

The bakery boxes float along and I lean close to Wrath and grab his arm. "We need to go through the kitchens to the hallway door and take a left. The basement door should be at the end. That's where I bet we can get the jump on him."

"I would say lead the way but I don't want you going first, not yet," Wrath murmurs and moves to step in front of me. We've only gone a half step before someone shouts at us.

"You there! Stop!"

Wrath and I freeze. "I'm going to throw the baked goods at them. You run," he says simply. But before he can, I stop him.

"Wait, just wait. They can't kill me, not with you being my husband, remember?" I whisper to him and then turn with a bright smile on my face. "Why hello there! How can I help?"

A man with graying hair and a pinched look on his face glares at us. I've never seen him before, which is...interesting. Since when are Outsiders allowed to work in Sweet Tooth?

"Grab a tray. Why are you not in uniform? We need more hands taking the hors d'oeuvres to the guests."

Wrath crosses his arms and glares back at the man. "What did you just call my wife?"

I put a hand on him when he looks like he's going to take a step forward. "Hors d'oeuvres, ah, they're food. It's okay and um, we're with the bakery?"

His eyes flick over to the floating boxes. He doesn't look phased when he sees them in midair. "It's about time. I thought we were going to have to drive down there. Put them on the table behind you. Move it, I don't have time for your funny business. Not today. All of you in this creepy little town are too much for me," the man snaps and thrusts a tray at Wrath who takes it with a begrudging sigh when I give his arm a squeeze.

"Low profile," I remind him before I take a tray from the man. "So sorry! We'll get right on this for you.

"Fine, but I'm not wearing a uniform," Wrath says with a sniff and turns on his heel.

I duck my head and hurry along with my tray. I already know I'm spilling things when I bump into the table Wrath just dumped the boxes on with a crash.

"Watch it! There are tarts!" The Outsider yells at us.

I don't say anything but I do raise an eyebrow at Wrath's pleased smile as we slip out into the hallway. "You really need a lesson in chill," I tell him.

He shrugs. "I found him disagreeable."

I might think to tell him that sometimes you have to go along to get along, but I'm here to murder a man and probably take out my parents so I don't think I have much room to talk. We head down the hallway in relative peace. I'm relieved when I see the basement door up ahead. It's big and brass and the doorframe is set in stone with runes etched into it.

Funny how when I was here with Callum I chalked it up to Founder's Circle things and never thought twice about what Old Man Rossi might be hiding down in his basement. What if it's the Blossoms?

What if that's why all of these people are here? Sunday said we had two more days, plus possibly more if we needed it, but what if she got it wrong?

"Come on, we have to hurry," I tell Wrath and set off at a jog. The glasses on my tray clink and thunk as some fall over and spill their contents. I bet I'm leaving a trail of booze behind me, but I don't care. I have to get in that basement and I have to do it now.

I come to a skidding stop in front of the door. That's when I notice there's no door knob.

"Oh, what the mulberry?" I whisper, staring at the smooth shiny surface. "What do we do?" I ask Wrath when he comes up beside me. He takes one of the drinks off my tray and sips from his glass with a pensive look on his face.

"It's dwarvish," he murmurs and takes a step closer. "It's doable, but it will take some time. Don't worry, I'll handle it," he says, throwing back his cocktail with a hum of satisfaction. "Now, that terrible man in the kitchen might get on my nerves, but these drinks are superb. You have to try one," he says, holding one out to me. I bat his hand away. "I bet these little bites here on my tray are delectable as well but I have no idea what this is." He holds out the tray. What looks like small spoons made of bread stuffed with melted cheese and meat are artfully arranged.

"What do you think? Tiny lasagnas? Or would this be pizza?"

"Wrath, the door." I tap a finger against the door as I consider the food on his tray. "It looks like pizza to be honest but in a bread spoon."

"Pizza bread spoon then." He shoves his pizza tray off onto a side table and holds his hand out to the door, beginning to chant. I don't understand the language but the runes do. Each one of them lights up when he moves his palm over them. Before long, the runes along the doorframe are glittering gold in the low light of the hallway. Wrath steps back and plucks another drink off my tray. I don't know why I'm still holding it. Probably because I don't know what else to do with my hands while I wait for him to work his magic on the door.

How am I going to kill anyone?

"The enchantment will take a few minutes to work but I wager we'll be in there before I can catch a buzz."

"What are you two doing in here?" A head pops into the hallway. This time it's a woman, but there's no smile on her face to soften her sharp tone. She's glaring and frowning and I stare at her in shock because, just like the man in the kitchen, I don't know her either.

She's an Outsider, too.

"Oh my god are you *drinking the cocktails*?" She stomps into the hallway with a dark look on her face and I can't look away from the sight. She's like a car accident you see coming and can't look away from. Instead of it being because I'm horrified, it's because her frown is one of the most beautiful things I've ever seen.

She's so free in her displeasure that my heart stutters in my chest and I have to take a step closer to her to get a better look. She whirls on me when I do and points a finger in my face.

"Back up you weirdo townie or I'll put the hurt on you."

"Sorry," I whisper and fall back a step while Wrath drinks his cocktail and ignores her.

"Would you like me to send her to the sixth dimension for you, beloved?"

"No, please don't do that."

"Very well."

"What the fuck are you two talking about? I swear to god I hate this town and these jobs. But I need the money so of course I drive my ass out here and on a school night too. I swear, if either of you costs me this gig because you're getting drunk on the job I'm going to throttle you!" She grabs the drink out of Wrath's hand and drops the glass into a potted plant.

"Now, get your pretty butts out there and serve those culty freaks," she orders and points a finger towards the dining room.

I don't want to leave but the door isn't showing any signs of opening. The runes are still glowing, which I guess means they're working. Wrath did say it would take a few minutes. The woman isn't being quiet and I bet she'll tell the man in the kitchen about us, which would only get us thrown out. There's only one solution to this problem, which is going to suck seeing as my parents are in that room. And I know they're not expecting to see me when I should be dead.

"Right, you got it," I say with a bright smile and nod at Wrath to follow me. "We won't let you down."

We're going to have to serve the party. *Oh, mulberries.*

CHAPTER

EIGHTEEN

"Beloved, I know I said I would follow you anywhere but this is risky, even for us. Especially for a first outing as a harbinger."

"You said you would follow me anywhere?" I ask Wrath. He blushes before he looks away. "Really?"

"Well, maybe I thought it," he hedges before he looks back at me. I smile at him.

"That's so sweet."

"I am a very sweet demon when I have the mind to be."

I beam at him. "So I've noticed. As much as I adore it, we should make moves," I say and move away from him when he looks like he's going to kiss me. "I don't want her yelling at us again while we wait for the door to open. How long do you think it'll take by the way?"

"Not long, one circuit here and it should be done. I'll know when the magic is completed and we can go back that way."

I nod and follow him into the dining room. It's a big room

with high ceilings and a sparkling chandelier. There's classical music playing from a string quartet set up in one corner. The long dining table that's normally here is gone. Instead, there's a circle in the middle of the room with runes that look like a mirror image of the ones on the doorway.

"Perfect. But until then, please lay low. We need to blend in. That means no more eating or drinking off the trays and—what the heck is that?" I ask him with a nod towards the circle and runes.

"Oh very well, but I'm taking my fill once we're done here. And *that* is a summoning circle. A very big one. If it's what I think they're bringing here, they are going to need *a lot* of power," Wrath pauses and looks around the room with a hum. "Interesting choice of venue, seeing as it's so small."

"Why is that?"

"Those look like the runes for a stone troll. I could be mistaken, my dwarvish is rusty at best. I was only ever conversational on account of them not being easily swayed by my charms. Much like the staff we've encountered. Perhaps they're dwarvish too."

"A stone troll? What the heck are they going to do with a troll? I swallow hard. The smile on my face takes on the normal strained feeling it did when there was conflict in the cult or I was tasked with something I didn't want to do. "Am I going to have to fight a troll? H-how do I fight a troll?"

"When you're you, Buffy, it's an easy thing. You'll see when the time comes. The only thing you will have to do is listen to your instincts."

He's confident. I know, because I can feel it sure and as plain as day. Wrath believes I can fight and beat a stone troll. One that he thinks won't even fit in this room. Until today, I didn't even know there were stone trolls. Now I have to fight one?

"Instincts? I don't have any instincts." I was brainwashed by a cult to smile when I'm upset. How do I have instincts Wrath is confident in? I shake my head and the tray in my hand trembles. "You keep saying that, but-"

"Oh, I'm dying for a drink! Give me three." A woman nearly takes Wrath out in her sprint to get to me and snags a drink in each hand. "Come on, Darla, get a drink. You're in the big leagues now. You'll soon see these brunch things are a chore without one or five of these in you."

Darla.

My mom.

I try to turn away but I'm pinned against the wall by the woman that's double-fisting cocktails and blocking me from leaving before my mom has a chance to get her own drink.

I know Wrath feels my distress when he shoots me a look over the woman's head but before he can ask me what's wrong, I hear her.

"Buffy?" It's my mom. She's in front of me and she looks shocked to see me, even if her lips are turned up in a smile that lies. I guess they didn't tell her I wasn't dead after all.

"Hey," I offer up. I don't use any replacement words or fight the urge to call upon the god I worshiped all my life. I give in and call on Wrath in my mind.

Wrath, help me. Wrath, please. It's my mom.

That's all it takes before I feel him in my head.

I can kill her before anyone notices, he offers.

It's tempting but I know that won't help me get close to Old Man Rossi. I don't know where my friends are either.

It's all right. You can deal with her later. I promise. I just need you close.

The smile he sends my way makes me relax enough that when I look at my mom, I have no problem smiling or pretending that I'm not angry.

"Hey? That's all you have to say to me?"

"Mother," I say and offer her the tray with a flourish, "would you care for a refreshment?" More than one of my drinks has spilled and my tray drips onto the floor while I wait for her to take a glass.

She swallows hard and slowly plucks one off the tray. "You know I don't like it when you call me that," she tells me. I hear the same old reproach she always sent my way when it looked like I was stepping out of line.

I used to cave when she spoke to me like that. I bent over backwards to hurry and do the *'right thing.'* But now I don't. I stare back at her with a smile and ignore her displeasure while the dripping from my tray keeps time with my pounding pulse. My hand shakes and I daydream about throwing the drinks in her face.

Do it.

I sigh. I know that's Wrath talking, not me. Maybe I *will* take on this stone troll with the anger that's waking up in me. Fury makes my blood hot, my skin prickle and my palms itch. The urge to throw drinks and cause a scene bubbles to the surface but I tamp it down and do nothing.

I can't. Not while they have my friends. I have to find Old Man Rossi and knock his block off before I can make a scene.

"But it was what you were to me," I tell her, taking care to stress the past tense before I turn to Wrath. "It's so very lucky for my mother to meet my husband." I incline my head to Wrath and just like Ms. Donna, my mom seems to fall right under his spell. She offers him a genuine smile. The woman beside her nearly chokes on one of her drinks as I turn their eyes to Wrath.

"That's not Callum," she whispers to my mom before looking at me. "I thought you said she was marrying Callum."

My mom opens her mouth to speak but I cut her off. "I *was* marrying Callum but that was before he had a little...accident," I answer, watching my mom's face pale. She knows what happened to Callum. Maybe she did know about me getting away before she saw me today.

"Accident?" The woman asks and looks between all of us. "What do you mean by *accident*? Blossoms marry their intended. It's the only way that Sweet Tooth is able to-"

"Bernice, that's enough," my mother snaps, cutting her off with a thin smile. She never was as good at hiding her true feelings, not like the rest of us. Being an Outsider only takes you so far when it comes to Sweet Tooth. She'll never be as good at hiding what she feels like the rest of us that were born to it.

Wrath steps in front of me and affection fills my heart for him and his strategic move to shield me from my mom and her friend. "It was no accident, but the details about what happened to Callum are not fit for polite company. Especially not at a fine brunch such as this," Wrath tells them, bowing forward and offering my mom a pizza spoon. "Would you like one? They look very good but Buffy tells me I'm not to have any."

My mother takes a pizza spoon immediately. I get it. Wrath's voice is smooth, deep and soothing. He has both of the women eating out of the palm of his hand. They both reach for one while he smiles on encouragingly. But through our bond, I feel his anger.

I will avenge you, beloved.

"We have to be going. I promised I would help with this," I say and lift my leaking tray. "It was good to see you," I tell them, backing away. I only make it a step when she calls out to me.

"I didn't want it to happen this way. Y-you weren't supposed to find out the way you did. I wanted to tell you before, because you're a good girl, Buffy. You would have done what they asked you to do. You would have been a Blossom all on your own, even if you'd known. I told your father, but he wouldn't listen. Buffy, we had to do it. The money was too good."

The tiny shred of hope I had that my parents didn't know what was going to happen to me on my wedding night dies. All those years they lied and let me believe that I would move away to the city. Not die in a bloody mess with a knife in my gut. They did it so easily.

And over money?

They never loved me. They couldn't have. How could anyone lie to someone they loved like that?

I pause and look at her over my shoulder. "I don't know what you're talking about," I say and I watch her smile wobble. It nearly breaks but a quick jab of Bernice's elbow to her ribs has her shaping up and it's a smile that sends me off to make my rounds around the dining room with Wrath beside me.

"I don't see Old Man Rossi," I tell him while I look around the room. "He's got to be downstairs. Do you think the door is open by now?"

"Buffy..."

"Let's go back that way and see if the coast is clear."

"Buffy, are you all right?"

"I'm fine," I lie.

"Don't lie to me, beloved."

"She knew," I whisper and tears prick my eyes. I have to blink double time to keep my composure when a woman saunters up and takes one of the remaining cocktails standing on my tray. Wrath shoves a pizza spoon in her hand before he turns his attention back to me.

The tenderness in his eyes makes me ache. "Let me kill her. I'll do it now. I'll paint this room red with her blood," he vows and I fall a little more in love with my demon husband.

"My friends," I tell him and shake my head. "I can't leave them. No."

"I hate these people." Wrath frowns and looks past me with a scoff. "This is by far the worst brunch I've ever been to." He shoves his tray off to a random guest and takes my arm. "Let's be off then. The magic holding the door closed should be drained by now. The faster we rescue your friends the faster I'll be able to cut down your sniveling parents. I plan on taking my time when I'm finally let loose on them, beloved."

Right on cue with Wrath's words, I see my father. He's with my mother and their heads are bent close together while she talks to him. I know she's telling him she saw me. What else would they be talking about?

A half second passes and he lifts his head to look in my direction. I watch his face go pale when he sees me. He looks so...*different*. They both do. We were modest in everything, never having enough to truly splurge on things like clothing, not when there was more work sent our way because my father chose to marry an Outsider. Now you'd never know it.

Gone are the sturdy and plain dresses my mother favored and the reliable and worn leather shoes my father always wore. He's in a suit with shiny black shoes and perfectly combed hair, and my mother...now that I have the distance to look at her, I see she's wearing a royal blue dress with a slit on the side and white pumps.

They don't look like themselves at all. They're like a shined up penny someone put on display and I know why.

"The money was too good."

They sold me out and got rewarded. This party is part of the reward package. I want to scream at them both. Was this what they thought about while I was stupidly gushing to my friends about how dreamy I thought Callum was or worried that I wasn't going to be able to drive in the city properly when I kept running into curbs in town?

"I wanted to tell you before, because you're a good girl, Buffy. You would have done what they asked you to do. You would have been a Blossom all on your own, even if you'd known. I told your father, but he wouldn't listen."

They really thought I was going to lay down and die for them. For this town. Because I was a *"good girl."* My stomach lurches, because I know she isn't wrong. I would have done anything and everything for this town, for this cult. That was before I knew the truth.

Now I'm going to end it all.

"It's going to be alright," Wrath tells me and steps in front of me, blocking me from my father's sight. "Now, let's go see about that door."

CHAPTER

NINETEEN

When we leave the dining room and enter the hallway I breathe a sigh of relief and sag against Wrath. It's quieter here, darker too and I can breathe again. Wrath hooks an arm around my waist and holds me up as we approach the door.

The runes aren't flashing and have gone dark now.

"Is it open?" I ask him and he nods.

"It is. Dwarvish magic is all about the lights, beloved. If you see those runes and they're lit up, there's magic. When they go dark, it's dead. I've disabled the locks for now but they won't hold. Especially not if this Old Man Rossi is looking to summon a stone troll soon. All that power coming through here will kick this right back on, so let's be quick."

"If it comes back on, does that mean we're locked down there?"

"For a while. I'll get us out but it won't be easy. Dwarvish magic is potent stuff and now that I'm free of Ichabod's hold, my power is still regenerating. I won't be up to full strength for a while longer."

Wrath sounds disappointed. When I look his way I see the slight slump of his shoulders and the worry on his face that tells me he's blaming himself for not being as powerful as he could be.

"Hey, you're doing great. You rescued me and you made me a harbinger, remember? I'm sure that wasn't easy. We'll be alright. I'm strong enough, remember? Now, get behind me, I'll go first."

Wrath raises an eyebrow at my bold words. I don't feel strong but I'll pretend if it gets the worry off his face. "Buffy, what are you-"

I jerk a thumb back at myself. "I'm the harbinger, so let me harbinge" I tell him, leaning up to kiss him. I smile when he falls silent and kisses me back.

"I don't think harbinge is a word but I'm on board if you kiss me like that." He reaches past me and touches the center of the brass door. There's a soft click as it unlocks. "I'll be right behind you if anything goes wrong. Don't worry, Buffy."

I wave a hand and roll my shoulders. "Listen, nothing is going to go wrong. Besides, I got this," I lie again and take a shaky step forward. The truth is, the only reason I'm going first is to make him feel better. I trust Wrath. I know he wouldn't tell me I was ready for something if I wasn't but after seeing my parents, I can feel the doubt and fear that clung to me like a second skin and I can't take it.

I have to change.

I have to become the harbinger Wrath says I am. I have to be different. That means I go first when I'd rather let him take the lead. I'm not exactly one hundred percent on the mechanics of demon marriage and harbinger biz, but I'm positive it took a lot of out of Wrath to make me into one.

He did it for me.

He did it because he knew I was scared. He did it to give me power. He did it to keep me safe.

And now I'm going to do the same for him.

I take a steadying breath and look back at Wrath with a bright smile. "I'm sure there's nothing down there anyways. Sure I'll have to take on the troll—but still, let's do it on three, okay?"

Wrath nods and steps beside me so we're side by side. We both put a hand on the door's surface.

"One," I count and tense. I'm ready to kick this door down now that my adrenaline is moving but I keep counting.

"Two."

I take a deep breath and let it out before I say, "Three!" and shove the door open with Wrath.

The second we open the door I realize how silly I was for even trying to say there was nothing down here. The basement is medieval, nothing like the chic and polished upstairs and the fancy brunch taking place. This place is arcane and old.

The basement makes me think of the Founders' Circle but it feels different here.

I remember being excited in the Founders' Circle. Even when Callum and his dad were trying to gut me it didn't feel like this. The air is *heavy*. There's a metallic scent in the air that's unnatural. Breathing feels hard, like every bit of the oxygen here is weighty.

The basement feels evil.

And the evil basement is full of hooded cultists in the middle of a ritual. And they're all looking at us. At least, I think they are from the way they're angled towards the stairs. It's tough to see exactly where their eyes are trained because of the hooded cowls that hide their faces in shadow. High above them, a chandelier flickers, full of flames. It casts the room into dim light and shadows. There's an altar at the middle of the floor and I bet money that Old Man Rossi is the one standing over the altar with his arms above his head, mid-chant.

"Oh mulberries," I whisper.

One of the cultists lets out a shout and points at Wrath and I. *"Get her!"*

Chaos breaks out when two cultists spring forward and charge towards the stairs. We only have a few seconds before they're going to be on us.

I feel the tug of our bond and it forces me to stand tall, even with two bloodthirsty cultists coming for me. "Trust your instincts, Buffy. Trust yourself. You know what to do."

Laughter floats to us from the brunch my parents are still stuffing their faces at and my body comes unlocked. If the cultists get their hands on me, it's game over. They have an entire upstairs full of acolytes who won't hesitate to take me apart if they think it's going to get them ahead with the Founders' Circle.

I know what to do.

I always have.

"We can't let them get help. Shut the door," I order Wrath, eyes scanning for a weapon but there's nothing on the stairs for me to use. The only weapon I have is myself, so I do what Wrath told me to do and I listen to myself. When a cultist gets close enough, I throw myself forward and kick him hard enough in the chest that his hood snaps back and I see his face. There's a look of surprise and I realize it was the mailman that ran from me earlier.

"I knew it!" I point a finger at him. "I knew you knew, you sneaky little rat!"

He groans and falls against the railing, barely managing to grab hold of it. He staggers towards me as his friend tries to shove past him. The pair of them don't make it any further before I launch myself at them. We all go over the railing, except I don't hit the stone floor like a broken egg the way the two men do. My body moves on its own and I grab the railing, catching myself from falling. I swing back over the railing and up onto the stairs in a crouch.

Wrath applauds while the men below us howl with pain. "Very nice," he says and warmth washes over me at the praise. I feel powerful and strong, like I'm capable of taking on the basement full of killers and winning. The smile on my face is one hundred percent real when I kick the railing as hard as I can. The railing never stood a chance and immediately cracks in half. I rip the two broken pieces free before turning to look at Wrath. Below us, the cultists are screaming and scrambling like ants pouring from a kicked anthill but I don't care about them. They'll come by the dozen until this is over. What I care about is Wrath.

I twirl my makeshift weapons and gesture down the stairs with the pointy ends. "I'm going to make with the harbinging now," I tell him.

Wrath chuckles and saunters down the stairs to me. "You're doing beautifully. Mind if I take a few of them apart for you, beloved?"

The stairs shake under the pounding footsteps of the cultists coming for us. There's so many that if they weren't forced to come in pairs because of the narrow stairs, they'd be on us by now.

I lift my chin and stare them down, even if there's only shadows where their faces should be. "The more the merrier."

"Harbingers first, then." Wrath bows and gestures to the cultists running up the stairs with a flourish but he stops me a second later. "Oh and Buffy?"

I recognize the first two men. One of them was a teacher at my high school. His name is Rick and I hated his History of the Founders class. The other is Mike and he's one of the supervisors in charge of laundry duty that always gave Meadow and I the worst jobs.

I'm going to enjoy this.

"Yeah?"

"You're going to walk out of this just fine, because you have me. I might not be as strong as I was, but I'm plenty strong enough to protect you while you rampage."

Rampage. I've only ever heard the word used when it comes to storms or earthquakes. Sometimes it was used to describe Wrath's power over our lives if we were to step out of line but the word has never been used to describe me.

I think I like the word rampage.

I turn to meet the cultists. They're people that I've grown up with, people that I've seen on the streets of Sweet Tooth day after day, but they're killers. They've always been killers and now they want to kill me.

"Buffy! You little bitch!" Rick lunges for me and I crack him over the head with the railing I'm holding.

"I never liked your class," I tell him, but he doesn't hear me. Rick's eyes roll back in his head and he instantly falls back and crashes into Mike, who catches him clumsily before falling onto his knees while he swears and screams at me.

160

"You selfish, stupid girl! I'm going to kill you. I'm going to rip your eyes out of your-" Mike's words are cut off when I slam the wooden spikes I'm using into either side of his throat. I rip them free and blood splatters onto the next cultist's face, who looks shocked at what I've done.

"I don't think he's going to be doing much of anything that doesn't involve bleeding out. What do you think?" I ask them and I watch panic wash over my next victim's face.

"Wrath!" They throw their hands up and try to stop but their momentum carries them forward right where I want them. They look up at the ceiling and I smile down at them. "Wrath, save me! I beg you!"

"He doesn't care what happens to you," I tell them. When I move, it's with grace. The kind that I never knew before now. I know I'm only moving my limbs because I'm Wrath's Harbinger —*his wife*. I swing the spike up and through the begging cultist's jaw. The wood cuts them off and the gurgle of their words turn to wet gasps while Wrath hums a song I don't know behind me.

"I'm glad to say there won't be a bit of protection for any of you. I'm far too busy watching my ruthless little wife's show," Wrath calls out to them and leans over the railing with a cheery little wave that has the cultists dropping to their knees.

"Beg all you want. She's going to kill every last one of you and I'm not going to lift a finger to save you."

I look over at him and see that he's dropped his human form. It's their god, the one they worshiped and killed for, that's smiling down on them while I butcher them. I kick another down the stairs so hard they bounce when they hit the stone floor.

"Where are my friends?" I scream. When one of the men tries to run, I throw one of my wooden spikes at their back. I watch them go down like a sack of potatoes while the spike comes out the other end and embeds itself into the stone wall.

I'm at the bottom of the stairs now. I turn to face the basement full of murderous cultists now turned coward at the sight of their god turning a blind eye to them.

"What did you do to them? Where are my friends?" I ask again. I raise my voice when my eyes lock with Old Man Rossi who's frozen at the altar with his arms above his head. Old Man Rossi, isn't really that old at all. He's the same age as my father, but everyone calls him Old Man Rossi anyway. He's blond and fit, a head taller than me. I've watched him beat guys my age at pick up games of basketball, which is where I think he gets his nickname.

I was always nervous around him because he was part of the Founders' Circle, because his family planted the seeds of this town. Now I know just how rotten the roots of it all are.

He looked powerful before, scary even. Now he looks like a puppet someone's cut the strings off of. I'm not scared of him anymore.

How can I be, when I'm on a rampage?

"Where did you take them?" I look around the basement and it's nothing but the cultists and some bookshelves. A room off to the side catches my eye, so I point at it. "Are they in there?" I ask.

"You're supposed to be dead," Rossi says as he lowers his arms finally and clears his throat. He draws himself up. I know he's trying to regain control here, which is laughable considering I've just taken down half a dozen of his men and his "god" is backing me up.

I pull a feigned look of shock and smile brightly at him. "Jeepers, really? Do you think anyone else has noticed?"

"Buffy, I don't know what little game you're playing at, but it's not going to work, little girl."

Little girl.

It's something I've been called many times before. Belittling, of course. Always belittling by the leaders I was told to follow.

"I'd say something snappy about you calling me a little girl when I'm mowing down your men but I don't give a shit enough to do it. So I'll just act out like this." I throw the remaining wooden spike as hard as I can. Cultists scream and drop to the floor but Rossi doesn't. That's okay, because I was aiming for him.

The spike slams into his shoulder and hits him so hard he's thrown back into the altar.

"You insolent little *bitch!*"

"You know, a lot of you keep calling me that. I don't think I should be the one to remind you that it's *against the rules to swear!*" I grab a man by his robes and throw him one-handed at Rossi. The pair collide and I hear the crack of stone before the altar crashes to the floor.

"You've defiled this place!" A man moans and I send a mean smile his way.

"I'm going to do a lot more than that before I'm done with all of you. Now, where are my friends? The Blossoms. Where did you take them? Are they in there?" I jerk a thumb back at the room I saw and then snap my fingers at the nearest person.

"Open that door or I'll use your head to do it."

They bob their head and scurry towards the door but not before they let out a quick. "Yes, ma'am."

"Thank you," I say, because even if I am running through the cultists like one-ply, I was raised to have manners. The man that opened the door bows low to me as I walk past him. I don't hear anyone inside but that doesn't mean I'm not going to look all the same.

"There's no one in there, ah, ma'am? I mean, do you want me to call you ma'am or is there something else like your highness? Perhaps your excellency?"

"What? No, that's-don't call me your highness," I tell him and duck into the room. "I'm not the Queen."

"No, but you are *my Queen*," Wrath calls out to me and I hear the terrified moans of the cultists. For being so in love with sacrifices, they don't seem like they can stomach much of it when it's on their end. "I order you to call her your highness."

I smile at his words while I take in the small and windowless room. There's nothing in here but a writing desk and more bookcases along the walls. That doesn't mean that I didn't read all the same mystery novels that Meadow did or sneak time watching prime time tv when our moms thought we were memorizing our verses.

Little hidey-holes like this are prime real estate for stashing people in—of course, in the shows it was to hide dead bodies but close enough considering the trail of bodies I've left in the other room.

I stomp on the floors just in case there's a trap door and knock on the walls, looking for a hidden door. There's nothing. When I exit the room the cultist I left is still bowing low and holding the door open for me with shaking hands. Wrath is casually leaning against the railing while he keeps an eye on the men huddled and crying on the basement floor.

His tail gives an irritated flick as he watches them. "You're all crying far too much to be my acolytes. It's a mercy I've brought her here to end you all."

Someone sniffles. "But why? Why would you bring her here?"

"Because she's my wife and she does as she pleases. Even if she was not, she would deserve to bring you to the low vermin you are, because she has withstood far more than any of you here are able. Just look at you!" Wrath sweeps an arm out across the room and laughs—but it isn't the laugh I usually like.

It's not warm and kind. It doesn't make me think of sunshine and cinnamon rolls.

This laugh is mean. I've never heard it before from him but I like it almost as much as I do when his laughter is joyful. The cultists cower and Wrath descends the steps as he speaks.

"You're all weak. You tried to break her and failed. Here she is, twice as strong and ripping you apart for the pleasure of it. Her sacrifices bring me strength. You foolish men couldn't even do that right. Now, *where are her friends*? Tell her now."

No one speaks. I'm not even sure anyone dares breathe after Wrath finishes speaking. I fight the urge to tap my foot as we wait.

I look at the cultist next to me. "What's your name?"

"Elijah," he squeaks, looking up at me before he drops his eyes again, "I mean, my name is Elijah, your highness."

"Don't call me that."

Elijah's eyes flick to Wrath and I don't miss the way his eyes dart from his horns to his tail before he swallows hard and looks back at me pleadingly. "He told me to, your highness."

"Buffy is just fine."

"You are not just Buffy," Wrath rumbles.

"I am," I argue.

"You're the Harbinger," Wrath corrects and I have to agree, he does have me there.

"Fine, call me the Harbinger, Elijah."

"Yes, your high-I mean, yes Harbinger."

"Elijah, you wouldn't happen to know anything about the missing Blossoms, would you? Because I'm looking for my friends. And *your* friends," I point to the basement of cultists, "took my friends and I really want to get them back."

Elijah is shaking now. "Are you going to kill me, Harbinger?"

There's fear in his voice. Even though I probably should like that, I can't. I'm not a bully. Not even when I was raised by them I couldn't be like them. Hearing that hitch in Elijah's voice makes my stomach turn.

I take a deep breath and look at Wrath who's just reached the bottom of the stairs and watches me carefully. "I might," I answer Elijah truthfully. "But if you help me, I have no reason to hurt you. The only thing I want are my friends. I have to get them back. As soon as I have them, I'm gone. I promise."

"No!" Someone shouts. I hear the telltale scrape of metal against stone. "She can't take the Blossoms. If she takes the Blossoms, Sweet Tooth perishes."

Elijah can see who's yelling, I know it when his eyes go wide. "Look out!" He surprises me when he throws himself forward to push me out of the way but I'm already turning. There's a man with a sword, an honest to god sword. Like the ones I've seen in the documentaries and period dramas Meadow and I watched with no sound on to keep secret. The man wants to kill me, it's the only explanation for the frenzy I see in his eyes. The rage I hear in his voice. But he's too slow.

I know where he's going to move, how the sword will arc, because the swing is wide. He will miss me by just enough that I'll be able to take it from him and split him in two. I step forward, fury moves me and it feels good. I'm smiling at him but I don't mean it. At least, not the way I was raised to. We both know it. I can already feel the weight of the sword in my hand and how it will feel to cut him down but I never get to do any of it, because the man vanishes.

Or rather, he explodes.

CHAPTER
TWENTY

One second the angry cultist is coming down on me with his too slow sword and the next there's no trace of him and I'm snatching the sword from the air. The only way I know he exploded is because his robes look like someone took a weed whacker to it. There's nothing left of him but thread and lint raining down on all of us like confetti. Well that and the sword I'm now holding.

I hear Elijah moan and I worry he's fainting. But when I look back at him I see him staring at Wrath with adoration. "Oh, Hallowed Destroyer!" Elijah falls to his knees and ends up face down with his palms extended to Wrath in supplication. "You have blessed us, Wrath! Our god, our king. Please, grant me mercy and let me serve you and your Buffy."

"She's not just my Buffy, she's my wife, acolyte."

Elijah lets out a muffled affirmation and keeps his nose pressed to the stone floor as Wrath approaches me. The rest of the basement is so still you'd think the cultists have been turned to stone. I wish it was all of them. How nice and neat to end all of this here and now, but it's not. Sweet Tooth might be a small town, but one basement isn't going to hold all the devotees.

"You made him explode."

"He was going to touch you. Of course I made him explode."

I hold up the sword. "I would have been just fine with this," I tell him and twirl the blade. "I could have handled him."

Wrath stops in front of me and tuts. "It's the principle, love. No one touches you. Not a single inch of you. Well, unless they're me, of course." His silver eyes flash as they slowly move from my face to my body. Wrath hums and nods. "I'm the only one allowed to touch your beautiful curves."

The blood lust that powered me before turns to something far simpler—lust. I need my demon husband. The shyness I felt earlier when touching him, the uncertainty, the newness of it all, isn't so scary anymore. Not when I've done what I just did to the cultists.

"Do you want to touch me now?"

Wrath smiles and just like that, the golden thread between us snaps and he's in my space, his hands sliding gently down my sides to cup my hips. "Oh, yes. Touching you is the finest pleasure I can imagine. Second to tasting you, of course. Can I taste you, beloved?"

"Yes," I answer him, fully ready to climb Wrath like the jungle gym I spent an entire summer hanging from when Meadow and I thought we were going to leave Sweet Tooth together and join the carnival. I fell a lot then, skinned my knees and hands but it was worth it. I think, as nervous as I might have been to be intimate with Wrath before the events of the past half hour transpired, taking the next step with him will be well worth it, too.

Hopefully I won't end up with scraped knees like I did when I was dreaming of tightrope walking but even if I do...that will be worth it, too. I wrap my arms around Wrath and let the bond we share expand until it's all I feel around me. It's only the whimpering cry of a cultist that has Wrath and I both freezing.

He frowns and shakes his head. "Mortals..." he grumbles, looking at the remaining cultists. There's ten or so, maybe a couple more if they are hiding somewhere in the bookshelves at the far end of the basement.

"We have to do something with them," I say and then heft my sword. "I'll take care of it." I'm not particularly in the mood to kill, not when Wrath tasting me is on the table but I'm not adventurous enough to go any further with an audience. I'd rather kill them now than have to make awkward eye contact after I come to my senses and realize that I do indeed have skinned knees and they all know why.

Wrath takes my hand and holds it up. "If you allow me to siphon some of my power back from you, I'll be able to make neat work of them."

I squeeze his hand and nod. "Do it," I tell him. There's a tingle in my palm before Wrath closes his eyes and takes in a deep breath. The tingle spreads from the center of my palm to my entire hand. There's a warmth that weaves itself between our fingers and into my arm. It moves up my arm and through my body until it pulls at the place the bond we share sits above my heart.

Wrath opens his eyes and when our eyes meet the warmth in my body quickens until it's the familiar heat that always wakes in me when Wrath touches me.

Wrath turns to the huddled crowd. "Right then, does anyone

know the whereabouts of the Blossoms? They're about, oh I dunno," Wrath uses our joined hands to point at the top of my head, "yea high. I think we all know the Blossoms were meant to be married to me. However, seeing as I'm a one woman kind of demon, Buffy is the only one for me. My bride has a particular aversion to her friends being sacrificed for your amusement. Now, where are they?"

"We did it for you," one of the cultists chokes out from where they cower on the floor and Wrath bares his teeth in a snarl.

"I have *never* heard your prayers. I have turned a deaf ear to each and every one of you sniveling fools. And as you do not have the information I seek, there's little reason for me to keep you in one piece." He steps forward still holding my hand and extends his other hand out to the cultists. "You've given your lives to me and it is only now that I will deign to hear your cries and pleas, because it is I that will tear you limb from limb for what you've done to my beloved."

I grab his arm. "Not Elijah."

Wrath inclines his head that he heard me while a ball of light forms in his palm and he smiles down at it. The cold blue light of it washes over his features as he speaks. "I want you all to know I'm going to enjoy this very, *very* much."

The air stills and the pressure goes wonky. It feels like my ears need to pop and everything is muffled when the screaming starts.

I look up when blue light expands out and shoots towards the cultists, tearing through their robes before it cuts through their bodies and limbs. Everything slows down as I watch on while the men scream. Blood pools and splatters across the stone floor when their limbs hit the ground. I know I should feel remorse.

I should feel disgusted or sick. Horrified, at the very least, but I don't.

I don't feel anything other than joy while I watch Wrath tear the men apart. I smile and Wrath holds my hand tighter. The screams grow louder, sharper. The blue light brightens so quickly that I have to shut my eyes against the flash of it. I blink against the afterimages and the room falls into silence when I open my eyes.

The sight of broken bodies and limbs in places I didn't think I would ever see greet me.

"Holy shit," I whisper, taking in the carnage. "You really did a number on them."

"My honor demanded it. No one tries to touch my wife and lives to tell the tale."

My heart gives a flutter in my chest and I reach for Wrath. I know what I need and it's him. I wrap my arms around him and kiss him but there's still one thing I have to take care of before I lose myself in Wrath's touch.

"Elijah, wait outside," I order. Elijah leaps to his feet and races towards the stairs.

"Yes, your highness Buffy."

"I'm glad I spared that one," Wrath rumbles and picks me up.

"I like him," I whisper against his mouth, wrapping my legs around him. My body craves closeness with Wrath. Every inch of me that isn't touching my husband is wrong. I move and wriggle closer before I lock my feet behind him and slant my mouth to his. Wrath opens his mouth and I take my time exploring him. I trail my fingers up the side of his neck and bury them in his thick hair. He holds me close, hands curled around my thighs while I take my time learning his taste until I've had my fill and pull back to look down at him. He's holding me higher, just above him. Looking down at him is a heady thing. Wrath's eyes shine silver and bright in the light of the basement as he stares up at me.

"You are exquisite, Buffy."

"So are you," I tell him, which earns me another kiss and a wink before he hums and kicks one of the bookcases over. Books and papers fly out around us when it topples over and a second later he lays me down on the side of it.

He chuckles and leans over me to kiss my neck. His lips move against my skin as he peppers kisses in a trail up my neck. "I'm evil," Wrath whispers again into the curve of my neck and I feel his hands on my hips. He slides his hands to the top of my pants and the warm brush of his calloused fingers against my skin has me arching my hips up with a moan.

I grab onto his shoulders and bite my lip when Wrath's lips graze my ear before he nips it. "Evil is good."

"It's really not, beloved. For you though I can attempt good," Wrath murmurs, his voice low and hypnotic in my ear. "I'll be so very, *very* good."

I turn my face towards Wrath but he moves before I can kiss him so I reach for him. "Come back."

Wrath slides down my body and drops to his knees in front of me. "Ah, ah, patience is a virtue."

I don't want to be patient. Or virtuous. Wrath makes me greedy but I force myself to not move when I feel his lips graze my stomach. My heart races. The thundering of my pulse turns to a roar in my ears when he slides the skirts of my dress up my hips and the cool air of the basement hits my thighs.

"Wrath," I whisper and he stops to look up at me.

"Yes, beloved?"

"I-I've never done this," I tell him while my cheeks heat up from embarrassment. I know there's no reason to feel this way, not when I know Wrath wants me. Not when I've been living the way that I have.

The cult hardly left me alone enough with a man to do anything more than steal a few hand holding sessions. Even if that weren't the case, I know embarrassment has no place here.

It's a leftover from the cult, from this place with its claws in every part of my life—they turned my body into a dirty thing that didn't belong to me. It was theirs.

But this, here? With me, with Wrath?

This is just for me and there's nothing dirty about it. Hot and sexy, yes. But dirty? No. Never.

"I'll be gentle," Wrath promises and the smile he sends my way is dark. Gentle or not, I don't know if I'm going to be ready for what he's about to do to me but I'm hungry for it. I raise myself up onto my elbows and look down at where Wrath's head is bowed over my thighs. His onyx horns shine in the light and his thick hair slides over my thighs as he comes closer.

"You are more beautiful than I could have imagined, Buffy," Wrath says. My toes curl at hearing him say my name. He hooks his fingers into my panties. I raise my hips to help him slide them off, but there's no need. Wrath rips them from my body.

My mouth goes dry at the sight of him holding the scrap of ripped fabric in his big hand. "*Mulberries.*"

Wrath directs a wicked smile up at me and I'm glad he's in his demon form. I've gotten used to his human form enough, but for this? Only his demon will do.

"I think," Wrath leans down and kisses the top of my bare thigh before he turns his face and inhales deeply over my aching cunt, "I quite liked it better when you were saying my name, beloved. What do you think it will take before I have you screaming it today?"

"Not a whole heck of a lot," I answer him truthfully. My clit pulses. I can feel my arousal building and I almost forget how to breathe when Wrath grabs my thighs and yanks me towards him. My arms give out and I fall back onto the bookcase with a thud. Above me, I see shadows moving. At first I think it's from the flickering candles in the chandelier, but they're not.

These shadows move on their own. These shadows move as if they are a living thing with a mind of their own. I watch them dance across the ceiling above me before they swoop down towards me.

I should scream, but I don't. The shadows are Wrath's, I know they are. When they're close enough to me, I reach a hand up towards them and watch as they wrap and swirl around my fingers and slide down to cover my arms.

"You smell like fresh strawberries," Wrath whispers. His warm breath puffs against my skin, "did you know that?"

The shadows pulsate. The darkness of them deepens and spreads over my body. It feels like fingers stroking and teasing my skin. My breath hitches when I feel the pluck of fingers on my nipples.

"No," I choke out and the word comes out strangled. Shadows play across my body and wrap themselves around me. The inky darkness moves to join where Wrath has settled himself between my thighs and when he drops his mouth to my aching flesh, I cry out. He moans against me and I buck my hips when he eases a finger inside and the shadows dance across my skin.

It feels like there's another here with us. And another and

another. There's kisses pressed to the column of my throat and another claims my mouth. I feel fingers caress my hair as the underside of my breasts are stroked. I don't feel the bookcase under me when the shadows gather me up and bring me higher for Wrath to devour.

"Such a sweet, sweet wife you are for me. I have waited hundreds of years for you, Buffy. Every part of you belongs to me."

Wrath takes his time. Slowly, ever so agonizingly slowly, he covers me in kisses. All across my thighs and over my aching puffy lips. When he's done kissing, he moves to tasting me. The hot drag of his tongue followed by the gentle strokes of his teasing fingertips and shadows before he licks into me has me thrashing. The only thing keeping me in place is the darkness enveloping me. I hold my breath, waiting for Wrath to give me what I want the most, to touch me where I want him the most, but my demon husband loves to play.

Wrath smiles and bites my thigh while his shadows play over my aching body but he never goes near my clit. He continues to pump his fingers into me and I moan when his darkness joins his fingers and stretches me all the more.

Wrath has me ready to beg, so I do.

"Ungh, Wrath, please."

"Such pretty words from you, sweet wife," he croons and rewards me by sinking another finger into me. The stretch of it makes me whimper and the sound urges Wrath on. He moans against my body, tongue circling my clit closer and closer still until I'm going out of mind, knowing that the next drag of his tongue could be over my aching clit.

The darkness rises and the shadows lift my hands up. I watch as they bring my hands to Wrath's horns and I know exactly what the shadows want me to do. I wrap my hands around the thick width of his horns as Wrath groans and finally gives me what I've been hungering for.

He captures my clit between his lips. His tongue works it over with maddening flicks that have my eyes rolling into the back of my head. My stomach tightens and pleasure starts to roll through my body. My skin feels too tight, like my insides are molten. Like they're moving in a gravity all their own. It has me crying out with exhilaration.

The shadows lift me higher still and nothing feels real. I've never felt this way before. It starts in my chest, the warm and frenzied feeling that I know is only awake in me because it's Wrath with his mouth on my body and his fingers inside of me. I pull him towards me, my grip iron on his horns. When I pull harder, Wrath sucks my clit in kind.

I pull as hard as I can and squeeze my eyes shut with a smile on my lips. "Wrath! Yes." I roll my hips, chasing the feeling he's giving me. I need more. There's nothing else in the world that I want more than Wrath's tongue, his lips, his hands. Those wicked, delicious hands. He moves closer, big shoulders forcing my legs further apart and brings me down from where I've been floating. He anchors my body to the bookcase with an arm over my hips, because the shadows haven't stopped holding me. It feels like I'm in a tug of war between two greedy lovers. When they try to lift me away, he digs his fingers into me and keeps me in place.

I hope his touch leaves bruises.

I want to look at my body and remember exactly what he's

done to me. "Wrath," I sob, hips moving faster. Wrath lets me do it.

"Use me, Buffy. That's my ruthless little wife," he rumbles against me. He turns his face to kiss my thigh before he bites the too sensitive flesh. "Give me your pleasure, wife. Give it all to me."

He crooks two fingers inside me and shifts the angle ever so slightly. The next roll of my hips has me seeing stars. "Oh, ungh, yes, there. Don't stop, *please* don't stop."

"Try and stop me." Wrath partakes of my pussy like I'm the feast that's been just out of reach and now he's finally allowed to eat. I dig my heels into his back and lift my hips and Wrath helps me. The arm over my hips moves to hold me up and wrap my legs around him while I pull him close by his horns. Wrath bites down on my clit and everything is gloriously intense. My world narrows down to his teeth and my body. All around us, the gloom has risen and the only light there is comes from the bond between us. It flares bright and golden. The light of it pushes back at the hungry shadows and then all at once, it shatters around us and everything goes dark.

"Yes, oh, I-Wrath. *Yes.*" I scream and orgasm. My body shudders in his hands for a second before I go boneless. I laugh when I open my eyes and see him wiping his mouth and standing from where he's been kneeling between my legs. He plants a hand on either side of my body and raises an eyebrow as he watches me.

"Feeling good, dear wife?"

"Amazing. Never better. Ten out of ten from me. I think my soul left my body and I can't move." I lift and drop my hand onto the bookcase with a thunk for emphasis.

Wrath grins and reaches for me. He helps me sit up and

brushes my hair away from my face. "You were exquisite to watch."

I swallow hard and shyness rears her annoying head. I duck my head and nod. "Thank you."

"I mean it. I have never and will never see anything more beautiful than your face in rapture."

"Is that what they're calling it these days?" I joke and he rests a finger under my chin, tipping my head back to look up at him.

"I mean it, Buffy. Don't hide from me now. What we just did was very special to me."

"I know, I'm sorry...it's just all new to me. I don't think anyone I know has ever had it done with shadows before," I tell him and look around the room to see if any of the handsy shadows are nearby but everything in the basement looks normal enough. Give or take the bodies still littering the floor.

"No, I don't suspect they have. It's a perk when you're married to an Arthas demon."

"So it was you. The shadows, I mean. They're a part of you?"

He nods and slides my dress down over my thighs before hooking an arm around my waist and lifting me to bring them completely up. "They are, in a way. I control the darkness you see, to do as I will. Though, with my recent employment, my use of shadows has never been this enjoyable."

"Ichabod," I spit out and cross my arms. "I'm going to kill him, you know."

"You'll never see him, beloved. But I appreciate your sentiments on the matter."

I want to tell Wrath that I'll find Ichabod. That it doesn't matter how long it takes me, I'll have his revenge as well but that's putting the cart before the horse, considering I still need to carry out my own revenge first.

Ichabod will have to wait until I take down the cult and rescue my friends. Which is totally fine, because I do my best work under pressure.

CHAPTER
TWENTY-ONE

"Do you think," I pause and look towards the door, "the party upstairs—do you think they've noticed no one's come to summon that stone troll?"

Wrath's tail flicks in annoyance and he holds a hand out to me. "If they haven't, they most likely will very soon. We should leave quickly."

Quick isn't that fast when there's body parts in the way. I almost trip over a foot but Wrath holds me up. When we exit the basement, Elijah is the first thing I see. He's arguing with the man from the kitchens.

"I don't care what your timeline says. *No one* is to disturb the summoning," Elijah snaps and draws himself up. It's then that I notice he's tall, like *really* tall. Easily six foot five, muscular and broad-shouldered. He's blond and blue-eyed, exactly the definition of All-American and wholesome.

"I'm not going to have Outsiders ruining a sacred ceremony for the sake of your little *schedule*," he says and stares down at the man who yelled at Wrath and I earlier. I remember the man from the kitchens as being scarier but right now he looks small. That could be because he's next to Elijah, who is a big muscled man I had calling me highness, Buffy and ma'am.

Neat.

"Fine," the Outsider throws his hands up and practically stomps his foot in annoyance but he does back up when Elijah takes a step towards him. "But if this comes back on me, I'm going to make sure you're the one doing the explaining."

"For my Harbinger, I'll do any and all explaining. I am loyal," Elijah says and my mouth falls open when I realize he means me. I'm the harbinger he's talking about and publicly pledging loyalty to. "Now, away with you. I'll not have you look upon her."

"You know what? I don't even care about this job anymore, it's not worth it. You want the ice sculpture to melt and the souffle to fall? Fine by me. I'm going on a smoke break." He stomps off and when the kitchen door slams behind him, Wrath and I exit the basement.

"You covered for us. You just said you're loyal to me?" I ask.

Elijah inclines his head. "I am. There is no greater honor than to serve you, not after I witnessed your might."

"But I thought you served him," I say weakly and point to Wrath, who grins at me.

"Oh, I can spare the follower. Well done on collecting a follower your first day as a harbinger. You never forget your first," Wrath says, clapping Elijah on the shoulder, "A fine choice you've made. I could not have picked a better idol than my wife. If you need any pointers on how to serve her, let me know. I'm the Buffy expert."

Elijah brightens and I know without a shadow of a doubt that he's about to take Wrath up on his offer, so I wave my hands at them to bring them back to reality.

"We need to get out of here, like yesterday. Before that kitchen man comes back and blows our cover or anyone else looking for that troll they're waiting on. Now come on." I take off at a power walk for the kitchens. I can't risk my parents seeing us if we use the front door.

"There's no troll," Elijah tells us when we duck into the kitchen and weave through the chaos towards the side door. Staff run back and forth. Some of them look like they're praying over the souffles mentioned and in the corner I see a collection of animals that I think resemble the topiaries we hid in earlier. It's hard to tell with how quickly they're melting into sad little puddles.

"What do you mean there's no troll? Didn't you say there was a summoning circle for one?" I ask Wrath and hip check a server into the bakery boxes still piled high on counters.

"Yes, but there are other uses for such a circle..." Wrath mutters as he gets a faraway look in his eyes. He's human again and his emotions are harder to read but I know he's worried.

I want to ask him what it is but I don't. I keep walking, shoving open the kitchen door and taking the side steps two at a time. Elijah and Wrath follow close behind. We nearly barrel into the Outsider Elijah tussled with. He's smoking and on his phone and looks like he wants to scream when he sees us.

"*You*," he snarls and points his cigarette at me. "Oh, I've had it with you. I'm going to make sure you never work in this town again, missy!"

"Oh, mulberries," I whisper and edge away towards the front of the house. "We're leaving, so don't-" I start but stop when

Elijah decks him. The man goes down without a sound and his phone bounces away from him. He's knocked out cold. I hear a staticy *"Hello*?!" float up from the phone. Wrath has to pick me up because of how shocked I am.

I point to the man on the ground and then to Elijah. "You punched him!"

"He was threatening you," Elijah says simply.

"I really like you," Wrath tells Elijah and tucks me under his arm. "I like him, beloved. He's a great addition to the team."

"A team? We have a team now?" I ask.

Elijah preens. "I thank you for the compliment, my lord."

"I can't believe you just hit him."

"You killed an entire basement of men before we shared an intimate moment and that one punch is the thing that shocks you?" Wrath asks me. I fall silent, because he does have a point.

"I just didn't expect it from Elijah. He called me ma'am," I tell him after we've been walking for a minute. We're back in front of the house by now and almost to the sidewalk. Wrath puts me on the ground the second we hit the sidewalk and then points at Elijah.

"Ditch the robes, acolyte. You're attracting too much attention."

"Certainly." Elijah tosses them without hesitation. He's wearing a nice pressed dress shirt and dress slacks, which makes sense considering the Founders' expectation of neatness and conformity when it comes to ceremonies, which their little basement party definitely was before Wrath and I went on a rampage.

"Where are we going now, my Harbinger?" he asks me and I blink in surprise.

"I, uh, I don't know. I'm looking for my friends. You really haven't seen them or heard anything about them?" I try, taking a step closer to him. "We're pals now, right, Elijah? You can tell me the truth."

"I don't know anything. If they talked about the Blossoms, they didn't do it where I could hear them." Elijah sighs and his big shoulders drop forward when he slumps down. "If I had any information, I would give it to you a thousand times over," he tells his feet. I immediately feel bad for asking for information again.

The poor man sounds despondent over not knowing what I want to know.

"I, ah, I know that. Thank you." I edge closer to Wrath as we walk down the street and lean close to him to whisper. "What am I supposed to do? I don't know what to do with an acolyte. I've always been the follower, not the leader. Look at him, he's so sad. What am I supposed to do with him now that I made him sad?"

Wrath tilts his head and watches Elijah continue to mope. "You could always tell him to do what your leaders would do. Maybe that would cheer the big guy up?"

My stomach goes tight just thinking of that. The Founders tried killing me. They created a cult where my parents sold me and lied to me my entire life.

I shake my head. "I can't. Never. He deserves better."

"Then what would you have wished you had been told to do?" Wrath asks. That feels lighter to me. Better.

"I like that...okay, I can do that." I nod and look Elijah's way. He's still down but he's moving now, walking along and scanning the street carefully when anyone comes too close to us. I should probably tell him to leave, set him free and tell him not to try and follow me because I'm figuring it out as best I can, which doesn't seem like quality leader material. But I don't.

I know what it's like to decide to follow something—follow someone. If I told Elijah to leave he'd be devastated. If he is like the old me, there wouldn't be a day of his life where he hasn't followed someone else's rules.

He wouldn't know what to do if I cut him loose cold turkey. I'll have to ease him into free will if I want it to take.

"Um, hey, Elijah?" I ask and instantly his eyes leave the old lady he was just eyeing up and down and come to me.

"Yes, highness Buffy?"

Yup, increments. Very tiny, small baby step increments if I want Elijah to successfully leave me and not follow the first person he comes across.

"You know the house on the hill? Wrath's Embrace?"

He nods. "Of course, it's only one of the most hallowed places in Sweet Tooth."

"You ever been inside?" I ask and Wrath makes a disgruntled sound. He knows where I'm going with this. I know I'm going to have to remind him that he just said he liked Elijah if he kicks up a fuss.

Elijah shakes his head and goes visibly pale. "What? No, I-of course not. My family doesn't rank. We're barely allowed to participate as it is. I would never be fit to enter it."

"Well, I live there and seeing as you're going to be following me, you're totally going inside."

"*What*?" Elijah and Wrath say in unison.

"I want you to go there and wait for us. Keep an eye on things, okay? Make sure no one tries to get past the wards Wrath put in place."

Elijah looks uncertain but he gives me a bow. "If it is your will, I will go at once."

"It is," I say and loop my arm with Wrath's when I catch him opening his mouth to protest, "you just said you liked Elijah. What was it you called him? Oh, yes, a 'great addition to the team,' that was what you said, right?" I remind him. Wrath sighs at me and then reaches over to flick Elijah's nose. "You booped him?" I ask in confusion.

"It was a necessary boop," Wrath grumbles. "Now the wards will recognize him. Anyone else that tries to enter will be cut to pieces."

"Shall I make my way to Wrath's Embrace, your hig-"

"It's just Buffy, please. Try it out for me, I bet you'll like it."

Elijah makes a pained face but manages it. "*Buffy,* shall I make my way to Wrath's Embrace?"

I nod. "Yes, go now and-and don't come out, okay?" I shake my finger at Elijah who looks like a naughty puppy I just smacked with a newspaper, which isn't great for my leading capabilities at all. "I mean, you know you have to stay put so...so you're a secret weapon for the team, okay? I don't care who comes, just, you know," I wave a hand at him, "hide until I'm back. You'll be safe there until we return."

"I will await your return, Harbinger." Elijah gives me another deep bow. I expect him to head off towards Wrath's Embrace but he doesn't. Instead, the big man hesitates and clears his throat. "There is one thing I should tell you before I leave," he says. "Even though I really shouldn't on account of it possibly being a trap."

"What is it?" I immediately ask while Wrath goes tense at my side.

"What do you mean a trap?" Wrath asks.

"I know I said I didn't know anything about your friends, but there *is* something." Elijah shifts from foot to foot before he forges on ahead. "The Autumn Festival. If I were you, I would try going there for information but-but you have to be careful. It's not safe. I know it's not."

"What do you mean it isn't safe?" I ask. "What do you know?"

"I know the Founders were excited about the festival. I know they were planning something with the game booths but I don't know what." He holds up his hands and gives me a pleading look. "I swear, I didn't hear a word about the Blossoms. It was only a little here and there that I overheard about the games. They told us to keep an eye out for a surprise tonight."

"A surprise?" Wrath groans and looks up with a sigh. "That's definitely a trap all right."

I shrug. "We're totally going."

Wrath drops his eyes to look at me and nods. "Obviously, beloved."

I clap my hands. "Perfect. I can't wait to show you around. They have the *best* funnel cakes. No disappearing those."

Wrath grumbles but nods at me and I beam when he says, "Understood."

"Perfect! Thank you for the information, Elijah. We'll go on to the festival while you keep watch over, um...over headquarters."

Elijah's eyes go wide. "I'm in charge of headquarters?" he asks and stands a little straighter.

Wrath wags a finger in his direction. "She said keep watch, not in charge of, acolyte."

Elijah nods and smiles but I know he isn't listening to Wrath at all. "Right, sure. I can do that. I can make sure headquarters is in tiptop shape for your arrival. You won't regret putting me in charge. I promise you Highness Harbinger Buffy, this is the best decision you have ever made. Just you wait and see!" He calls over his shoulder before he takes off at a jog in the direction we came from.

I hide my smile while Wrath glares at Elijah's back. "I take back what I said about him earlier."

CHAPTER
TWENTY-TWO

"He said the game booths. Those are towards the back of the festival grounds," I tell Wrath. We've just arrived at the Sweet Tooth Municipal Park, which sits just outside of downtown and serves as the perfect spot for a festival meant to lure in Outsiders. It's impossible to resist with the Ferris wheel and two roller coasters rising up out of the trees along with the lights and signs from the maze of mirrors and the haunted house.

Sweet Tooth's Autumn Harvest Festival is famous. There's going to be no less than five tour buses pulling in tonight. Before I knew the truth, I always thought the festival was a celebration, a way to share in the Blossoms' good fortune and bless them on their way to a new life.

I was blind.

How could I not have noticed that none of the Blossoms were ever seen again? That any time their husbands returned to town, it was without them. That there were no families born to

Blossoms. No babies or daughters and sons returning to Sweet Tooth with their fathers. There was nothing, just letters and supposed calls. The odd parent that swore they were visiting their daughters in the city and coming back with word of happy days.

Lies, all of it.

This night wasn't about celebrating with the Blossoms, it was about fleecing the Outsiders. It was about putting more coin in the coffers of the Founders and letting them play god. As soon as night falls the park is going to be lit up like the Fourth of July, with the perfect avenue of downtown to funnel Outsiders and Sweet Tooth residents this way after the float parade and marching band take Main Street.

It's going to be the picture perfect small town night where nothing bad can happen but that's a lie too. I'm the bad thing that's going to happen. Anger runs bright and hot in my veins and I have to take a calming breath to bring my heart rate down. Holding my smiles is starting to get so hard.

It was never this hard before.

"Are there churros here?" Wrath asks, looking around hopefully. "I had those a few times and I quite like them."

"A churro? Yeah, they're past the games. Come on," I say and grab Wrath's hand. Even though it's not the prime time hour for the festival, everything is set up and the game booths are lively with plenty of takers already enjoying themselves. The food stands are just past the games but as we pass them I slow down. There's a crowd at the Dunk o' Fun water dunk tank where people are lobbing baseballs at a bullseye. If they hit the bullseye trigger just right, it will drop in poor Mrs. Landry sitting on the little perch into the water below. Mrs. Landry was my cooking class teacher in my last year at school and she shivers while she sits looking half drowned.

I lift my hand in a wave to Mrs. Landry. She was always kind to me and showed me how to chop an onion without crying. Who knew a matchstick could be so magical?

"A friend of yours?" Wrath asks before another one of the baseball players nails the bullseye with a victorious 'whoop' and the seat Mrs. Landry is on drops out from under her. She hits the water with a splash and the crowd goes wild but I feel bad.

"She was my teacher and yes, she was my friend," I tell him.

The dunk tank was always the booth people were sent to when they were on the outs with the Founders. Mrs. Landry did something to deserve her stint getting dunked...but what? I always remember her being kind, a smile always present on her face while she instructed all of us Blossoms how to be the very best hostess and cook.

I never amounted to much in the kitchen other than dry roasts and too soggy pies. Even then she never made me feel bad about it. Not even when I made a mess of the cake I wanted to make for Callum's birthday when I got the salt and sugar mixed up. The cake had been an inedible disappointment but Mrs. Landry had cheered me right up.

"Not to worry! Not everyone is meant to be a cook. Your talents lie elsewhere, that's all Buffy. Look here, I have a gift certificate for the bakery! Now, why don't you go pay Ms. Donna a visit and see what she can do about a cake for Callum."

I never knew why she had that gift certificate at the perfect moment but she'd saved me that day. It had been one of the few times I'd defied my parents to spend time with my friends and I had sworn I'd bring 'the best cake anyone had ever tasted' to Callum's party.

Ms. Donna had made me a triple German chocolate three tier cake that Meadow had to help me carry to the Founders' Circle where we'd had Callum's party. I don't think I would have been able to face everyone with my salty mess of a cake but Ms. Landry had made sure I'd been okay.

I have to do the same thing for her now.

"Come on. We have to help her," I tell Wrath and make a beeline for the dunk tank. "Something isn't right about this."

"What do you mean? Isn't this the sort of thing humans do at these festivals?" Wrath asks as he dodges a man's wild swing with a turkey leg. "This town is strange. Stranger than most but I can endure it knowing there's churros out there somewhere."

"If you're talking about the turkey leg that almost took you out, I think that's normal but I can't be sure," I admit, because I've never been to a festival in any place other than Sweet Tooth. "I've never been anywhere else, so my measure of strangeness is a little skewed with the cult and all."

"You've really never been anywhere else?" Wrath asks and the surprise in his voice stops me.

"No, my father has always lived here. My mom was an Outsider but I don't know where she came from. We never," I pause and glance around us to see if anyone is listening but everyone is too focused on turkey legs, funnel cakes and who's going to throw the next baseball at Ms. Landry's Dunk 'o Fun tank.

Wrath scowls and the sight of it warms my heart. "Ah, yes, your illustrious parents. I'm going to enjoy gutting them for you."

"That's really sweet of you."

Wrath beams at me and the sight of his smile is like the sun breaking through the clouds after a thunderstorm and I have to force myself to focus.

Focus, Buffy. Ms. Landry. Dunk 'o Fun tank. Focus.

I take a steadying breath and look back at the dunk tank. Something is off, something is wrong, but what? "Look for anything suspicious. Ms. Landry was a model cultist, you hear me? But this tank is where they sent people as a punishment. She must have done something to end up here and I have a feeling there's a clue in the tank."

I remember the looks people would get when they mentioned having to take a shift in the Dunk 'o Fun tank when the Founders rolled it out during a festival. I remember the summer my dad had to do a round in it. He never said a word about it but I heard my mom crying that night while my dad tried to calm her down.

"It doesn't hurt that much, Darla. It'll be fine by morning."

There had to have been a reason but what was it? Why was my mom crying and my dad saying it didn't hurt too much? Falling in the Dunk o' Fun couldn't hurt you, could it?

"What's that?" Wrath asks and nods towards the tank.

I step closer to him and try to see but I don't see anything but the baseball team slapping hands and paying for more coupons to the dunk tank. "What's what?" There's another round of cheers as Mrs. Landry hits the water again. This time I see what happens when she's underwater through the glass. Before I was too far away but not now.

Mrs. Landry screams. Honest to Wrath, opens her mouth and screams. Bubbles form and float to the surface, Mrs. Ladry's scream is muffled and lost under the cheering and clapping of the crowd gathered. There's music floating in the air from the fun houses while a game buzzer goes off. I hear balloons popping in the distance but none of it registers.

I hear her.

I hear that scream. Feel it in my bones. My heart drops.

Wrath dips his head to whisper in my ear. "There's something in the water. See the sheen? It's green. I think it's poison. There it is, do you see it?" he asks and points to the corner of the tank.

I follow his finger and I finally see it. There's a dark green liquid being pumped into the tank from a valve in the corner. It's so dark that it almost matches the shade of blue the back of the tank is painted but not quite. It's only visible for a second, one little floating cloud, before it vanishes into the water, no doubt helped by Mrs. Landry's thrashing as she pushes herself back up to the surface.

I watch while she gasps and gulps, hands slapping against the tank sides. Fury rises up in me, because she smiles when she looks out at the crowd that's so eager to send her under again.

"Got another bullseye for you, Mrs. Landry!" The captain of the baseball team hollers. His name is Jack and I never liked him. I like him even less now that I know he's about to send Mrs. Landry back into poisoned waters while she smiles at him like everything's okay.

"Don't wear your arm out before the big game, Jack," she calls out. Her voice shakes and I can't take it anymore.

"This is now a rescue mission. We need to break that tank and spring Mrs. Landry," I tell Wrath.

"As long as we get churros after this, I'm game." Wrath looks around the crowd and hums while I watch an ember come to life in Wrath's palm. "I can break the tank with magic. Give me just a second."

195

I clap my hands over his and snuff the fire out. "You almost got clocked with a turkey leg, what do you think they're gonna do if they find out you can use magic?"

"I'm supposed to be a mage, dear heart. This is something a mage would do."

"Even so, I think we need to be more subtle. Elijah said to come here for info and we aren't going to get anyone to talk to us if they're scared of you because you can fireball them."

"Fair enough. But for the record, I wasn't going to use a fireball."

"Weren't you though?"

"It may have crossed my mind," Wrath admits with a sniff, "but only just. Now, what would you prefer if not a fireball to save your teacher?"

I bite my lip and think. What else if not a fireball? Because watching Jack wind up and show off for his buddies is making me reconsider. What's one fireball in the grand scheme of things, if I get to put him on his ass?

Jack raises the ball over his head and the crowd goes silent. They all expect that bullseye to land and for Mrs. Landry to take the plunge again. That's when I realize what's better than a fireball.

"Make him throw wide."

"That's it?"

"That's it."

Wrath snaps his fingers. "Done."

Jack throws the ball and I watch his arm move at an odd angle before the ball goes flying over the Dunk 'o Fun and straight into the funnel cake stand. A collective gasp rises up from the crowd and there's the faint sound of a few shrieks and pans banging when the baseball finds a new target.

"Nice," I whisper to Wrath and watch Jack turn red. He's ticked.

"That was...there was something on the ball. That's all. It was a bad ball," Jack explains loudly to the crowd and holds his hand out for another from the dunk tank attendant. "Give me another ball, Tim and make it a good one this time or else."

I hear the threat in the *'or else'* and I don't particularly like it.

"You know what? Break the lever, the one he's trying to hit. I swear on all the mulberries in the universe that he's lucky I'm not breaking his arm."

Wrath chuckles. "I love the way your mind works, my ruthless little wife. Consider it done." I watch him snap his fingers again and I raise an eyebrow.

"Do you have to snap to make spells happen?"

"No, but it's satisfying."

"It also looks neat."

"A bonus to be sure."

There's a thunk when the baseball hits the lever and nothing happens. I turn back to the scene of our magical sabotaging in time to see Jack almost pop his top with how angry he is. "I hit the bullseye, Tim! What the h-" He starts, but a friend of his claps him on the back and jerks him away from the dunk tank.

"How about we take a break? Maybe cool off and get a drink?"

He looks stressed and I know why. The Founders don't like cursing, anger or outbursts. Not even from men. Especially not at an event where Outsiders are present. Sweet Tooth has a reputation for being, well, sweet. Jack having a fit over the Dunk 'o Fun isn't exactly doing our town image any favors. He might even end up taking Mrs. Landry's place if he isn't careful.

Jack blinks like he's waking up from a dream and then swallows hard and nods. "Yeah, a drink sounds good, uh, thanks."

Jack and his friend are swallowed up by the crowd when the baseball team moves as one towards the concessions stand. For a second no one moves, everything goes quiet. Water sloshes up against the tank sides while Mrs. Landry slides back into her seat and clears her throat before she raises her hand and waves cheerily out to the crowd.

"Who's next to take a turn? We're raising funds for the school's cooking club. Won't you take a chance and see how you do?" she calls out to the crowd and I step forward. Her eyes widen when she sees me and she leans forward to press a hand to the glass in front of her.

"Buffy? Oh, Buffy, it's you."

She didn't know. I know that from the way she's smiling at me with a mix of relief and wonder.

"Morning, Mrs. Landry," I call out with a smile and head for Tim, the attendant. I've only ever seen him in passing. He's older than me and waits tables at the diner in town. He seems okay, even if he's in charge of running the poisoned dunk tank.

"It's five bucks for a turn," Tim says and I wave them off.

"The tank is broken. I'm not paying you and no one else is either. Get her out of there."

Tim blinks in surprise and then narrows his eyes at me. "Aren't you Buffy? Why aren't you-" he catches himself, pauses and then clears his throat, "why aren't you in the city?" *Oh, he knew.* The man has no finesse at all. Of all the people to let in on the murder plot, they chose Tim? But I guess that does track with the poisoned dunk tank duty he's currently pulling. Tim immediately goes on the list of people I do not care if harm befalls them in my little quest to get Meadow and the rest back.

I cross my arms and smile at Tim. "I just do. Like you just happen to know where I should be right now," I say and watch Tim's face pale. "Go ahead and check the tank if you don't believe me. It's broken."

Tim's eyes go to Wrath where he's standing behind me and he nods quickly before he mutters, "Yeah, okay," and goes to check the tank lever. I watch him push the button and Mrs. Landry freezes. I know she's expecting to hit the water but it doesn't happen then, not even when Tim hits the button again with both hands and pushes on it. Tim grunts and throws his shoulder against the lever and still nothing happens. That doesn't stop him from trying. He kicks the lever, once, twice, three times. Wrath sighs beside me.

"How much longer do we have to watch that mortal struggle?"

"Dunno, maybe a few minutes. Can you quit saying 'mortals'? You're a mage, remember? Not a god."

Wrath sniffs. "No, not in this world, sadly."

Tim finally gives up when he nearly falls and he turns to the crowd with a frown. "Tank's closed. It's broken!"

Chaos erupts and I smile.

"I had tickets to throw for this one!"

"Are you serious?"

"You better get that working. I was promised two throws today by Old Man Rossi."

"Let's help her out. My dad was in this thing one time and he was pretty weak from it." I take off at a jog for the little door I see at the back of the tank. Wrath follows a step behind.

"We're coming, Mrs. Landry!" I call out when we get to the door. "Just a minute."

"Buffy! Buffy, it's really you."

There's a padlock on the latch keeping the door shut. I don't see any keys, so I reach up to the padlock and twist. It comes off in my hand and I toss it to the side before I rip the door open. I hear the creaking sound of hinges giving a second before the door comes off.

"Oops," I whisper when Wrath and Mrs. Landry stare at me in surprise. "Ugh, I didn't mean to."

"That door was ugly. No loss," Wrath says and grabs it from me. He chucks it behind him without looking and it slams right into Tim who just rounded the corner. "Problem solved, see?"

"Problem not solved! Mulberries! You took Tim out!" I yell and point at Tim while Wrath just looks annoyed and toes the door with a sigh.

"Where did he come from?" Wrath mutters and stares down at Tim where he's facedown in the dirt. Tim moans when the door slides off him. Wrath points to him with a triumphant smile. "See, beloved. Not to worry, the mortal lives. All is well."

"Who is that?" Mrs. Landry whispers, her eyes on Wrath. I get it. He just hit Tim with a door. A small door, but a door all the same.

"My husband."

Mrs. Landry's eyes snap to me. "You have a husband? Oh my, Buffy! Really?" I nod and watch her smile. "I'm so happy, Buffy. You deserve this."

I know what she means. All I've ever wanted was to be a wife.

To be married. I thought it was my only purpose in life but that's not what I want anymore, not now. But I do want Wrath, so I nod and return her excited smile.

"Thank you, Mrs. Landry." I hold my arms out to her and motion for her to come towards me. "Come on, let's get you out of there, okay? I-we came to rescue you. I know something is in the water. Are you okay?"

"Buffy, it's terrible. I didn't know it would be like this. It hurts so terribly and I-I didn't mean to do it."

"Do what?"

"Go against the Founders. I just—I couldn't do it, I couldn't," she says as I lift her out of the tank and place her on her feet beside me. She sways slightly but I keep an arm around her shoulders. "It's okay, I've got you."

Mrs. Landry pats my arm. "Were you always this strong? It's nice."

"Ah, I've been working out," I lie, helping her take a shaky step from the tank while Wrath drags Tim by his ankles in the opposite direction.

"I'm just going to get rid of this," he says on his way past.

"Where is he going with Tim?" Mrs. Landry asks.

"The churro stand probably," I tell her while I watch Wrath head off with Tim towards the food stands. Whatever he's going to do, I'm not going to pry. "Now, what did you do?" I ask and kick over a crate for her to sit on. "Sit here and catch your breath."

Mrs. Landry sinks down onto the crate with a groan. "Thank you, Buffy. I don't know what you did but you did something to the tank, didn't you?" she asks and looks up at me with hope. "You stopped it. I know you did."

"Not me, um, my husband did. He's a mage," I lie. I want to

tell her the truth, that Wrath is Wrath and that he's a demon helping me find the Blossoms but I can't. Even if Mrs. Landry was always kind, she's still in the cult. She's still loyal and I don't know how deep it runs. For now, she gets the same lie as everyone else about Wrath.

"A mage? But I thought they all died out?"

"Apparently that's just a Sweet Tooth thing for how, ah, off course we've gotten as of late. He's here to keep an eye on things for a bit. The Founders are going to have to tighten up around here, because Wrath isn't happy. Not even a little bit."

Mrs. Landry leans forward and slaps her hand on the crate. "I knew it! I knew something wasn't right when they put in a cake order with me."

I tilt my head to the side and think over Mrs. Landry's words but it's not making sense. "What? The cake order? I don't understand."

Mrs. Landry waves her hands at me excitedly. "No, it's on me, dear. I-I know I sound like a mad woman and you might not believe what I'm about to tell you but I'm going to anyway. Because I trust you and because I believe your life is in danger."

"Oh, yeah, really?" Mrs. Landry shocks me with that one and I stumble over my words but I keep trying. "I mean, why do you think that?" I ask, taking a seat next to her on the crate. If anyone hears her telling me this, there's going to be more than the Dunk 'o Fun tank that she has to deal with.

"Normally, the Founders take the Blossoms and their grooms to the city for a feast but they didn't this time. Mrs. Donna twisted her ankle, so they had me do the cakes for them but the order was all wrong."

"You keep saying that. Why?"

"There weren't enough cakes. There were twelve of you girls, twenty-four counting the grooms. But they only wanted me to make twelve cakes. I thought they were meant to be joint cakes, so I asked about the portion. They said, no, the portion was just for one person each. There would only be twelve grooms in attendance for the feast. That made no sense, not when it was the most sacred night of the year. Not when it was the *wedding night*. I-I asked if I should make anything special for the Blossoms, I said I would be just dandy delivering it to them if need be, to make sure you girls all had a sweet treat. And-and..." Mrs. Landry's voice trails off and I watch her focus on the gaping door of the dunk tank.

"They didn't like you asking questions about girls they were going to kill," I finish for her.

Mrs. Landry grabs my hand and her eyes fill with tears. "They *did* try to hurt you, didn't they? I knew it. Oh, Buffy, I'm so sorry. I tried to—I *tried*. I went looking for you. I swear I did but they found me in the Hall of Worship. That's when they sent me home and posted a guard outside. I watched them all night until he brought me here for my turn in the dunk tank."

"It's poison, isn't it?" I ask her. "In the water, I mean. We saw something being pumped into it. I knew I had to get you out."

Mrs. Landry nods and sniffles. "I don't know what it is, but it burns. Every time you get sent under is worse than the last. It's still burning but it's better now that I'm out of the tank."

"What?! You're still—I mean, it's still *burning* you?" I look Mrs. Landry over but I can't see anything on her skin. "Hold still, I'll get my husband and he'll take care of it. I promise he will fix this."

"You rang?" Wrath's voice makes me jump. I spin to see him

strolling up to us with a box of churros in one hand and a water bottle in the other. He holds the water bottle out to Mrs. Landry. "I got you this, thought you might be parched. There's churros too, once you've had enough to drink."

"Thank you," Mrs. Landry murmurs and takes the water from Wrath with the same look I saw Ms. Donna give him. Interesting.

"She's still in pain. The poison or whatever it is, is still on her."

"That won't do. One moment." Wrath and tucks his box of churros under one arm. "Give me your hand, Mrs. Landry."

She only hesitates for a second before she slips her hand into his. Wrath lets out a hiss. "Ohhh, Naga poison. This town is just full of surprises, isn't it?"

Mrs. Landry looks like she's going to burst into tears. "*Naga poison*? What is that? Am I going to live? Oh Wrath. I'm going to die, aren't I?"

I shake my head and wave my hands at her to try and calm her down. "No, no, of course not," I tell her and then shove my hands over her ears. "She's not going to die, is she?"

"This mortal coil ends for all humans, beloved."

"Wrath. I'm serious," I whisper-scream, my blood pressure rising with each second that ticks by with me pawing at Mrs. Landry's ears. "Is she going to be okay?"

"She won't die from the poison. I expect she'll make a full recovery by this evening now that we've intervened. You can drop the ear muffs if you like."

"Thank you."

"Always, beloved."

Wrath smiles at me and it's hard to think but I do my best. I start by dropping my hands from Mrs. Landry's ears and standing up. "You're going to be okay. Nothing bad is going to happen to you, I promise, Mrs. Landry."

"Oh, Buffy." Mrs. Landry's eyes well up with tears and she grabs both my hand and Wrath's. "I don't know how to thank you. I already feel so much better. It doesn't hurt at all anymore. I can't repay you for what you've done for me."

"No, not now but there will be a time when you will," Wrath tells her and we both look at him in surprise.

"What are you talking about?" Mrs. Landry presses her hands together and takes a deep breath. "If it will help the girls, I'll do it. I'll help now and I tried to before, Buffy," she says and gives me a searching look. "I wanted to help you and all of the Blossoms. That's why I went to your mother."

My blood turns to ice and my heart turns to stone. "My mother?" I whisper.

"Yes, I went to her first thing to ask about the order. I thought she might know where you would be, that it would be a nice surprise to cheer you. But she said she didn't know. I saw her this morning but she didn't mention seeing you."

I grit my teeth and think of ten different ways that I want to end my mother. *Darla.* She's not my mother, she's just some woman that sold me out for a new wardrobe and invites to stuffy stone troll summoning parties. And if she sold me out, I know she did the same to Mrs. Landry. *She* was the reason Mrs. Landry ended up in the Dunk 'o Fun tank getting Naga poisoned to next Tuesday.

"She must have been in a hurry this morning. There's a party at the Rossi's," I tell her and Mrs. Landry nods.

"I heard about the party."

"And yet, no invitation for you," Wrath sniffs and gives her an awkward pat to the shoulder and Mrs. Landry almost swoons from the simple touch. "No good deed goes unpunished, I suppose."

What is it with women in the cult and Wrath?

I keep Mrs. Landry upright with a hand. "Thank you for trying."

"I'm sorry I didn't do more. I knew, well I've known things haven't been right here for a very long time." She sniffles and pats at her eyes with her damp blouse, but it does nothing with how soaked she is. I'm thankful when Wrath magics a handkerchief out of the ether and hands it to her. "I'm so sorry, Buffy. I'll do anything. I promise I will be there when you need me."

Mrs. Landry is smiling at me but I see the determination in her eyes. They sparkle with it. It doesn't matter if her promise means she's going toe-to-toe with a stone troll or trying to help me fix a birthday cake disaster, she's going to do it. And she's going to do it with a smile on her face.

I smile back. "When the time comes," I say, repeating Wrath's words. She nods.

"When the time comes."

We say our goodbyes and leave Mrs. Landry looking ready to punch the next person that crosses her, which is an improvement. I think about walking her home, but I don't think we're done here. Something feels like it's just out of reach. So Wrath and I keep walking. We do our best to blend in and it's easy enough with how many Outsiders are here today.

We do keep attracting curious glances from the townies that recognize me. Of course, Annie is among the first and Wrath was right. I can tell she's forgotten all about our morning run in with how she bounces up to me and finagles an introduction to Wrath with a starstruck look in her eyes. The interaction is harmless enough with Ron shooting us the stink eye before he drags Annie away in a huff.

Nice.

Little by little, I relax. The sun is high in the sky and I'm one funnel cake and half a hot dog in while Wrath has polished off his box of churros when he freezes and goes to attention, like one of those English hunting dogs. If he was in his demon form, I'd expect to see his tail shoot straight out to complete the picture.

"What is it? What do you see?"

"Beanbags. *You have beanbags,*" he tells me like it's an unbelievable thing. The bean bags are really filled with rice and stitched out of the hand-me-downs brought to the Hall of Worship. I know because I was one of the ones that stitched them together with the other Blossoms.

"What?"

"There," he says and points ahead of us to a game stall. I see milk jugs in pyramids and tin cans stacked high. "I cannot believe I found it. We have to play." He grabs my hand and starts to drag me towards it with the kind of speed I never in my life have seen anyone associate with bean bags.

"The bean bag toss? You're excited about the bean bag toss? *Why?*"

"Who wouldn't be? Such a sacred game and to be enjoyed *here* of all places."

"Wait, what?"

We come to a stop in front of the bean bag stall and Wrath slaps down a wad of cash. "I'll take all the bean bags."

"Where did you get that money?"

"Magic," he replies and takes the first crate of bean bags with a satisfied nod. "This is a good start, keep these coming, good sir."

I look at the good sir and I recognize him. His name is Charlie and he was two years behind me in school and kind. He spent a lot of time tutoring everyone at the library in Calculus–me included. I never was the best student.

Wrath snatches up a bean bag and lets it fly, which would be okay with anyone else considering it's just a rice filled scrap of shirt he's throwing and that should be totally harmless but not in Wrath's hands. The first bean bag hits the back of the stall so hard it shoots right through it. Charlie jumps and gives me a '*did you see that?*' look so I nod that I did, before I turn back to Wrath.

"Can you at least *pretend* to be human?" I ask while he picks up another bean bag and gives it a smack.

"What are you talking about? That's exactly what I'm doing. Though I might add, the gods of the Kroas Dimension are going to be *livid* that you've made bean bags available so easily. Not a sacrifice in sight," Wrath gives a little *tsk* before he chucks the beanbag in his hand at the pyramid of tin milk jugs with enough force that it leaves a permanent indent in the milk jug it hit and sends the rest of them flying. One of them shoots towards the booth worker and nails him in the side of the neck.

I clap my hands over my mouth as Charlie drops like a sack of stones. "No, you're not! Oh my-oh my mulberries. You took him out!"

"He's fine."

"He's *not* fine. His name is Charlie Vallencourt and he has *anemia*," I quietly shriek at Wrath before I leap over the booth counter and hurry towards Charlie. Charlie is laid out on his back in a dead man's pose when I get to him but at least he's conscious.

"Are you okay?" I ask and drop to my knees beside him.

He blinks and shakes his head. He doesn't look fine from where I'm kneeling but he does his best and gives me a thumbs up. "I-I'm okay, Buffy."

Charlie pushes himself to sit up and I wrap an arm around his shoulders and help him. But the second I touch him, I feel a sharp tug on the bond that nearly jerks me backwards. I hiss and look over my shoulder at where Wrath is hopping right over the counter and into the booth.

"What are you doing? Chill."

"I'll chill when you get your hands off that mortal."

I sigh heavily at Wrath and give him a brittle smile. "My, what a totally human thing to say, darling," I say between clenched teeth. He either doesn't care or he doesn't pick up on my *start acting a semi-sane human, and not a hot demon vibe* I'm sending his way.

"He's fine," Wrath grumbles and reaches down a hand to Charlie. "Aren't you, Gamemaster?"

"Damon, I really think that-"

"Y-you think I'm a-a gamemaster?" Charlie stammers and takes Wrath's extended hand. When I look at him, I see that he still looks dazed but it's a lot less from getting nailed by a bean bag and more of the might be in love dazed kind of look. He swallows hard and stares at where Wrath is still holding his hand.

I sigh. I get it, Charlie. Wrath more than likely has me looking like this twenty-four-seven now.

Wrath gives him a nod. "Certainly, what else would you be?"

he asks and gestures around the booth with a sweep of his hand. "You are the master of this booth, this game, are you not?"

"Well, yeah, but this isn't," Charlie rubs the back of his neck and drops his voice, "this isn't the *real* game, you know? I run a game circle and I'm good at it, even if they put me here because they know if they let me take over one of the bigger games I'll be unstoppable."

"Ah, you thirst for power. Admirable."

"Charlie isn't thirsting for anything," I tell Wrath but then I pause, because Charlie is still holding Wrath's hand and he looks thirsty for something all right. "I mean, at least not power."

"No, I do, I do want power," Charlie blurts out. A few fairgoers look over at us before he drops his voice to a whisper and lets go of Wrath's hand. "I do want power. But they're keeping me down. You know how it is here, Buffy."

"What do you mean?" I say carefully, because I didn't know how it was, not until my eyes were truly opened. It took the Founders trying to kill me and kidnapping my friends for me to finally understand that everything wasn't for some greater good.

"I-well, you know how they don't let us do anything we want. It's like, if we do what we want, they lose power or something. I don't know why they can't just-"

"Let you choose the path of your own mortal demise?" Wrath asks and he drops his voice an octave that has me yanking on the bond with a sharp look.

"Tone it down," I whisper.

"Sorry, I told you, until last night, I was on the job. This is all very new to me. Charlie here would be a fine candidate to make a deal with."

"A deal?" Charlie breaks in and we both look at him. "What

210

kind of deal?"

"There's no deal, he's just...you know, a mage," I say quickly. "Mages don't make deals."

Charlie's eyes go wide and he looks at Wrath. "You're really a mage? I heard whispers from the bakery this morning about how you made all the fritters vanish but I didn't believe it. Mages are extinct."

"Dormant, not extinct. And only here, young Charlie. Why, there's a whole wide world out there just waiting for you to discover it. A world full of mages and games to play. A world where no one will stick you in the corner at a lackluster game. Now, tell me, what is it you truly desire?"

"Damon," I try, but he holds up a hand and sends a wink my way.

"Trust me, beloved. My instinct tells me Charlie here is a fine ally to make."

"You need allies, because the Founders want you gone, right?" Charlie asks and my blood runs cold.

"How-what are you talking about, Charlie?"

"Callum," he says quietly and then motions for us to follow him out of the booth and around the back of it. It's quieter here and there's no one around. "Everyone knows Callum's dead. Mister O'Hare isn't going to let you live because of that. That means the Founders want you dead." He looks at Wrath. "That's why you married him, right? For protection? They can't kill a married woman."

Wrath hums in appreciation. "I told you, dear wife. Charlie is indeed a valuable ally."

I cross my arms and ignore the puppy dog look Charlie sends Wrath's way. "Let's say you're right," I hedge, not willing to come right out and say what Charlie is. "Why are you telling me any of this?" I wasn't programmed this way, speaking plainly is for men. Even if Charlie is timid and nervous, he's still something more valuable to the cult than I ever was.

He's a man.

"Because I know what happens at the Founder's Circle."

"How? Who else knows?" I ask him.

Charlie shakes his head. "It's just the elders, some of the families, I guess. I don't know how many people know. I thought I was the only one that wasn't an intended that knew the truth, but it doesn't feel that way anymore. More people know what happens there."

Charlie is right. There are more people who know about what happens to the Blossoms and just like him I have no idea how far it goes or who to trust.

"I know you're supposed to be dead."

Wrath and I go silent and time slows around us. "How do you know that?" I whisper.

"I snuck out there," Charlie swallows hard and looks down at his feet. "I went there and I saw. I thought, well, I thought something was wrong, because none of the Blossoms ever come back from the city and none of us are allowed to leave Sweet Tooth. I posted about it on the forums and they told me to go see what was really happening."

"Forums? What forums?" I ask in surprise, because there's no forums that I know about. There's an intranet we use in Sweet Tooth that provides enough Wi-Fi to Outsiders when they visit town, but there's no forums on it.

"On the internet," Charlie says and then adds, "well, the *real internet*. Not our wacked out cult internet. The real honest to goodness thing. There's all kinds of people on there to talk to, Buffy. When I started telling them what happened in the Creepy Life 'n Stuff Forums they said to follow y'all to get answers."

"Did you tell anyone here about it?"

Charlie shakes his head. "No, I didn't know who I could trust. It's not like any of that actually matters, because look where they put me," he says and sweeps his hand to the booth behind him.

"At the fair?" I ask, because I don't get it. But I guess Wrath does, because he gives a sympathetic hum.

"Truly a travesty, Gamemaster."

"Thank you! And they put *Sylvie* front and center at the Shoot 'Em Up Booth. Like, what? I'm not good enough so they stick me back here with the *bean bags*? I can handle firepower, I really can."

"It's a bunch of BB guns, Charlie," I tell him while Wrath continues to nod along sympathetically.

"I'm sure this Sylvie is abhorrent," he says and I feel like I'm the only sane one, which is saying a lot.

Charlie throws his hands up in the air. "The absolute worst, thank you! That's what I've been saying but no one is listening and here I am with a bunch of bean bags and I nearly got knocked out."

Wrath steps in front of Charlie and holds up a finger to me with a conspiratorial wink. He's working on Charlie but why? I go quiet and watch him work his demon magic on Charlie.

"What if I told you that I could get you all the firepower you'd like, Charlie."

Charlie's eyes go wide as saucers and he grabs Wrath's hands with a desperate little gasp. "The Shoot 'Em Up Booth?"

There's a flicker and I almost see the outline of Wrath's horns before they're gone again. "Absolutely my friend. Say the word and Sylvie is nothing but a memory and you'll be in your rightful place. The only real suitable place for a gamemaster such as your-self." Wrath's eyes are hypnotic, low and slow. The pitch of it sends a thrill through me and settles into my belly. "Is that some-thing you'd like, my ambitious friend?"

A glow appears around Wrath. It's so subtle that if I wasn't staring right at him, I wouldn't see it. I know Charlie doesn't notice it. There's no way with how he's currently losing himself in Wrath's eyes. The shimmering sphere spins and moves and it encircles Charlie. When he speaks it flares bright and vanishes.

"Yes, I want that. I will do anything you want for that."

"It's a deal," Wrath says and the shimmering light winks out of sight when he extends his hand to Charlie. "A gentleman's deal then? I give you Sylvie's spot and you, my dear, curious friend, find out a little something for me."

Charlie shakes Wrath's hand immediately. "Done."

"Splendid, my friend. What I require is something very simple. The location of the Blossoms. Where are they?"

I expect Charlie to drop away when Wrath gives him his terms but he doesn't. Instead, he reaches into his pocket and pulls out a phone. We aren't allowed to have phones. No one is, unless they're part of the Founder's Circle. Where Charlie got one, I have no idea but he swipes away on it with an ease that tells me he's had it awhile.

"Here," he says and thrusts the phone to Wrath. "Nick Aguirre has them in his little torture chamber of secrets. There's the proof if you don't believe me."

Wrath juggles the phone and then winces when he catches sight of the screen. "I see."

"Where did you get a phone?" I blurt out, snatching the

phone away from Wrath before he can stop me.

"Ah, I, well there is a black market for things, if you know where to look..." Charlie says, but I'm not listening to him anymore. There's no way I can when I see the video that's playing on the screen. It's grainy and dark and the movements of the camera are jerky at best but I can see the Blossoms.

My friends.

They're chained in a dark stone room. None of them seem to notice Charlie but it's probably from the angle he's crawling while he tries to hide in the shadows. The camera shakes in his hand and the only sound I can hear is his ragged breathing while he crawls along on his hands and knees. He drops his phone but when he picks it back up the first face I see is Meadow. She's chained to the stone floor and still wearing her wedding dress. It's tattered and stained and I can tell she's crying from the way her shoulders are shaking.

I grab the phone from him. "When did you take this?"

"I-uh, this morning," Charlie stammers.

"What were you doing there?" I grab Charlie by his shirt and lift him off the ground with one hand and give him a shake. "What were you looking for? How do I know you aren't in on this?'

Charlie yelps and tries to get free but it's no use. Not with me holding him a foot off the ground. "I was looking for a-a book. There's a book that I heard Aguirre has."

Wrath steps up beside me and looks at Charlie. He doesn't have to look up into his eyes like I do with how I'm holding him. They're more at eye level now. Wrath snaps his fingers in front of Charlie when he opens his mouth and it looks like he might scream.

215

"No screaming for help, friend. My wife is still testing her strength and I have to tell you, I don't know what she'll do when she realizes just how easy it is to snap a head off. Now, what's the book on?"

"You mean like Callum's?" I ask and Charlie looks like he's about to faint.

"I knew that was you! You killed him?" he asks with wide eyes and Wrath holds up his finger in answer.

"No, that was me but she could do it to you, too. Now that she's my harbinger. She's very formidable."

"I thought you said she was your wife."

"Same difference," I interrupt and give Charlie another shake. His head bounces like one of the knickknack bobble heads of Ichabod they sell in the souvenir shop to Outsiders. "Focus on me, Charlie. What book and where are my friends being held?"

"The book, I-I, it's a magic book. One that makes whatever you write in it happen. I want it for one of my games."

I tilt my head to the side and give Charlie a once over. "There's a book capable of making whatever you want possible and you want it for *games*?"

"These are important!" Charlie blurts out. Excitement makes his voice rise and I have to shush him and shake him to get him to lower his voice before anyone hears him. "Sorry, sorry! Look, I know it seems dumb but the games are important. The biggest one of all is coming up and I'm going to prove that I'm the Gamemaster to beat. I need that book to make the best Dungeon Manual *ever*."

"I only understood about fifteen percent of the words you just said but okay."

Wrath settles a hand against my lower back and it's hard not to lose focus when I feel the warmth of his hand through my clothes. "He wants the book for a minor mischief. Worry not, beloved."

Charlie swings his legs and nods at Wrath's words. "That's right, just a little mischief. I just want to show everyone what I can do. That's why I went down there today, I swear it. I'm not in on any of the plans they have for the Blossoms. I promise."

"Then why did you take the video?"

"I-I was," Charlie hangs his head and I hear the hard swallow he takes before he speaks again, "I didn't know what to do, okay? I was scared. I thought that I'd find someone that could help them. Maybe an Outsider, anyone. I just-I didn't want them to just disappear like all the rest."

Like all the rest. I understand what he means. He wanted someone to know to look for them, even if he was too scared to do it. I'm no better, not when I ran from the Founders' Circle while Meadow and the other Blossoms fought.

I let go and drop Charlie in a heap at my feet. "Fine. I'll help you get that book but I need more than a little video. You need to show me where the Blossoms are."

"D-deal. I can draw you a map. If I leave the fair, they'll know something's up. I'd never leave my booth. B-but there's one other thing, I mean, if it's not too much trouble. I have something else to ask and seeing your husband is a mage and y-you're really strong now, Buffy, do you think you could help?"

I cross my arms and look down at Charlie. He sounds serious, whatever it is, it's big. "What is it?"

"I hate to be a stickler but there's still the matter of Sylvie's booth. I want it."

I groan and squeeze my eyes shut. "Are you serious? The book isn't enough?"

Wrath puts a hand on my shoulder and gives it a gentle squeeze. "He's entitled to it, beloved, as the deal was initially struck for Sylvie's booth. We're bound to honor the quest. What you've done now with the book is simply creating an addendum, not a replacement."

Charlie snaps his fingers. "See, Wrath said it, so it's true. The deal was for Sylvie's booth and if you must know, *it is a big deal*, okay? What if something happens to you and you don't make it out of that dungeon? If I don't get that book, at least I'd have Sylvie's booth to show for what I'm about to do for you. If they find out I helped you I'm dead and no one is going to look for me. Not here. You know it, Buffy."

"He's got us there." Wrath holds a hand down to Charlie and pulls him to his feet. "As my lovely and vengeful wife offered, we are happy to sweeten the deal and retrieve the book for you, valued informant. I know it was you that Elijah sent us here to find."

Elijah.

I groan and rub my temples. "We have to get back to check on Elijah." I send a silent prayer up to whatever deity doesn't accept sacrifices that Elijah is safe and the house is still standing.

Charlie pouts but he's giving Wrath puppy dog eyes again so I know he'll listen to the demon. "I'm not a-"

Wrath hustles him back towards the booth with a sweep of his arm. "Right this way before Buffy throws you through your booth. Now, get in there and start drawing and we'll be on our way to pay Sylvie a visit. I want a masterpiece for my bride or you'll be spending the rest of your days in gaming obscurity." He practically tosses Charlie back into his booth but pauses before he follows him and shoots me a wink that makes my cheeks go hot.

"This will just be a minute, beloved," Wrath calls back to me and I nod stupidly, because he's not in front of me. There's no way he can see it but I'm just as taken with my husband as the rest of the cult members that seem to fall under his spell everywhere we go.

I can't help it.

"S-sure thing!" I stammer out while this morning dances through my memory. Wrath knows the effect he has on me judging from what happened between us after we cleared the basement and dealt with Old Man Rossi, I don't think Wrath wants me to fight it, either. He feels the same way. I can feel it humming away happily through our bond just as surely as I felt his hands and mouth on me this morning.

My blush spreads and I know I'm flushed all over. I fan myself and pull my pastel skirts away from my body to give myself some breathing room. All the flouncy layers seemed like a good idea this morning when Wrath made me something to wear and they certainly felt like the right idea when Wrath had me floating with his head between my thighs but now I *know* it was the right move. If I was wearing pants, I'd be burning up thinking about what my husband did to me.

Husband.

When I summoned Wrath and he first kissed me by the hot springs, I would have let him do anything to me. And when we laid together in bed last night the only thing I wanted was the comfort of his touch but I wasn't so sheltered by the cult that I didn't know what was expected of me on my wedding night.

Of course, that was when I thought I was going to survive it.

I survived and now I'm married. And the only thing on my mind is how long until I'm able to explore exactly what it means to have a true wedding night.

"I am an Arthas demon. I am skilled at pleasures of the flesh. Carnal delights as it were and that is what Lethos chose to employ me in."

My skin prickles knowing Wrath was forced to do anything against his will but with us?

It's different when it's us.

"Wrath." I whisper his name partly out of habit but also because Wrath's name on my lips feels right when I think of him like this. When I think of us together and how easily he took me apart with just his hands and tongue. Yes, we did have bloodlust on our side but it wasn't the room full of slain cultists that made it exciting or intoxicating. It was my husband. I don't know how I'll survive the night in Wrath's bed...though, the prospect of coming to an end because of his demon *talents* is intriguing.

I take a deep breath and let it out slowly before I take another and repeat it. I'm on my third exhale and shaking out my skirts to achieve maximum ventilation while I try not to burst into flames over my husband, when someone clears their throat. I look up. It's Wrath and he's smirking at me.

"Hot, my ruthless little wife?"

I drop my skirts and straighten up. "It's unseasonably warm today."

"I'll bet it is," he says and his gaze slowly moves down my body with the kind of intent that tells me precisely what he would do if we were alone. I swallow hard and press my hands to my thighs.

"You called me. I heard you," he says and taps a finger to his temple. "But I imagine you wanted me to hear you, isn't that right?"

I open my mouth to say I hadn't thought to call him but I don't, because he's right. I did say his name. I did mean for him to hear me while I thought about him.

"Yes. I-I did call you. I meant to."

Wrath's smirk turns mellow. It morphs into the beautiful curve of his lush mouth that I adore. I stay still when he crosses the space to me. His dark eyes flash in warning and my breath catches.

"If I were you, I would take care what you think of when you call on me. Private or not, I have no problem making your desires real."

"You would touch me? Out in the open like this?"

"Oh, if you intend to keep tantalizing me with your memories of my mouth on you, tasting you. If you dare think to me what my fingers buried in your delicious body felt like, or what you hope I do to you tonight when we're alone. If you do all that, I promise to do more than touch you." Wrath's voice is low and hypnotic, it weaves and winds itself around me, the grip of it tightens and I gasp when Wrath continues on, voice just above a rasp, "I'll have you, Buffy."

All around us the festival is in full swing. I hear laughter and children shrieking in the distance. The sound of games and the twang of music playing in the square floats on the air to us. It's a picture perfect day with the sun shining down on us and a crisp blue sky overhead.

No one would ever know what Wrath is promising to do to me.

Or just how close I am to letting him do it.

CHAPTER
TWENTY-THREE

"What are we doing again?" I ask. I'm following Wrath through the crowd, Charlie is up ahead. I catch sight of his mop of brown hair every now and then before he turns to look over his shoulder to check we're following him. There's a manic light in Charlie that wasn't there before. He sticks out with how he's rubbing his hands together like a villainous fly as he darts through the festival crowd to Sylvie's booth.

"He's going to get us caught. Look at him. Are you sure he's the reason Elijah wanted us to come here?"

"He is. I know it, beloved. He's eager, that's all. We'll make quick work of this and be on our way to see how Elijah is managing."

"I hope he's okay." I feel bad for sending Elijah on his own the way we did but it was the only way I could think to keep him safe. It was the right thing to do. I know that after Mrs. Landry and the

Naga poison but I'm still worried about him. "You don't think he's lonely or anything, do you?"

"He's just fine. He knows to lock the doors and keep to himself. There's nothing to worry about. Ah, I think we've reached our destination." Wrath jerks his chin ahead of us. The Shoot 'Em Up booth is just up ahead. Even though I don't remember it much from the other years I came to the festival, Charlie wasn't lying about just how popular it is. It's three times the size of the bean bag booth Charlie manned. There's a long counter with ten seats along it. The targets are about thirty feet off from the counter. Each target hangs from a carousel that whirs loudly as it brings fresh targets in for the newest BB gun enthusiasts.

There's old west music piping in from speakers that I can't see and a raised platform with a few cactus cut outs along with a pair of fake saloon doors where the person running the game can oversee the shooters comfortably. A neon sign proclaiming Shoot 'Em Up! flashes overhead.The line here is easily twenty people deep. The Shoot 'Em Up booth is a world apart from the empty bean bag booth we found Charlie at all right.

"What's the plan?" Charlie asks, popping up at my elbow. My heart nearly bursts out of my chest.

"Don't do that!" I jump in surprise and turn to face him to see him looking unbothered.

"Don't do what?" he asks.

"Materialize out of thin air when we're planning crime on your behalf," Wrath answers and puts an arm around my shoulders. "She's a bit jumpy after the other night."

"If by the other night you mean my near sacrifice on my wedding night? Then yes, I am jumpy after 'the other night'."

Wrath chuckles but doesn't say anything about my sass. From the smile on his face, I'd say that he enjoys me talking back to him. Which...is new. I've never been with anyone other than Meadow that liked me sassy and it sets a warm and happy glow that has nothing to do with our bond in my chest at knowing my husband does.

"Can I help? With the crime, I mean?" Charlie asks with a hopeful look. "I'd like to be a part of Sylvie's downfall, if I can."

"What did she do to you? Break your heart?" Wrath asks and Charlie snorts.

"As if I would care about that," he says with a blithe wave and turns to face the Shoot 'Em Up booth with a glare. "Sylvie used to be my teacher, back when I was new to games and all. She stole that booth from me in a series of betrayals so deep and dark it would make your toes curl to hear in the light of day. I told her she would rue the day she stabbed me in the back and now the chickens have come home to roost, haven't they Sylvie?"

Wrath and I go silent and exchange an '*uh oh*' look.

"The chickens have done what?" I ask.

Charlie steps forward and crosses his arms. "Look at her there, thinking she's won and banished me to the *bean bags*. Too bad for Sylvie she counted her chickens before they hatched. Looks like you put all your eggs in one basket when you double-crossed me."

I turn to Wrath and grab his arm. "Listen, whatever you're going to do, do it fast before he makes more poultry references. This is starting to feel really serious."

"I'm gonna put you out to pasture. It's my time to shine," Charlie growls.

"Right, I'm on it. He's definitely heavy on the pastoral

warpath," Wrath mutters and steps forward to grab Charlie back to us. That's when the unthinkable happens.

Sylvie spots Charlie and uses her big loud megaphone to call out to him. "Charlie Chicken, is that you?" she asks and tips back her cowboy hat to get a better view of us. "And you brought friends, too!"

"That's not my name!" Charlie whines.

I snap my fingers. "Ohhh, I get the chicken thing now."

"Don't try to show off for your friends, Charlie Chicken! You can't hide who you are from me. Isn't that right, folks?" Sylvie asks the crowd of thirty waiting for a turn at the Shoot 'Em Up booth and they all shout in agreement.

"Charlie Chicken's back!"

"*Bock*! *Bock*! Charlie Chicken!"

A few people in line make chicken wing arms at Charlie and I watch him visibly shrink into himself. The sight makes my heart hurt, even if I was shaking him like a bobble head doll just minutes before, I wasn't going to hurt him. These people are all about hitting Charlie where it hurts the most.

Emotionally.

"Why are they calling him that?" I ask Wrath and look around to see that most of the people in line seem to know Charlie. It makes sense, seeing as we grew up here with the cult members that are now jeering at him, but...why Charlie Chicken?

"Charlie what happened?" I try but he doesn't hear me. Charlie looks pale and like he might pass out. Wrath steps close to him and moves to support him when a girl speaks up.

"He choked," a girl near me explains with a smile. "They let him run the booth last year but he didn't even last an hour before he was done. Stage fright had him choked up so bad that Sylvie had to take over for him."

Charlie whirls to face the girl. "That's *not* what happened! Sh-she tricked me. I was nervous but I was excited to do the Shoot 'Em Up booth, okay? Everything was going fine until *she* came to see me and brought me lunch. Th-that *cursed chicken sandwich.*"

I clear my throat and shoot a quick smile to the girl who's trying to edge away from Charlie now that he's taking a trip down memory lane. "That seems...nice," I try.

"Nice? It wasn't nice, it was diabolical, Buffy. She told me I could take a break to enjoy my chicken sandwich, so I did. I didn't have anything to drink, so I went to grab a pop from next door. When I came back, she'd replaced me. Told the organizers and even the *Founders* that I had a nervous breakdown. That I chick-ened out!"

I watch Sylvie. She's still squawking away on her megaphone but I'm listening to Charlie, not her. "Charlie, that's terrible."

"She made that nickname for me. She got me banished to the bean bags and now I want her to pay."

"Charlie Chicken, come on up here, I've got something for you."

We all look to see Sylvie holding a chicken sandwich in her hand.

I press my hands to my temples and take in a deep breath. "Oh, mulberries..."

"She better not be doing what I think she is," Wrath growls when Sylvie lifts her hand and cocks her arm like she's about to chuck the chicken sandwich at Charlie.

Charlie moves away from Wrath, squares his shoulders and

lifts his chin to meet the soon to be airborne sandwich. "Oh, she's doing exactly what you think she is. This time, I'm not moving."

I have to give it to Charlie for standing his ground. He doesn't even move when Sylvie throws the sandwich and the crowd lets out a collective gasp. "Wrath, sweetheart, do something. Please," I beg, because I can't stand to see Charlie get chickened in front of everyone.

"As you wish." Wrath snaps his fingers and the chicken sandwich loops back on itself and hits Sylvie in the face with a satisfying *splat*. Her arms fly out at her sides and she pinwheels on the raised platform that overlooks the shooting range for a second before she pitches over the side and vanishes from sight. There's a loud thud and the only thing left of Sylvie is the cowboy hat that got knocked off her head and landed on the platform.

Everyone goes silent and stares at us. Well, everyone but Charlie. "I didn't run. Did you see that?" He runs for the booth with a holler and vaults onto the platform. "I'm not Charlie Chicken! I'm Charlie the Gamemaster!" He shouts and raises the cowboy hat over his head in victory. "How do you like a face full of chicken sandwich, Sylvie? I'm gonna call you Sandwich Sylvie!"

Nobody looks Charlie's way, not even with his tirade. They're all still looking at us.

"He's a mage," I offer quietly, which doesn't improve our situation any. I grab onto Wrath's arm. "I think we should go."

"Why? I'm quite enjoying watching Charlie up there. He's losing it, don't you think?"

"Yes, he is losing it and we're going to be losing it if this crowd turns on us."

Wrath looks out at the crowd and squints at them for a beat

before he shakes his head. "They won't make a move. We're protected by the Founders, at least for now."

"Are you sure they know that?"

"It doesn't matter if the crowd knows it, because they do," Wrath says and nods off to the side. I turn to look and at first I don't see who he's talking about but a second later I do.

The robes kind of give them away.

The Founders are here. At least, the Aguirres are. I swallow hard and watch them watch us. There are five of them, but I'm only concerned with one of them.

Nick Aguirre, the Aguirre patriarch. The man that I'm going to murder for every little thing he's done to me and my friends in this cult. He's older than Old Man Rossi and my parents, but not by much. He's not a nice man, at least not from what I know of him. He once made Ms. Donna cry. Her smile broke after he laid into her about a cake mix-up. I don't know the particulars about the cake or why it was so important, but I do know that I was there the next day with Callum trying to cheer her up over the ordeal. Ms. Donna gave us watery smiles and sweet cupcakes for coming by to comfort her about it, but she insisted she was fine. Just disappointed in her weakness.

"You're both so sweet. You'll make a lovely couple. I don't deserve you here on my account."

He's here with his sons but out of those there's one that stands out. Roy. Meadow's intended. He looks fine, maybe a little sleep deprived if the shadows under his eyes are anything to go by. I guess that's what happens when you try to sacrifice your fiancée to a demon and now she's chained up in your dad's torture basement.

"Nothing will happen if they're keeping watch."

I smile at Nick Aguirre when he glares at me. "That means we can't kill them either." I'm going to enjoy breaking him the way he did Ms. Donna's smile.

"I'm going to consider our work here for Charlie done. We'll get the book and complete the deal." Wrath turns me away from the Aguirres and leads me through the crowd. When I dig my heels in and look back towards Nick Aguirre and his brood, Wrath leans close to whisper to me. "Not yet. We have the map and we have time enough for you to enjoy your revenge, dear wife."

"Good, I like that. I seriously *don't* like him."

"I know, I feel it here," Wrath murmurs and taps his chest just as there's a chirp from inside of his jacket.

"What's that?" I ask.

"A text from Charlie."

"A what?"

"A text from Charlie," Wrath repeats. "I'm assuming it's the Gamemaster on account of him being the only one to have this number."

"A text? When did you get a phone? Am I the only one without a phone now?" I ask and lean close to get a look at the device in Wrath's hand. The text is a photo of Charlie leaning over Sylvie and the sandwich that took her out with a thumbs up.

"Earlier when Charlie drew the map he procured me a device. He's quite resourceful and look at him, he's reclaimed his power as the Gamemaster."

I smile at Charlie's photo. "Yeah, he did." I'm happy for Charlie, even if he scares me a little.

CHAPTER
TWENTY-FOUR

The entire walk back to Wrath's Embrace passes in a blur on account of me trying to make sense of how close I came to asking Wrath to take me in public. I don't even care when Annie and Ron pop up when we're halfway there and make a show of following us to the bottom of the hill to Wrath's Embrace.

Although, all it takes is one look from Wrath for Annie to scamper off into the bushes.

"I thought you wiped her memory?" I ask, watching Annie nearly trip in her dive to take cover. Ron doesn't make a run for it and stands awkwardly on the road behind us, looking like he wants to evaporate. Which I understand, on account of Annie rolling around the bushes like a raccoon.

Wrath lifts his hand in a wave to Ron. "I did."

"Ah, so it's just her natural nosey state, then."

"Looks like the measure of it."

I nod and wave at Ron too before he shuffles off to help Annie get loose from the bushes. "Let's go, I think they're going to be stuck there for a while and I'd rather be inside before she gets free and tries to follow us again. I don't want her to see Elijah and go around telling people that he's with us now. Do you think he's okay?"

"He's a grown acolyte and capable enough. Worry not, beloved."

"But we've been away for half the day," I counter and pick up my pace until I'm practically sprinting up the hill to Wrath's Embrace. Wrath runs beside me like it's the easiest thing in the world for him to do, which I guess it is. I'm not winded at all. Being a harbinger is definitely something I can get used to.

We don't see anyone on our way to the house, which I'm grateful for. I hadn't realized just how tense I was being under constant watch by everyone in Sweet Tooth but I feel it by the time we hit the stairs to the porch. I stop and raise my hands over my head, taking in a deep inhale. I feel lighter, like a weight has been lifted off my shoulders and it's bliss.

"It feels better up here," I tell Wrath. "There's too many people watching us in town."

Wrath opens the front door for me and I step inside with a happy sigh. "There are many eyes on us in Sweet Tooth but what you're feeling are my wards. The protection they bring will settle your soul and give you respite."

I lean into Wrath's side and relax. He's right. Each second inside of the house relaxes me a little more. "Some respite right now sounds amazing. I can't wait to get settled in and just relax. Maybe we can make dinner and see if Elijah wants to join us for a nice and peaceful-"

"Hello, lovebirds! We've been expecting you," Sunday's voice trills.

I stop walking so fast that I nearly trip and fall but Wrath catches me. "Oh my mulberries! What are you doing here?"

Sunday's smile obliterates every thought I had about a nice quiet dinner at home. She's sitting prim and proper with Nina in the living room while Elijah pours her tea and holds a three-tiered cake stand stuffed to the brim with tea cakes, sandwiches and fruit.

"What are you doing here?" I ask.

Sunday rolls her eyes at me. "We were invited, so don't get that look on your face, hellcat," she says and then nods at Elijah. "Thank you for the tea. This is delightful."

"Invited?" I take a cautious step into the living room and scan the room looking for anyone else that might be here but it's empty. "Who invited you?"

"Your acolyte did, of course. I have to say, you picked a quality follower with this one. And on your first go, too. Color me impressed. Did you know he bakes? The best cinnamon rolls I've ever had."

I give Elijah a searching look. "You invited her in? What part of 'keep a low profile' did you not understand?"

The lights flicker and there's a sharp crack that makes me think of when the ice on the lake in town splinters and cracks at night after a warm day. We all look to Wrath to see he's returned to his demon form. Elijah whimpers at the sight.

Wrath's eyes flash silver. "*This will not do*," he growls and steps toward the trio while Elijah looks like he might faint. Sunday doesn't look concerned and Nina's too busy grabbing tea cakes to really get a good look at Wrath as he stalks towards them.

I hurry after Wrath. "Let's hear them out. We're working with Sunday, so her being here is okay, right? We're all on the same... you know, team. Isn't that what you said we were?"

"I *will* have satisfaction." His tail flicks. He points a finger at Elijah and I stop trying to get him to calm down. "Get in the kitchen. *Now.*"

"The kitchen?" Elijah squeaks and then looks at me. "Harbinger, I humbly ask for your protection from your husband."

"I dunno, he looks kind of ticked. Maybe go in the kitchen," Sunday chimes in and plucks a strawberry from the serving tray Elijah is still holding. "I mean, what's the worst that can happen? You end up covered in oil? Maybe they have to take their shirts off, too?" She leans back in her chair and feigns a look of horror. "That would just be so terrible."

"He could die," Nina pipes up and gestures with her tea cup between Wrath and Elijah. "I mean, he could kill him easily. Not that it takes much to kill someone..." she says, her voice going soft at the end. I make a mental note to see how she's doing, but first?

First, I have to make sure Wrath doesn't murder my acolyte.

"Hold that thought, Nina. I'll be back, okay?" Nina gives me a nod before I dash into the kitchen after Wrath and Elijah. When I burst into the kitchen I'm not sure what to make of the scene, because it's not what I expected to find.

"Don't...don't hurt him?" I try, because I don't think putting a hurt on Elijah is on Wrath's agenda, not when they're both putting aprons on.

"I just wanted to make a good impression, my king."

Wrath arches an eyebrow and snaps the strings of his apron into a bow. "Oh, *king* now is it? You've finally remembered that you originally served me? All it took was one harbinger for you to forget."

"She's very formidable, my king. I've never seen anything like her fury."

"You speak true enough. For that you may keep your life."

"This is because I invited the Witch of the Woods, isn't it?"

"Partly."

Elijah whimpers and I snap my fingers at them both and they freeze. "Hey, none of that! No killing in the house."

Elijah slumps against the counter but puts his apron on all the same. "This *so* isn't fair. All I wanted to do was make a good impression while I was in charge of headquarters! I thought, maybe, just maybe, the Witch of the Woods would be a good ally. She was so convincing when she came to the door."

"I told you not to answer the door," I groan and look over my shoulder. Sunday and Nina are still at the table enjoying the tea spread Elijah made them. I lower my voice when I speak. "Sunday is already on the team but she's a loose cannon, okay? Inviting her in probably wasn't smart."

I'm not lying. Sunday is unpredictable at best, even if she did save me and offer to hold the moon to buy us more time. There's a reason she's interfering at all and so far she's not telling us why.

Whatever it is, I know it's for her own gain and I don't know how close I like having her when the entire town is watching us. If we were seen cavorting with the Witch of the Woods, they might not abide by my being married to Wrath as a reason not to hit us all at once and kill the other Blossoms before I can find them.

The big man taps his chin thoughtfully. "She seemed so innocent," Elijah murmurs.

Wrath barks out a laugh. "You thought *Sunday* looked innocent? I may support your devotion to my wife, acolyte, but Sunday is the furthest thing from innocent and you'd do well to remember that."

Elijah pulls a face but doesn't say anything. He crosses his arms and takes a deep breath. "I'm ready to face my challenge. I will dedicate this win to Sunday–The Witch of the Woods."

"Did someone say my name?" Sunday asks, popping up from the other side of the kitchen island. Elijah and I grab each other with a scream while Wrath sighs and stares up at the ceiling.

"If we could stay focused on the matter at hand, please? There's not much time to put things right and I will not have this day end with my honor at stake."

"And how is it at stake, exactly? Because this hunk bakes better than you?" Sunday asks and shoots a wink to Elijah who blushes and looks away. "Aw, look, he's shy. I like that in a man. Don't worry, sweetie, I don't bite unless you ask me nicely."

"You really thought she was innocent?" I ask Elijah, who blushes so deeply his ears turn pink.

"I accept your challenge, King Wrath. The Bake Off starts now!" He declares and throws his hands up.

Wrath claps his hands. "Finally." He heads for the pantry while I try to process what I just heard.

"Did you say Bake Off?"

"Verily," Wrath replies and practically rips the pantry door off when he jerks it open and grabs a sack of flour. "My honor as the most talented baker of cinnamon rolls will *not* be challenged by an upstart like your acolyte."

"His name is Elijah."

"Acolyte Elijah," Wrath says, "will not best me. *I am The Baker*. That is my role, that is my place, and I will accept nothing less."

"You're a demon an entire town worships. You're on a revenge spree through town with your unhinged wife and that's the role you choose?" Sunday asks and hops up on the counter while Wrath and Elijah sprint around the kitchen. Elijah has an armful of bowls and a carton of eggs while Wrath is busy measuring flour and milk.

"Did we preheat the oven?" Wrath asks and Elijah stops what he's doing. The pair exchange a look before Elijah charges towards the oven.

"On it!"

I watch them for another second before I leave the trio to it and head back into the living room where Nina is. She's still at the table making her way through the platter of bonbons with a happy smile when I slide into the seat across from her.

"Hey, Buffy." Nina's smile is real. I can tell because it reaches her eyes.

"Hey, Nina. How are you?"

"I'm great," she says and holds up the bonbons.

"Are you sure?" I swallow hard and shift in my seat. I can feel the corners of my mouth trying to pull up into a smile—it's my default response, the one that's been conditioned so thoroughly into me that even now when there's no one to care if my smile breaks or not, I still do it.

Nina pauses her bonbon eating and looks back at me. She doesn't smile, she frowns. "I mean, the death thing kinda sucked but I'm good now. At least, mostly."

"Your smile," I start and I hate myself, because why am I bringing it up? There's no one to make us say what I almost said and yet...why is it so hard to let go?

"Is mine now," Nina says and puts the bonbon platter down. She leans forward and looks me over. "Are you okay? How are *you* holding up?"

"Okay, I think...at least, mostly. I'm mostly okay."

"Kinda intense, what you're going through."

"Same as you," I point out.

She nods. "Yeah but there's nothing and no one depending on me. My parents sold me out to the cult and I died like I was supposed to. No one expects me to be the one that saves them. No one in town has even seen me yet. They think I'm dead."

"Oh."

"You, though. You're a different story, Buffy. You always have been."

"What do you mean?"

"You cried when you were little," Nina says and drops her eyes to where her hands are clasped in her lap. "It was over your dog."

"Blossom," I whisper.

"Yeah, that's the one. Crying over losing a dog is normal but you did it where everyone could see. You didn't care, not even when I heard my parents talking about how it was going to get you kicked out of being a Blossom. They were excited, because they thought I would take your place."

The familiar feeling of losing Blossom swirls in my chest and realization hits me. "That's the year you got picked."

She smiles, eyes still downcast. "Yeah, it was a month after you lost Blossom that I became one. I think they were going to take it from you but something happened and they didn't. My parents were furious and I just didn't understand. They wouldn't stop talking badly about you, but you were so nice. You felt everything when the rest of us were scared to."

"Nina, I-"

"And that didn't change, not when we grew up and went to school. The rest of us didn't really feel a lot for our grooms but you were head over heels for Callum. You made it into a fairytale that I wanted to believe. You lit up the room when you entered it. I always wanted to be like you. You were braver than me, braver than most of the others, because of how you saw people. Remember when Ms. Donna's smile broke? You were there first thing the next morning with Callum. If you hadn't done that I don't think she would have kept her job."

Nina's right. When a woman's smile broke, the repercussions were always harsh. The Founders made an example to the rest of us. I'd gone there with Callum on account of wanting to protect her. If Callum was friendly with Ms. Donna then I knew nothing would happen to her. Mr. O'Hare wouldn't be able to remove her from the bakery if Callum was involved. It worked, too.

"No one else was brave enough to do that but you were."

"I had too. I couldn't let them hurt her more than Aguirre had."

Nina looks up at me. "That's the thing, you didn't have too. Just like you don't have to now, Buffy. You have a demon husband that can protect you. Not even that, you're a harbinger. Do you know what that means?"

"A little but I'm still figuring it out," I admit. "I'm strong now though." I'm more than strong, I felt invincible today in the basement. There wasn't a soul that could have escaped me but I keep that to myself.

"I did some reading. Well, a lot of reading. When you're dead, you don't sleep anymore. Lots of time for books, Buffy. Learned a lot about what you are now and our current situation."

"Like what?"

"You'll never be scared of anyone again. Not ever. You're powerful now. *You* are the thing the Founders fear and nothing can stop you. Only the oldest magic could and I'm not even sure it exists anymore. If you wanted to, you could leave now and carry on, safe and happy with Wrath and no one would ever know."

"I would know."

Nina hums. "And that's why you're different. That's why Wrath chose you for his wife and that's why you're going to win." She swallows hard and then smiles at me. "When my parents told me I was going to be a Blossom, I was scared. My smile broke. I-I was so scared for *you*. I ran to your place, I had to make sure you were okay. That they hadn't done anything to you. When I got there, panicking and afraid—you were just fine. There you were, standing in your yard with Victor Marsh and his dog Lady. I knew that even if they had tried to do something to you that you would have still cried for Blossom."

My chest aches. I remember those tears. I cried until I had nothing left. The sorrow left by losing Blossom felt so bone deep I thought I'd never get over it. Nina is right, even when my mother begged me to stop and warned me what might happen, I didn't stop mourning Blossom.

I couldn't.

"You were so sad but the second you saw me? You invited me in. You're good, Buffy. Your heart, the good in you? That part of you that can't stand by while someone is hurt? That's your strength, you can't forget that. Not even when things get their darkest, Buffy, because they will get dark. Stay true to your heart. Promise me, promise me that you will."

Whatever books Nina is reading have to be heavy. She sounds like Sunday did when she used to haunt me with her cryptic little sayings and warnings, but I don't bring that up.

"I promise."

Those two words hang in the air between us for a beat before there's a crash and I hear Sunday scream bloody murder. Nina and I rise from our seats to go see what the rest of the team is getting up to in the kitchen.

TWENTY-FIVE

"This one is my favorite." I say and pull my blindfold off to see Elijah grimacing and grabbing his chest like I just stabbed him through the heart. Considering the stress and work that went into this impromptu bake off with Wrath, it might feel that way to him.

I shoot Elijah an apologetic look. "It wasn't yours, huh?"

He shakes his head remorsefully. "Nope. Again, it wasn't mine. I've failed you, Harbinger. Don't look at me. Not like this." Elijah throws up his hands to hide himself from me while Sunday tuts and pats his shoulder, stealing a bite from the plate Elijah's cinnamon roll is on.

They just blind tested me, with a blind fold and everything, for the second time. The verdict is still the same. I prefer Wrath's cinnamon rolls to Elijah's. On the bright side, Sunday thinks Elijah's are the best.

"Sunday likes yours better," I remind him while Wrath puffs

out his chest in victory and comes to my side. "And it's really quite good, it was so close."

"But you still like mine better," Wrath clarifies.

"Correct," I tell him and kiss him. I reach up and run my hand along the base of his horn and the change in him is instant. He shivers and leans closer to me with a barely muffled moan that has Sunday raising an eyebrow while Nina continues to eat her cinnamon roll.

"Get a room, you two. Horn fondling? Right here in front of everyone? I didn't take you for a minx, Buffy."

I blush and drop my hand. "Sorry, I just-I miss his horns when he's all human," I say, wiggling my fingers longingly at his horns. Wrath opens his eyes and crosses his arms at me, which means I might have said the wrong thing. "But I love your human form. I love all of your forms, really. I promise."

"Oh, is that so, wife?"

"It is, because I love you," I tell him in a rush. The world tilts beneath my feet and I feel like the room is spinning, because I just told him that I love him in front of everyone while I'm pretty sure I still have cinnamon roll icing on my face.

Wrath's face breaks out into a smile. "I love you too."

Holy shit. He loves me.

Nina sighs and clasps her hands together with a dreamy smile on her face. "How wonderful," she whispers while Sunday gives us both a pleased look.

"I knew you would be a good match. I approve. Don't you?" she asks Elijah, who looks like he might faint from happiness.

"Oh, yes, love is magical," he tells her and Sunday slides closer to him.

"Ah, you're a romantic, are you? I love romantics," she purrs but I'm not looking to see Elijah's reaction to her. I only have eyes for Wrath.

"You love me?" I ask him. I manage to get the words out far easier than I would have ever thought and for a wild second I'm proud of myself, before I realize what I've done. I've not only told him I love him but I'm asking if he really loves me. In front of everyone.

Oh mulberries.

"I mean," I swallow hard and my skin burns hot, "I mean, uh, let's just forget that I-"

"Of course I love you." Wrath reaches up and his fingers slide along our bond. The stroke of his fingers is gentle but it makes it light right up between us. "Your body is mine and mine is yours. That includes my heart, Buffy. I would promise you my soul, but I haven't had one of those in quite some time. What is left of me is eternally yours, beloved."

My eyes prickle with unshed tears and I'm not so embarrassed because now I can't see if Nina and the rest of them are watching me. I lean into Wrath's touch and press my hand to his chest where our bond sparkles and shines.

"I love you," I whisper to my husband.

"Do you think they're all asleep?" I ask Wrath. I just tiptoed into our bedroom after I handed off a fresh set of bed linens to Nina. I know Sunday can teleport them right out of here if she wanted, but for now the witch is content to stay put.

As much as I don't trust her, it's nice to have her nearby. If Sunday is here it's not just Wrath and I protecting the others.

Though, Nina did confirm she's dead now, so I guess it's really just Elijah that would need protecting if anyone made it past the wards like Sunday did.

Whatever magic she's wielding, it's powerful to get past Wrath.

Wrath pauses where he's turning down the bed and tilts his head to listen. The house creaks and shifts like a centuries old house ought to in the night, but we both hear a laugh from down the hall. "Sunday is taken by Elijah," he says.

"As long as she doesn't hurt him. He's, you know, sweet."

"And a second rate baker," Wrath adds smugly.

I sigh and cross my arms. "Be nice. Not everyone has had an eternity to master the finer points of baking cinnamon rolls."

"No, but they are missing out. Though, not so much as I right now," Wrath rumbles. His eyes go dark before a shine of silver colors them and I shiver. I know what that look means. Even if I didn't, I'd feel his hunger for me through our bond.

Wrath has to be feeling the same thing coming from me. My lust and need for him is on a hairpin trigger and ready to go.

That doesn't mean that I don't ask.

"What do you mean?"

He grins and takes a step towards the ensuite bathroom. "I think I'll show you after you've bathed. I'll prepare the bath now." He moves with grace so at odds with his large size, horns making it inside the bathroom with a quick duck of his head.

"Will you join me?" I call out to him and I hear him bump into something.

I tense, barely daring to breathe while I wait for him to speak and then finally, Wrath does. "Yes, beloved." I hear the squeak of the taps in the tub turn on before rushing water sounds. I wait, frozen in place with the knowledge that I'm about to not just be alone, but alone, wet and very naked with Wrath in just a few minutes. When they taught us about our wedding nights, about the most pleasing way to attract our grooms, how we should look, what we should do, all of it was geared to being the perfect bride.

Performing perfectly for the men we wed. That's not what's happening tonight, because the demon I've married only seeks to please *me*. It is freeing and exhilarating, but it's also scary.

I have zero clue what to do. I was never trained for accepting pleasure. I look around the room in a panic, trying to think my way through how to get in the tub with as much finesse as possible. In the end, when the bath is prepared and ready, I'm rummaging through the closet Wrath magicked my clothes into. I have just settled on a white robed dress that looks equal parts pretty and slinky enough to pass as seduction wear.

Wrath clears his throat and I jump a mile high, my dress pressed to my chest and a smile barely clinging to my face.

"Is the bath rea-adheeeyy, *mulberries*." I choke out, ending the last word on a whisper. I almost scream and faint, because Wrath is certainly ready for the bath. He's naked and proud.

He stands in front of me with the ease of someone comfortable in their own body. Which I understand, because the demon is gorgeous. He looks like what I thought an angel might look like, what the photos in the books the Founders approved for our schooling showed us of perfect sculptures.

Broad shoulders, a muscular defined chest, a tapered waist with honed abs, thick thighs and strong legs. Of course, the first and only cock that I've ever seen as well. Wrath's cock is beautiful, just like the rest of him. Thick and long, slightly curved with a

245

fat head. It hangs heavy between his legs and lust electrifies my body. It zips right through me, from my toes to the top of my head. My clit aches knowing I will be on my knees in front of him soon enough. What he did to me in the basement today?

I want to do it to him. I want to explore every inch of him while I am the one on my knees in worship.

"See anything you like, dear wife?" Wrath drawls and moves toward me. The same grace I saw before is there again. His movements are languid and swaying and it makes me want to move with him, so I do. I meet him at the foot of the bed with my dress still clutched in my hands.

"You know I do. You're beautiful."

"Not as beautiful as you."

I bite my lip because I know Wrath won't let me say a word against him, so I just nod. "Thank you."

Wrath's big hand joins mine where I clutch the dress. "Is this what you would like to wear tonight?" he asks, running his fingers along my knuckles to touch the fabric gently.

I shiver and nod. I've never wanted to be a slip of fabric more than I do right now. "I thought I could wear it after our bath."

Our bath. Oh mulberries. The way it sets my cheeks on fire. I must sound so inexperienced to him. When I lift my eyes to meet his I see that he isn't looking at me like he's noticed any of the things I'm worried about.

Adoration.

That's the only word to describe the look in his eyes. He catches the dress and takes it from me and a simple nudge from his fingers sends the bond wrapping tightly around me.

"A fine choice for my beautiful bride. Come with me, there's so much of you I wish to see and touch." I follow him into the bathroom where he carefully folds my dress for me. When we get to the tub, I let him undress me.

I shiver when the cool air kisses my skin and try not to shrink away when Wrath's eyes move over me with each piece of clothing he strips off me. One by one my clothes end up on the floor at my feet until I'm left shaking. My body hums with the electricity I used to feel when the Founders trotted me and the others out as examples of what the others should be—anyone hoping to become a Blossom was meant to think, act and talk like me. It was such a rush to be held up as the ideal in such a small, small world.

I bought into the lies so easily.

There are no lies here now. Just the bare and aching truth of who I am and how I feel for Wrath. Truth's bite is sharp and quick, enough to make me raise my arms to try and cover my bare breasts from him, but he catches my hands and stops me.

"You are perfect, Buffy."

Perfect. He thinks I'm perfect. I've never been perfect for anyone and yet...

To him, I simply am.

Everything around us softens in the gentle glow of the bathroom and it's then I notice there are candles everywhere.

I drop my arms and smile, but it's hard to meet his eyes. "You lit candles," I whisper. Everything is turned up to eleven and I'm grateful I can hide in the shadows of the candlelight.

"I did."

"Why?"

"You deserve candles, beloved."

I lose the battle against the tears I've held off since we exchanged '*I love you*' and the first tear slides down my cheek and onto the floor with a little plop. The sound of it is deafening in the silent bathroom. The only thing I can hear is that tear hitting the floor and the steady thump of my heart.

Wrath's fingers are gentle on me and he moves his thumb across my cheek, swiping away the next tear with a sigh. "Buffy."

I expect him to tell me not to cry, but he doesn't. He only gathers me close. The warmth and bulk of his body grounds me in the moment and I let him hold me. I sink into Wrath and soak up his strength like a dying plant. It feels like I've been in a storm so long that I've forgotten what tenderness, what *safety,* can soothe. What it feels like to simply be. I take in a deep breath and smile despite my tears.

"You are a gift," I tell him.

Wrath rubs my back and hums in response. The sound of it is low and when the pitch rises I realize it's a song. Each note rises and falls and the melody is sweet, but there are no words. I sway with Wrath as he hums his song to me. We stand like that for a minute or so more before he falls silent and kisses the top of my head.

"That was pretty. What song was it?"

"I don't know. It's ancient, a tune I heard once when I was young on a walk through meadows long made fallow on a planet that no longer exists. I've never known the words but it's sweet and you deserve sweet, beloved."

Lust is a capricious thing that I've not yet managed to understand. The shift in the energy between us is almost instant. The sweeter Wrath is with me, the hotter my blood grows for him, and the more I need him to demonhandle me.

I have a great need for my husband at this moment and I'm

not going to worry about doing it right or how awkward I might be. I'm going to seize the day and do something about it.

My hand shakes but I reach for him, just the graze of my fingertips along his hip before I slowly drop my hand lower. "And what if I want more than sweet?" I keep sliding my hand down until my fingers are touching his dick. I circle my fingers around him and slowly start to stroke. Wrath goes still and sucks in a deep breath when I give him an experimental squeeze.

I freeze and stare at where my hand is wrapped around him. The sight of his dick, the thick length of it in my hands, makes my clit ache and I press my thighs together to try to keep it together.

"Was that bad? I mean, did I hurt you or-"

"No, no, that was very, very good. You're a very quick study. Why don't you give it another try, hmm?" He lowers his head and kisses my neck. It's only a second before I feel his teeth in my flesh and I cry out, my grip tightening around his dick out of reflex.

"Buffy," he moans and gathers me close. "You don't know the power you have over me."

"I like that." I drop my other hand down to stroke the underside of his balls. After a few tentative touches he moves his hands down to mine and shows me exactly how to touch him.

"That's it," he encourages me when I cup his balls and he leans down to spit on his dick for me. "Mmm, tighter, just like that. You're a natural. About to bring me to my knees."

I preen under his praise and drop down to my knees myself. I stop before I taste him and look up at Wrath. "Is this okay? I want-I want to do what you did to me earlier." I hold myself back from touching him until he answers me.

An expression that looks like pain flits over his face before he swallows hard and stokes the crown of my head. "Yes, oh yes, my ruthless little wife. Take from me what you please tonight. I invite you to make my body yours."

He invites me. That's better than a yes if I ever heard one.

I waste no time after hearing Wrath's free-for-all invitation and lean down to lick the head of his dick. There's a bead of precum on his head. I've heard all about this from the other girls but it's not salty, musky, bitter or even sour like I heard it could be. It's pleasant, sweet without being overly so. The taste reminds me of what fresh baked sugar cookies smell like. Inviting, warm, a hint of vanilla with a smooth finish. I moan and grip him tighter as I lick the underside of his mushroom headed dick and take him back into my mouth.

Vanilla explodes on my tongue as I take another inch of him and another until it's hard to breathe and Wrath's head hits the back of my throat. Wrath's hand is still at the crown of my head and the weight of it sends a flood of pleasure through me. I start to move, slowly at first, with the guidance of his hand encouraging me faster or slower as I please. I bring my other hand up to move with the first, palms pressing firmly to him, my fingers curled tightly around him and still not meeting in the middle. He's so thick that it makes the muscles in my jaw and cheeks ache from the stretch of him, but I don't stop.

I can't. Not when I feel every little delicious shake and shudder that my movements send through Wrath. When I flex my fingers he whimpers and when I suck him harder, hollowing out my cheeks from how intently focused I am on him, he shakes. Spit and precum make a mess of me but I don't care. Even in my messiness, Wrath finds delight.

"Buffy," he groans, breath ragged and raw. I love hearing him say my name like this, as if there's no other thought that could ever exist in his mind but my name. That I am, in this moment, the be all and end all for my demon. He swells, his dick becoming fatter than I thought possible and I slide free from him with a messy pop that has me choking and coughing. It's not sexy, but it's real. Though, maybe it *is* sexy from the way Wrath grabs my jaw, the whole of his hand encompassing me to tilt my head back as he devours my lips in a messy kiss.

He yanks me to my feet and I flail before I grab on to him. He steps forward, his still hard dick bobbing between us and poking my belly from where it's pressed between us. He lifts me higher and I think for one delirious moment he's going to bring me down on him, impale me right on his hard length but no, he doesn't.

Instead, he holds me tight and lowers us into the still steaming bath that pulses purple and blue around us.

Magic. He's used magic on the bath and it's not just to keep it warm. I know that when I feel the heat of it make my muscles heavy and relaxed. There's an electricity to my skin that can only come from the water and when I lift my hand out of it, color clings to my fingertips.

Oh yeah, definitely magic water.

I lower my hand back into the pastel bath and wiggle closer to Wrath with one aim. I want to ride him until I'm cross-eyed and can't remember my name. The closest I can come to taking him inside of me is slotting the curve of his dick between my thighs. I undulate my hips and my eyes nearly roll into the back of my head when my clit slides up and down the width of him.

"Wrath," I try and shake my head before I roll my hips again, faster this time and grab hold of his shoulders. "*Please.*"

The bath pulses a deeper color now. Fuchsia and jewel-toned teal dance around us and my skin lights up with the change.

"Patience, beloved." Wrath kisses me deeply. He steals my breath and I gasp and move as fast as I can. I lose my rhythm in my desperation but only for a moment before his hands go to my hips and my frantic, jerky movements are slowed. He shows me how to move my hips in time with his. I forget how to breathe when I feel the familiar roll of pleasure start to build in me. It's the kind of exhilaration that starts at the bottoms of your feet, like before the rollercoaster you're on plunges from the top of the tracks or when you've spun and spun in circles and finally come to a stop. This is that moment when the world still flies right on by and you feel weightless, limitless. When it's impossible to know up or down right before the world and gravity force you back into your body and you remember everything again.

Water sloshes around us and I hear it hit the floor with a splash as the dance of shadows over our bodies paints a haunting picture that makes me smile. I close my eyes and press my face against Wrath's chest. I follow his direction, the press and grip of his hands on my body that show me the steps of this dance we're locked in.

I couldn't stop now if I tried, so I don't try. I smile against his slippery skin as his tail moves close. It slides along my back and takes the place of his hands, the muscle in it flexing and anchoring itself around my waist.

Wrath dips his fingers down between my thighs and I keen high, head falling forward until my forehead presses to his chest for support as he slides two fingers inside of me. It's so, so good.

"That's it, my darling wife. Look at you, come apart for me

now. Let me see you, Buffy." He scissors his fingers, curls them and strokes a place inside of me that has me gasping.

"Wrath, yes. *Yes*." I dig my fingernails into him. I know it's going to leave marks but the thought makes me proud. I lean forward to use the leverage as best I can. I rise and fall with a satisfied moan as I take Wrath's fingers deeper. I repeat the motion and my thighs shake and start to burn but I tune it out and listen to my body. Wrath slides an arm across my back and curls his fingers around my shoulder to add more punch to my downward motion even as he lifts his hips to meet mine. The fingers inside of me only whet my appetite for his long, hard dick between my thighs. The curve of him hugs close to me and the head of it nudges against my ass every time I move.

I close my eyes and bite my lip while I imagine the fingers inside of me are what I want most— Wrath's dick.

The people that raised me meant to have me killed and still they raised me to be shy and docile, to give in to whatever it was that my husband was going to ask of me.

Right now, with Wrath, I'm anything but.

Water swirls around us and droplets slide down our bodies. Rivulets glow where it touches us. It makes me think of stars. Stars painted on our skin. I shift closer and Wrath helps me, his strong hands holding my hips and helping me move. Shadows play across his face but Wrath's eyes shine silver back at me. He has such beautiful eyes, not even the darkness around us dims his light. I come closer like a moth drawn to a bright and shining flame.

"Wrath," I sob out, his name uttered like a prayer for the very reason I meant it like that. I cling to my husband as I feel him brush up against my mind. All it takes is that single touch of

Wrath's consciousness for me to tip over the edge and I cry out his name in a choked gasp.

"Wrath!"

My body spasms and I lose control of my limbs. If Wrath wasn't holding me, I'd slip beneath the pastel water and drown blissfully right now. I whimper and squeeze my eyes shut while the aftershocks of my pleasure roll through me and leave me shivering in Wrath's arms.

He gathers me close, slowly brushing my wet hair away from my face and smiles down at me. I'm not looking at him, but I know he's smiling. I can tell by his voice.

"Stars, is it, beloved? I will give you more than you can count."

I smile in return and open one eye. "Didn't you just do that?"

"This?" he asks and gives the water around us a flick. It shimmers like the glitter we use on the centerpieces for the Blossom Banquets. That stuff always got everywhere and even a week later you would be finding glitter in the oddest places.

"What do you mean *this?* Of course this," I say and splash him with the technicolor sex bath. "What else is there but this?"

"Why, the real thing, Buffy."

"Show me."

TWENTY-SIX

"When you said the real thing and I said *show me*, I think, well, I think I was overzealous," I say. I'm standing in front of the window in my slinky dress and staring out at Wrath. I'm staring out because he's outside.

Floating outside, that is.

"There's nothing to fear, Buffy. Come with me now. I'll keep you safe." Wind ruffles his hair and the moonlight shines bright like a spotlight crafted especially to highlight the perfection of my husband. When he moves, the light shifts and makes Wrath glow like an angel.

Or the god his cult thought him to be.

I take a shaking step closer to the window and eyeball the hand he's holding out to me. "I think...maybe in here is good, though. You know, when I think about it, I don't think the virtues of the great indoors are extolled enough."

I've never been good with heights but even if I was, floating outside as easily as you please would still probably have the same effect on me. That effect being that I'm scared. I rub my sweaty palms on my thighs and edge a little closer to the window. I don't know why I'm stalling. I'll give in to him eventually.

"Do you think I'll drop you?"

"No, of course not.'

"Then come here, beloved."

My damnable feet have a mind of their own and I end up in front of the window. "We're really going outside?" I ask and look past him to the night sky.

"We are and when we do, you will see how good it can be to let go. To let me take over is ecstasy, Buffy. Don't you want to know that?" he asks and floats closer to the window. He holds a hand out to me once more. I'm helpless to resist him.

I slip my hand into his. "Yes."

Wrath moves back and I'm halfway out of it already, because I refuse to let go of him. Wrath holds out another hand to me and lovesick woman that I am, I reach for that too and step out of the window.

I don't fall. I knew I wouldn't with Wrath but still the fear was there. Humans aren't meant to fly, after all but I'm not exactly all human anymore. Not as Wrath's Harbinger.

We rise up in the air until we're high above the house. Sweet Tooth is spread out in front of and I can see the lights of the homes and businesses twinkling like stars. So close, yet so far away. It could be the distance or the fact that I'm in Wrath's arms that the town I've known all my life looks harmless from here. I'm almost certain it's the latter.

Nothing can hurt me with Wrath at my side. I look at him and relax the death grip I have on his shoulders.

Wrath nods encouragingly at me. "I'll never drop you, beloved," he whispers in my ear and I shiver. Wind caresses my skin and the nightgown I'm wearing billows out around me. The silk of it flares around us and wraps around our legs. I let my hand drift lower and my fingers explore Wrath's warm muscled body. The water from our bath is long gone but I trace the path I remember the water took. He moves with me and my husband's hungry touch devours every part of me while he consumes me one kiss at a time as the ache of my clit begs for more. He moves close and strokes me gently as we continue to rise through the air. Wind rushes around us and I smile up at him. The clouds move, they rise and fall until I can't see Sweet Tooth anymore.

Wrath kisses me and the air changes temperature. It warms until my skin heats and the next stroke of his fingers inside of me has my dress melting away to nothing.

He moves forward and he's on top of me, Sweet Tooth at my back below. Wrath moves down until he's beneath my thighs. The first thrust of his tongue inside of me has me grabbing his horns tightly and crying out.

"You belong to me, Buffy." Wrath's grip on my hips is tight and when he jerks me to him to devour me, I moan. He circles my clit, moving closer and closer while working his fingers inside of me, faster and faster until he finally takes my clit into his mouth and gives me friction where I've wanted it the most.

"Wrath!"

"Every part of you is mine. Your heart, your soul, *this body*." He growls the last word against me and I climax with a scream.

"Your screams are so sweet to me. Give me another, *wife*." He crooks his fingers inside of me and urges me to move until I roll my hips and grind against his face. "That's it. More. Give me more."

I'm so wet and when I look down my body Wrath lifts his head to look at me. His full lips shine in the moonlight with my spend and I dig my heels into his muscled back. There's nothing here but us now. Peace settles in my heart and the only thing on my mind is the hunger and need I feel for my husband. I've waited long enough for him. I tug on his horns, pulling him up my body.

I wrap my arms around his neck and lean in close to him to whisper in his ear. "I'm ready."

We move together. His arms circle me and moonlight paints our bodies. Everywhere I touch him shadows move and dance. The thick head of Wrath's cock nudges at my entrance and when he rocks forward my demon steals the gasp that comes to my lips with a kiss.

He kisses me slowly, hands gentle on me while he thrusts into me. I rake my nails down his back when he speeds up. Wrath fucks into me with force until I have to hold on to him to keep my bearings.

"Wrath!"

"That's my wife. My ruthless little wife." He wraps his arms around me and rises up enough to look down at me. It's when our eyes meet that I come undone again. Pure love shines back at me from my husband and I surrender my body wholly to him. Over and over I move to keep up with the pace my husband has set, but there's no prayer of me matching him when I can barely breathe from the pleasure he's pulled out of me once again. It's bliss and when Wraths follows after me with a hoarse shout, it's with love.

He holds me to him, our bodies rising and falling together in shared breath.

"You are the only thing I have ever wanted for myself."

CHAPTER
TWENTY-SEVEN

When I wake up the next morning it's not to the security alarm going off, which is a plus. I'm also not alone, which is an even bigger plus. Wrath is asleep beside me. Sunlight pours in through the window and the demon I call my husband looks almost heavenly in the early light. I reach out a finger and stroke it along the curve of his horn, though I'm careful to keep my touch light. Even if his horns look like weapons, I remember just how sensitive they are and I don't want to wake my husband up.

Not until I've had my fill of him.

I turn on my side and move closer to him. He shifts and I freeze. I practically hold my breath while I wait for Wrath to settle back into his sleep. One second passes and then another before his breathing evens out and I resume my exploration of him. Last night, in the moonlight with the world at our feet, Wrath was bare to me, but I couldn't take my time to look at him like I am now. Last night he took me apart and put me back together, which really didn't leave me with more than a single coherent brain cell. I curl a lock of his snowy hair between my fingers and wrap it around my finger. His hair is soft and silky and I lose the battle with myself to take my time with him. I bury my hand in his hair and grin when his eyelashes flutter and he opens his eyes.

"Can't keep your hands off me, can you, wife?"

"To be honest, no," I answer him truthfully and roll into his arm when he holds it out to me. Wrath draws me in and I cuddle closer to his side. "I wanted to touch you while I could think."

His hand moves across my back, his touch light. "An admirable decision, but I think I like you addled."

"What are you-"

Wrath moves quickly, bringing me with him and settling me beneath him. The warm weight of him on top of me definitely has the effect he knew it would and it's hard to think of anything other than where we touch.

He leans in close to me, a hand drifting down my side and I moan when he grips my hip. "My ruthless little wife," he whispers into my ear.

So much for thinking. I'm done for.

I lift my leg intending to wrap it around him, but a crash in the hallway makes us both freeze. Wrath lifts his head and looks towards the door. "What was that?"

"I thought you said the wards were in place," I say.

"I did. They are."

"But Sunday-"

"Has no ill intent and is a powerful witch. The cultists in

Sweet Tooth," Wrath scoffs and sits up straight, taking me with him. "Those fools wouldn't know the first thing about my wards. Something else is amiss."

"Right then," I sigh and clap my hands against his shoulders before I point to the door. "Let's go investigate."

Wrath stands and kisses me. "I like it when you're commanding."

"I'm commanding?" I ask and preen under his attention. I've never been commanding in my entire life. At least I wasn't until Wrath. "That was commanding, really?"

"Truly." He opens the door and sticks his head out. "What's going on out here?"

"Who wants to know?" Sunday hollers back.

"I do!" I shout down the hallway from my perch in Wrath's arms. Sunday's head pops out of a room down the hall.

"Oh, why hello there hellcat, so sorry to have awakened you. I was just showing dear Elijah here a little maneuver I learned last century. Would you like to see?" There's a thump and a muffled moan that has me waving my hand at her.

"Go back in there. Do not show me."

"Suit yourself," Sunday sighs and slams the door.

"Do you think he's okay?" I ask Wrath who shrugs and puts me down.

"If he's lasted this long, I think he's enjoying it."

"Fair point."

"So then where are you two off to this early in the morning? The sun's hardly risen." Sunday has her back to me, a pot of coffee in her hand while Elijah cooks bacon with a serious case of bed head.

Wrath and I have eaten breakfast already, or at least I have. I don't think he needs to eat, even if he does enjoy baking. Nina was already waiting for us at the kitchen table with a book in her hand when we arrived. She's since finished that book and moved on to another, so she's definitely making the most of her new situation.

"You're going after the Blossoms, aren't you?" Nina asks and I nod at her.

"Yes. Charlie Vallencourt showed us a video of where the others are being held. They're with Aguirre now. We have a map that Charlie drew for us to show exactly where they are."

"Where are they?" Nina asks and I shudder.

"Charlie called it Aguirre's 'little torture chamber of secrets' so wherever it is, it can't be good. We're going to go now and get a head start on things, seeing as the full moon ends tonight."

Sunday waves a coffee cup at me. "Not really. I can buy some time, hellcat. I am inclined to be useful after your acolyte's attentions."

"Um, thanks?" I offer to Elijah who looks like he wants to drop through the floor. I get it. If anyone brought up my evening air show with Wrath I'd feel the same."

Elijah clears his throat and puts a plate of bacon down on the table. "It was a magical evening."

Wrath unfolds a piece of notebook paper and puts it on the table. "Here is the map Charlie supplied. It looks like the place the Blossoms are being held is past the festival grounds," he says and taps the paper. It's the familiar shape of Sweet Tooth with X marking the spot where my friends are being held.

"That's where the greenhouses are," Nina says and tilts her head to get a better look at the map. "I never knew there was anything else out there."

The greenhouses are where the prize flowers Sweet Tooth is known for are grown. The Zinnias grown in the greenhouses are bigger, more vibrant. The smell reminds me of candy—sweet and cloying. I never cared for it, but there are people that come from all over to buy a bouquet of them. No one goes out there except for whoever is on the garden rotation and that's a select few with how important the flowers are.

"That's because none of us were allowed out there on our own. It's the perfect place for them to keep a dozen girls without anyone getting suspicious." I don't mention Mrs. Landry, because I know Nina will worry. "Wrath and I are going to investigate and rescue the Blossoms. It's going to be a quick in and out, just like we did yesterday at the Rossi's.

"You were spectacular. Truly sensational. I am confident in our victory today." Elijah stands with a proud look on his face and I know he isn't going to like what I have to say next.

"You're not going, Elijah."

His face falls. "What? Why not? I'm valuable. You need me on the team."

"I do, but I need you here more," I tell him. I hold up a hand when he looks like he's going to argue. "If any of the Blossoms come to the house, I need you here and I-I can't risk you, okay?"

If anything happened to Elijah, I don't think I'd be okay. I've already lost too much and I will him to understand that. He frowns and looks down at his hands before he sighs.

"As you wish, Harbinger."

"Thank you, Elijah. I really do mean that I need you here. Who else is going to keep this place running? If you weren't here, who knows what Sunday would be doing."

Sunday sighs and leans back against the counter with her cup of coffee. "She's right. I'm a menace."

Elijah doesn't look convinced but that's when Wrath tosses him a pouch. "What is this?" Elijah asks, barely managing to catch the pouch before it hits him in the face.

"That is a summoning stone. It functions more or less like the bond she and I share. As her follower you are now entrusted with it and will use the summoning stone to contact Buffy if anything goes wrong. Simply tap it three times and say her name. She'll hear you immediately."

Elijah takes the stone out with wide eyes. It's a deep purple and cut into a square shape almost the size of Elijah's fist.

"Is this because I'm the only one that doesn't have a phone?" I ask and Wrath grins.

"Maybe," he says and makes a show of taking his phone out in front of me. There's a text from Charlie waiting for him and I give his screen a swat. Before I can ask what Charlie wants, Elijah falls to his knees in front of me.

"I swear to use the summoning stone with the utmost care. This is an honor that I can never repay, Harbinger. If there is any news to share, you will know." He raises the stone above his head. "You can trust me, I swear it."

"Thank you, but get off your knees." I reach for Elijah but Sunday sails past me.

"I quite like him like this. Now, you two get out of here and rescue those Blossoms and stop spoiling my morning fun."

I back up and grab Wrath's hand, pointing at Nina who is already scrambling towards the door. "Let's go before we see something we shouldn't."

TWENTY-EIGHT

"I feel bad for Nina."

"She'll be able to be free once more. Once we deal with this sordid little cult she can come out of hiding," Wrath says. He's walking in front of me, squinting down at the map as he walks through the forest behind the fairgrounds.

"Why should she have to hide at all?"

"Because her existence is tied to Sunday's magic."

"And that means what, exactly?" There's a note of irritation to my words and I know Wrath hears it too when he stops walking and looks back at me. "I'm sorry, it's just...why can't she help us? She talks around it but I know she can't interfere directly. You haven't told me either. It feels like a secret between you two and I-I don't really like secrets after my entire life was one."

He frowns and comes to me immediately. "Beloved, there is a secret but it is not mine to tell. There's magic at work that keeps the why of Sunday hidden, even from her. I do not think she could tell you even if she wanted to."

"You mean like she's got a hex on her stopping her from telling me?"

Wrath nods. "Lethos' mark on this world runs deep. Sunday was not spared, the same as I, but our wounds are different. There are reasons Sunday cannot interfere and in time, you will know."

I sigh. "I shouldn't feel angry about it then you mean."

"Something like that."

I rub my temples but take a deep breath and nod with a smile. "I'm not going to push it right now, with the murder and rescue we're about to lay down on Aguirre and whoever else is there. I'm not going to let it go, either."

"I would expect nothing less of you, my ruthless little wife."

I smile at his words. "Don't try and flirt your way out of this."

Wrath's eyes move over my face and down to my lips and when he licks his bottom lip, my entire body heats. I know exactly what it feels like to have that tongue on me and I lean right into him when he strokes my cheek. "Oh the things I would do to you if we were not constrained by time."

My eyes flutter closed with a sigh. "I'm going to kill them twice as bad because of this."

"I like your enthusiasm for the hunt. It's going to come in handy in a moment." I open my eyes and Wrath hands me the map. "According to Charlie's map we will be coming upon the Blossoms soon."

I straighten up. "Right. My friends. Retribution. Let's go."

The woods we're in are dense but well traveled, at least by the few allowed to the greenhouses. There's a paved road from Sweet Tooth that leads right out to the greenhouses. Wrath and I started our trek alongside it but from the look of Charlie's map we cut through the woods to reach where the Blossoms are being held. The building is at the far corner of a cluster of buildings on Charlie's map and when I rack my memory for it I can't think of what it might be. Until I push past a tree and I see it.

"It's not a greenhouse. I know this place," I whisper, staring at the stone building. It's small and low to the ground, which is why I thought it was just a shed, really. I always assumed it was where the tools and things were kept. Every time I saw someone enter and leave the building it was with a pitchfork or a scythe, some-times a pair of shears or some other tool. I never thought there was anything sinister about any of it but now I know better—Charlie's map tells me so. A bird caws overhead and then there's a shift in the light. Everything goes...gray.

It's like a veil has fallen over everything and it reminds me of what it was like the night I met Wrath. The air has the same kind of charge to it. The world has gone heavy here and when I take a step forward it sounds muffled. I frown and look down at gravel beneath my feet. I give a rock a kick and it skips along but hardly makes a sound.

"Something isn't right."

Wrath nods and takes my arm. "There's a dark enchantment on this place. Let's go. The sooner I can have you away from this place the better. It's tainted."

"Dark enchantment? Tainted? Sounds about right for the people holding my friends," I mutter and take a deep breath before I take off at a jog towards the not garden shed. I stop in front of the door and roll my shoulders. "Whatever happens, just get my friends out."

Wrath goes still beside me and I'm not surprised when he reaches for me. "Buffy-"

I turn to him and grab the hand he has extended to me. "I

mean it. Please. You have to make sure Meadow gets free."

His brow furrows and I watch him turn into his demon self. The human facade of him fades as quickly as mist in the morning and the ball of nerves in my stomach loosens some. It's easy to not be terrified when Wrath looks normal.

"Who is Meadow to you? You speak of her often."

"She's my best friend," I whisper to him and swallow hard. "I-I think you'd like her."

"Best friend?" he says like he's testing the word out. "You consider this Meadow to be your sister, then?"

"I do."

Wrath inclines his head. "Then I will see to her safety, beloved."

I smile at him and like all my smiles for him, it's real. "I love you."

It's always real when it's Wrath. It always will be.

I throw my arms around him and kiss him. I put my entire soul into the kiss and let my love flow for him through our bond. The beauty of his demon form means there's no hiding it and it shines bright when I pull back from him. I don't make it a step though before he kisses me back, his lips brushing against mine when he speaks.

"I love you more. Now, go fell your enemies."

I beam at him. "Gladly." I turn to the door and consider it. The door is made of metal, maybe iron, but its surface is rusty and the hinges have turned practically orange-red from it. I lean close and inspect the door, looking for an easy way in. There's no way it'll open without a screeching sound loud enough to wake the dead.

"They'll hear us coming. There's no way this is going to open quietly," I tell Wrath, who hums in agreement. Then I do the only reasonable thing anyone would do in my place.

I kick it in.

Metal gives under my foot like paper and the hinges scream in protest but the door comes right off. It slams against the wall and I take a step in.

"How was this quieter?" Wrath asks, following me inside.

"It's not but at least it's my choice."

"Bold."

"Thank you, sweetheart." Wrath blushes at my words, but I don't get to enjoy the pretty picture he makes before someone yells.

"You there! Stop right now!"

I sigh in disappointment when I see the room from Charlie's video. The stone building isn't a garden shed like I thought. It's also not as small, either. "Bigger on the inside, huh?" I mutter and look around the room that's easily a hundred times bigger than the outside.

"Charlie could have warned us about this," I say, gesturing out at the sprawling space crawling with cultists. I scan the room quickly but don't see the Blossoms anywhere. There's not a single shackle or girl in this joint. Just robed, feral cultists as far as the eye can see.

Wrath sighs and starts to text on his phone. "He will be hearing about this."

"Are you *texting* him?" I ask, watching a cultist lift a crossbow. A second later fire blooms at the tip of it as they notch the arrow and swing the weapon our way.

"Well, it really is an inconvenience. Just look at this." Wrath gestures with his phone and shakes his head. "The young Gamemaster has a lot to learn about communication. Even a simple legend for scale on this map would have done wonders."

The cultist fires the arrow and it moves fast, whistling through the air towards Wrath. I'm faster. I catch it from the air about a foot from my husband while Wrath continues on texting without a care in the world.

I glare at the cultists. "*Who shot this at my husband*?!" I scream so loud the stone walls of the room echo and shake. The cultists around the robed figure that fired scurry back and I even see a few fingers pointed his way.

"Larry did it," someone calls.

"Come here, Larry," I order.

"No!" Larry shouts, taking a step back as he tries to melt into the crowd but the group at his back shoves him forward so hard he stumbles and nearly falls. "I only did it because he said to!"

I take a step forward and twirl the still flaming arrow between my fingers. "Who?"

"Them!" Larry points up and that's when I see the balcony above us. There's two figures there—Nick Aguirre and Derek Marsh.

"Two for the price of one." I nod and smile before I launch the flaming arrow back at Larry. It hits him square in the chest and he goes down without a scream, just a muffled *oomph* and a thud when he hits the stone floor.

"Get her!" A cultist yells and I take a deep breath. *Wrath*. I really should have come with weapons. Any weapon at all would be better.

"Mulberries," I whisper when a row of arrows lights up and the cultists notch their crossbows to fire at us.

"Here." Wrath holds a golden trident out to me. The tips of it are curved and shine in the low light of the room.

"Not the weapon I was expecting, but I love it."

"I knew you would," Wrath tucks his phone into his pocket and rolls his broad shoulders. "Now, by my estimation, there's only three dozen or so of them here. We'll clear them out and you can have your fun with those three."

I test the weight of the trident and twirl it. I've never been graceful in my life, but it has to be my inner harbinger taking over with how smoothly I handle the weapon. I watch a cultist frantically run across the line of crossbows and wave their arms to gather everyone's attention. They look like they're in charge. They trip on the edge of their robes and fall down.

Yup, definitely in charge.

"Three? I only saw two," I tell Wrath, who chuckles.

"The third was hiding himself, beloved. He fears you. Cowered behind those two you'll find Felipe Smith."

Three Founders are here. My heart skips a beat at the possibilities. I only managed to take down Rossi yesterday, but I can make ground up now. If I take them all down, then there's only O'Hare left and I have a feeling about him.

I don't think he's going to make me go after him at all.

How can he, when Wrath ripped his son's head clean off? He doesn't know it was Wrath that did it but he knows it was because of me. He'll come for me before the full moon is done. Sunday won't even have to play for time if I can manage to get through this.

O'Hare will find me and when he does, I'll be the one to take him apart and end this nightmare.

"Fire!" The cultist still on the ground and fighting with their robes shrieks. I hear the crossbow triggers click before a rain of fire cuts through the air towards Wrath and I.

"I won't spoil all your fun," Wrath tells me. "Do as you please and know that I am at your back."

"Love you too." I smile at him and again I see the blush I glimpsed earlier return to his face. I'll have to carve out time to find out all the ways that make my husband blush when we're done with this. I raise my trident and spin away from him and towards the flaming arrows. My first swing of my weapon sends six arrows to the floor. They bounce, fire flying from their tips and into the air as they splinter and break. Wrath sends his arrows neatly back with a flick of his hand and I watch a dozen cultists fall to his magic before another group fires as quickly as they can on order of the cultist still on the ground.

I run towards them. If I don't close the ground between us there will be no way I can show the Founders watching us exactly what is in store for them. I want them all to cower like Felipe. Funny that he's the one hiding himself. He's the biggest of all the Founders, a head taller and broader than any of them. At six foot six he always walked about town like he was a king.

How easily he's dropped his crown when it's me that's come knocking.

I spin my trident and send two arrows into the wall. I push my body to move faster. I'm within striking distance and before the cultists can reload, I jab my trident forward. The prongs are sharper than they appear or maybe it's that the men I attack aren't as strong as I believed them to be.

In either case, the blades of my trident cut smooth and sure when I sweep my weapon to the side, cutting them in two. I'm rushed by a man and the anger in his eyes makes sense, I recognize the rage I see. It's what I feel in my heart, after all.

I smile at him and swing my trident up. The prongs slam neatly into his chin and jaw and all it takes is a quick jerk to send them straight through his head. He gargles and thrashes, the anger I saw so quickly fades and goes dark. I rip my weapon free and blood splatters on my chin and chest but I pay it little mind. I turn to look up at the Founders high above me and I'm not surprised at what I find there. I wipe at the blood on my chin with the back of my hand and smile up at the solitary figure.

It's Aguirre, because of course it is. I should have known. He's the only one mean enough to try me. I take the measure of the balcony. It's small, little more than a recessed area into the stone wall, with a few feet's worth of standing room. There's a small staircase cut into the stone leading up to it and the railing comes to hip height, but it doesn't hide much. I can see Marsh hiding with Smith on account of his shaking shoulders. Good, but not great.

I wanted them all to fear me.

Guess I'll have to work on that.

Screams echo and mingle with the sounds of bodies hitting the floor. The cultist that ordered the fire in the first place moans pitifully somewhere near my feet but I keep my eyes trained on Aguirre. All my life I've looked away from men like him, too terrified to attract their attention. Mean men with callous hearts have trampled on the people of Sweet Tooth for too long, people like Mrs. Landry, Ms. Donna and Nina.

I'm never going to look away from a man like Aguirre again.

I smile, knowing I'm safe with Wrath dutifully working his way through the room as promised. I put a hand on my hip to meet Aguirre's stare. He doesn't so much as flinch when I point at him, or at least he doesn't until I frown.

"I'm going to kill you now," I tell him.

CHAPTER
TWENTY-NINE

I don't think Aguirre hears me, at least not at first. He's zeroed in on my frown, though. I tilt my head to the side and watch him.

"Your smile," he finally rasps, knuckles white from gripping the railing in front of him.

"You know, for a man whose spine I'm about to rip out, you sure do focus on the details." I wave my trident at him before I let it drop. The butt end of it thuds on the cultist squirming at my feet. They moan and paw at my trident, but it's over when I flip the trident in my hand and slam the blades of it into his neck. There's a squelching sound when the weapon sinks in and I yank hard, severing his head from his shoulders and in one neat motion, send his head sailing towards Aguirre.

Blood drips and splatters along the stone floor as the man's head hits Aguirre smack in the chest. He staggers back and falls to a knee, frantically batting at the head. "You insane bitch!"

"If I'm insane, I think you have a big part to play in that, don't you think?" I ask and throw my arms wide, "I mean, sacrificing me on my *wedding night*? You think a girl comes out of that the same? Because, spoiler alert," I hold up a finger to make my point, "she doesn't!"

"You should have *never* been a Blossom. I told them. I *told* them you were wrong," Aguirre snarls and lobs the head back at me with surprising accuracy. I swing my trident, connect and send the head right back at him. This time it lands on Smith with a thud and the big man howls in fear and throws himself as far away from it as he can. He presses close to the wall and squeezes his eyes shut.

"I'm sorry!" He screams and Aguirre groans in annoyance.

"*Not good enough!*" I scream back at him, hefting my trident high and taking aim. I focus every bit of the power I can muster into my throw. My golden trident whistles through the air before it slams into Smith. The blades crack into the wall, sending mortar falling to the ground as it impales him into the stone. His legs kick and he grabs at the trident, but there's not even enough breath in his lungs for him to scream, not with the way the trident is buried in his chest. I cross my arms, watching the blood bubble up out of his mouth. I frown at the sight of him.

I wanted it to last.

"Wrath! Save me, Wrath!" Marsh sobs and raises his hands skyward. "I call on you to avenge your faithful servant.

"I don't answer to you." Wrath steps up beside me, tossing a severed arm behind him as he does. "I answer to *her*."

Marsh looks ready to faint when he looks from the ceiling to Wrath and I see the realization finally dawn on him. He clasps his hands and pleads. "I have been your faithful servant since birth. How can you leave me like this?"

"You have served no one but yourself. You made a deal with my master. Like him, you are just as greedy, vile and beneath my wife. I'll not save you this day. I will delight in her vengeance and wrath. I will watch her stand over your lifeless, decaying corpse and think her more beautiful than the night I first saw her. No, there will be no escape or relief for you. Suffer her wrath and know I am behind it all."

Wrath puts a hand on my shoulder and a surge of power moves through me. It's so mighty that my knees buckle and I have to grab on to him.

"What are you doing?" I gasp.

"Powering you up, beloved."

"For what?"

"Creativity, of course," he says with a wink and when I lift my hands, they glow.

"Oh, I have magic now."

"You do. Now, what will you do?"

I look back at Marsh and Aguirre with a wicked smile and jump up in the air. Instead of landing back down a second later, I hover where I am and all it takes is a little flick of my hand to send me right where I want.

Wrath sighs below me but he's smiling when I flit by him. "Flying. Of course you choose to fly."

I laugh and spin in the air before I dive towards Marsh. "All humans want to fly, it's a fact," I tell Wrath and watch Marsh scream and trip towards the stairs. He barely makes it to the first step before I grab his shoulders and yank him off the stairs.

"No, put me down!" He swings at me. I give him a shake that has him slipping from his robes. "You stupid, worthless girl."

I grab his robes and twist them, forcing them into a rope

around his neck and spin. I spin so hard and fast that it's only when everything is a blur around me and I feel dizzy that I let him go with a flourish and 'oops'. Marsh slams into the wall with a splat, his head cracking open. The mess it makes marks the entire wall.

"Sorry! I'm just a stupid worthless girl." I wiggle my hands at Aguirre and drift closer to him, albeit in a slight diagonal, because I am well and truly dizzy. I give my head a shake. "You know how easy it is to drop things."

Aguirre scoffs. "I'll make a deal with you, Buffy."

"I thought I wasn't right," I say, repeating his words. "What's changed now that you want to make a deal, Aguirre?"

He raises an eyebrow, and looks at Wrath. "You went and got yourself a demon husband."

"Yes, that."

"How did you manage it? In five hundred years no one has seen this demon and you-you do it? The girl with an Outsider for a mother? The girl named *Buffy*?"

I wag my finger at him. "I happen to like my name, *Nick*."

He flips me off. "Listen here, girl."

"I'm going by Wrath's Harbinger at the moment but fine, I'm listening," I lie.

"You let me live and I'll take you to your friends."

I steeple my fingers and pretend to consider him, but I know it's a trap. Of course he wants me and the Blossoms together, it's the only way he'll be able to complete the ritual. I know that's why he's offering me my friends, but the offer tells me just how dumb Aguirre truly thinks I am. He *would* think I would take the bait without thinking.

"How about you tell me where they are and I won't make your death that icky. I'll keep it tasteful."

"You'll never find them without me. Not even your husband is going to be able to help you do it. Not where they are, not where the almighty Lethos spirited them away to."

Lethos.

"Motherfucker," I whisper, because *that* I didn't know. I wince when the bond between Wrath and me jerks. When I glance down at him, I see he looks like he's going to be sick. Anger wells up in me because my beautiful, strong husband looks queasy from knowing Lethos is here.

"How do you know Lethos?" I ask.

"All who serve Wrath know Lethos. Lethos is eternal, he is the well from which all power springs, including your husband's power." He leans over the balcony to glare accusingly at Wrath. "How could you taint yourself with humanity and take a human wife? Where did your darkness fail you?"

Wrath straightens up and looks at Aguirre, blue fire flares around his hands when he speaks. "You dare address me, mortal?"

"You have betrayed the Almighty Lethos. He is darkness eternal. He is your maker."

"To make a demon you must be able to undo him," Wrath growls and when he moves, it's so fast that I barely track it. The only way that I really know Wrath moved is that his hair floats behind him when he appears in front of Aguirre. Quick as a viper, he grabs the man by his neck and lifts him. The blue fire still circling his hands blooms and spreads across Aguirre's neck in a bright flash before it moves over the man, consuming his body inch by painful inch.

281

Aguirre screams and I wince at the sound, but Wrath *tuts*.

"Quiet," he whispers and Aguirre's cries fall silent. His mouth doesn't close and I know he still screams even as fire licks and consumes him, even as it fills his mouth and blackens his eyes, turning his skin to ash. Aguirre falls to pieces in Wrath's hands. Bones and skin fall to the floor in a pile of blackened soot.

"Do you feel that?" The blue fire flares brighter still and I have to squint to keep watching what he's doing to Aguirre. "That is the humanity being burned out of you. You are being unmade, cleansed of the humanity you loathe. Is it everything you wished it to be, human?"

I lift my hand when everything goes bright and the last bit of Aguirre that was solid goes '*poof*.

"And the only soul capable of undoing me is my wife," Wrath mutters to the pile of Aguirre. He steps on it when he turns to look up at me where I'm still floating. "Lethos' arrival has complicated things."

"Agreed. I'm still going to kill him."

"A pleasure it will be to see that, beloved," Wrath says, dusting his hands on his pants of whatever is left of Aguirre and heads for the recessed wall of the balcony. He slams his fist into the stone and a second later pulls out a leatherbound book.

He holds the book up to me. "Even if your friends are not here, we satisfied the Gamemaster's request. The deal is fulfilled once we deliver this to him. Let us leave this place and end our terms with Charlie. No doubt if there is information available, he will know." He vaults over the railing and starts for the door. Gray and dreary sunlight streams in and frames him so beautifully. He looks every bit the hero striding to his destiny and my heart feels full at the sight, but there's one little problem.

My juice ran out. Whatever power up Wrath gave me isn't powering me up anymore. I wince when I bump against the ceiling and hold my hands over my head to stop me from hitting the ceiling again. I try to reach for the power that got me up here in the first place but there's nothing there but a void. I sigh and bump along the ceiling like a half-inflated balloon.

"A little help here?" I call out to him and with the same time blurring speed, Wrath stands directly below me. I reach for him, trying to turn and brace my feet against the ceiling, but it doesn't help. "I don't know how to get down and-" my words die and I scream when Wrath snaps his fingers and I fall like a bag of hammers.

I turn to land on my feet but there's no need. I should have known better. Wrath catches me and kisses me before I've even processed what's happened.

"I have blood all over me," I whisper when we part.

"I think it's okay. I have a lot of his dust on me," Wrath tells me.

I giggle and turn into him when he throws me over his shoulder. "Yeah, I think that balances things out."

CHAPTER
THIRTY

When we emerge from the building everything is dark and I stare up at the sky. "Huh."

"What is it?"

I point up at the evening sky. "That's what. It's nighttime now." The full moon shines down on us, but even its light is muted here. "This is some magic nonsense, isn't it?"

Wrath considers the sky for a moment and then looks back at the building with a hum. "This place has a time warp enchantment on it. I don't know why I didn't sense it earlier."

"A time what?"

"Warp," Wrath explains and draws his hand through the air. The arc that travels in the air glows and he nods to himself while looking at what looks like glow in the dark gibberish. "Any time spent in the building slows while everything out here proceeds at a normal speed."

"Why would anyone want time to go slower while everything else is going faster?"

"It is useful when there are moments you wish to escape or seek safety. An hour inside of the building may buy you half a day like we have seen here. A day inside of the building, though? Why, when you emerge the danger has long passed and it took little resources for you to hide."

"Danger to hide from? What danger is there to..." my voice trails off, because the look Wrath gives me tells me everything. "Oh, *I'm* the danger to hide from."

"Indeed you are and I have never been prouder to be your husband."

I blush and look down at my feet. "You said I was even more beautiful than the night you saw me."

"When you are in your vengeance? Oh, yes, you are." My belly tightens at the drop in his voice and I have to force myself to stay focused. I cannot think about throwing myself at my husband.

I take his arm when he offers it to me. "You are very sweet."

"It's easy to do when it's you, beloved."

Wrath's words have me walking on air, but then I remember what Aguirre said before Wrath dusted him. "Lethos is here."

"Indeed he is." I feel Wrath's energy change. The playfulness is gone and something darker and somber settles over him. He frowns and stares ahead at the tree line we're walking towards but he stops us a second later.

"We're going to have to kill him," he says and looks at me.

"I know."

"You will not sacrifice yourself to do it."

"Wrath, listen. If I have a shot at him, I'm going to take it."

"Buffy, no."

"Buffy, yes."

We stare at each other in silence and I frown at him. I point at my face when I notice he sees the frown and I pull at my lips. "You see this? It means I'm pissed. I'm not smiling a stupid fake smile I don't mean. I'm mad, I'm frowning. I smashed my stupid smile to pieces back there and if I can kill Lethos, I'm going to do it."

"I can't risk you."

There's a tug at our bond that begs me to be softer but I ignore it. I take a step back from him. "My life is mine to risk and if I want to do it to protect you, I can do that. You can't stop me."

"You are my wife. You are mine to protect. I will die before I let Lethos take you from me."

I glare at Wrath and step into his space. "You are not allowed to die. End of story."

Wrath steps in with me until we're toe-to-toe and leans down to glare right back at me. "And neither are you. There is no story without you, Buffy."

Oh. My heart squeezes and my eyes prickle with tears so quick and fast I have to blink to keep them from falling.

"That's not fair," I whisper and poke him in the chest.

Wrath covers my finger with his hand and pulls me toward him. "I'm a demon. We do not play fair. When it comes to your life I will never play fair, Buffy." He wraps his arms around me and holds me tight.

I relax in his arms and as much as I want to argue that I'm going to rain unholy hell on Lethos and make sure the sick look I saw on my husband's face never happens again, I don't. No one has ever cared so much about me they would tell me there's no story without me. No one has fought this hard for me. I know Wrath, he means exactly what he's saying.

It's not just pretty words and empty promises because, just

like always, the bond between us shows me his heart. Wrath will gladly end the world to keep me safe. There's never been a luckier woman than me and I hug him tight.

"I love you so much," I whisper to him as I pour my love for him through our bond to show him that I would rip the world apart for him.

~

WRATH THUMPS the book down in front of Charlie and nods at it. "We've procured your book, Gamemaster."

The lights of the Shoot 'Em Up game booth blink and dance behind Charlie and I try to tell myself the manic light I see in Charlie's gaze is due to the lights and not him. There's no way a normal human could look that deranged all on their lonesome, right?

Charlie scoops up the book with coo. "My precious little angel. I knew you were there, I knew it." He strokes the book and sighs with pleasure. "We are going to make them all pay."

"Hey," I snap my fingers at Charlie, "I thought you wanted the book for, quote 'minor mischief,' end quote." I look at Wrath and point between them. "Didn't you both swear this book was just for petty things and not 'make them all pay' level grievances?"

Wrath nods at Charlie. "We did make such a promise, Gamemaster. Agree to it now."

Charlie pouts but nods. "Fine, I won't make them all pay, literally. I'll just make them all pay in the game, is that okay? Can I at least ruin their fiction and fantasy lives?"

"Of course that's okay, but keep it light, keep it fun, or I'll be back to lay the hurt on you."

"Jeeze, what happened since I last saw you? You're definitely more bloodthirsty now," Charlie observes, adding a quick, "which I totally support and condone. It's a new millennium, harbingers can be as bloodthirsty as they like, but you were always so..."

"So what?"

"Sweet," he says and I flinch.

Of course he thought I was sweet.

"Well, when that is what a girl is brainwashed to be," I mutter with a frown. Charlie's sharp intake of breath at seeing it is all the reward I need, but it also ruins the effect because I give him a toothy grin.

"Something the matter?" I ask, hoping that he'll bring up that he saw my smile break but Charlie just shakes his head.

"No, nothing," he says, eyes on his feet. Then I feel bad. Of course, Charlie wouldn't mention my smile. If he saw a woman's smile break in Sweet Tooth he wouldn't say a word about it. It's not his fault that he thought I was sweet.

I clear my throat. "Okay," I say quickly, turning away from him and Wrath, who steps in quickly and taps the book in Charlie's hands as if the tense moment never happened.

"Listen here, Gamemaster. Minor mischief only. The only ruination I want to know about through the use of this book better occur in your games and nothing more. If there's anything more, I'll let my wife loose on you."

"Aw, come on, Wrath. I swore I'd get you play with us this week, just don't let Buffy hurt me."

I keep an eye on the crowd, watch the faces I've known all my life slow down and pause in front of Charlie's booth. They aren't used to seeing the Shoot 'Em Up booth at a standstill, but after

Charlie's ascension to power I'm sure they're willing to excuse it when I send a frosty look their way.

"Now that our deal is complete, I have one more question for you," Wrath says and my ears perk up. He's going to ask about my friends. Charlie better not lie to us. There's no time for it. I look up at the night sky and bite my lip at the sight of the full moon.

Sunday might be able to hold it off, but she can't do that forever. If we don't find the Blossoms, how long until the cult gives up and sacrifices them to Lethos? Why wouldn't they? He is the start of all of this.

"Shoot," Charlie says and I roll my eyes but keep my focus on playing bodyguard. Nobody is getting near Wrath and Charlie right now.

"Where are the other Blossoms?"

Charlie clears his head and drops his voice. "I don't know."

"You must have some way of investigating the matter. You are knowledgeable and well connected, Gamemaster."

"Getting a phone is one thing, but this is something else entirely, Wrath. The Blossoms were with Aguirre the last I knew, but I haven't heard a peep about it since then," Charlie pauses and then says, "I can try asking around, but I don't know how many people are going to talk to me. Not with them knowing I'm friendly with you and Buffy. I'm not so invisible anymore, not like I was before."

I look over my shoulder at him and raise an eyebrow at the neon lights flashing and the glittery cowboy hat Charlie is wearing. "You think we're the cause of you not being invisible?"

He crosses his arms and pouts. "Listen, the Shoot 'Em Up booth is a very prestigious appointment to have at the Autumn Festival."

"Your hat looks like a Christmas ornament."

"Fair point," Charlie concedes and uncrosses his arms. "But this is different. You're a wanted woman, Buffy. Everyone can't stop talking about the fact that you're with a mage." He gestures at Wrath who puffs up his chest proudly. "I mean, I know he isn't just a mage and anyone with half a brain cell does too. They probably had the Blossoms moved because they knew you were coming and the odds that they're gonna tell me about it are nonexistent now that people know we're friends."

I hold up a hand. "Wait, we're friends? I wasn't expecting friends."

"Neither was I, but that's what we are now. I know things are getting serious and I'm with you both on this."

I smile at him. "Thanks Charlie."

He dips his head in acknowledgment. "I also wanna be part of the gang. Something flashy with authority but I'm willing to work my way up the ranks."

I rub my temples and groan. "Elijah has been here, hasn't he?"

"He's very enthusiastic about his role in the gang."

"There is *no gang*," I groan.

"That's not what his girlfriend said."

"*Sunday*," Wrath and I both say in unison.

"She was pretty scary," Charlie tells us.

I move closer to them. "Yeah, that's kind of her thing, but there is absolutely no gang."

"Buffy come on, I'm no snitch. Let me in and I'm a lifer."

"A lifer? A lifer for what?"

"*Your gang,*" Charlie says and holds up his hand when I go to tell him he's out of his mind, "I'm dependable and resourceful and I'm a-okay with indoctrination. Look at me, here in an actual cult. You know without a shadow of a doubt that I'm a follower for a cause. Take me on, Buffy."

He's got me there. We both know it. It doesn't help when Wrath leans in close to me with a quick, "All very valid points."

"But we don't have a gang, darling," I remind Wrath through clenched teeth.

He winks at me. "But we could."

I look between Charlie and Wrath, and weigh my options. When I tried to send Elijah away nothing went to plan. If people are connecting Charlie to me now...well, that's more of the same. I can't let him go out in Sweet Tooth alone with a target on his back.

"Fine, you're in."

Charlie tips his hat to me. "You won't regret this, ma'am."

"Please stop calling me ma'am."

CHAPTER

THIRTY-ONE

"That was a noble thing you did, Buffy."

We're walking through the festival, eyes peeled and ready for clues but I wasn't expecting Wrath to say that. "What noble thing?" I ask him.

He raises an eyebrow at me. "You took the young Gamemaster under your wing." The lights from the rides around us paint his face in pinks and purples and the colors war with the night shadows that slide across Wrath's features like ink.

He really is so beautiful. Even in his human form.

I reach up and brush his hair away from face, savoring the drag of my finger across his high cheekbone. "I couldn't let him face Sweet Tooth alone, but now we have a gang."

"That is more formidable than a team," Wrath points out and I grin.

"True."

We turn and keep walking but we both don't say the thing that I can feel moving between us.

Now what?

We don't know where my friends are, Wrath's big bad master is around and the full moon is supposed to be ending tonight.

"Aguirre knew he had to try and get me with the other Blossoms," I tell him softly. "That means they're going to try and kill us all together, just like Sunday said."

Wrath wraps an arm around my waist and tugs me close. "They can try, but no one is laying a finger on you."

I lean into him and let him take my weight. I feel so tired suddenly that it's a relief. "Right back at you."

We walk for another minute before we end up in front of the Coaster of Fun. I rode this last year with Callum and he held my hand in line when no one was looking.

"We'll be in the city next year, Buffy. Next year it will be us that gets married."

My hands clench into fists at the memory. That little shit knew.

"Don't like this ride?" Wrath asks me and I shake my head.

"Bad memories," I confess. I don't want to talk about Callum. Not when I'm with Wrath and not when I can't really make him pay more than he already has for the lies he happily let me believe.

He lost his head, which kind of put revenge against him at an end.

Unless Sunday can resurrect him like she did Nina? Hmmm, now that is a thought. The witch is just chaotic enough to think about doing it.

"Then how about we make new ones?" My husband asks before I can go too far down the *resurrect my old* fiancé *so I can destroy him again path* and holds his hand out to me. A saner me would say no with everything we have to accomplish tonight, but a saner me probably wouldn't be killing her way through the cult, either. Plus, the sight of him offering me his hand so freely when last year I had to hide to be close to Callum, does something to me.

Callum is dead and so is the girl that I was last year, but there's room for me to be someone new with Wrath. I take his hand and step into line for the Coaster of Fun with a smile. Why can't I pretend I'm carefree and a girl that still gets to have fun?

The cult took enough from me. They don't get to take my fun.

"I'd love to."

Wrath and I hold hands while we wait and ignore the curious looks from the people around us. There are enough Outsiders here enjoying the festival that it doesn't entirely matter. No one would ever say anything to us, not even with what I just did out at the greenhouses.

No one would know about that yet. At least, I don't think they would, considering we've taken out nearly every last one of the heads of the Founders' families.

Rossi, Smith, Marsh and Aguirre.

All of them are dead and gone. Only O'Hare remains, which isn't bad considering where we started the day. What could one little roller coaster ride hurt in the grand scheme of things?

Draven O'Hare will still be there waiting for me to end him when I get off this ride.

"Step right up!" The worker waves us forward and holds out his hand for our tickets, which Wrath just so magically happens to have, because of course he does. He leads us to the front car of the roller coaster and we slide onto the hard bench seat together. I know the roller coaster is old and small compared to the newer ones out there from the conversations I've overheard from Outsiders but it's always been one of the most exciting things I was allowed to do in Sweet Tooth. I swallow hard when my thigh is pressed up against Wrath's. After the worker yanks the safety bar down, Wrath puts his hand on my leg and my heart starts to pound.

Yup. This is still the most exciting thing to do in Sweet Tooth.

Wrath flexes his hand and I shiver. "Excited for the ride?"

I swallow hard and look at him. Even with the lights of the rollercoaster and the full moon shining down on him, his eyes are different. Silver, but in the darkest of ways. His gaze moves over my face slowly before he leans in and kisses me. The ride lurches forward and I grab onto his arm to keep me upright.

He smiles against my mouth and rubs his thumb across my leg. That's when I realize Wrath just used his magic on me. My pants are gone, but there's a skirt in its place—a pretty, pastel, flowing skirt that tells me my demon husband is up to something. Good. I can't wait to see where Wrath takes this.

"I'll keep you safe."

Adrenaline moves through me like it did when I was raining unholy terror on the cultists, but this time there's a sweetness to it that wasn't there before. I shift closer to him and smile.

"I know."

The hand on my leg moves higher until it's on my thigh and when the roller coaster turns its first curve and starts its steep ascent to the drop, Wrath's touch moves higher still and slips beneath the hem of my skirt. I suck in a sharp breath at the sight of his hand beneath my skirt and when the roller coaster jolts up in this climb of the rickety wooden track, the familiar ball of butterflies that always settled into my stomach sets up shop like clockwork.

I almost ask him what he's doing, but I don't. I know what he's doing.

Wrath's fingers skim the inside of my thigh, his knuckles brush across the front of my panties and he leans in close to me. "Let me in, beloved."

My legs fall open without a single thought in my head and the dark chuckle he gives me is all the reward I need to know that I'm going to do exactly what Wrath tells me to do.

Someone laughs on the roller coaster behind us and I hear shrieks and voices below us. Music floats on the air and high above us the moon shines on, but it's all background noise with Wrath touching me.

I suck in a breath when he slides two fingers inside of my panties and I squeeze my eyes shut.

"You are breathtaking."

The fingers stroke me slowly and I tilt my hips up to take him deeper inside of me. Wrath shifts closer and his thumb circles my clit. I grab his thigh when he curls his fingers just right and starts a steady stroke. The thrust of his fingers has me seeing stars and I squirm on the seat beneath me. The roller coaster keeps moving, the steady rise matches the heat building in me and when I open my eyes, we're nearly at the top.

"You bloom so beautifully for me, Buffy."

I turn my head to look at Wrath and his eyes meet mine the second I do. "Don't stop."

"Never dream of it."

Wrath speeds up, his knuckles dig into my inner thigh when I squeeze them tight around his hand and drop my hands to cover

296

his. I squeeze his hand, urging him to move faster while the view in front of us opens up and the entirety of Sweet Tooth is laid out in front of us. I can see every street and building from where we are.

From here it looks innocent, like an ordinary small town without any darkness or secrets.

I know better.

Sweet Tooth is built on lies and I'm going to be the one to drag its sins into the light if it's the last thing I do.

The roller coaster pauses at the very top and the feeling of neither here nor there, the anticipation that drew me back to the ride over and over again shows up. When our car finally moves into its freefall, I'm dragged right along with it and fall headfirst into my orgasm. The world becomes a blur of lights and noise, the sound of rushing air fills my ears and I hold on tight to Wrath. Our bond hums along, the warmth of it makes it easy to let go of everything and just feel. It holds me just as securely as Wrath does while he works me through my orgasm and forces more from me with each and every twist and turn of the roller coaster until I can't tell up from down. It's only when the ride slows that I can open my eyes. I sag against him with a smile.

"I thoroughly enjoyed that," Wrath says with a happy sigh.

The ride comes to a clanging stop and the safety bars unlock with a snap that startles me. "My brain is mush," I tell him and point to my head, "I have mush brain from that."

"My poor, darling, wife," Wrath coos and stands from his seat. He hops out easily and scoops me out of the ride without losing a step. "I'll have to tend to you then until you gain your bearings, won't I?"

I lean against him and walk. "That would be the only conscionable thing to do."

"I have been and always will be a conscientious husband. I am at your bidding."

"We should check on the others. We've been gone all day. If Sunday and Elijah were here then I want to make sure they're back at headquarters where I know they're safe."

"All right then, let's be on our way home."

Home.

I never thought home would mean a rambling Victorian I shared with my demon husband, an over eager acolyte, my undead friend and the Witch of the Woods, but to be fair I've also never really had a home either.

"Yeah, let's go home." I smile and let him lead me away from the roller coaster on shaking legs and everything feels so right.

But this is Sweet Tooth and I was raised in a cult, so I really should have never trusted that feeling.

CHAPTER

THIRTY-TWO

O ur walk back to headquarters is relatively peaceful.
The most eventful thing that happens between the
Coaster of Fun and Town Square is that Wrath
magics my pants back into place, which sort of causes a stir when
an Outsider catches sight of it and nearly trips.

But other than that? Perfectly peaceful. We pass excited
Outsiders and cultists when we cross the Town Square and walk
down Main Street. I window shop with Wrath, because if I'm
going to indulge in acting normal why not go the whole way,
right? Ms. Donna waves to us brightly when we pass the bakery
and I see Mrs. Landry inside with her, drinking a cup of coffee and
petting Velma. I'm happy to see Mrs. Landry looking better than
when we left her. She's smiling and looks like she's recovered
from the Naga poison enough to enjoy a fritter and Ms. Donna's
company.

I think about stopping to get a box of treats to take back to
Sunday and the rest but then I decide against it. Best not to tempt

Wrath and Elijah into another baking challenge. I don't know if they would survive another round of it so soon.

Wrath holds my hand as we walk and I tilt my head back to look up at the moon. It's silly, but I just pretend that we aren't locked in a revenge death match with the cult in town. I pretend that my friends aren't being held somewhere as prisoners or that I'm going to have to face off against some old god that imprisoned Wrath for who knows how many centuries.

I glance his way and see that he looks relaxed. I know he's not though, not really. There's a hum of energy in our bond that hasn't been there before. It feels like a bowstring pulled too tight, like any second it's going to snap and take someone's eye out.

"You okay?" I whisper to him.

Wrath squeezes my hand. "I'm fine, beloved. It's just things are..." his voice trails off and I finish his sentence.

"Too quiet?"

He nods and scans the street. I can see Wrath's Embrace ahead of us at the top of the hill but it's still a ways off. We've just stepped off of Main Street and it's quieter here.

"Things should not be this quiet. Not now."

He's right.

"It's okay. I'm sure they're all just at the festival," I say, trying to keep my voice even but it's difficult. Wrath's agitation flows down our bond and for once, when I reach for it, there's no steadying energy for me to sink into. I tug on his hand and he looks at me. "Nothing bad is going to happen," I lie. I'm used to lying. I've done it all my life. I've lost count of how many times I lied to myself that things would be okay.

Finding the will to lie to Wrath now is easy. I'll do anything to ease the distress I feel rolling off of him but the bond works two ways. Wrath sighs and gives me a kind smile and I know he can feel the lie but he doesn't call me on it.

"Of course not, Buffy."

We keep walking down the deserted street and it's only when we're at the foot of the hill, Wrath's Embrace looming over us, that I see the first figure step out from the side of a house. A second later another figure appears across the street. Then another and another until they're flooding the street.

Wrath sweeps me behind him and looks around the street. There's more people behind us and when I look up the hill I see more cultists rushing out to block the road to Wrath's Embrace.

I move and take a step back until my back bumps against Wrath's. We move in a circle together, back-to-back and I lift my hands ready to fight. When I get out of this, I'm going to make good on carrying a weapon with me.

"They're everywhere."

"Buffy, run."

"Absolutely not. No. I'm not leaving you."

"Buffy, there's too many of them."

I take in a deep breath. *Wrath.* I think his name and reach for our bond. I wrap it around my wrists and throat until I can't take a breath without feeling the press of it.

They could bring an army down on me. I'm not going.

There's silence from Wrath's end and then he rushes in to soothe me. He reaches for me and I feel his fingers brush against mine.

My ruthless little wife.

I smile and take his hand in mine. "This is going to get nasty, isn't it?"

"Yes, but I'm with you until the end. We are coming out of this. I promise you."

My heart pounds against my chest so hard that I wince. "Of course we are."

"But first, you were wanting a weapon, isn't that right?" Wrath asks and there's a shimmer in front of me before two swords appear. "Will this do?"

I grin and reach for the blades. They're not quite daggers and not quite long enough to be true swords but they feel balanced and sure in each of my hands.

"Oh yes," I say and twirl the swords in my hands. "This is more than enough."

"I'll do my best to keep you safe. If this goes wrong, Buffy-"

"It won't," I interrupt him and lift my chin to meet the eyes of the cultist I see stepping forward. I recognize the set of his shoulders. When they push back their hood, I'm not surprised to see it's Draven O'Hare.

The last cultist I need to end the Founders Circle.

"Buffy," Draven says when he's close enough to be heard while speaking but still far enough that I can't reach him.

"Draven."

"Mister O'Hare to you," he corrects.

I roll my eyes. "You don't tell me what to say. Not anymore, you monster," I spit and flick my blade at him. The flinch from Draven makes me smile. "What's wrong? You look nervous. You know who else was nervous?"

He doesn't want to ask who but I know he just can't help himself.

"Who, you little bitch?"

"The Founders I paid a visit to today and you know what? They called me a bitch too, before I cut them to pieces."

"I'm not afraid of you, because unlike those unbelievers, my god has not abandoned me."

Wrath holds up a hand and there's a whoosh as his demon form takes over. "Hi, that would be me and I certainly have abandoned you."

Draven scoffs. "Not you. I'm talking about the *true god*. We have served you in vain but that time has come to an end, false god that you are."

Wrath's tail switches and he growls low. "Lethos," he mutters.

Draven smiles and he looks every bit the villain he is. "Correct. Lethos has returned to bring us home and to offer us honor."

"Honor, huh?" I tighten my grip on my swords and stare him down. "And what do you have to give him for that honor?"

Draven splays his hands wide and starts to pace with a smug smile on his face. "Oh why, nothing of value at all, really, Buffy. All our god wants is you."

"You know what? I'm a little busy, so I think I'm going to have to take a rain check on a meet and greet with your god."

Draven glares and spits at me. "No you," he snarls and points past me to Wrath. "I'm talking about him." He snaps his fingers and motions for the mob around us to move. "Take them. I don't care if she dies, but the demon must live."

The demon must live.

I have half a second to process what Draven orders before the cultists rush towards us. The first cultist lunges for Wrath and I swing my swords with all my strength in a sweeping arc. The metal glints in the moonlight before I slice through their arms.

"You're not touching my husband!"

Their arms hit the ground with a thud and I move forward, cutting my way through the mob of dark figures. Wrath stays with me and we keep a circle around us clear but every second that passes our fighting space shrinks. I dodge and spin away from their hands, I force them all away and there's nothing but the rhythmic swing of my swords. One by one the cultists fall in front of me, but the second I drop one another appears in their stead. After the first dozen I realize the body my blade rips through isn't human.

Instead of blood, sand pours from their wounds. There are no bones in their bodies for me to crush, it's only sand and straw that I see when I tear them apart.

I sever a cultist's head and rip their hood back. "What? No." Sightless cloth and straw stare back at me.

"They're poppets!" Wrath calls to me, tearing one in two. He throws its limp body at another and takes down another dozen with a blast of magic but there's no reprieve. The destroyed bodies either get back up or more poppets materialize in front of us.

I force myself to keep going, to keep fighting but it's no use. For every poppet that falls another five take its place.

"There's too many." I turn to look for Draven and see him at the center of it all. I have to get to Draven if there's any hope of us escaping. I push forward and try to pull Wrath along with me, there's tension in our bond before I feel him move with me. My muscles scream and burn from how fast I have to fight but I do it with Wrath at my back.

I'm almost to Draven and I crouch low to leap at him when I

hear Wrath grunt behind me. I look over my shoulder to see him on one knee.

"Wrath!"

"I'm fine, Buffy." He holds his hand out at me and smiles. "I'm going to give you my power. Fight your way free. Get to the house and tell Sunday what happened. She'll know what to do."

"No." I shake my head but there's no stopping the blast of power that fills me and fear makes it hard to think. I know if I'm getting stronger that Wrath is getting weaker. One of the poppets takes his back and he's slow to shake it off.

He isn't going to last long now that he's given me his power.

I have to end this now or I'm going to lose my husband.

I hesitate but only for a second before I turn and start running for Draven. It's easy to move, I'm as fast as Wrath was earlier today. In the blink of an eye, I'm in front of Draven and bringing my swords forward. They should hit him square in the chest but they never slide home. Magic stops them an inch from Draven's heart.

Magic is the only thing that can stop me and I glare at him.

"Fuck you," I snarl and pour more of Wrath's power into the blades in my hands. I move forward an inch, but that's all.

Draven winks at me. "You're not the only one with power anymore, you cunt. Compared to your washed up demon boy toy, Lethos reigns supreme. There's no winning against me."

Rage fills my body and I scream at him. "I'm going to rip your heart out and feed it to you." My arms shake, the strain of pushing against the magic keeping me back makes my muscles burn, but I refuse to give up.

I can't give up.

Not now.

Not when I'm this close to completing my revenge.

"You can try, but it seems like my god is more powerful than your husband." He makes a show of flicking invisible lint from his robe sleeve. "There's still time for you to serve Lethos, Buffy." Draven looks up at me, eyes glittering in the moonlight. "He's taken an interest in you, though I told him you're no more than an idiot girl bred to die. He thinks you have potential."

"I'd rather be buried alive than serve your god. My soul belongs to Wrath." I break free, the magical vise Draven had wrapped around me vanishes with a snap.

"Buffy, run!" Wrath orders me.

I do the opposite and force my blades home. I sink them right down to the hilt into Draven's chest, but nothing happens. No blood, no screams. There's not even any sand pouring out like from the poppets.

He smiles and looks down at the twin blades sticking out his chest. "Oh, ouch. This is supposed to hurt, right?" He asks and flicks the blade with a finger. I stare at the swords. They should have dropped him.

I try to jerk them back to try again but they don't come loose. "What the fuck, Draven?"

He tuts with a sigh. "That's Mister O'Hare to you. Where are your manners? You were going to marry my son, weren't you, Buffy? Now be a good girl and drop the swords or I'm going to kill him."

He doesn't have to say who he means when he says him. I know exactly who it is. There's only one *him* that matters to me at all.

Wrath cries out behind me and my heart nearly stops. Our bond feels weak. The energy that's usually a live wire between us feels different now. It's hardly there and I have to concentrate to feel it. I look over my shoulder and see why.

Wrath is on his knees with more poppets than I can count bearing down on him. Their sand filled hands hold him down and there's a knife shining at his neck. They force his head back and he winces.

"Buffy, get out of here!"

"No, I'm not leaving you!"

"As touching as this scene is, I have a god to serve and he wants your demon's power, so we really need to be on our way."

Draven says something else but his words don't make any sense to me. I'm too focused on Wrath.

Our eyes meet and the silver light in his glows brighter before I feel the bond surge. There's so much coming through that I nearly fall to my knees, but I keep my feet. Wrath doesn't though, his eyes go dark and he sags forward in the poppet's hands and I understand what he's done. He didn't just share his power with me like he did before.

He *gave* it to me.

All of it.

It feels like I've swallowed the sun and I feel dizzy. My hands slip from the swords and I stagger forward. I start to fall but I don't hit the ground. Draven catches me and peers down at me while my vision goes fuzzy.

He chuckles and the sound of it is distorted. I try to take a swing at him but I can't lift my arm. I can't even focus on what I'm seeing.

"Buried alive, you say? I think we can arrange that."

Everything goes dark.

CHAPTER
THIRTY-THREE

When I wake up, things are weird.

It's pitch black and I can't move, at least not by much. I'm laying on my back and when I lift my hand it smacks right into something just a few inches above me. My hand makes a thud and my brain tells me it's wood above me while my heart leaps into my throat. I bring my hands up and feel the smooth wooden surface above me.

Whatever it is, it's big.

"Stay calm, Buffy," I whisper and slide my hands along whatever is above me. I try to raise my leg and bump my knee against the wood but when I try to turn to the side, it's no dice. There's more wood there to bump my shoulder against. I slide my hand along the side of it and find that it only goes a few inches out on either side of me. When I push my feet against the base of it, the top of my head smacks into more wood.

"It's a goddamn box."

My lungs nearly seize up and I squeeze my eyes shut, not that it matters. There's nothing but darkness all around me. Closing my eyes makes no difference.

"They put me in a box, those fuckers."

Buffy!

For one wild second, I think it's Wrath that's calling to me but it's not. I know the voice, though.

Harbinger, please! Where are you?

It's Elijah.

"Elijah!" I scream and open my eyes and start to shove at the wood above me while I try not to think about the fact that it isn't just a box they put me in. There's only one box this size and shape.

"Buried alive, you say? I think we can arrange that."

Fucking Draven. He did it. He really did it, didn't he?

"Elijah can you hear me?!" I bang my fists on the wood but there's only silence now. There's a hum that tells me magic is afoot but it's weak. I'm on my own.

I grunt and try to get enough leverage between my hip and the wood to help me shove but it's no use, I can't even turn on my side.

"Open! Open you stupid thing."

It's a coffin.

It's not going to open.

I suck in a ragged breath and try not to cry. I'm not going to cry. I won't do it, I can't. I reach for the bond. I try to grab hold of it like I've always been able to but this time it slips through my fingers. Wrath is there, but barely. He's normally so bright and strong, the emotions he sends to me nearly bowl me over with how strong they are, but now?

I can hardly feel him at all.

309

He's weak. Whatever they're doing under Lethos' orders is working and there's no one to stop them with me buried in the ground. I swallow down my fear and send what I can through the feeble bond to Wrath. I send him love, reassurance but most of all, I send him the bright white heat of my anger. Wrath answers me. He knows I'm here, he can feel me and the slight brush of his fingers against the bond fuels me even more than my hate and anger.

My beautiful husband loves me. He wants me to live. I know he would tell me not to come. He would want me to run and save myself.

I was raised to obey the man I would marry, to be a dutiful wife. Just like I was raised to be a docile daughter, but I will not listen to Wrath now.

I will not let evil, cruel men break and destroy the only being I have ever truly loved.

Lethos won't win, Draven's greed will not prevail, the weak and heartless men that lived like kings will not see another sunrise. I don't care that they've buried me alive, I won't let the men that have shaped my life to their liking break me.

They've had their fun and now they have my husband.

"I'm coming," I growl and suck in a deep breath. "I'm coming and vengeance will be yours," I promise him. My voice echoes in the coffin. I don't know how it echoes, but it does. Maybe it's my mind already playing tricks on me but I push that aside and work with the space I have.

"I'm going to kill them all."

I draw back my fist and slam it into the wood above me, there's a splintering sound and I feel the wood give under my fist. I don't feel pain when I punch again and again. There's no such thing as pain for me with Wrath's power humming in my veins. They might be draining my husband dry but they don't have all of his power, not without me.

I could probably stay put and the idiots would come dig me up but where's the fun in that?

I want to hear them scream.

I snarl and bare my teeth to the darkness around me. "I am Wrath's Harbinger and they should have fucking cut my head off if they didn't want me to get back up."

I punch up. I slam both fists into the wood above me and there's a groaning sound before dirt starts to fall through the opening. I grab the edge of the hole I've made and start to pull. This is going to get messy with the dirt that's about to come down on me but it's fine. I don't need to breathe. I take a deep breath and hold while the dirt tries to shove me down but I fight it. I'll make it out of this and the next person to be put into the ground is going to be fucking O'Hare.

I'm going to kill him like Wrath killed his son.

"A gift for my darling wife."

Tears prick my eyes when I remember Wrath appearing out of the dark and saving me. He'll be upset that I've walked right back into the trap to save him instead of running but I don't care. He's going to have to just deal, because I'm not leaving him. Wood breaks and dirt rushes into the coffin in a wave that instantly makes me deaf.

There's nowhere to go with the earth itself now trying to swallow me whole, but it could be a mountain above me and it would still not be enough to keep me from my husband.

I kick the wood, my rage burning bright. The fuel of it makes it easy to do what I need to and I start to claw my way up. I grab a handful of dirt and rocks and force it out of my way, I dig my feet in where I can and try to push myself up, but most of my progress is from me digging. Handful after handful of dirt, I grab and shove down again and again and *again*.

Time melts away and the only thing is the darkness around me, the dirt filled gasps of air I manage to suck in from the pockets left from the loose dirt they used to bury me. I keep a careful watch over the bond and fragile as it is, it's a golden thread in the darkness that I follow up and up *and up* until my fist punches out into the night air.

I kick and push, shoving my other hand through and scrabble at the dirt to lift myself out of the grave.

I groan as cool night air fills my lungs and blink, trying to clear the dirt in my eyes. I shove my hair out of my face and look around. There's no one here with me in the graveyard. Cute. They actually put me in the graveyard like this is a proper burial. I press my palms down and lift the rest of my body out of the grave, throwing myself onto the ground to rest for a second.

My body aches, my muscles feel like they're on fire and my lungs hurt from the air that's filling them, but I'm out.

I did it.

I smile, press my palms to my face and take in a shaky breath. I really did it.

"There you are! I thought I was going to have to add more time to the clock for you."

I yelp and jackknife up at the irritated voice that I would know anywhere.

"*Sunday?*" I don't see her immediately but it's because she's climbing out from behind a mountain of dirt with Nina right behind her. They both have shovels in their hands and Sunday drops hers to the ground with an exhausted groan.

"Harbinger? Harbinger, is that you?! I told you she wasn't in this grave! I didn't feel you through the soulstone, but nobody on the team ever listens to me!" Elijah screams and I spot him a few rows over with a shovel in his hands. There's a pile of dirt next to him and he's waist deep in a hole.

"Oh Harbinger, I tried to find you. I tried to let our bond guide me to you but I failed," he says holding up the purple soulstone Wrath gave him. "I don't know why the stone didn't work. I've been digging for hours."

Hours?

I shake dirt out of my hair. "I heard you, but it was weak. I-I couldn't answer but I tried." Wrath gave Eliah the soulstone. If it's weak, it's because so is my husband. I can't think about that now. I look around and see the dirt piles all around the graveyard and my eyes go wide at the sight. "How many graves did you dig up?"

"I was prepared to turn this graveyard inside out," Elijah tells me.

"About three dozen," Nina answers, wiping her hands on her pants. "It's been a creepy night."

Sunday hums in agreement. "Zombie girl is right. It's been a weird night."

Nina stomps her foot. "I'm not a zombie!"

"Tomato, potato." Sunday stretches her hands over her head and kicks the shovel next to her. "They didn't bury you too deep, did they?"

I shake my head. "Didn't feel like it."

"They were in a hurry then." Sunday gestures around the

313

graveyard with a scowl. "Probably because they knew we'd be coming to find you. They went all over this graveyard and dug them all up to confuse us. There was no way to find you."

"Couldn't you just have found me with magic?" I ask and stand shakily. The energy in my body is still too much and everything is off kilter. I groan and lean against a gravestone while Sunday walks over to me.

"I'm not allowed to interfere directly," she says and shrugs. "I'm more of a third party in this with a heavily vested interest but magic is a direct interference kinda thing. By the time I figured out what was going on they were already leaving the graveyard, but I know who's here. I can feel him."

"Lethos." I flick dirt out of my hair and wipe my nose, but it's hard to breathe with the amount of graveyard dirt I think I've swallowed. "I'm going to kill him."

"Not just him."

"Who else?" I frown and stand straight with a groan. "Don't tell me it's Ichabod," I say, conjuring up the worst case scenario I can imagine. The last thing I need is the actual founder of the cult in on this action.

"Nailed it. Ichabod is in on this one. Seems like they've got the band back together, oh Harbinger of Doom."

"Wrath," I correct and cough up another mouthful of dirt with a groan. "I'm the Harbinger of Wrath."

Sunday gives a little bow. "My apologies," she says and I cross my arms, watching her. I don't trust her. Wrath said to watch myself around her and now here she is when he's weak and held hostage and I just crawled out of a grave.

"What's your play, Sunday? Talk fast, because I'm feeling cranky after my dirt nap."

Sunday smiles at me and I see her teeth are sharp in the moonlight. They look like knives and I'm surprised there isn't blood on them. She takes a step closer but I don't shy away from her when she points a finger at me.

"Power suits you. I like you sassy."

She knows something. I can tell from the way she's looking at me. I'm tired of her games but she knows something I don't and she did come to dig me out, so I stay put while I focus on taking hold of my bond and marking the direction it leads. It's south of here, towards the Founders Circle.

He has to be there. Of course they would take him back to where this all started.

I stay quiet and she raises an eyebrow at me.

"Stoic now too, how very chic of you. As I said, Ichabod was with them but you have more than enough bite to you to take that little warlock down now. He's never been very powerful and it's Lethos now that you'll have to contend with if you want to rescue your darling husband the way I know you're about to risk it all to do."

I curl my hands into fists. "He's mine . I-I have to protect him." The only thing I can think about is the sick look on Wrath's face when he found out Lethos was here. It's that look that helps me rally for what I'm going to have to do next.

Sunday inclines her head with a wince. "I know what you're thinking. Big bad time and you're right, he is the very biggest of bads. I know you might–" she starts to talk but I'm not listening. I know where I'm going. I turn on my heel and stalk off through the graveyard.

"What the hell, Buffy?" Sunday yells and then runs after me with Nina a few steps behind. "Where are you going?" she asks.

"To get weapons," I tell her, shoving open the rusted gate of the graveyard so hard it snaps and falls off. "That makes the police station my first stop. Then to kill Lethos and anyone else that gets in my way to get my husband. I don't care if God himself comes down, I'll kill him too." I rub my hand against my chest. The bond feels tight, like it's about to snap and I know I don't have much time.

"Hey! Where are you going?" I stop long enough to see her make a grab at Elijah who runs past her to me with his shovel.

"You stay here," I tell him and force him back.

Elijah shakes his head. "Where you go, so do I." He looks determined, absolutely resolute and I know he would follow me into hell if I asked him to.

But I can't ask him to follow me. Not when I don't know if I'll survive it.

"Elijah, no."

"Harbinger, you-"

"Please. I can't lose you too." The pressure in my chest thumps hard once, twice, then it falls to almost nothing and I stagger from the loss of it. "I don't have time for this. Wrath, he's dying," I say and double back to the graveyard gate, ripping off a couple of the iron bars. I flick my wrists and give them a spin so they give a satisfying whistle as they slice through the air. That's good. They're still strong enough for me to put them through Lethos' eyes.

"Wrath is in the Founders' Circle but he's weak. I don't know how much longer he has and I'm going to have to travel fast. I can't bring you with me," I tell Elijah before turning to Sunday. "I know you said you can't interfere but do what you can. Hold the moon off," I gesture to Nina and Elijah, "keep them safe, do anything to help us. Please."

For once the witch looks worried. I've never seen her like this. I should probably rip more bars off the fence. Sunday bites her lip and then nods. "I can do that, but I didn't say I couldn't interfere, I said I couldn't interfere *directly*. Of course, that means that I can still do this."

"Do what?" Nina asks just as I open my mouth to tell Sunday now is not the time for any of her cryptic riddles, but that's when I see the flash of steel in her hand.

"This," Sunday says and twirls the blade with ease before she holds out the sword to me. It's big and ornate, something that I wouldn't ever be able to lift, let alone have a prayer of using in a fight if I didn't have Wrath's strength coursing through me. It's long and wicked, the blade of it glitters and shines bright under the full moon. Its hilt is gold with a large cut red ruby inset in the pommel.

I take the sword from her and lift it with one hand to look at the blade. There's runes inscribed along the steel and the markings glow bright when the moonlight hits them.

"What's it say?" I ask, because I know words have power. Words built the rotting kingdom that crushed me and my friends beneath its weight, words brought Wrath to me and words are the reason my husband was taken from me.

Sunday rocks back on her heels as she answers me. "Ruthless Little Bride. I thought you might like to carry something like that with you tonight. Besides, Ichabod and Lethos can read the runes. They'll fucking hate it."

I chuckle and look down at the big sword. "There's nothing little about her, but I'm glad for it." I raise the blade with its shimmering runes in front of me. The moonlight hits the ruby and it glows like it already contains a soul. "Now that's pretty," I breathe.

Elijah falls to his knees and holds up his hands. "Harbinger, you are a deadly and holy sight."

Nina smiles at me. "He's right. You look great."

Sunday comes to stand beside Elijah and ruffles his hair. "It's some of my best work." She jerks her chin at the sword in my hand. "I want you to take that damn sword and cut their fucking heads off, Buffy. The souls you claim will go right in this soul-stone," she says and taps the ruby stone.

I consider the stone. It looks different than the one Wrath gave Elijah. Elijah's has a functional air to it, big and sturdy, but this soulstone is delicate.It's pretty. Definitely made for style and looks like it should be on a necklace a debutante would wear, not my sword.

I let out a low whistle and stare down at the twinkling gem. "I like it. Nice and sparkly one you got me."

"Indubitably. Now beat it, hellcat. Go get your demon back. Nina, Elijah and I will meet back up with you after. Ta!"

Nina lifts her hand in a wave. "Kick some ass, Buffy."

"Wait, no!" Elijah tries to push to his feet. "Harbinger, take me with-"

There's a whooshing sound and I know Sunday and the others are gone. Just as well. I've wasted too much time as it is. I heft my sword up over my shoulder and take off for the Founder's Circle at a jog. I have a husband to rescue and men to slaughter.

CHAPTER
THIRTY-FOUR

I t's for the best that Sunday gave me a soulstone sword and I didn't decide to raid the police station, because when I jog past the side of it, I can see something is going on. Every light in the station is on and there are officers spilling out onto the street.

I recognize most of them. Mostly because they're from the Founders' families, even if they're not the power players I am after. I pause in an alleyway and watch for a few minutes. They're getting into cruisers, a whole fleet of them from the looks of it. One of the Marsh's comes out holding a megaphone.

"The last patrol confirmed her grave has been exhumed. She's considered armed and dangerous! She will be after the Blossoms. If you do see her, do not engage. We're going to need more fire-power than any of you have."

The *she* they're after is totally me.

"*Mulberries*," I whisper and drop into a low crouch. The force ready to go after me are still getting into their cars while I decide how best to cut across town to get to the Founders' Circle when a woman screams.

"There she is! She's right there!"

I wince and growl before I turn to see the one person in all of Sweet Tooth that, if I was going to be caught and tattled on, it would be by them.

"Annie, shut up!"

Annie's standing across the street in her housecoat and slippers. She clutches the front of her housecoat and glares at me.

She shakes a finger at me while hollers go up from the officers and lights start to sweep in our direction. "Don't you talk to me like that!"

I flip her off and she gasps. "You're a snitch, Annie Bustos and you always have been!" I turn and sprint down the alleyway. If my cover is blown there's no use in trying to be sneaky. I may as well use my speed to my advantage. I can feel Wrath's power humming away in me and unlike the time I got stuck floating, his power doesn't feel temporary.

It feels like it's mine.

I don't really want to think about why it could feel like it's mine. I wrap the silken cord of our bond around my wrist like a bracelet.

"I see her!" A light sweeps the alley behind me and I put on a burst of speed and round the corner. I'm in the alleyways behind Town Square and I think about scaling the building to access the roofs. Maybe I can hop buildings until I get to the edge of Main Street and make a run for the Founders' Circle. I slow down and grab hold of a window ledge and am about to pull myself up when a door opens and someone whispers to me.

"Get in here, Buffy. Get in here now."

Mrs. Landry.

I forget all about my plan to roof hop and hurry towards the open door. She's holding a candle and the warm glow of it beckons me forward. I'm behind the bakery and didn't even realize it. Mrs. Landry holds open the door for me and ushers me inside. Ms. Donna slams it shut and slides the lock home before she turns to look at me in the flickering light of the candle she holds. We're in the kitchen, the ovens are cold and silent and I can smell the ghost of sugar and flour in the air.

"Oh sweet girl, what have you done?"

I shake my head but avoid the women's eyes. "Nothing." Velma is there watching the three of us, her eyes glow in the candlelight and I squat down and offer her my hand. The cat pads forward and sniffs my fingers before she bumps her head against my hand.

Ms. Donna nods at the sword hilt showing over my shoulder. "That sword doesn't look like nothing."

I pet Velma and offer a weak smile. "Uh, well that is something but it's...a, well-would you believe that I'm holding it for a friend?" I try as I stand. Both women look at each other in dismay.

Mrs. Landry gestures with her candle. "We have to help her."

Ms. Donna waves her off. "Of course we do. I know that."

Velma meows her agreement and winds around my legs.

My heart sings at their words. "You're...helping me?"

Mrs. Landry smiles at me. "You helped me, Buffy. I won't forget it and of course we are. All I've ever wanted was to help you girls. I wanted, well, I wanted better for you than Sweet Tooth," she says, surprising me. I thought she was happy here, although no one would be happy after doing a tour in the Naga poisoned dunk tank, but I never knew she felt like this. "We know you're going to help the other Blossoms, aren't you?"

I nod. "Yes, I'm going to save them."

Ms. Donna crosses the kitchen and peeks through to the front of the bakery. "How are you going to do that? And where is that handsome husband of yours?" Ms. Donna asks.

There's muffled shouts of the officers tracking me. They're close and we all fall silent when we hear them right outside the door.

"She was here!"

"Go that way!"

We hear the sound of boots on pavement and I don't dare breathe until it fades. Only then do I clear my throat and look at the other women.

"I'm going to kill Draven O'Hare."

"You can't kill them, Buffy. No one can."

"I've killed all the other heads of the Founding families." Ms. Donna claps her hand over her mouth to muffle her gasp while Mrs. Landry whispers a soft 'oh my'. "They have the Blossoms, but they need me to complete the ritual. At least, they did until they took Wrath."

I bite my lip and frown as I work it out. "There's an old god here now but I don't know what he wants or why they took Wrath for him. We thought they wanted the power that comes with killing the Blossoms..."

Why would Lethos want Wrath? Whatever it is, it's for a bigger gain than even the sacrifice of the Blossoms if they were willing to bury me alive.

"I think there's something g-"

"Your smile," Mrs. Landry whispers and I realize why they've been quiet. They've been staring at my frown.

"Is finally mine," I tell her and smile genuinely. "I don't smile because they make me. I don't smile out of fear or worry and I never will again. My smiles are my own to give."

"You've done something neither of us could ever manage." Ms. Donna smiles as she dabs at a tear with the corner of her apron. "Oh, Buffy. I'm so proud of you."

"So very proud," Mrs. Landry says in an echo and stands taller when I look her way. "Where are you going then? How can we help?"

"The Founders' Circle. They have my husband there and I know they're planning to sacrifice him, so I don't have much time." I press the heel of my palm into my chest and frown at the dull ache there. "I can feel him here and he's getting weaker by the minute. I was trying to get there but then Annie Bustos told the cops where I was."

Mrs. Landry tuts. "She always did have a big mouth."

"Nosey as the day is long," Ms. Donna adds.

"Exactly, but now they're out there looking for me. I don't think there's a street between here and the Founders' Circle that isn't being watched."

"Let's go." Ms. Donna waves a hand at me and shoos Velma away when the cat tries to trip me. "They'll be looking for someone on foot. No worries, we'll drive you."

"That's a wonderful idea," Mrs. Landry agrees and grabs her coat. We can take my car. Afterwards, I'd like to stop by the McAllens. They're saving us a spot at bingo tonight. They've been worried about me after the dunk tank fiasco. Buffy, do you not have a coat? It's getting chilly at this hour."

"What? Uh," I pause and look between the two women, who aren't paying the least bit of mind as they get ready to go out.

"Your coat, Buffy. Where is it?"

"I don't have one."

"Young people, always taking risks with their health, isn't that right, Velma?" Ms. Donna asks the feline and gets a slow blink and a tail swish in answer. "You can take my spare. It's just there by the back door, but let's hurry. There's bingo to be played."

I do as she tells me and pull on a thick flannel-lined coat that's a lot too big on me in the best of ways—it helps me hide the sword I have strapped to my back.

"Perfect! You're ready now."

What Ms. Donna thinks I'm ready for other than a brisk autumn night, I don't know, but I nod at her all the same and fall in line behind her, Mrs. Landry and Velma bringing up the rear.

"Are you sure it's safe out there?" I whisper when Ms. Donna unlocks the door and the older woman nods.

"They won't think to look for three. We'll get there just fine. When we do, I want you to kill them all. You make them pay for what they did, especially Draven O'Hare." My mouth drops open at Ms. Donna's words. I've hardly heard the woman utter a harsh word against anyone and now she's asking for retribution. "Do you hear me?" she asks and looks over her shoulder with a raised eyebrow.

"Yes, ma'am."

"That's more like it, sweet girl. If we see Annie, you just leave her to us. If she wants to stick her nose in other people's vengeance she can deal with the pair of us."

Mrs. Landry hums in agreement and I shut my mouth with a click of my teeth. I'm more scared of them than I am about taking on Lethos. Annie is in big trouble if they find her.

We leave the bakery and walk single file down the sidewalk to Ms. Donna's station wagon. It's a familiar sight from the years I've seen her rolling around town in it. Hunter green with a ding on the back bumper from when she backed up into a fire hydrant two Autumn Festivals ago. She'd set off the water main. It's comforting to have such a normal part of my life here with me while I'm on my way to face certain death. When I slide into the backseat, I'm relaxed. It smells like cinnamon with a slight hint of mint.

Velma hops up onto the seat next to me and rushes to the window to look out as Ms. Donna starts the car and backs out onto the street.

"Is Velma just a cat?" I ask, watching her scan the street. "She seems smarter."

"Of course she's just a cat. What else would she be?" she asks and turns down the street leading to the Founders' Circle. Velma slaps her paw on the glass when a squad of officers comes into view and I slouch lower in my seat.

"Are you sure?" I press and Velma growls low at the officers when we turn the corner and pass by them. Their flashlights shine in the window and move over us and I squeeze my eyes shut, waiting for them to yell at us to stop while Velma goes nuts on them, but nothing happens.

"Cats are just like that," Ms. Donna says and rolls on by the officers with a wave while I sink lower into my oversized coat and

Mrs. Landry turns on the radio. There's two approved stations in Sweet Tooth and this one is broadcasting a football game.

She groans and checks her watch with a sigh. "I forgot it was Sports Hour."

We drive on and the women I've looked up to and known my entire life chatter idly. Velma stalks the back seat and throws herself at the window every time she sees an officer. The more it goes on, the more I suspect it's because she wants to smack their flashlights out of their hands and not because she has a personal vendetta against them but I could be wrong.

When the car comes to a stop in front of the Hall of Worship I can't believe it. "We're here!" Ms. Donna says cheerily and throws the car into park with a jerk of her hand. "I told you it would be just fine, didn't I?" she asks, turning to look at me in the backseat.

She did say it would be all right, so I nod. "You did," I answer, even though I can't understand how it's all right. I have the might of the Cult of Wrath after me. Every street is being watched and an old god has my husband captive but somehow I was able to hitch a ride with the town baker and my old Home Ec teacher?

"Now Buffy, I want you to be careful out there. I know you're stronger than you were before but that's no excuse to take any needless risks, you hear?" Mrs. Landry asks me.

"Yes, ma'am. Thank you for the ride." I get out of the car and both women wave to me with smiles on their faces. When I smile and wave back, it's not forced or fake.

"Have fun getting your vengeance dear and make sure to let us know when you're home!" Ms. Donna calls out and pulls away from the curb with Velma going wild in the back seat. The last I see of them is the silhouette of the cat launching herself into the front seat before the red glow of the taillights turns the corner and vanishes.

I stand there for a second. The sound of the wind rustling the trees and my flapping oversized coat are the only thing I hear on the empty street as I stare after Mrs. Donna's station wagon before I laugh.

THIRTY-FIVE

The Hall of Worship is empty.

Not a single light or soul is in the joint from what I can see as I circle the building and peek in the windows. I stop in the shadows and close my eyes to concentrate on my bond with Wrath. I let it guide me like a compass and when I take a step away from the Hall of Worship and towards the Founders' Circle, it gets stronger.

I can work with that. There's a hill that rises up on one side of the Founders' Circle that will give me the high ground. I don't know how big Lethos is, but being a god makes me think he's, well, *big*. Trying to get up high is the smart play to make here. I'm working the buttons on my coat to get it off when a shadow darts to the side and I freeze, doing the mental math on how quick I'll be able to rip my sword free with the coat still on me, when I hear a weird sound.

"*Pssttttt.*"

It's like the air is being let out of a balloon. What on Earth would make that sound?

I tilt my head to the side and watch the bushes across from me. The sound has to be coming from there. "Who's there?"

"*Psssttt.* Buffy, it's me."

"Who is me?"

There's a sigh and I jump when Charlie comes tumbling out of the dark with a grumpy look on his face. "You can't tell it's me when you hear me?"

"No, not when you're invisible, Charlie."

His pout vanishes and he smiles. "Pretty cool, huh?"

He looks so proud of himself that I nod. "Yeah, it's pretty cool, but why were you invisible and what are you doing out here?"

"I came to help you."

"Help me how?"

"With this. My games book," he explains and holds the book up, "I can make anything happen, remember?"

"Charlie, you promised to only use that for minor mischief. You said it was just for your wizardry games."

"I know, I know and I promise, it's going to be for games like 99% of the time-"

"*Charlie,*" I groan, but he rushes on and cuts me off.

"I can use some of the wizard game power for you, Buffy. You're going up against that big god they've got out there and he looks seriously twisted. You need help."

That makes me go still.

"You've seen him?"

"Yeah, dude looks like a walking disease center." Charlie shudders and opens the book. "I'm going to write something to help you and then I promise I'll go right back to tabletop games and you won't have to worry about me using this for evil."

"Do you pinky swear?" I ask and hold up my pinky.

Charlie instantly hooks his pinky with mine and nods. "I pinky swear. I'm going to be a hero just this once before I go back to ruining people's lives in the realm of fantasy."

"Well, all right then. Thank you."

"You're very welcome. Now, with that thing I saw you're going to need to be faster. Like, a lot faster and stronger than you already are." Charlie bites his lip and starts to scribble in his book with a determined look. "And you'll need fire. Lots of fire. Yeah, fireballs...that's good. I like that."

My palms tingle and go warm. "Charlie chill."

"Trust me. It'll feel weird but it's part of the process. Hey, what about lightning? You wanna throw that around some?"

"Yes," I say without hesitation, because of course I want to control lightning. Who wouldn't? "What else are you writing in there?" I ask, leaning close to him. There's a bullet list Charlie's working on and my eyes go wide at the sight of it.

Buffy's Super Hero Upgrade

- *Inhumanly fast and strong enough to throw cars*
- *Able to shoot fireballs out of her hands*
- *Can produce and shoot lightning*
- *Definitely immune to diseases*
- *Bulletproof (?)*
- *Cannot be mind controlled*

"Mind controlled?" I jab my finger at the paper. "What do you mean *mind controlled*? And diseases? Do they have guns?"

"Well, like I said, the god looks like he's a plague god of some kind, so I thought you not being able to catch diseases would be good. I don't know how this works in real life. I can't just write + Divine Immunity here, okay? I'm working with what I can."

"Divine what?"

"You have so much to learn, Buffy and so little time." I roll my eyes at Charlie but he doesn't care because he's back to scribbling in his book. "Immunity to all poisons will be good to add, because that god is *rancid*."

"Where did you get eyes on Lethos?"

"The hill, but they weren't calling him Lethos."

"What were they calling him?"

"Ichabod."

"That wasn't the god," I tell Charlie and his eyes go wide.

"That wasn't a god? But he was...he was so-I mean, he *scared* me, Buffy."

"That's the founder of Sweet Tooth."

"*That Ichabod?*" Charlie clutches his book to his chest and nods. "You know, now that I know it's the original Ichabod and the reason we're all trapped in a cult, I get why he looks so rotted. Guy's been around for like what? Five hundred years?" Charlie asks and he misses the light I see turn on inside. It looks like a candle, the gentle glow of it shines just out of sight of the main room of the Hall of Worship.

"Yeah, something like that," I say, leaning to the window for a closer look.

"Listen, I don't want to freak you out, but he's a giant zombie mess."

"Uh-huh." The light glows brighter and I see it's a torch when it swings into view. I hear a dull thud and then another. More of the torch comes into view and that's when I realize I'm hearing footsteps.

"I bet he reeks too. I couldn't smell him from where I was, but no way he doesn't."

The full torch shows and then I see the hand holding it and it's...big, just like Charlie said. Easily three of my hands would make up the width and length of it. The torch in their hand looks tiny and I keep watching as a grotesque and rotting arm appears before a massive bulging shoulder until finally the being enters the Great Hall.

All my life I've thought of the Great Hall as massive. A place meant to inspire a feeling of smallness, a reminder that I was insignificant and the cult knew all. The Hall of Worship never failed to remind me of my place in the world, but it seems incredibly small with Ichabod's rotting form in it. He's easily twelve feet tall, maybe more. When he turns to look around the room, I grab Charlie and shove him down.

"Get down."

"What is the big deal-"

"He's here," I whisper and jerk my finger back at the window. "Ichabod."

Charlie pales and looks up at the window. "Fuckity fuck."

"Totally."

"What do we do? Oh my god, Buffy. I'm not brave. I'm not like you, I'm a gamemaster and-"

I grab his face in my hands and squeeze. "*You are brave.* You hear me? You're brave and good and you didn't have to come help me but you did. You're here with me and nobody else is because this is a death mission."

I hear the telltale thuds of Ichabod's footsteps in the room. They're slow, even. It sounds like he's pacing.

Charlie looks like he's gonna puke. "What? A death-what?" he squeaks.

"Death mission and only the very brave and the very stupid would go on one. You're not stupid which means you're brave. Do you hear me?" I give his smooshed face a shake and he nods.

"Yes, ma'am."

"Good. Now, I'm going to go fight that zombie monster and you're going to go find Wrath. You're going to use this book to help him. Whatever you need to do, do it. Can you do that for me?"

Charlie's shaking, I can feel it but he nods. "I promise I will."

"Good man." I smile at him and give his face another squish. "Now, I'm going to circle around the back and-"

The sound of Ichabod's footsteps stop and I freeze and look up. The flame of his torch is bright, too bright. "He's right there, isn't he?"

Charlie nods and I'm still holding his face when the window shatters and a hand reaches down to grab me and yank me back inside.

"Buffy!" Charlie yells and for all his talk of not being brave, the Gamemaster tries to climb in the window after me but I kick at him.

"Stay there, Charlie! I mean it!" I order and wave my hand. A small lighting bolt shoots out and hits the wall beside him and we both scream.

"It worked!" Charlie looks gleeful, so I shoot another bolt off while Ichabod raises me high above his head.

"Get to Wrath! I mean it!" I say and fire. The bolt goes wide and zips out the window.

"Okay, okay!" Charlie throws up his hands and vanishes from sight.

Ichabod snarls and shakes me before he speaks. "You insolent creature." His voice sounds old. It rumbles and shakes the floors and overhead the crystal chandelier trembles.

"I go by Buffy these days," I snap and reach for my sword but that's when I realize I still have the coat on and my sword is trapped beneath yards of flannel. "Oh not now." I swipe at my coat but Ichabod holds me under my arms so it's tricky for a second, until I remember I can shoot lightning from my hands and I fire off twin bolts at Ichabod's rotting arm.

He howls and his grip loosens just enough for me to raise my arms and wiggle free of the coat. I land on my feet with my sword drawn.

"Can we get a do over on my introduction? Something a little more snappy, a little less caught in a coat?"

Ichabod growls and flings my coat to the side. "You wretch! My cult, the vision I have nourished for hundreds of years, is in danger because of *you*? One insignificant girl? How dare you?"

"Oh, I very dare." I swing my sword and manage to cut into his leg before I dance away, but not before the smell of rotting flesh hits my nose and I dry heave. "You founded our town and you smell like that? Are you telling me Lethos has just been letting you curdle like milk this entire time?"

"This is my chosen form. I have no need for pleasing appearances, not like that whore of a demon you bonded yourself to. Tell me, do you know how many he's touched? How many have given themselves to your husband, only for him to betray them?" He laughs. "Poor, stupid girl," he spits the word *girl* at me like a curse and I flinch, "you think that demon loves you. He's just using you. Even now he serves our dark lord faithfully. You've been led to your demise like a lamb to the slaughter."

He's trying to get in my head, I know that. He wants me to not trust Wrath or our love. He wants me weak and confused, ready to give up, but his words do none of those things.

"My husband loves me," I growl and raise my sword again. I point it up at his chest and smile. "But you wouldn't know what love is, even if you had a heart that wasn't halfway decomposed, would you?"

"He's a *pleasure demon*. Do you know what pleasure demons are made for? They fuc-"

I lift my hand and will something to happen. Anything at all, because I don't know how to control the abilities Charlie just gave me. A fireball blasts out and hits Ichabod square in his mouth. His words die but the scream that bubbles up out of him is music to my ears.

I smile while he staggers back and paws at his flaming mouth. The smell of putrid burning flesh fills the room and black smoke makes me wave a hand in front of my face.

I circle my mouth with my finger and give him an apologetic shrug. "Sorry, couldn't quite hear you around the fire mouth thing you have going on."

Ichabod lurches forward and when he does, he moves faster than he has so far. He brings both of his fists down and I barely manage to dodge them. Marble cracks beneath his massive fists and he takes aim at me again, punching through the air so fast they whistle.

I roll again and lose my grip on my sword and it goes sliding across the floor towards the stairs. I roll to my feet to run after it but this time Ichabod strikes true and he catches me in the stomach. He hits me so hard that I fly back into the wall. I hit an oil painting, taking it down with a crash.

The heavy frame and canvas are on top of me and I shove them off with a groan. "Lucky hit. I'll give you one of those."

Ichabod grabs me and squeezes. I wince and try to pry his fingers off of me, but it's no use. He's too strong. How is he this strong when I have Charlie's power-up working on me? There's a crack and I scream. Something definitely broke, maybe a rib. I suck in a ragged breath and barely have time to brace myself before Ichabod throws me in the air and punches me again. His fist connects with a *thwack* and my ears are ringing from the force of his punch that sends me slamming into the staircase railing. A few of the wooden pieces from the banister come free and the marble cracks under my back. I taste blood and slide down the staircase with a groan. Black spots dance in my vision. I bet I have a concussion or whatever it is that happens when a five hundred plus year old plague monster punches you across the room.

The floor trembles, the vibration of each step Ichabod takes towards me makes me shake and I hate it. I grit my teeth and push myself against the staircase. When he comes to a stop in front of me I spit the mouthful of blood I have at his feet and tip my head back to look up at him.

"Hey," I say with a bloody smile. "Nice arm."

"You're ash under my heel. You lay with demons. You treat your body like trash, *Blossom*. You're rotten to the core."

I point a finger at him. "You know there's an old adage about pointing fingers, but I'm going to do it anyway, because speaking of rotting, have you looked in the mirror lately?"

Ichabod glares as pus slides down his face when he blinks. The open sores weep blood when he leans down into my space. "I'm going to rip your petals off, Blossom."

Fetid breath rolls over my face as he reaches for me. Twisted and gnarled ham hands almost close in on me but I surprise him and lift my hands to meet his.

"I said, I go by Buffy." I grab his hands and let the power in me loose. The mix of Wrath's might and Charlie's power-up twist and meld into one and I light Ichabod up from the inside.

His eyes go wide and he looks down at his hands. They glow bright as my power moves under his skin and he realizes what's happening. "No!" He tries to rip his hands away but it's too late. The power I've shot him up with is already seeded and it explodes with a sickening splat.

Ichabod's hands explode and I throw my arm up to shield my face from most of it. There's blood and sinew clinging to me when I stagger to my feet. Ichabod falls back and roars with anger as he waves the bloody stumps that used to be his hands in pain and I smile.

"Ouch, that looks like it hurts. On the bright side, your hands aren't rotting anymore."

He falls to a knee and spits at me. "Hands or no hands, I'm going to kill you."

I sway on my feet with a wince and pick up my sword. "You're not the first-" I pause and gesture at him with my blade, "-*thing* that's tried to kill me today, so be my guest."

Ichabod opens his mouth and the sound that comes out of

him sounds like a thousand voices screaming, a thousand souls being ripped and torn to pieces. I clap my hands over my ears and run for the stairs. I have no idea where I'm going, maybe I can get the chandelier to drop on him if I'm lucky, but I run. He lunges after me and the steady thud of his feet makes pictures fall and windows crack on the bottom floor. I make it halfway up the stairs when Ichabod slams one of his bloody stumps into the stairs and catches me on the shoulder.

I go down with a shriek and lob a fireball at him. Ichabod spits at me and warm green liquid hits my leg. The material of my pants disintegrates and smoke rises from where he hit me with his loogie. Definitely poison, though other than my ruined pants, I'm safe.

"Good job, Charlie."

I keep running and leap over another one of Ichabod's swinging, rotting stumps. I hack at his arm when he tries again and he falls back enough that I can barrel roll to the top step and land in a crouch. There's nothing really up here. I see a few doors on the opposite end of the hallway but there are no doors where I currently am.

There *is* a floor-to-ceiling window offering a birds eye view of the area. I'm sure I can see the Founders' Circle from there. If things get bad enough here with Ichabod, I can at least jump out of that.

"I'm going to make you pay. Your screams will be my lullaby." Ichabod is only a few feet away from me and glares. The milky irises of his fetid eyes move from my leg to my face to my sword and I see the realization hit him that this might not go his way.

Good.

I twirl my sword in my hand and point it at him with a smile.

I'd rather he know his demise is on the way. It's more fun that way.

"What *are* you?" He rises another step and smashes the banister so hard that it splinters and breaks. Ichabod is feeling creative because he kicks the smashed banister at me like a spear but I cut it in two with a neat swipe of my sword.

"Didn't you guess it already? I'm Wrath's Harbinger. You know, that whore of a demon you were talking about?" I create a fireball and smile at him.

"Wrath is nothing more than a puppet. A whore. You are foolish to-"

I suck in a breath and interrupt him, each word growing louder until I end on a scream. "Watch how you talk about *my husband.*" I toss the fireball in the air and swing my sword at it. The blade slices the fireball in two and quicker than my eye can follow the fire shoots towards Ichabod.

Apparently the fire is also too fast for him to follow, because it catches him square in the chest. "Aughhh!" He flails, bloody stumps pawing in vain at the fire that's caught and spreads over his skin like it has a mind of its own.

I smile and flick my fingers and the fire moves with my gesture. So, the fire doesn't have a will of its own, but it does obey mine. I sweep my hand in an arc and the fire consumes Ichabod in seconds. Never one to give up, the founder of Sweet Tooth and the Cult of Wrath makes a run for me.

Kind of works out, because I return the favor and run straight at him. We collide a few feet in and I cut right through him with a jerk of my sword. The two halves of Ichabod land on either side of me with muted thuds that feel anti-climatic after what I just went through.

I cough and wave the smoke away from Ichabod's bonfire of a body and stagger towards the window at the end of the hallway. I clear the smoke away and brace a hand on the wall to steady myself. The soulstone in my sword lights up and I lift my sword to look at it. There's a light moving inside of the stone, flickering and moving from side to side frantically.

My soulstone sword *ate* Ichabod's soul like Sunday said it would. At least it's pretty.

"I can't believe I just cut the town founder in half." I look over my shoulder at his flaming remains. "What a day."

I close my eyes and reach for the bond but nothing changes. Wrath isn't here. The pull I feel towards him is directly ahead of me. I squint and look out the window towards the Founders' Circle. The full moon makes it easy to see and there's not a cloud in the sky to block its light. I have a clear view of the Founders' Circle and I see a few things that concern me.

First, the Founders' Circle is ablaze with torches. There are twelve torches ringing the circle and I see Blossoms and cultists at each of them. Second, I see Wrath. He's up on the altar I prayed to and watched all those nights ago when I was a bride and a Blossom.

And the worst one of all, is that I see my parents. Even at this distance, I'd recognize them—Darla and Lorne Martinez. They follow behind a robed figure and I'd bet my magic sword it's Draven O'Hare.

The love match that made me. The parents that sold me out for status. The people that were supposed to protect me and love me above all else.

Out of all the betrayals I've had handed to me in Sweet Tooth, theirs is the one that should hurt the most.

It doesn't, though. It feels like all the rest, but it does fill me with rage. Anger hits me quick and hard when I see my parents holding hands as they approach my bound husband. I don't know what their part in all of this is, but I do know I won't let them near Wrath. Not if I can help it.

I don't have time to take the stairs when my parents are here and Wrath is laid out like a birthday gift for them.

They sold me out to be sacrificed. They'll have no problem watching Draven end my husband.

"Right." I sheath my sword back across my back and take a few steps back before I take off at a run towards the window and leap.

CHAPTER
THIRTY-SIX

Whatever the window is made out of, it's not glass. I hit the window so hard that I nearly knock out a tooth. I practically bounce when I hit the floor and it knocks the air right out of me. I lay gasping on the floor and roll over onto my back with a groan.

"Ohhhh."

I suck in a choked breath and then manage another before I open my eyes and stare up at the ceiling.

"I hope no one saw that."

"It's bulletproof."

I wince at Charlie's voice and sigh. "How do you know that?"

Charlie leans over me and holds up my sword. "The dark web, Buffy," he says, holding a hand out to help me up.

I take his hand and have to concentrate on not keeling over when Charlie pulls me up. Everything spins for a beat and I hunch over, hands on my knees, to get my bearings.

"You didn't mention that before."

Charlie's hands go to his hips. "Didn't have time before the plague monster ripped you a new one. I might have if I knew you were going to try to jump out of it. You too good for the stairs now?"

I stand shakily and head for the damn stairs. "I thought it would save time but apparently I was wrong." I look back at him and frown. "What are you doing here? I thought you were going to help Wrath."

Charlie hesitates and leaps awkwardly over a broken set of stairs to follow me down. "I did. Wanted to make sure you were okay." When he almost trips, I reach out a hand to him.

"Come here, Charlie."

He eyeballs my hands which is understandable because they're covered in blood and guts, but he eventually comes to me and I pick him up and toss him over my shoulder. "Ohhhhkay, I think I'm into this."

I laugh and leap down the last few stairs to the bottom. "Don't let Wrath hear you say that." I put Charlie down and then point up the stairs. "And you know, about the whole window thing, if you just wouldn't mention that..."

Charlie crosses his heart. "Secret dies with me."

"Appreciate it."

"Anytime, oh Harbinger of Wrath."

We walk out of the Hall of Worship and I motion for Charlie to head towards the hill. "I'm going to go down there and get Wrath back. Whatever you do, just...just make sure Wrath gets out of this."

Charlie hugs his book to his chest and frowns. "Buffy...I don't think that's what he would want."

343

I shake my head. "I mean it. Wrath walks out of here. I'm not important."

Charlie opens his mouth. He wants to say more but I don't wait for him to speak. I lift my head and start out for the Founders' Circle. It's still the same stone path that I took with Meadow a few nights before with torches flickering through the trees and the moon high in the sky, but the world was different then.

I was different then.

I'm close enough to the circle that I don't even have to reach for the bond. Wrath pulls on it, just a tug but it settles me some. I pause just inside the trees to look behind me, Charlie's gone. Good. I hope he has enough time to get settled for what's about to happen. I scan the circle and nothing has changed. Wrath is still on the altar and the cultists are still at their posts with the Blossoms in chains in front of them. I don't look for Meadow. If I do, I might not be able to stay calm long enough to figure out what Lethos' game plan is. Blacking out from rage at my best friend being held hostage means I'm no good to anyone. I take a deep breath and lift my sword. When I walk into the circle everyone freezes. I hear a few Blossoms cry out and the clank of chains but I keep my eyes on Draven at the center of it all.

"You came," Draven says with a raised eyebrow and hums. "I thought you'd at least try to catch us off guard but you're just delivering yourself to us. How splendid."

"Eat glass."

"You have no right to this place!"

"Oh, am I interrupting something? I mean, if you didn't want me to crash, you should have dug deeper."

"Insolent little b-"

"Ah, ah, ah that's no way to speak to our guest of honor, now is it Draven?" The voice that speaks is old—feels old. It's like music, low and melodic, the kind of harmony that makes you relax and ache to lose yourself in it. A man materializes in front of Wrath's altar and my mouth falls open.

He's beautiful.

Achingly perfect.

He looks like he's been carved from marble with how flawless his skin is. Thick auburn hair and dark eyes meet mine. He smiles at me and I want to return the expression. Full lips and high cheekbones give him an angelic look. Unlike Ichabod, there's nothing rotting about him. He's dressed perfectly. The suit he wears reminds me of the one Wrath wore when I first met him but instead of midnight black, his clothing is spotless white. When the moonlight hits it he glows like an angel. I almost have to shield my eyes from the blazing amulet he wears at his neck to complete his angelic facade.

It shines just as bright as the moon. Interesting.

"Allow me to introduce myself." He takes a step towards me. I should move, but I don't. I want to see what he does. Want to hear what he says next. Everyone else does too by the way they hold their breath and stay statue still until he finally speaks.

"My name is Lethos."

"Our most holy on high!" Draven O'Hare throws himself down into a bow so low he nearly bangs his forehead on the ground and the spell of beauty that got its dirty little fingers on me lets go. I give myself a mental shake—just because demons and old gods are beautiful doesn't necessarily mean they're friends.

I watch Draven try to right himself and I actually feel a little bad for what's going to happen to him. Then I remember he buried me alive and demon-napped my husband. He's dead the first chance I get.

I narrow my eyes at Lethos. "I'm Buffy."

Lethos taps the amulet and smiles at me. There's something so familiar about the amulet, but what? I stare at it for a second longer before I realize what it is.

It's a soulstone.

"There's a lot of news about you, Buffy."

I twirl my sword. "So you've heard of me. I'm flattered," I say and nod at the amulet. "Nice accessory."

"Oh, this old thing?" He tilts his head and a halo of moonlight forces the shadows back. "I'd tell you where I got it but I want to talk about *you*. One doesn't forget a name like Buffy. I like it. It has character."

"You hear that, mother? Lethos just loves your taste in names." My eyes slide her way. She's pressed close to my father with a bright smile on her face. This one doesn't look forced. She's either finally getting better at playing the cult's game or she truly is happy with how things have turned out.

I can't believe I ended up with such horrible parents.

"You will address him as his holiness!" Draven screams from where he's still contorted into a pretzel trying to bow.

I roll my eyes. "Look, I don't know what your plan is here, especially with the whole 'angel look' but I'm not into it. I'm here for my friends." I flick my swords in a circle and then gesture at Wrath. "And my husband. Hand them over and I'll let you get back to your worship party."

I'm playing for time. Lethos' power comes from the soulstone, even if not all of it does. I know getting it away from him will weaken him. Who knows how many souls he has trapped in it? Hundreds, maybe thousands, from the way it shines.

Lethos chuckles and crosses his arms. "You're a spirited girl, Buffy and strong-willed. You're not even affected by my charms, are you?" He sparkles a little brighter then and I have to look away.

I look to Wrath where he's bound on his altar. He's on his knees and looking right back at me with his arms behind him. There's a length of chain beside him and I want to rip every link apart and make Lethos choke on it.

"No," I answer and it's the truth. My eyes are for one soul and one soul only.

Wrath.

There's blood on his face and running down his neck and I see the tip of one of his horns is broken. Whatever they did to him, he's bleeding down his side. His shirt is stained, the black material darker than it should be and stuck to him. I swallow hard and don't think about what I'm going to find beneath his shirt when I look after all of this.

I send love and reassurance his way through our bond and his back straightens. The tremble that I noticed before vanishes and he smiles at me.

Our bond feels better now that I'm closer to him but I would be a fool if I didn't see that he's in rough shape. I hope Charlie is coming up with something to help him while I deal with Lethos.

"Such an unusual girl." Lethos sighs and I force myself to look back at him. He's beautiful, but where I thought him perfect, I see there's no soul. It's hollow and empty. Too perfect to be true.

I tilt my head and there's a shimmer that tells me magic is being used and a second later I see the crack in Lethos' mirage. It lifts and shifts wrong. When he moves it stays and I see what he really looks like.

Instead of beauty and light there's nothing but darkness. The soulstone he wears goes dark and Lethos transforms into a pure void that sucks in everything around it. My breath catches. Lethos isn't a shadow, he is *darkness*. Pure darkness and nothing more. There are no features, just the shape of his body, an outline really that's colored in with emptiness.

"Not any more unusual than you," I tell him and his magic snaps back into place, the void I saw is gone and he's angelic once more.

"It's not nice to peek behind the curtain, Buffy. Didn't anyone ever teach you manners?"

"My parents sold me out to a cult to be sacrificed, so I honestly think I'm behind the curve on that one."

For a moment there's no reaction from Lethos and then he throws his head back and laughs. The sound is discordant. It matches the void version of him I saw and I wince at the harsh, grating sound of it. The Blossoms around the circle whimper and cry, some of them fall to their knees and clap their hands over their ears. I can't help but look their way. I see Meadow then. She doesn't give in like the girls trying to hide from Lethos' laugh. She stands tall and true. She looks so brave, even with a knife to her neck. The cultist at her back is Victor. I should have known.

I wish I'd killed him when I had the chance.

"They did, didn't they?" Lethos says before he snaps his fingers at my parents. "Parents of Buffy, come here."

My mother comes forward first. She has to practically drag my father who looks like he's finally realizing that being part of a murdering cult is a bad idea. He puts his hand at her arm to stop her but there's no stopping Darla Martinez.

"Your holiness," she purrs and drops low into a bow.

"You sold your daughter."

"For you as a gift, of course."

"If you sold her, then she's not a gift, is she?"

"I-what?" My mother looks surprised but Lethos ignores her and looks at me.

"I thought of using your parents as collateral against you. I know what you did to poor old Ichabod in there," he says, waving at the Hall of Worship. He grabs my mother by her throat and jerks her forward. "I see now that was a mistake. You don't care about them at all, do you?" He squeezes hard, I know from the strangled sound that comes out of my mother.

I shake my head and answer him truthfully. "Honestly, no." Lethos lifts my mother off the ground and she starts to kick and slap at his arm.

"Buffy, please," my father begs and holds his hands out to me. "We're your parents."

"*And I was your daughter.*" The scream comes out of me so fast and quick that it leaves my throat raw and I shake my head. "You're not my parents. You're monsters. Cruel and terrible souls that I wish never existed. I hope he kills you both."

There's a snap and my mother stops kicking. Lethos drops her body to the ground. My father tries to run but he's too slow.

"Wait, no! Buffy, tell him to-" My father never finishes, because Lethos snaps his neck and tosses his body at my feet.

Lethos sniffs. "That wasn't even fun. What a pity."

I expect to feel something looking at my dead father but I don't. Not even seeing my mother's sightless eyes makes me feel what I know I should. I feel nothing and the truth of that comes from me wishing I'd been the one to do it.

"Now what?" I look up at Lethos. "We know what I want. I want my friends and my husband and I want to go free from this twisted nightmare, but what do you want? Why are you doing this?"

"Why not?" Lethos answers and I want to sock the god.

"*What?*" I ask, because I couldn't have heard him right. *What the Wrath?* My entire life has been a lie and now I'm fighting for my friends' lives and that's his answer? "What do you mean 'why not?'"

Beloved. Tread carefully.

I look at Wrath and see him looking at me with a pleading look. Right. Our mind link. Oops.

Fine, but I don't like him. He's a void monster.

Correct, but at least he killed your parents.

You're not supposed to make me like him. Charlie is going to help us with his book. Hold tight. I'll get us out of this.

"Answer me," I snap, looking to distract Lethos. I don't want him knowing I've been talking to Wrath. I focus all my attention on Lethos and shut Wrath out. He's just going to try and talk me out of this.

Lethos shrugs. "Gods are notoriously pernicious. I'm no different, so 'why not' is my answer. There *is* a little something of a motive, if that makes you feel better. Would you like to hear it?" He moves towards me and I move too. We circle one another and I lift my chin in defiance. I have to get that damn necklace off of him or else.

"Only if it's not a villain monologue. I hate those."

He glares at me. "You will learn obedience, Buffy. I see why

Wrath is charmed by you and your mouthiness, but I'll not tolerate it in my wife."

My eyes bug out and I forget my game plan to snatch his soul-stone, because I almost cough on my own spit. "I'm sorry. *Your what?*"

"*Wife,*" Lethos says again, waving his hand at me and my limbs freeze. "How lucky for you that I've chosen you. What a pretty dress I've given you, too." I look down at the dress I'm wearing and my heart stops.

It's my cult approved wedding dress.

An exact replica of the one I wore when I last set foot in this circle. The familiar feel of the material against my skin makes me sick. I try to scream but nothing comes out, the sound dies the second I try and Lethos tuts at me. He takes a step towards me until he's close enough to touch me. The shimmer of magic that nearly entranced me before brightens and I can't break the hold he has on me. I know what he is underneath the beauty and perfection, I know what he is, but still...it's so hard to look away. His magic wraps around me like a poison and I can feel it eating away at the bond I share with Wrath. It's already so weak and Lethos is a force.

He leans to the side and smiles at me. "You have such a beautiful smile, I know you do. Show it to me now." I smile at him. Lethos hums in pleasure. I hear Wrath's voice, but he's so far away. The pull of our bond is nothing but a pinprick against the weight of Lethos' magic.

It's unrelenting and endless.

Magic so old I know it was here before Sweet Tooth or this world. There's no end to Lethos.

He holds out his hand to me. "Give me that sword." My hand

squeezes tight and it's with a smile on my face that I don't give him the sword, even when he narrows his eyes.

"Give me the sword, Buffy."

I don't answer him. Words don't form the way I will them to, the way I want them to. Everything is so unimportant with Lethos looking at me. *But my sword.*

I can't let that go.

I need it, even if I've forgotten why. My reason is almost there, it flits in the shadows just out of reach and the longer I stare into Lethos' eyes the further away from me it gets.

"Wrath chose well with you." He sighs, leaning to the side. I mirror the movement. Anything to be closer to him. "I will break you until you answer to me and me alone. Just give me time." He raises a hand to touch me. My world narrows down to the hand in front of me and I close my eyes.

"Get away from my wife."

There's a snap of metal on skin before Lethos is jerked back from me. I open my eyes and instead of his soulstone necklace, I see there's a thick chain around his neck. It's wrapped tight and digs into his skin. Another rip of the chain breaks the skin. Shadows spill forth from the wound and the perfect, unmarred skin around the shadowy gash flakes and falls away.

Wrath rises from his knees and Lethos' soulstone necklace floats in front of him. When he speaks it cracks and goes dark.

"My wife answers to no one."

Wrath's voice shakes the ground beneath my feet. He whips the chain to the side and Lethos with it. The magical haze that blinded me lifts. I suck in a choking gasp and fall to my knees, my sword still in my hand.

Lethos gives Wrath an irritated look. "You never were good at sharing, now were you?"

Wrath wraps the chains in his hands around his knuckles and lifts them. "You'll not touch my wife if you want to live to see another miserable day. God or no god, I will unmake you now." The chain he holds glows metallic, a brilliant white and when he pulls, the metal pulses before it forces more of Lethos' skin to char and fall.

Lethos grabs the chain and growls. "You are a *pleasure demon*, nothing more. Your power comes from me and it is me alone that commands you. Drop the chains," he commands, but Wrath does not obey him.

His power. The one thing the cult wanted from Wrath no longer lives in him but with me. I never had a chance of fighting him and winning with the whole of Wrath's power in me.

I almost laugh when I hear Wrath speak.

"The power that sustains me is written into being. Your power is gone and your hold over me with it." He moves then and I can hardly follow his movement. One second he's there and another he's grappling with Lethos. Demon and god collide, the deadly chains Wrath wields rise and fall, the length of them catching Lethos and wrapping tight. And when Wrath rips them away, he pulls away another bit of the perfect facade hiding Lethos' true face.

When they part, Wrath ends up at my side, bloody shining chains still in his grip. "Are you all right?"

"Yeah," I whisper.

We both watch the shadow form of Lethos move, squirming and expanding, filling the space with night as the moon falls dark. There's a cry from the cultists and I hear Blossoms start to scream. Only the light of the torches illuminates the circle and I see the rise of the knives the cultists intend to use on my friends.

I know what I have to do.

"Kill him," I tell Wrath and cup his cheek. "I'm going to save my friends."

He turns his face, leans into my touch and kisses my palm. "I would destroy this world, the next, the universe for you, beloved."

I blush at his words. "You always know exactly what to say. Now, have fun destroying the god."

"Be safe, beloved." He winks at me and if there wasn't a cult waiting to murder my friends or a shadow god bearing down on us, I would beg my husband to do unseemly acts to me, but as it is-

I take a deep breath and turn to face the chaos of the circle. Cultists are dragging my friends into place. I watch a knife rise over the head of a girl closest to me, it's Lylah.

"Get away from her!" I close the distance and drive my sword up through the cultist with a jerk. He falls to his knees, a gasping and sucking sound coming from the hole I just put in his chest. When his hood falls back I see he's an Aguirre. He grabs at me but I swing my sword again and take his head off. His body falls with a splat as I help Lylah to her feet.

"You're going to be okay. I promise."

Lylah laughs and hugs me. "Buffy! You saved us!"

I hug her back. "Not yet, we aren't safe yet but we will be." I press the knife meant to take her life into her hands. "Take this and fight."

Lylah takes the knife with far more gusto than I thought she would and nods. "You got it." I watch long enough to see her launch herself at the closest cultist with a scream and the Blossom he was assigned to turns on him, too. They steal his knife and he goes down with a terrified scream as the women cut into him.

"All of you, fight them!" I order, my voice carrying on the still night air. "There are more of us than them. Listen to me and fight them!"

I'm lying, there aren't more of us than them but it doesn't matter. We will win. We will have our vengeance and when I turn to grab the next cultist and slam him into the altar my words don't feel like a lie.

There might only be a dozen Blossoms fighting for their lives in the Founders' Circle we were raised to die in, but I don't feel that way. I fight my way through the men in front of me and it's like the spirits of all the women that went before us are here now.

I cut down another cultist and that's when Draven appears. The man that I thought would be my father-in-law, the one everyone feared in Sweet Tooth.

I remember him looking intimidating before but now I'm the Harbinger and things are different.

"You're going to pay, do you hear me?" He roars and pulls a knife out. "I'm going to cut out your tongue and-"

I thrust my sword into his gut and he goes silent.

I grab his shoulder and jerk him forward, impaling him further on my blade. Blood spills from his mouth and onto the ground at our feet.

"And do what?" I whisper.

Draven doesn't answer me. He can't.

I rip my sword free and move on. Draven O'Hare is just another dead body to bury and nothing more.

"Mercy!" A man falls at my feet and he looks up at me. It's Victor. Meadow stands over him with a bloodied knife and I see he's already got a stab wound in his side. She's torn his robes in two. "Please, don't do this, Buffy. *Buffy!* You know me, you know that I'm not like this. *They made us.*"

I want to believe him. I want to do the thing that killed so many of us. The girls I wanted to be like when I was younger, the women that I thought left for the city, the ones that would have believed a man like Victor.

"Buffy, I swear I'll make it up to you, just don't-"

"He's just as bad as them. Worse even, because he's a coward but I don't think I can do it." Meadow interrupts and looks at me. She's like my sister and I nearly lost her.

"Don't worry, I can." Meadow holds her knife out to me and I wave her off. "Thanks, but I've got my own."

So many Blossoms have died and bled here. They lost their lives for nothing.

This blood belongs to them too, so I give it to them.

Victor might be as bad as the rest, but I make his death quick. My sword rises and falls, flashes in the torchlight as I bring it down and plunge it through his heart. He's gone in an instant, sightless eyes staring up at the dark sky as I rip my sword out of him without a second look.

"Are you all right?" I ask Meadow and she nods but I can tell differently. She's trying to be strong. Her lip wobbles and her eyes water so I hold my arms out to her and she throws herself forward with a sob.

She clings to me. "I was so scared, Buffy. Buffy, I knew you would find me."

"I'm sorry, oh Meadow, I'm so sorry." My heart breaks and I

remember why I didn't let myself look at her before. I start to cry and hold her to me. "You're safe now, I promise. You're safe, you're safe."

"*Buffy.*"

I let Meadow cry while I keep her safe.

THIRTY-SEVEN

"That's your husband?" Meadow whispers with wide eyes. "You married a demon?"

"Well, a demon that we all thought was a god, you know?" I smile proudly and nod. "Isn't he great?"

"He's beating that shadow to a pulp."

"To be fair, he deserves it."

Wrath has Lethos on the ground. The chains have multiplied and wind around Lethos. He's utterly bound, there's no way for him to escape and I know he knows it when he begs.

"You owe me," he insists. His shadow flickers and moves and if not for the chains wrapped around him, I would lose him in the dark.

Wrath snarls at him, his handsome face contorts into something I've never seen before. Pure rage. His teeth look sharp as knives and the silver of his eyes has gone dark.

This is not my husband.

This is a demon possessed.

Wrath's fire burns bright and I welcome it. After barely being able to feel him, the surge of energy and power is a blessing.

"For centuries you owned every inch of me and made me your puppet. You ripped my soul from my body and kept it in this." He holds up the soulstone necklace. The stone is dark now but it shines bright under the moonlight.

"I owe you?"

He lifts his hands, palms pressed together and the chains follow him. They rise up, the metal links gleaming, before they snap tight and drag Lethos up with them.

"You thought you could force me back under your control? That I would let you bind me to you again?" Wrath squeezes the soulstone and it shatters with a sharp crack. He opens his hand and the shards float from his hand and begin to circle Lethos.

"You tried to touch my wife."

The shards speed up, their movements are frenzied and they start to glow until they remind me of the embers that sparked hot and popped during the summer bonfires the Founders held for the Blossoms. Then, we were worried about a loose spark burning our clothing or smelling like smoke in case we ran into our intended grooms. Those worries seem so small and far away, yet they're here with me now. They step up beside Meadow and I, the red glow from the soulstone shards dancing across our faces and it's like no time has passed at all.

Just enjoying another summer bonfire while my demon husband gets his vengeance on an old god.

"My wife."

The charged shards spring forward and embed in Lethos face and neck. He screams and twists in the chains to get free but it's no use. Whatever magic holds him is stronger than he is. The red of the soulstone pieces flare crimson, the color made all the more bright because of the shadows they pierce.

"Buffy, your sword!" Wrath calls to me, "Use it now and end this."

"I thought you'd never ask." The chains keep him sitting pretty for me while I skip up to Lethos with my sword raised high.

His shadows writhe and snap. "Get away from me you miserable bitch!"

"Aw, that kind of hurts. I thought you wanted to get married. What's the matter? I thought you were going to break me. Guess we'll never know what that looks like, huh?" I raise my sword and slam it home, burying it in Lethos' chest. The shadows try to shrink back from it but there's no escape with the chains holding him.

Sunday's soulstone sparkles while Lethos thrashes. "No, no! You can't-*no*." Lethos screams, each word more frenzied until Wrath throws his arms wide and just like they did before, the chains follow him and rip Lethos apart. For a second nothing happens and I'm too shocked to move, but that's before I'm knocked backwards from a charge of power that lays me and the rest of the Blossoms out. When I open my eyes the only thing left of Lethos is my sword standing straight in the ground from where it landed and lights dancing in Sunday's soulstone.

"Are you shitting my dick?" Meadow groans nearby and I laugh.

I roll onto my back and manage to find her. "I told you it had something," I wheeze.

She smiles at me. "You were right. I thought we went over this before."

"*Beloved.*"

I smile and struggle to sit up. "Come here, I love you." I hold out my arms and a second later Wrath is there. He sweeps me up into his arms and hugs me tight.

"I thought I lost you," he murmurs and kisses my forehead and then nose. He covers my cheeks with kisses and cradles my face in his hands.

"Hey, I wasn't the one in chains. I thought I lost *you*," I tell him.

"They *buried* you," Wrath whispers. His eyes shine with tears and my heart breaks when he says, "And I was powerless to stop it. I watched them put you in the ground. I thought you were dead and so I-I let them."

"You let them what?"

"I didn't fight. I let them bring me here. I am ashamed to say I gave up when I thought you were gone. There was no reason for my heart to beat or my soul to be free without you."

I hear the pain and truth in his voice. I rise up onto my knees and it's me that kisses his cheeks and forehead now. "*Wrath*. No, that will never be true. Even if I'm not here, you still have to live."

"I won't. I refuse it. Even if the gods conspire to take you from me, I would follow you into the underworld in this dimension or the next and I would find you. I would bind myself to you for all eternity even if that meant my soul was damned to walk the worlds in darkness."

"That was so romantic," Meadow whispers loudly to us and when I look her way, I see the other Blossoms are gathered around her and staring at us with dreamy smiles. "I get why you married a demon." The Blossoms all murmur in agreement and I blush.

"I am honored to gain the favor of Buffy's friends. We have labored long to ensure your safety, Blossoms."

"Are you all okay?" I ask.

Meadow nods. "We are. They left us alone, mostly. They moved us around a lot so we knew something had them spooked but we didn't know it was you."

"They were scared of me?" I ask and the Blossoms all nod.

"You're all they would talk about," Betty Marks tells me proudly. I did choir with her for four years and last year she was the runner up for the Autumn Harvest Festival Queen. "But they didn't call you by your name. They called you the-"

"Harbinger!" A voice shouts and I jump. We all turn to see Elijah sprinting down the hill I told Charlie to hide on. He followed directions to a tee, because a second later he bursts out of the trees and trips after Elijah. Nina and Sunday saunter out a few steps behind the men.

Meadow snaps her fingers. "Yeah, that's what they called you, but the harbinger of what?" she asks and I draw myself up with a pleased smile.

"I'm the Harbinger of Wrath."

Everyone's mouths fall open and they look to my husband. "He's Wrath, isn't he?"

"Yup."

"Oh my Wrath, I thought...well, oh my god, you meant he was the demon we thought was a god and I didn't know you meant him...I didn't put it together, I'm so embarrassed," she whisper-screams to me like Wrath can't hear her. "You actually married Wrath? That is totally worth nearly getting sacrificed."

I have to agree with her on that one, even if the first part kind of sucked.

"It's an honor, your holiness."

"Wrath!" A Blossom falls to her knees and holds her palms up in supplication and Lylah practically passes out.

"What do I do?" Wrath is panicked. Positively flustered and I love the sight of it, so I step back and let the Blossoms descend on him. "Buffy, I'm scared."

I wave him off. "Just smile, it'll be fine. I'm right here if you need me!"

"I need you," he insists, but the Blossoms have closed ranks and I'm pretty sure one of them stole a pen off one of the dead cultists, because she's asking him to sign her arm.

"Harbinger, are you all right? You were victorious, just like I knew you would be!" Elijah falls at my feet and holds up my sword.

I take it from him and pull him up off his knees with my other hand. "Thank you but please, no kneeling. I thought we went over that."

"Are you sure, he looks so pretty when he's like that."

I glare at Sunday. "Yes, I'm sure. That's for you two."

"More for me, yippee."

Nina groans and covers her eyes. "I'm going to get sick if I hear any more unholy sounds from the pair of you. Is there no rest for the undead?"

Charlie nods at where Wrath is being mobbed by starstruck Blossoms. "Is he going to be okay? Should we help him? I can write something else for him if he needs it."

That has my interest and I go to Charlie to get a look at his book. "What did you write for him before? He was incredible, did you see what he did to Lethos?"

Charlie beams and opens his book to show me. "Go big or go

home, am I right?" he asks and my mouth falls open when I see the words on the page.

The Wrathinator

- *Wrath is a god of infinite power.*
- *Wrath is no longer a demon, plus Celestial Divinity and Heavenly Origin.*
- *He is a storied god of unparalleled worlds with infinite power to unmake beings with his words.*
- *VERY OP.*

"You made him a *god*?!"

"I mean, he kind of already was, at least around here. So I thought, lets keep it simple and stick to the storyline. That way it's more believable and makes for a more compelling campaign."

I look at Wrath. He still looks like the husband I know and love, but I know his power. He did unmake Lethos for almost touching me. Ripped him right apart and now I have his soul in my sword. I heft my sword and consider the shining soulstone.

"Is he going to stay a god?"

"Yeah. I mean, unless you want me to take it away."

All my life I've been at the mercy of men with no souls. Greedy, ugly, cold-hearted men who broke others for their own gain and convinced us all they were good and right. They controlled us through fear and manipulation until not even my smile was my own.

I smile and look at Wrath. He turns and our eyes meet.

"Wrath," I whisper and let him into my mind. The brush of him is familiar and constant, it's the comforting and safe place I have always known my husband to be. The demon with a heart of gold, the demon that saved me from the men that would kill me.

"*I love you, beloved,*" his words come to me instantly.

"If anyone should be a god, it's a demon," I tell Charlie and nod at his book. "Make it permanent?"

Charlie clicks his pen. "Done."

When I go to my husband, Nina comes with me. The Blossoms welcome her with open arms and hugs. Dead or undead, she is still one of them. I leave her with our friends, smiling and laughing as she introduces them to the others.

"I want you to meet the gang," Nina tells them and leads them over to Sunday, Elijah and Charlie.

This time I don't tell her there is no gang. I'm too happy watching them all meet and Wrath rests his chin on my head.

I lean back against him and tears prick my eyes but I blink them away. "Are you happy?" I ask.

"Of course, I'm happy. I have my wife in my arms and victory in my heart. Plus, I think I'm a god now."

"You are," I confirm.

He kisses my cheek. "An unexpected development but even without it I would be the same, which is happy. And you? Are you happy, Buffy?"

I watch Elijah shine my sword and hold it up to inspect it in the moonlight. Next to him, Sunday makes the Blossoms laugh while Charlie scribbles in his book and Nina peeks over his shoulder.

Everyone I care about is safe and for the first time I know I'm strong enough to keep them that way. My heart feels full and everything is perfect.

"I am so very happy," I whisper.

EPILOGUE

One Month Later...

"So you're saying there's still a Cult of Wrath."

I look up from the laundry I'm folding and shrug at Sunday. "I mean, yes there's a cult, but it's like *a nice cult*. Like a "hey, it would be nice if you joined us and we all work together and share what we have but no pressure at all if you don't want to join us, please have a nice day." That kind of cult."

"That's what they call a commune."

"What's a commune?"

"A cult."

"Oh, okay, then yes, there's still a cult."

Things have settled in town. With the Founders gone there was a power vacuum and all it took was me seeing Annie Bustos make a play for power along with some of the surviving men from the Founding Families to tell me we couldn't go.

"If we leave them now, it's going to go back the way it was. We can change things. You're a god now and I'm me."

366

THAT TIME I TOOK DOWN A CULT

"You are perfect."

"You know what I mean."

"Fine, we'll stay, but only if you agree with me that you're perfect."

"I'm perfect," I grumbled and my husband beamed at me.

Who knew a demon turned god's cooperation could be earned so easily?

Sunday squints at me and then sighs and picks up the basket of whites in front of her and brings them over to me. "You know what? I think you're actually going to try and not make this a sacrificing cult, so I'll help you."

"You're joining our cult?" I'm so excited that I drop the sheets and hug her. "Elijah is going to be so happy!"

The pair have been courting, or at least I think they have been, from what Elijah has told me excitedly during our morning coffee times. He likes to get up early to make breakfast for the house while the others sleep in. Wrath refuses to wake before sunrise now.

Sunday flails in my arms for a beat before she hugs me back with a sigh. "I'm joining as a consultant. Every cult needs a witch, everyone knows that, so don't get any bright ideas. I'm doing you a favor."

"Of course you are."

"I mean it, Buffy. Elijah is going to think I've decided to join his cult to you when he hears I'm staying, but I'm not. I'm here on a consultation rotation."

The gang is still staying with us at Wrath's Embrace and it's been a comfort to have them close. I know Elijah's been worried about Sunday vanishing one day.

"The Witch of the Woods is tied to no one and nothing but the woods. What if I wake up one day and she's gone?"

367

I turn over Elijah's words and step back from her. He's right. Sunday has never been attached to Sweet Tooth. It was always the woods.

"Then why didn't Sweet Tooth have one? Why the woods? I mean, you could go anywhere and do anything but you chose here."

Sunday sighs and picks up the sheets I dropped. She starts to carefully fold them when she speaks, "Because I lived here a very long time ago. I-I was here when Sweet Tooth was just being formed. My parents came from the East hoping to strike it rich. Ichabod was a nobody then, but that all changed overnight."

I freeze. Sunday was here at the beginning of Sweet Tooth? I stay silent and she keeps talking.

"He was just a farmer, someone I saw in passing but didn't think much of. Then he won over the mayor and then the town council, suddenly he was everywhere. One night he came to my house." Sunday clears her throat. "My father brought him. He was there to ask for my hand in marriage. We were married that night under the full moon. I think you know how my wedding night went with his track record. Wrath wasn't on duty then, it was Lethos that came for me."

"Oh Sunday," I whisper and cover my mouth with my hand.

She looks up at me and the witch's eyes are bright. "So you see, I was the first wife but even though he killed me, I didn't die. Lethos likes pretty things and he brought me back. Kind of like I did with Nina."

"What was that?" Nina calls. She's meticulously scrubbing at the grass stains on the football uniforms of the youth city league. "I heard my name so don't pretend you didn't say it."

"Just talking about my origin story and how you and I are

more alike than it seems."

Nina sends a smug look our way. "I'm telling you, zombie girl nights should be a thing, Sunday."

"We aren't making a club for zombies, Nina. For the last time, we are not zombies."

Nina rolls her eyes and waves a box of baking soda at us. "Oh, but it's fine when *you* say it. I see how it is."

Sunday sighs and rubs her temples. "Do you mind? This is dark trauma time story hour with Buffy."

"Sorry, sorry."

"Now, where was I?" Sunday taps her chin. "Ah, yes, the depths of my despair where I tell you that just over five hundred years ago I was the first bride, the blood sacrifice that brought all of this," Sunday swirls her finger around the room, "into being and became forever tied to Lethos."

I remember Wrath's words about Lethos'.

"For centuries you owned every inch of me and made me your puppet."

The night I met Wrath he was free of Lethos' control but Sunday was not.

"He still controlled you, didn't he?"

Sunday nods. "He did, but I'm smarter than he ever was. I found my ways around his orders not to directly interfere, because I knew if anyone was going to bring his ass down, it was you and I was willing to risk it. It's not like things could get more boring for me wandering around these woods for the next few centuries. So I thought 'let's take a risk, Sunday', and you proved me right. Which is why," Sunday holds out her hands and wiggles her fingers, "I'm joining your cult."

"In a purely consultation role."

She winks at me. *"Obviously."*

WHEN WE'RE DONE with laundry it's time for lunch. From the pull of our bond, I know Wrath is waiting for me at the front doors of the Hall of Worship. We fixed it up thanks to Wrath's newly found powers of divinity and now it's the home base of operations for the new Cult of Wrath.

The Cult of Wrath 2.0 as Charlie calls it.

He's in charge of communications and he's been working on getting the rest of the townsfolk phones. There's been a steep learning curve with social media, which is why I think he's holding a presentation in the Main Hall. Ms. Donna and Mrs. Landry are front and center, squinting at the projection screen Charlie has rigged up and dutifully taking notes. I wave at Charlie on my way past and nearly run right into Elijah, who is rushing past me back to the laundry room.

He looks handsome, hair neatly combed and wearing a pair of pressed slacks and a starched colored shirt with a bouquet of roses in his hand.

"Looking for Sunday?" I ask and he turns red.

"Yes, Your Holy Terror," he says. He's been trying this title out and I like it more than his slips of your highness Buffy and ma'am, so I let him keep going with it. He's been actively recruiting more acolytes to join him in following me and I let him because it makes him happy. There are about two dozen Acolytes of the Harbinger now, so at least I know Elijah keeps busy.

I jerk a thumb over my shoulder. "She's in the laundry room with Nina."

"Thank you, thank you. It's our one month anniversary tonight," he tells me and shows me the flowers. "Do you think she'll like these?"

"They're lovely. She'll love them."

"If you say it, then I know it to be true, Your Holy Terror."

"Have fun tonight. Happy anniversary." Elijah gives me a weepy thanks for my 'blessing' and I have to tear my hand away and force him down the hallway before I'm free to meet Wrath.

"He's zealous in his devotion to you. That pleases me."

"He's sweet," I say and take the hand Wrath holds out to me. He's human today. It's for the best when we're out in the open and there might be Outsiders. I don't think the world can handle knowing there's actually a demonic god roaming the countryside with a whole town in his thrall. It's one thing when they thought we were all delusional and following a fairytale, they were happy to come and spend their money in town then but if they knew it was true?

I have no idea what they would do. So for now we keep it our secret.

"What would you like to do, beloved?"

Wrath and I leave the Hall of Worship and head towards downtown. It's a crisp afternoon and the sun is shining brightly on Sweet Tooth. We have a town play to attend later and there's the communal dinner in the town square, but other than that we have nothing to do and nowhere to be.

"A walk through town, maybe?" he asks. The wind blows and ruffles his hair and I'm struck by how beautiful my sweet husband is. He smiles at a group of children that run by laughing and I squeeze his hand.

"A walk sounds lovely. We have all the time in the world."

Acknowledgments

That Time I Took Down A Cult is what happens when you love Buffy and the 90's so much you want to write an ode to it, plus you definitely did join a cult that one time and it all has to come out somewhere.

It's also what happens when you spend a night laughing, plotting and scheming with Kimberly Lemming and make a deal to let them name your next book if they make the cover. *PS: You always take that deal when its offered.*

Kimberly, you are without a doubt one of the most supportive, kind, creative and genuine souls I have ever met. I'm really glad we joined that one online cult way back when because our friendship has been a blessing. Thank you for always being there, I'd probably lose it without you. Brittany, since we've met you've been my number one supporter and our friendship has grown into something with deep roots. I wouldn't have been able to finish this book without you, just like so many other books I've written. I'm happy that we have been able to grow together for every wild turn life has shown us both. I love you. Desi, you are amazing beyond compare and I am blown away at how our friendship has blossomed out of reader and author to genuine friends. Your help with this book is irreplaceable and I know that

I can count on you for a water and sanity check. Your presence in my life has been such a light.

And last but not least, dear reader, thank you. You took a chance on my book and it means the world to have you here with me at the end of this book that brought me to tears more than once. Happy tears but tears all the same. I hope that there was something in Sweet Tooth for all of you to love, that Buffy and Wrath live rent rent free and happily ever after with you as much as they do with me, and that I'll get to share more stories with you.

About the Author

Hi, Bestie! I'm Rebel Carter, I write a lot of romance and there's never been another thing I've ever wanted to do than to be a romance writer. It's my calling and when you pick up one of my books, I hope you get swept away enough to forget about the world for a little while. I write all sub-genres and heat levels as Rebel Carter, deliver on the Dark Romance as Darcy Dahlia, and bring the alien omegaverse romance adventure as Jupiter Belle. (I really meant it when I said that I write a lot of romance, bestie!)

I'm most active on TikTok and you can ***<join my newsletter>*** to know what chaos I'm getting into next.

Love y'all and thank you for being here with me!

Also by Rebel Carter

Oak Fast Fated Mates Series

Small Town Cozy Paranormal Shifter Romance

Barista and the Bear: PNR Fated Mate Romance

She's a Luna: PNR Fated Mate Romance

Fairy Suited: PNR Fated Mate Romance

Very Bearly Mated: PNR Fated Mate Romance

Librarian and the Bear: PNR Fated Mate Romance

Gold Sky Historical Series

19th Century Historical Romance

Heart and Hand: Interracial Mail Order Bride Romance Gold Sky Series Book One

Hearth and Home: Interracial Mail Order Groom Romance Gold Sky Series Book Two

Honor and Desire: Friends to Lovers Gold Sky Series Book Three

Three to Love: A MMF Romance Gold Sky Series Book Four

Leather and Lace: A Lesbian Historical Novella Gold Sky Book Five

Pride and Passion : Enemies to Lovers Romance (Gold Sky Book 6)

Rose and Wicked: Marriage of Convenience (Gold Sky Book 7)

The Cairn Series

Daddy Kink + Hades x Persephone Retelling Romance

Come To Daddy

Honey, Honey

Bitter Desire

Sweet Rule

The New Girl Series

Older Woman Younger Man Romance

New Girl In Town

New Girl In the City

New Girl In Play

The Golden Duet

Reformed Bad Boy + Good Girl Romance

Once Bitten

Twice Shy COMING SOON!

Stand Alone Romance Novels and Novellas

Auld Lang Syne: A Highlands Holiday Novella

Sugar and Spice: A Christmas Novella

Love And Gravity:A STEM Romance

Made in the USA
Middletown, DE
22 September 2024

61303532R00231